the

DAYDREAMS

LAURA HANKIN

BERKLEY

NEW YORK

BERKLEY
An imprint of Penguin Random House LLC
penguinrandomhouse.com

Copyright © 2023 by Laura Hankin
Penguin Random House supports copyright. Copyright fuels creativity, encourages
diverse voices, promotes free speech, and creates a vibrant culture. Thank you for buying an
authorized edition of this book and for complying with copyright laws by not reproducing,
scanning, or distributing any part of it in any form without permission. You are supporting
writers and allowing Penguin Random House to continue to publish books for every reader.

BERKLEY and the BERKLEY & B colophon are registered trademarks of
Penguin Random House LLC.

Library of Congress Cataloging-in-Publication Data

Names: Hankin, Laura, author.
Title: The daydreams / Laura Hankin.
Description: First Edition. | New York : Berkley, 2023.
Identifiers: LCCN 2022037540 (print) | LCCN 2022037541 (ebook) |
ISBN 9780593438183 (hardcover) | ISBN 9780593438206 (ebook)
Subjects: LCGFT: Novels.
Classification: LCC PS3608.A71483 D39 2023 (print) | LCC PS3608.A71483 (ebook) |
DDC 813/.6—dc23/eng/20220815
LC record available at https://lccn.loc.gov/2022037540
LC ebook record available at https://lccn.loc.gov/2022037541

Printed in the United States of America
1st Printing

Interior art: Star and spotlight © hugolacasse / Shutterstock.com
Book design by Kristin del Rosario

For Dave,
who helped me believe in second chances

One

· · · · · · ·

2018

We all had our roles to play, and I was The Bitch.

Or, to rephrase in the family-friendly language preferred by the corporation that aired our TV show: The Mean Girl. A villain with devious plans and that devastating eyebrow. One slow raise of it, and I could turn even the most poorly written insult into the kind of taunt that keeps a person up at night. (My eyebrow got a workout.)

Liana was The Best Friend, supportive and true and allowed to be a little bit funny, her face always right outside the spotlight's glow.

Summer and Noah? They were The Stars, and The Star-Crossed Lovers. Golden, beautiful teenagers practically designed in a lab to sing and dance their way into your heart. Summer swooned for Noah, and a million girls swooned with her. Noah longed for Summer, and a million men longed for her to turn eighteen.

We played a group of fictional high schoolers who started a band together. Over the course of the show's two seasons, the special concert appearances, and the live finale crafted to set us up for a blockbuster movie, story lines switched between the band's budding music career and high school drama that was so heavily sanitized, we seemed to live in a world where babies were delivered by stork.

The show was called *The Daydreams*, and in the thirteen years since our live finale went so spectacularly wrong, I've been trying to leave it behind me. Yet here I am hiding in my office, squinting at a video link that I fear will plunge me right back into the mess I've worked so hard to escape.

I'm a lawyer now, by the way. I'm on the partner track, and I wear skirts from Banana Republic, and the people I meet assume that I am the boring, real-life version of the big-city girlfriend in a Hallmark movie who doesn't appreciate Christmas. Sometimes, though, my disguise slips. I forget and use the devastating eyebrow on a difficult client whose kid used to watch the show, or whose assistant was a preteen girl at just the right time. It clicks into place for them: Katherine, who patiently responds to all the urgent emails they send at nine on a Friday night, is actually Kat, who for a couple of strange, glorious years was one of the leads of a television phenomenon. They take a new interest in me, asking why I left Hollywood, if I'd ever go back. "Being a movie star has nothing on mergers and acquisitions," I say with a smile, and usually that works.

Once, though, a middle-aged businessman kept going. "So did you know that Summer Wright was going to—" he started. I knocked my coffee cup into his lap, and that got us off the topic.

Liana's got a new role too: A Wife. Her husband plays for the Texas Rangers and has been setting all sorts of records that I do not understand because I don't follow sports. She looks great in the stands at his games, more made-up and glamorous than she ever was on the show. She looks a little less great in the tabloid photos, underneath headlines wondering when she and Javier are going to have a baby.

But you want to hear about The Stars. Everyone always does.

I haven't spoken to either of them since the finale, and I have better things to do than sit around all day refreshing their social media pages. Still, I am a person living in the world, so I know this much:

Noah is the only one of us whose role hasn't changed. If anything, he's grown more golden, with an Oscar nomination in his pocket and all sorts of casting rumors about his next big project. All sorts of rumors about his love life too, now that he and his long-term girlfriend have broken up. I wish him nothing but the worst.

And Summer. Ethereal, wide-eyed Summer, who had all the potential in the world? She is The Cautionary Tale.

I don't want what I did onscreen back then to define how others see me, or what I did offscreen to define how I see myself. But now, I stare at the video on my phone, labeled Entertainment Wow Exclusive: Interview with Noah Gideon. My boyfriend, Miheer, sent it to me while I was in a meeting with a client, along with a string of text messages. You're having a moment online! was the first one, then, Uh, this thing is blowing up, and finally, I'll grab wine on the way home. As my client droned on, the buzz of my phone in my pocket grew increasingly steady—notification piling upon notification—until it felt like I was sitting on a vibrator. I made some excuse and escaped to my office, knowing that *something* must have happened with *The Daydreams*. Something big. Probably something bad.

My heart rate speeds up. I press play.

Two

· · · · · · ·

2018

There he is on my phone screen: Noah, with a closely trimmed beard and vivid blue eyes, sprawling in a chair. An interviewer—midtwenties, giggly, the kind of thin that I used to be before I left Hollywood and started eating bread—leans forward, almost panting with excitement. Her enthusiasm doesn't faze him. He's used to being worshipped.

"It's *so* fun to be talking with you today about your adorable new film, *Genius!*" she says.

"Thanks for having me," Noah replies.

The interviewer indicates the poster behind them, for some piece of CGI trash that will probably make a few hundred million dollars. "You voice a tech support worker who gets sucked into one of the computers he's trying to fix, and I obviously want to hear all about how you got into character."

Noah shoots her a charming smile. "It was tough, considering that my own tech skills max out at 'try turning it off and on again.'"

"Aw, I'm sure that's not true!"

"You're right, it's not," he says, straight-faced. "I'm also good at putting things in rice."

"*So* funny," she gushes. "But before we talk more about the movie, my fourteen-year-old self would kill me if I didn't ask you about *The Daydreams*."

"Oh boy," Noah says. "You sure you have to?"

"Us fans need closure, Noah!"

This happens sometimes, interviewers tossing him a softball question or two about the show before everyone moves on. (Not that I watch all of Noah's interviews! I try to avoid them, because it generally makes me furious to watch everyone fawn over him like he's a god descending from Mount Olympus. But it's been a long thirteen years, and sometimes I've slipped up.)

The interviewer turns to the camera. "I think we can all agree that the live season-two finale got a little, can I say . . . messy?"

"Sure, 'messy' is a fair word for it." Noah grins like he's in on the joke. This has been his strategy since the show imploded. He gets to be in on the joke while the rest of us are the butt of it. Still, there are some things you don't forget about a person if you used to be one of their best friends and also had a massive crush on them. Noah didn't get nervous often—the world had been too kind to him—but when he did, he transferred his anxiety into the heel of his foot. I look down—it's a wide shot—and sure enough, his foot is tapping away.

I'm certain he has a gentleman's agreement with the outlet not to talk too much about this. Besides, we all signed something long ago that ensured we wouldn't say anything to tarnish the Atlas brand, and any public comment about the finale that hasn't been heavily workshopped with a team of publicists definitely risks tarnishing. But still, the interviewer plows on.

"The speculation was that, by the end of the finale, we were going to get all sorts of plot developments to launch us into a movie. Maybe some redemption for Kat, a solo for Liana, a big record deal for the band."

Right after we'd all been cast, the show's creator changed the characters' names so that they were the same as our own. It was the savviest move he made, blurring the lines between fiction and reality like that. Our fans felt that we were playing versions of ourselves. That I actually did hate Summer. That Liana truly would do anything for her. And that Noah loved her in a pure, once-in-a-lifetime way. Some parts of that were true. But sometimes what happened behind the scenes was far beyond anything the censors would have allowed.

The interviewer continues. "But my fourteen-year-old self was most excited about the rumor that you and Summer were *finally* going to kiss, after coming so close all those times." She starts ticking them off on her fingers. "The almost kiss at the homecoming dance, right before Kat cut in! The almost kiss at the school carnival, when Kat shut down the Ferris wheel! The almost—"

"You know them all by heart, huh?" Noah cuts in.

"Obviously. There was even a confusing almost kiss in the broadcast, right before Summer went off script. And then the network cut the feed, so we never saw the end! Millions of us viewers were devastated. The amount of time I spent on fan-fiction sites, trying to get some closure . . . well, it's embarrassing. So can you *please* tell us more about what was supposed to happen?"

Noah swallows, still keeping that smile on his face. "You know, I can barely remember at this point. But what I do know is I'll be forever grateful to *The Daydreams* for launching my career." He deploys the Hollywood Pivot like a pro. "And speaking of, I can tell you more about *Genius*—"

"In a second! But first . . . we're living in a time of reboots. So, what do you say? Would you ever consider coming back for a reunion, and giving fans the ending that they've wanted for thirteen years?"

What is this interviewer doing? Some assistant must have forgotten to brief her on the list of off-limits topics. Either that, or she has gone rogue in search of a headline, throwing caution to the wind to get her face all over the internet, gentleman's agreement be damned. Noah's publicist is never going to let her interview him again.

"I guess I'd say . . ." He pauses for probably only a few seconds, but it feels interminable. His heel taps so fast he could lead a Broadway revival of *42nd Street*. Any other time, I'd love to watch him squirm in discomfort. But not now, not about this.

No no no, I think, even though I already know what his answer will be. He doesn't really have a choice. This giggly, enthusiastic interviewer has fenced him in. Noah leans back and casually utters a sentence that is going to make my life very difficult. "If the other Daydreams want to come back, I do too."

Three

· · · · · · ·

2018

Unsurprisingly, an overzealous fan has already started a petition—
Redo the Season Two Daydreams Finale!—and thousands of
people have signed it. In the time it takes me to scan the body of
it, another thousand people add their names.

Already knowing I'll regret it, I pull up Twitter; #Daydreams-
Reunion is trending. Amid the excited clamor, some people have
posted GIFs from the disastrous finale: a slow zoom in on my
shocked face, Noah looking like he's holding back tears, Liana
stopping her choreography mid-twirl.

And of course, one of the immutable laws of the internet, along
with "Even the most innocent-seeming website is harvesting your
data" and "If it exists, there is porn of it": anytime *The Daydreams*
trends, someone must post a clip of the last few seconds before the
network cut the broadcast. There on the screen, captured forever,
the curve of Summer's breast emerges from the top of her cute
yellow dress, and the online debate begins again—was that hint of
something on her breast a shadow cast by the light, or was it her
nipple?

Never fear, a bunch of horny guys have volunteered to solve
the mystery over the last thirteen years, zooming in and diagram-

ming Summer's skin with the kind of fervor normally reserved for detectives tracking serial killers.

I stare at the conversation online—the sick curiosity, the concern for her, the occasional take that *we should actually be judging Atlas, a corporation that makes kids famous and then rejects them the minute they grow up and show any hint of sexuality!*—until I feel sick, panic threatening to cut off my air supply. Then I go into a meeting with another client, a big bank suit who's being a stubborn ass about a contract demand. He regards me with a strange expression. Because I'm distracted, or because he's been paying attention to the celebrity gossip?

I clear my throat, anchor myself back to Earth, and lay out a plan for how he can most effectively screw over the smaller company with whom he's hoping to do business.

Yes, I know that corporate law is not the best place for a woman to go if she's trying to avoid the "bitch" label. Let me be clear: I wanted to save the children and/or whales. But even though the do-gooder nonprofit jobs don't pay well, they're the hardest ones to get. A lot of lawyers want to feel like a good person for a couple of years before spending the rest of their careers defending pharmaceutical companies. I applied to ten of the do-gooder jobs and went through rounds of interviews only to get rejected from them all. I applied to one midsize corporate firm and got an offer the next week, so here I am.

Besides, once I make partner, things will change. My mentor, Irene, the most senior woman at the firm, started bringing in pro bono clients for herself the minute she got partner power. She assures me that I can do the same, and that I'm so close. Soon, I'll be able to use the firm's resources to help people who wouldn't normally be able to afford our services. People trying to start their own business, say, who need protection from the predators lining up to take advantage of them. If I can make a real difference for even just a few people each year . . . the thought of that keeps me going. Thanks to *The Daydreams*, I know all too well what happens when the protectors are absent.

"Well," the client says, when I'm done, "I'm glad I've got the mean girl on my side for this." Celebrity gossip then. I grit my teeth in a smile as I usher him out the door.

When I come back to my phone I have six new voicemails, which I listen to hunched over at my desk—mostly journalists asking for comment. But my old agent, with whom I haven't spoken in years, leaves me a voicemail too: *Kat, darling! Atlas is very interested in this reunion now that they've seen the fan response. They're offering a good amount of money for a monthlong commitment, plus this will supercharge your brand, and could be a great launching pad for getting back into TV, or at least doing some commercials. I've always thought you could be a great fit for Geico. Call me back!*

I have no interest in supercharging my brand, or in hawking insurance. I text her instead: Sorry, but this is not right for me at this time. Also, FYI, it's Katherine now. Thank you, and I hope you're well.

Liana has already confirmed she's in and is very excited, so the only two we're still waiting on are you and Summer, she responds. At least promise me you'll sleep on it!

I pause, something holding me back from sending the outright refusal I know I should. Maybe it's worth it to wait until Summer turns it down too, so that I'm not the one jerk here. There's no chance she'll want to come back, not after the way everything ended. My hands are so sweaty, I need to wipe them on my skirt before texting back.

KATHERINE: Fine, I'll sleep on it.

Four

· · · · · · ·

2018

Miheer, that gem, is already holding out a glass of red wine for me when I get home.

"You all right?" he asks as soon as I come through the door of our Logan Circle apartment, and I don't say anything, just walk straight into him and lean against his chest. "That wild of a day, huh?"

I let out a guttural moan, and he laughs, handing me the glass. I chug it down with no regard for taste or texture or any of the things I normally pretend to care about, intertwining my free hand in his. "Thank you," I say, and hold out the glass for more.

"When are we moving to LA?" he asks.

"I was thinking . . . never?"

"Sounds like a great plan to me." He smiles, my lanky, handsome, solid boyfriend. (Although "boyfriend" doesn't feel quite right after three years together.) We plop down on our couch, and everything is so *normal*. We have a nice TV; and five houseplants that he waters every Sunday; and our quiet, easy routine. A few nights a week, I'm even home early enough to eat dinner with him. I put my head in his lap, and he strokes my hair.

"Do you think it'll feel weird if the others come back without you?"

"No, I've moved on," I respond, as if saying it firmly enough could make it true.

Miheer never watched the show growing up. Though he was born in the United States, his family moved back to India when he was ten and he didn't return here until law school, so he missed the phenomenon. He had no idea about my secret child star life until our third date, when I got the sense he'd be sticking around, and I decided to get the big reveal over with. I allowed him to watch one episode so that he could "understand" me but told him to please not bother watching any more. He respected my wishes. Or maybe he had no desire to watch more, because he is a full-grown adult who is more interested in things like environmental defense law than in plotlines about who is going to win the school talent show. He views my brief acting career as a funny bit of trivia about the teenage me. As if I'd taken a gap year, or gone through a goth phase.

And thank God he's never asked me to pretend to be my character during sex. I shudder to remember how many normal-seeming guys charmed me into their bedrooms when I was in my twenties, set the mood just right, and then told me to raise my eyebrow and say something awful to them. I shudder even more remembering that, a few times when I was particularly lonely or horny, I actually did it.

"You know what a fun distraction could be?" he asks, his hand still stroking my hair in that lovely way. "If the two of us went out of town for the weekend. We could get a nice room in a bed-and-breakfast, one of those places that looks like it was decorated by someone's kooky great-aunt?"

Miheer is awful at subterfuge. He has accidentally ruined more than one surprise party for our friends. And the semi-scripted nature of the kooky great-aunt line, the overly casual way he suggests going out of town like he practiced it in the mirror, gives away his game. This is a proposal trip.

The first time we talked about what our future together might look like, I told him I needed time to really gun for partner. Planning a wedding that would satisfy his parents, the trip to India to celebrate with his extended family, taking time off for a honeymoon, it would all put me even further behind the guys who came into the firm with me, younger guys who hadn't wasted the tail end of their teenage years trying to be famous. "Give me a couple years," I'd told Miheer, two years ago. So I've been expecting this. Looking forward to it. When I think of the two of us tottering around as wrinkly old people together, my hard little heart turns embarrassingly gooey.

But now, anxiety seizes me. Miheer assumes that the reason I don't reminisce about the "glory days" or regale people with stories of the show at dinner parties is that I want to be taken seriously now. Or maybe he thinks that I don't enjoy remembering how it ended—how I stood idly by, slack-jawed, while my friend melted down in front of millions of people.

It's more than that. I don't like who I was back then—not just a person who didn't help Summer, but a person who did her part to cause that meltdown in the first place. Miheer doesn't know that, because nobody knows. And I don't think he could love me in the same way if he ever found out.

He looks at me, pretending to be nonchalant, trying to hide the hope blooming in his eyes. Dammit, he's one of the best people I know, someone who actually *is* saving the children and/or whales, not just so that he can have an altruistic phase before going into Big Law but because he believes in noble things like leaving the world better than you found it.

The problem is that I fell in love with a good man who thinks that I am good too, who treats me with tenderness as if I am worthy of such a gift. But now, this stupid interview with Noah has resurrected something I'd buried deep inside myself: guilt. How can I let Miheer blithely tie his life to mine, how can I go off and celebrate, when there's a guilt zombie staggering around that only I can see?

So I feign ignorance. "I've got so much work right now, I don't think I can get away." His mouth turns down in disappointment, and I lean forward to kiss him. "Later in the month? It's a really nice idea."

Later in the month, this won't feel so raw. I just need to get as far away from this *Daydreams* mess as possible. Let the guilt zombie tire itself out and crawl back under the dirt where I can't see it. Then, Miheer won't even be able to finish getting the words out before I shout, *Yes, yes, a thousand times yes.*

I pull out my phone and fire off a text to my agent. **I don't need to sleep on it. My answer is no.**

· · · · · · · ·

The next day at work, I walk in with my head held high. Atlas can do the reunion without me if they'd like—I was important, but I wasn't Summer or Noah (a fact I was reminded of all the time back then). This office, this life, is where I belong.

An email from Liana comes in a couple of hours later: **Kat! Can't wait to see you again—this is going to be a really special experience for the fans! And maybe you'll finally get to meet my husband. Still can't believe I haven't gotten to introduce you—you'll love him, he's just the best.** I frown at it. Has she not heard yet that I've said no? Or is this her attempt to guilt me into changing my mind? I write back wishing her luck with the reunion and vaguely suggesting a phone call soon. She responds immediately, as if she's just sitting there staring at her inbox: You're so funny, now stop playing hard to get!! I ignore it.

In the late afternoon, our receptionist knocks on my office door, then sticks her head in. "Katherine," she says, "you have somebody here to see you."

"I have a meeting in five—"

"I know," she says, her face turning red, her tone strenuously professional. "But she's insisting. Oh! Miss, um—"

The uninvited guest has followed her to the door of my office. She walks past the receptionist, ignoring all her feeble, awed protestations, and sits down in the chair across from my desk. I register the cutoff jean shorts and oversized sweatshirt first, then the blond hair, all brittle from being dyed for too many years. My mouth goes dry. Only then do I focus on her wide, cartoon-princess eyes, locked on me.

"Kat," Summer says. "Let's go grab a drink."

SUMMER WRIGHT'S
TOP FIVE WILDEST MOMENTS!!

With the news that Summer Wright is heading back to rehab (round 2! We hope she's okay!), we're rounding up the most insane moments this roller-coaster star has taken us on, from the super scandalous to the semi-violent!

5. The Comeback Concert Fail, 2007—Who thought it was a good idea to let Wright do a live performance again? She showed up clearly drunk, forgot the words to her song (not that they were complicated lyrics—anyone should be able to remember "shame me, shame me, you can't tame me" repeated about twenty-five times!), and tried to compensate with some sad booty shaking that just made everyone feel uncomfortable!

4. Topless Canoodling, 2006—Wright engaged in some EX-TREME PDA on a trip to Mexico with her quick fling, reality TV star Ryan Delizza. Um, note to Summer . . . maybe don't take your bathing suit top off on a boat if you don't want people to take pictures of you??

3. The Big Gulp Fight, 2008—Who can forget the moment when Wright snapped and threw her Big Gulp in a paparazzo's face? Luckily, other paparazzi were there to document the whole thing. Wright totally ruined the man's expensive camera, and her straw ended up hitting him in the eye! He sued (wouldn't we all have done the same?) and she settled with him out of court.

Amount was undisclosed, but we have a feeling it was bye-bye, *Daydreams* residuals!

2. The Almost Wedding, 2010—Sure, we were all shocked when Summer announced she was going to marry her personal trainer, whom she had known for all of three months. But we were even MORE shocked when the wedding day came and, instead of showing up at the venue, she checked into rehab, leaving the two hundred guests to eat the cake and try to comfort the groom.

1. *The Daydreams* Finale, 2005—Could anything else really come in at number one? You know it, you love it. It's the moment of crazy that started it all. If for some reason you've been living under a rock, just watch the video <u>here</u>.

Five

· · · · · · ·

2002

There are certain feelings that you don't believe are real until you feel them yourself. Take anger so strong that you could kill someone. You cannot wrap your head around how a person could get to that place, and then something or someone overwhelms you with rage, and murder starts to make sense.

One feeling that I didn't believe existed until I felt it was total fulfillment, the sense that you are doing exactly what you should be. Before *The Daydreams*, I was a steady enough teenager. No grand fits of rebellion to keep my parents up at night. (They kept themselves up, with screaming matches I could hear through my bedroom wall.) I got good grades and ran track and kissed some boys whom I decided not to go any further with, but it was all a skimming-the-surface kind of life, filling the hours of the day until I could sleep, my alarm causing me an almost physical pain when it dragged me awake in the mornings. At restaurants, waiting for the food to come, I'd go to the bathroom even though I didn't have to pee because it was something to do, and maybe it would make the food come faster, and once the food came, we could eat and go home and I could go to bed again.

Some might say that it sounds like I was a little depressed, to which *I* would say . . . touché.

Auditioning for *The Daydreams* was just something to do too. I was out in San Diego visiting my aunt and her family for a few weeks, ostensibly to look at colleges, but really because my parents wanted me across the country while they finalized their divorce and fought over who got to keep the good china. My performing-obsessed cousin dragged me along with her to an open call in West Hollywood, despite my protestations that I had no experience beyond a stint in middle school choir. Maybe she thought I'd make her look good in comparison. I didn't even have a real headshot, just a picture that my aunt took of me with her disposable camera in her backyard. We printed it out at CVS.

The woman running the audition briefly sized up my cousin, then handed her some pages of a scene. "This character is the best friend, so think steady but fun." She glanced at me. "Okay, and here are the sides for the female lead." I reached down to take the pages from her, but she didn't let go. When I looked back up, she was studying me more closely. Then she made a decision I've spent countless hours wondering about—if this random woman hadn't taken a second look at me, what would have happened? Would I have failed to even get a callback, or might I have gotten Summer's role instead? "Actually, no. You're going to read for the mean girl."

When my turn came, I entered a bright white room where a casting director and a reader sat behind a table with a camera. The reader began to tonelessly recite the lines: "Wait a minute, that's not what we agreed to wear for the performance."

A strange sensation hit me: nerves, maybe. As I looked at the script, my hair fell in my face, tickling my cheek. I flicked it away, annoyed. What was I even doing here? But I flicked more dramatically than I intended, and the casting director chuckled. I looked up at him and the reader, and suddenly the strange sensation wasn't nerves. It was adrenaline.

"I forgot to tell you," I said, reciting my part. "This whole band thing has been cute and all, but I'm destined for solo stardom."

"You're quitting? Right before the big talent show? What are we supposed to do?"

"Sorry," I said, "but it's not Madonna and friends." I wanted more than anything to make those faces behind the table laugh again, but on purpose this time. The script in my hand became a kind of combination lock. If I managed to spin it just the right way, I could crack it wide open. I raised my eyebrow and gave the reader a withering stare. "It's just *Madonna*."

The reader snorted. The casting director blinked a couple of times, then sat forward as I read the rest of the scene, throwing everything I could think of at it, mugging and tossing my hair and stomping around the room. This is how performing would always feel to me when it was good, like a heist—adrenaline-tinged and thrilling. I was getting away with something, using my particular set of skills to pull off magic.

They had me come back a few days later to sing and dance. My cousin did not get a callback and refused to speak to me for the rest of my visit. Then: radio silence. I started my senior year back in Pennsylvania, where I narrowed down my list of colleges, quit track, and auditioned for the school play, shocking everyone by getting Annie in *Annie Get Your Gun*.

And then one day, when I was sitting at the kitchen table with my mother, her reading the newspaper while I flipped through the dELiA*s catalog, the phone rang.

"No," my mother said, after I hung up and breathlessly repeated the offer. "You'd have to drop out of school?"

"They'll have an on-set tutor!"

"Absolutely not. Tell them to call back after you graduate."

I took the legal emancipation forms to my father. He signed them, maybe ten percent because he was happy for me, and ninety percent to make my mother angry. After an immense pressure campaign from me (*"Dad's* okay with it! Why can't you be more like Dad?"), him ("Do you really want to deny our daughter her dreams just because *you* never followed yours?"), and some of the people at Atlas (making all sorts of assurances about how well I'd be taken care of), my mother capitulated.

The day I first met the others stands out in my mind, blazing bright. Liana was already there when I walked in for the read-through. The only Black girl in the room, she was highlighting her lines in a binder, her hair pulled up in two puffs on top of her head. Michael, the man who had come up with the concept for the show and was running the whole production, introduced us. Liana stood and threw her arms around me, then dragged me to the seat next to her. We sat and whispered while the adults bustled around, setting up.

"I can't believe this is really happening," I said.

"Is this your first show?" When I nodded, her round face lit up in a smile. "A little showbiz baby! How old are you?"

"I turn eighteen in the spring."

"Oh my God, you're so cute. I'm twenty, and I've been out here for a few years, so I can show you the ropes. You're never supposed to get your hopes up with shows. I've done like two pilots that didn't get picked up. But this one, it's safe to be excited."

She leaned closer to me, so close that I could smell her cherry lip gloss. "Don't look straight at him, but you see the man in the glasses, sitting in the corner? That's *Mr. Atlas*. Like, the guy who runs the whole network." I snuck a peek. He was in his late forties, maybe, perched quietly on a chair, one leg folded over the other, his fingers steepled in front of him, his spectacles resting on his nose. An ordinary-looking man, but with a force field around him, at once drawing all the adults' attention and keeping anyone from getting too close.

"I didn't realize the guy who ran it had the same last name," I said.

"What?" Liana looked at me, scandalized by my lack of researching. "Okay, so his dad started it, and then when he died, Mr. Atlas Jr. took over, and turned it from a movie studio to an empire, and—"

"Michael!" a voice called, full of bravado and ease. There are some people who belong on a poster, and this boy, with his floppy blond hair, walking into the room like a visiting god, was one of them. He carried a battered copy of *On the Road*, which now I might think was pretentious, but at the time convinced me that he was an intellectual. (I liked *On the Road* too! Or, well, I knew that it was considered genius, so I read it closely enough until I convinced myself I liked it.) The gorgeous intellectual and Michael gave each other a pound hug, slapping each other's backs. He was hugging the showrunner? I was terrified of the showrunner! Liana and I turned to each other, stifling giggles, communicating silently: *Cute boy, cute boy, cute boy!*

"Girls, this is Noah," Michael said. Noah flashed Liana and me a lazy, charming grin, the kind where he looked up at you from underneath his eyebrows, seemingly meant to seduce. It worked. He sat down next to me, and I blacked out for a second.

Summer was the last of the main cast to arrive, led into the room by a boisterous bear of a man who boomed out, "Don't worry, everyone, the star is here!"

"Dad," Summer said, peeking out from behind him, embarrassed in a pleasant sort of way.

"Sorry, you can't blame me for being proud," he said, grinning at her as she fiddled with the sleeves of her cardigan. She had such slender wrists, such a delicate beauty to her. Next to me, Noah snapped to attention. This time, his smile was different, not the charm offensive from before, but something so uncontrolled, his eyes went all squinty.

"Nice to see you again," he said to her as she took a seat next to him, smoothing out her skirt and crossing her legs demurely.

"You guys know each other?" Liana asked.

"They had us do a callback together," Summer said. "A . . . what do you call it?"

"Chemistry read," Noah said, too quickly.

Summer's father laughed, and clapped Noah on the shoulder. "Don't tell her boyfriend back home about that part!" For just a second, Noah's face fell, and then he rearranged it back.

We all went around and introduced ourselves, except for Mr. Atlas, who got his own special introduction from Michael. "We're very lucky to have our studio head here, Mr. Atlas, who has made all of this possible."

Mr. Atlas gave a nod. "There's much potential in this room. I'm looking forward to seeing where it goes," he said. His voice was low, mild. Still, every word landed, commanding attention.

"Do you think he has a first name?" Noah whispered to the three of us girls.

I stifled a laugh. "No, I think he was born a mister."

"It's Gerald," Liana said.

Michael was rambling now, a self-important speech about his

vision for the show. "We're spreading joy," he finished up. "Giving people a sense of wonder, the possibility that they too can live a life full of friendship, creativity, and maybe even true love. So, who's ready to get started?"

Summer, Liana, Noah, and I looked at one another, electricity charging through the air. Then, we began.

· · · · · · · ·

That night after the read-through, the three of them came over to my apartment, a one-bedroom that some assistant at Atlas had found for me on Barham Boulevard, a de facto Child Star Row. "The more you bond, the better the show will be!" Michael had called, sending us off while he took the adults to the bar for their own kind of bonding.

My apartment was the closest, and no one else would be there. (Summer still lived at home with her parents an hour and a half away, while Noah and Liana both had roommates.) But the barren apartment just screamed out loneliness and sadness. What if they thought its lack of personality reflected my own? That I too was soulless? Already I desperately wanted to impress them all.

On top of everything, there was the problem of the walls, which the person who lived there before me had decided for some strange reason to paint a muddy brown. The dingy color sucked all the light out of the place, making it feel like I'd moved to a gloomy swamp instead of sunny LA.

"It's not fancy or finished or anything," I warned them as I unlocked the door. "I just moved."

They followed me in, setting down their things, Noah flopping onto my futon. "Hmm," Liana said, registering the walls. "This color is . . . a lot."

"I know," I said. "It's so depressing." The way everyone had laughed at the read-through when I delivered the script's snarky one-liners motivated me to try one of my own. "Do you think the person who chose it was a masochist, or just color-blind?" The others smiled politely. I may have looked like a bitch, but I wasn't a natural. "Anyway, want to order pizza?"

"Wait, you can paint the walls, right? It's not against the rules?" Summer asked.

"Yeah," I said. "I think so."

Summer and Noah looked at each other, grins starting to spread over their faces, an unspoken communication passing between them. "There's a hardware store a few minutes away," Noah said.

Summer grabbed my hand. "Please, can we help you paint?" she asked, as if I'd be doing *her* a favor, her wide eyes locked hopefully on mine.

"I mean, sure," I said. "Really?"

"Yes!" Summer indicated Noah. "We'll grab some paint. You two order dinner." They disappeared together out the door.

I paged through the phone book for local pizza places, a heady rush of independence in the air around me while Liana looked at my CD collection.

"Kat. Really?" Liana asked. "Linkin Park and Sum 41?" It was a funny kind of judgment, not mean-spirited, just her believing in my potential to be cooler than I was. She opened up her over-stuffed messenger bag and began to rifle around in it, pushing aside makeup, magazines, and a portable CD player. "Here we go." She pulled out a case and unzipped it, revealing the CD collection inside. "We need some Mariah."

Summer and Noah came back half an hour later, lugging four paint cans along with some rollers and a tarp, breathless with laughter, nearly dropping it all on the ground.

"What are your thoughts on yellow?" Summer asked, her arms trembling with the effort of holding the cans. "I'm obsessed with yellow walls. But I got you other options too."

"I love yellow," I said, even though previously I'd had no opinion on it.

We started by painting the walls white, each taking a roller, stretching on our tiptoes, except for Noah, who was the tallest among us. We shimmied along to the music Liana had put on, and filled each other in on our lives, trading hometowns (Noah was from Boston and talked a *lot* about it) and favorite ice cream flavors ("dairy isn't good for your vocal cords," Liana said, "but Rocky Road") and stories about our auditions. This was what I'd imagined college would feel like, and here I was, getting to do it early.

"Are you, like, a child bride?" Liana asked Summer at one point, indicating a ring on her finger.

Summer reddened slightly. "Oh, no," she said. "It's a purity ring."

"Holy shit, so you're a wait-until-marriage, I-will-only-ever-have-sex-with-my-husband kind of girl?"

"That's the plan," she said. A quick flash of devastation passed over Noah's face.

Dizzy from the paint fumes, we tentatively began to fall in love with one another. Noah showed off in those stupid boy ways that girls ooh and aah over even though they're not impressive, housing four slices of pizza to prove to us that he could, then trying to balance a paint can on his head. We screamed at him to stop before it spilled all over the floor, giggling all the while. Liana gave up painting at one point. "I'll be the entertainment. I wasn't made for manual labor," she said. She began to sing into her paint roller as if it were a microphone.

Summer's cell phone, a blocky Nokia, rang. "Can I just have another hour?" she whispered into it. "Okay, fine." She hung up and turned to us. "My dad's on his way." Funny, the difference that six months or so could make—I was only a little older than Summer, and yet here I was, across the country from my family, living in an apartment all on my own while her dad was still coming to pick her up.

He came to my door smelling of alcohol—he must have gone out with the adults working on the show.

"Well look at this," he said, stepping into the apartment. "On top of all your other talents, you paint too?" We laughed. "Really, truly," he went on. "That read-through today was something special. Now, I'm not saying the plot is *War and Peace*." In brief, the pilot: Right before the big school talent show, I dropped out of the band that Summer, Liana, and I had formed together so that I could do a solo number instead. In a panic, Summer recruited the cute new boy at school, Noah, to take my place. Their performance was suffused with possibility, plus a whole lot of will-they-or-won't-they tension, while Liana lent her steady backup vocals. After the performance, a parent in the audience approached. He happened to work in the music industry, and wondered if they'd ever consider trying to go pro. As soon as I heard that, I forced my way back into the band as a fourth member, determined to undermine Summer and take my rightful place as lead singer, setting us up for a season of misadventures, sabotage, and fun. So yeah, not exactly *War and Peace*.

Summer's dad went on. "But the four of you, together . . . well, I can't predict the future or anything, but I've got a feeling." He put his arm around Summer, and she nestled into him. Even though she was annoyed that she had to go, she loved him too.

A tingling started up behind my eyes at his unabashed pride in his daughter, his enthusiasm. When I'd called my mother to tell her that I'd settled into LA safely, she'd merely sighed, then asked about the on-set tutoring situation. Sure, maybe Summer's father was teetering on the edge of being a Stage Dad, but I'd have taken that in a heartbeat.

As Summer's dad turned to go, Summer grabbed my hand. "We'll come back tomorrow to finish painting. Can we?" It was as if she didn't realize I had no other friends out here. A generous way of looking at me, assuming the best.

And soon I didn't need other friends, because I had them. The four of us fell into one another while filming the first season of that show. With so many people, it takes time to build intimacy. You make a relationship by stacking building blocks on top of one another, slowly but surely. The four of us built an entire home together that very first night, maybe because we'd all been thrust into such a new and intense experience, maybe because we were meant to be.

We all had our flaws: Summer could be holier-than-thou. Liana used the fact that she was older as proof that she knew the world better than us. (Although honestly, she usually did.) Sometimes Noah chafed at the softening of himself as an idol to preteen girls and did stupid things to assert his masculinity, like climbing bits of the set that he should've stayed off or flirting with every chorus girl who crossed his path. I could be insecure, worried that someone would discover I didn't belong and send me back to my skimming-the-surface life. And I didn't want to go back there, because for the first time I knew how it felt to spring out of bed in the morning, to wish a day could last forever. We were making something we hoped might be special, might garner us a devoted little fan base that would occasionally recognize us on the street, but what really mattered was that we felt alive. We belonged with one another. We didn't realize it, but soon we would belong to everyone else.

Filming the first season of the show was perfect. The second season was when it all went to shit.

Six

. . . .

2018

"No," Summer says at the door of the first bar I take her to, an upscale spot right near the office, the kind of place with fifteen-dollar old-fashioneds and soft jazz music playing in the background. She links her arm in mine, a glint in her eyes. "We're not old yet. Where can we go to have *fun*?"

When I hesitate, she opens her phone, does a quick search, and then leads me to a sticky-floored shithole, meant for twentysomethings who want to get wasted, with a table for flip cup in one corner and a karaoke setup in another. It's just after five when we walk in, and there are only ten or so other people there. Summer slides onto a stool. She leans forward and orders two gin and tonics, and the bartender mercifully does not recognize us. While she waits for our drinks, she toys with her split ends, nervous energy jittering through her.

I stare, trying not to be too obvious, my own nervous energy churning in my stomach. I have not seen Summer in thirteen years. Well, not in person. Though I've tried to wean myself off googling her, even gone cold turkey a few times, I always come back to looking her up, to hoping that something has turned around. Maybe *this* time when I type in her name, the first result will be a story about how she's founded a charity and gotten an exciting movie role and fallen in love with a devoted man.

As far as I can tell, she's been living off residuals, plus a few commercials she's done over the years, demeaning spots that play off what a mess she is. Literally. One notable vacuum ad featured Summer lounging around a trashed house while a spokesperson talked about how *this* vacuum could clean up even the biggest messes. The spokesperson hoovered up crushed chips and bottle caps, then sucked up a protesting Summer with the hose.

Summer hands me my drink. She's studying me too. Perhaps she's kept her own tabs over the years.

"So why are you in DC?" I ask. Summer is not a Washington, DC, kind of person. Last I heard, she lives in New York City, though she did a stint in New Mexico and one in Vegas. And a couple in rehab. Not for alcohol, so I think it's okay that we're getting drinks together. For "exhaustion," was the official party line. "Coke habit" was what the gossip blogs said. "You get an urge to see the monuments?"

She laughs, a little too hard. "I've missed you, Kat."

"Katherine now."

"What?"

"People just call me Katherine."

"Okay then, *Katherine*." She drums her fingers on her glass. Her fingernails are bitten down to the quick. "Why aren't you coming back for the reunion special?"

I groan, then take a large gulp of my gin and tonic. "I can't believe Noah opened up this can of worms. What was he thinking?"

"Noah just does what he wants and gets what he wants. Lucky him, huh? The only one of us to escape the show intact."

"Liana," I say. "Liana's doing well."

Summer snorts. "Right, with all of her posts about her husband's baseball team, and her flat-tummy tea." She chews on the lemon wedge in her drink. "She should've been more than what she is now."

"And besides," I say, "*I'm* intact."

"Congratulations." The bar door opens, and a group of twenty-somethings pours in, heading toward the flip cup and the karaoke. I check my phone, the flurry of emails from clients that I really should be responding to. Summer takes the phone from me and turns it facedown on the bar. "Not even going to pretend? 'No, Summer, you're intact too!'"

"I . . ."

She laughs, but it's a light, mirthless thing. "I'm kidding. I don't need you to bullshit me." She takes my hand, rubbing her thumb on mine. She was always very tactile, sweetly and thoughtlessly touching us all in moments of boredom or stress—a hand on our backs, a head on our shoulders. This time, though, she's looking me straight in the eyes. "I am doing better now, actually," she says. "And I want to do the reunion. For redemption. Maybe it could be a launching pad, you know? I could use one of those." A guy turns on the karaoke machine, starts singing a Whitney Houston song off-key for the growing crowd. Summer turns to watch him, an unreadable expression on her face. Then she says, in a low voice almost difficult to hear above the sounds of the music, "I don't want to go down in history as a joke."

I swallow, my heart beating in my throat. "Well," I say, careful. "I hope it happens, and that it turns things around."

"It can't happen without you."

"You guys don't need me."

"Don't," she begins, frustrated. "Don't do that. You've always undervalued how important you were to the show. And besides, if you bow out, Noah probably will too. He said if *all* of us wanted to come back."

"Summer," I say, shaking my head. "I've been working so hard to be a normal person."

"I can see that." She reaches out and touches the collar of my suit jacket, rubbing the fabric between her fingers. "You know how they say child stars stop maturing at the age they get famous?" She lets out a wry half laugh, gin on her breath. "I guess that's not true for you. You're such a grown-up now. That office of yours, it looked like the set of some show about a fancy career gal." More people spill into the bar, ready to take advantage of the happy hour specials, and Summer swivels around to look at them. "You probably appreciate fine wine and think about your retirement account and hate this place, huh?"

"It's not exactly my scene."

"It could be, though, if you'd let it. Remember how wild we used to get? Season two, I recall some drunken escapades." A smile spreads across her face. Downing the rest of her drink, she hops to her feet, spine lengthening. Then she strides over to the microphone as the Whitney Houston ends, brushing past a couple of women studying the booklet of songs.

"Hey," says one of the women at the song booklet. "We're supposed to go next—" She cuts herself off as she registers Summer's face. "Oh my God. Is . . . is it you?" She wobbles a little bit, her voice turning to a squeak. "Is it really?"

Summer winks at her. "Can you put in 'A New Kind of Wish'?"

"Obviously!" She elbows the woman next to her. "Find it!" The second woman flips through the book furiously for the code, then punches it into the karaoke machine.

Recognition hits the patrons in waves as the bouncy chords of the song begin and Summer tosses her hair, ready to sing one of her more famous *Daydreams* solos. A scream rings out from one corner of the bar. People begin to flock to the lip of the little stage, some of them clasping hands. "What?" a guy standing in front of me asks the woman next to him. "What's going on? I don't get it."

"*Mmm, yeah, you know it's true,*" Summer begins to sing. "*Something has changed ever since I met you.*" (Our lyrics did not win any awards.)

"Who is she?" that same guy asks his companion.

"It's *Summer Wright,*" she hisses back, before calling out to the stage, "My queen!"

Summer waves at her, then swivels her hips, closing her eyes as she continues. Her pure warble is raspier now, but there's something magnetic in her performance all the same. She can still hold a crowd in the palm of her hand, although not necessarily because of the sheer force of her talent. Maybe it's like watching a train wreck, or the awareness that a train wreck could be coming, because this particular train has a habit of speeding out of control.

"Who?" the guy says, and his companion lets out an annoyed grunt.

"Squeaky-clean teen TV star from *The Daydreams*?" He shakes his head. "She, like, ruined the live finale?" Another headshake. Her voice grows higher pitched with incredulity. "*Nipple-gate*?"

"She had a meltdown," another woman says, leaning in, "and we never got closure!"

"It was like . . ." the first woman continues. "Imagine that *The Office* unexpectedly ended right before Jim and Pam kissed, and you just had to live without ever seeing it."

"I think I'd be fine with that," the guy says.

"Okay, well, fuck off, Todd," the first woman says, and turns back to Summer.

"Sing along with the chorus," Summer shouts with a practiced ease, as if no time has passed since we pulled this move at our own special appearances. (Or maybe she sings *Daydreams* karaoke with strangers all the time.) It's not a huge crowd, twenty-five people or so, but the energy makes it feel like we're in a room of a hundred. She holds the microphone out, and people do sing, rapturously, with the purity of feeling that they must have had as teenagers. Many of them are recording on their phones. Summer stretches her free hand out toward the throng too, and some of the people reach up to grab it, to feel her skin even for just a moment.

"I'm *crying*," says one of them, and it's true, her eyes are welling up. Maybe those tears feed Summer—what a gift it is, to be the kind of person who can inspire such emotion in someone else. Maybe it doesn't matter if some of that emotion is pity or mockery, because it's *something*. To be the kind of person whose mere presence can so overwhelm someone that they cry . . . well, that can balance out a lot.

I'm frozen on my bar stool, watching. Hoping that no one will turn around and recognize me. Longing to be up on that stage too.

Summer finishes and takes a bow, flushed with pleasure as people whoop and holler.

"Do 'Shame Me'!" someone yells, and a few others laugh.

Oh God, please no. That one was *not* from *The Daydreams*, but from the strange, nightmarish period shortly afterward when Summer leaned into her bad-girl image, recording an album with some vultures who encouraged her to be the trashiest version of herself. If she was going to be sexual, she was going to be the *most* sexual, parading around singing a bunch of declarations that no one could stop her from being NAUGHTY! It sold terribly, inspired a bunch of mockery on late-night TV, and killed any shot she might've had at resurrecting her career.

"'Shame Me'!" more people call, and Summer blinks. I see it in the sudden slump of her shoulders: she knows that part of the reason these people have flocked to the stage is that they want to be in the front row for any drama. They're recording on their phones not just because this moment is special, but in case she falls down or says something ridiculous that they can post online later.

Suddenly I'm right back there, the day of the finale, Summer looking to us all to do something, anything. I didn't help her thirteen years ago, but maybe I can now.

"*Shame me, shame me, but you can't tame me!*" someone sings from the audience, while a couple of others cackle. I stand up and push through the crowd toward the table with the karaoke book on it. The same women who had control of it before reach for it, no doubt to look up the song that Summer doesn't want to sing, but I swoop in and pluck it up, ignoring their noises of outrage, flipping through the pages with a single-minded determination until I find what I'm looking for.

"Maybe that's enough for now," Summer is saying up on the stage, and a few people boo in protest, then start to chant the name of the song. This sudden shift of mood happened occasionally with fans of the show back when we were big. What starts as pure excitement from getting to be around you can turn, without warning, to anger that you won't give them what they want.

I plug the number 3945 into the machine and press play. As the first chord rings out, the crowd pauses in its chanting—have they gotten their demand? Summer recognizes the song immediately and looks to the machine, her eyes landing on me. Then the corners of her lips tug upward. She grabs a second microphone from a stool on the stage and holds it out. As the musical intro to one of our rare *Daydreams* duets continues, I step forward to take it.

I settle myself onstage next to Summer, trying to ignore the confused murmur from the crowd. I'm not as recognizable as she is, having stayed out of the tabloids for a decade, in my new uniform of business attire. Summer sings the first lines of the song, a folky acoustic number with shades of "Landslide" that I always found surprisingly beautiful. Michael had asked the songwriters to write something with gorgeous harmonies for me and Summer to sing during a brief moment of peace between our characters. The songwriters delivered.

As people catch on to what song it is, little squeaks of excitement start to burst from the crowd. "Holy shit, it's Kat," someone yells as Summer's solo lines end, and it's time for mine.

My hand sweats so much that I'm worried the microphone might slip out of it. I haven't sung in front of other people in years besides "Happy Birthday" at friends' parties. And even then, I practically whisper the words so as not to draw attention to myself. Now, I worry that I've lost any ability I had, that nerves will constrict my throat and only a croak will come out.

But Summer smiles at me like she did the first time we sang through this music together. ("We get to duet!" she'd said when we got the script for that week. "And it's so freaking pretty and I can't wait!") I take a deep breath and jump in, with the terrifying exhilaration of leaping off a high dive. My voice wavers on the first notes, but I push through and then we're at the chorus, our voices swelling in a tight harmony.

Singing can be pleasurable in two ways, when you're doing it right. There's the vibration of your vocal cords, a pleasant thrumming inside your skull. And then you hear yourself from the outside, or maybe you hear your voice blending with another's to make something greater than what you could have done on your own. The dual pleasures of hearing and feeling—sometimes it's almost too much to bear. And I'm not even *that* great a singer.

Summer and I face each other as our voices build, and the crowd is both there and not. Their energy feeds into ours, but I'm focused on the woman in front of me. She waggles her eyebrows and I nod, and then we launch into the dance that went along with this, which we somehow still remember from thirteen years prior, like it's been frozen all this time, perfectly preserved, waiting for us to bring it back out into the sun. The choreography is not the peppy steps of many of our other numbers, but a languid, graceful weaving. We must look ridiculous—Summer in her cutoff shorts, me in my skirt suit, singing a song meant for teenagers. But I don't feel ridiculous. I feel whole.

The song hits a musical break. Summer uses the time to turn to the crowd and indicate me. "Say hi to my friend Kat. Sorry, *Katherine*." I glare at her, and she smiles before turning back to the crowd. "You may have heard something about a *Daydreams* reunion special. Katherine is saying that she doesn't want to come back, but we can't do it without her, right?"

"Yes!" someone shouts.

"Kat, you *need* to!"

People are staring, eyes boring into me from all directions.

There are so many reasons not to come back. But I know that I'm going to say yes. It's not the peer pressure, or the glory that comes from a bunch of tipsy twentysomethings holding up their phones to snap a photo of me. I feel more alive now than I have in years. And, beyond that, I need to come back because Summer wants me to. Because this one month of my time could fix her ruined life, and I'm the reason her life spun so far off track in the first place.

Maybe the trick to dealing with the guilt is not to get as far away from it as possible, but to hurtle directly into the center of it. The center is where I can make things right. Then I can come home, my conscience free, ready to say yes to Miheer and finally, fully move on.

Besides, if Summer, Liana, and Noah get back together without me, who knows what they might manage to figure out?

"So," Summer asks into the microphone. "What do you say? Will you come back?"

She looks innocent—those wide eyes have that effect—and yet I'm not sure that I buy what she's selling me. I'm not convinced that her motives are entirely pure. But the music break is ending and the final chorus is coming back around. "Fine," I say into the microphone, prompting a roar from the crowd as Summer and I join hands and finish the song.

THE GIRL OF YOUR DAYDREAMS

BY CHRIS MATHESON

What accounts for the astronomical success of *The Daydreams*, a silly and utterly predictable TV show for tweens and teens that has grown into a religion for its younger viewers and a semi-ironic fascination for its older ones? Could it be the narrative tension or zippy one-liners? No, those do not seem to exist in the show's cotton candy world. What about the character growth? Unfortunately, its major players go through the same arc every episode with Sisyphean dedication. Sure, the fresh-faced cast is by and large appealing, performing the musical numbers each episode with an infectious (if bland) enthusiasm.

But for my money, the magic ingredient is the girl next door at the center of the show, Summer Wright. Though her name is Summer, the season she conjures is spring—that breath of fresh air arriving after a long winter. She buds, she blooms. Setting aside poetics for practicalities: Wright is an all-American sweetheart, blond and big-eyed with a healthy tan. Close your eyes, and it's easy to imagine her bouncing up and down, practicing cheerleading routines out in the sun. Tween girls around the nation may be putting up posters of Wright's costar Noah Gideon on their walls. But Wright has already received requests to pose for three different major men's magazines on the day she turns eighteen (just a few months from now, for interested parties). She turned them all down, confused by their interest. And therein lies the key to her appeal: her total lack of awareness of it.

"Sometimes," she tells me at a costume fitting for the show's second season, which is set to begin production next month, "I think, 'I'm a small-town girl. What am I doing here?' I should still be acting in my local community theater production of *Bye Bye Birdie*!"

The small town of which she speaks is located ninety minutes outside of Los Angeles. For most of Wright's childhood, a good time meant heading into Bakersfield for dinner. Weekends were reserved for theater practice (she got her start as Little Orphan Annie at age nine) and church with her family.

When I ask her about the church, she fiddles with a ring on her finger. It's a promise ring, she explains, given to her by her father to symbolize their commitment to their faith. Prepare to be dismayed and a tad titillated: Summer Wright is a virgin, and she's planning to remain one until marriage. Her personal life matches the show, where the high schoolers are chaste and the will-they-or-won't-they couple at the center hasn't even so much as kissed. Atlas, which produces and airs *The Daydreams*, has been accused of being too unforgiving to its child stars of the past. Who can forget the way they cut loose Amber Nielson, star of their previous hit show *Girl Powers*, when video surfaced of her snorting white powder at a private club? But Summer Wright swears her performance of innocence is no performance at all. She's a role model, which makes her the perfect fit for the Atlas mold.

And what about her boyfriend, a high school classmate who also attends the church? Does he mind the purity vow or the relentless interest in his girlfriend? A blush lights up Wright's cheeks, and she chews on her full bottom lip. "No, I'm really lucky that he's been so supportive of everything," she says, as if unaware that thousands of men would trade places with him in a heartbeat, purity vow and all.

Viewers of the show might assume that Gideon is one such man. Young fans have spun the romantic chemistry between the two into fantasies of a real-life romance. "Oh my gosh!" Wright demurs, putting her face in her hands. "No, Noah and I think it's funny when people say that! Because we're best friends, me and him and Kat and Liana." (Kat Whitley and Liana Jackson serviceably play the two major supporting characters on the show.)

For now, Wright's fame looks likely to only grow and grow. "I'd like to stay with *The Daydreams* as long as possible," she says, taking delicate bites of a watercress salad that an assistant has brought over. "And then, who knows? Maybe a solo album. Maybe a movie career."

Still, before we say goodbye, I notice a sign that Wright may already be on her way to outgrowing the show that's making her famous. While trying on one of the costume designer's selections for season two, a knee-length dress with a pattern of daisies on it, she rolls up the hem so that it exposes a few more inches of her toned, hairless thigh, the kind of thigh that could bring great men to their knees. "How about," she says to the designer, "like this instead?"

Seven

· · · · · · ·

2018

A month after my karaoke adventure, Miheer drives me to the airport.

The month has flown by in a rush of work and preparing. At my firm, Irene was befuddled, to put it mildly, when I told her that I was taking a leave of absence.

"Let me get this straight," she said. "You want to take a month off when you're so close to being considered for partner, not to clerk, or to do legal aid for an underserved population, or even because you're having a baby, but so that you can do a musical TV special?"

". . . Yes," I said.

"Good Lord, Katherine. I have to advise you against this." Irene has always looked out for me, assigning other junior associates to the true nightmare clients (well, most of the time, anyway). She and her wife, Leah, have Miheer and me over for dinner once a month, and we always stay for hours, gossiping and gorging and getting along like a house on fire. I love her.

"I know it might be unwise, but I have to go. It won't kill my partner chances, will it?"

"No. But it might . . . maim them. You know the guys here,

they're always looking for an excuse." Her eyes flitted to her office door—closed—and then back to me. "Those bastards."

"I want to show everyone that I'm committed, despite this." I gripped the edges of my chair. If I screwed up my shot at partner, I'd never get to do the pro bono work that I'd been pushing for. "Load me up. I'll do as much work as I can before I leave."

She delivered, assigning me so much that I had to pull multiple all-nighters. In the infrequent spare hours I had, I took dance classes at a local studio, remembering how to move my body, hopping around with a bunch of teenage girls and retired women.

Needless to say, Miheer and I had no time for a romantic bed-and-breakfast weekend. And the few other times he brought up going out for "a special nice dinner" or "even a lovely drink" with an increasingly desperate note in his voice, well, I told him there was no time for any of that either. I hate myself for dodging his proposal attempts. But I'd hate myself even more for accepting.

Now, he walks me to the security line. I wheel my suitcase and intertwine my free hand in his. My palm is slick. Or maybe the sweat is coming from both of our hands as we think about what waits for me on the other end of this flight, and what it will do to us. The sweet smell of sugared dough wafts from a nearby Cinnabon, and my stomach gurgles.

Normally when we're at the airport together, we pass through security and head straight to the kiosk with books. We each pick out a novel for the other person, and they have to read it on the plane, no complaining. (I always pick the most gruesome crime thrillers I can find for Miheer. I like seeing the adorable look of horror on his face as he reads the gory details, and cackle each time he asks, in increasingly plaintive tones, "Why are you doing this to me?" He picks me sentimental tearjerkers about noble pets who change the lives of their owners, determined to make me cry.) But this time, I'm passing through security alone.

We turn to each other for the moment of goodbye. He's wearing his black-frame glasses, which make him look so handsome I can barely stand it.

"Good luck out there," he says. "You're going to knock everybody's socks off."

"Thanks. I'll get you a ticket for the show, but truly, you do not need to come out and see it."

"You sure? I want to support you."

"It's going to be very stupid. Not your kind of thing."

"Well then, I'll see where I am with work and how easy it is to get away." He reaches out and squeezes my hand. "Hey, I'll miss you."

"It'll be weird, going to bed alone every night."

"How am I supposed to fall asleep without you furiously typing work emails next to me?"

"You'll have to buy a white noise machine. Maybe tape a picture of my stressed-out face onto it."

"If you could also send me a recording of you muttering things like 'stupid clients' and 'I've already told them this five times' at irregular intervals, that would be helpful."

"I'll get on it," I say, laughing. I step forward and kiss him, wrapping my arms around his chest. He tugs a strand of my hair gently, both of us not wanting to let go even though the security line is getting longer by the minute.

Reluctantly, we separate. "Well, goodbye," I say.

"One last thing," he says, and reaches into his pocket for a small box.

No no no, not now, I think as he starts to kneel to the ground, and then I'm not just thinking it, I'm saying it aloud, and he freezes part of the way down, his brown eyes filling with hurt.

"No, you don't want to marry me?"

"That's . . . that's not what I . . ." I stutter. He rises back to standing, blinking hard as if trying not to cry. "I mean not here, in an airport full of people, next to a Cinnabon—"

"Well, yes." His mouth tightens. "I know it's not exactly the most romantic of spots. I've been trying all month to do it somewhere nicer, but you've been so busy that I had no choice but to do Cinnabon—"

"It's not about the Cinnabon." I reach for his hand. "I mean not *now*, when I'm about to fly away for a month. I want to be able to enjoy this, not immediately worry that I'm going to get stuck in the security line."

He steps back, and now *I'm* the one blinking hard. "But don't you see that's why I want to do it? I'm trying to be supportive, but I'm really confused. You tell me you're not going back, then suddenly I get a Google alert that you've said yes to a bar full of strangers."

"Summer strong-armed me—"

"You say the show's not an important part of your life, that I shouldn't even watch it because you're embarrassed by it, and then you drop everything to fly to LA for a month. I'm . . . disoriented, and honestly kind of freaked out, and I guess I just want to know that you're not going to get sucked back into this Hollywood world and forget about our life—"

"How could I possibly forget about you? I love you so much."

Doubt about that crosses his face. No wonder. I just responded to him pulling out a ring like he was offering me a gigantic spider.

Why can't I tell him everything? Because I'm terrified of how his eyebrows might knit together as he says, *You're not who I thought you were.* Because I don't want him to withdraw his proposal in disgust. And because now is definitely not the time to bare my soul. We're in an airport full of strangers, including two young women who are staring at us curiously, whispering to each other. Shit, the last thing we need is for some rumor—*Kat Whitley and her boyfriend had a MASSIVE airport fight!*—to hit the internet. If the reunion doesn't work out the way I hope it will, I'll suck it up and tell him the truth, and pray to whatever god will listen that it doesn't change the way he feels about me.

"Hey," I say in a low voice, trying to keep a placid look on my face for any nosy onlookers. "Please know that this has nothing to do with you. You're the best thing in my life. I just didn't realize how much I needed closure. I'm going back to get that, and then it'll be done. Ask me again the day this is all over, okay?"

He swallows. Then he steps forward, hugs me tightly, and says, "You'd better not miss your flight."

Eight

· · · · · · ·

2004

The first time someone screamed at the sight of me, I was in a Walmart in Pennsylvania. It was two weeks before we were scheduled to start filming the second season of the show, and I was visiting my dad in his sad bachelor apartment (my mom had kept the house in the divorce). He'd invited a "nice new friend" of his to come have dinner with us that night. While he scoured the store for supplies—groceries and candles and, oh God, was he really putting *condoms* into the cart while I was right here?—I fled to the magazine aisle, flipping through the latest issue of *CosmoGirl* to take the quiz it promised on its cover: **Which Daydreamer are you?**

I got Liana.

A bloodcurdling shriek pierced the air, and I nearly dropped the magazine. Terrorism? A sniper? I looked up, ready to search for a hiding spot, only to find a girl, maybe twelve years old, staring at me and quivering.

"Are you okay?" I asked, scanning her for a wound.

"You're Kat!" she said. "Oh my God, oh my God."

My shoulders loosened as I realized what was happening. "I am!"

"Are the others here too?"

"Just me," I said, and then dropped into character. "And obviously I'm the best one, so you're welcome."

She laughed, her eyes shining, and I knew mine were shining right back. My mere presence had made her day, maybe even her week. She'd call up all her friends that night and tell them, *You'll never believe what happened to me!* and for a little while, she'd be the most popular girl in her group, everyone wanting to hear the story of her celebrity adventure. And all I'd had to do to make that happen for her was walk into a Walmart. I floated right up into the air.

"Do you want an autograph?" I asked, digging in my messenger bag for a pen as she squealed her assent. She looked around the aisle, picked a notebook for sale off the shelf, and handed it over to me. I scrawled a looping signature, one I'd practiced in my own notebooks when I was younger, never imagining that someone would actually want it, would treat a piece of paper like a prized possession just because my name was on it.

She hugged me and then ran off to find her mother. I stared after her, waving until she disappeared. Then I settled back with the magazine, looking down at the "Liana" description in the quiz results (*Congrats, you're the best friend a girl could have!*), my whole body buzzing. Vibrating with adrenaline. Oh, and something else— my cell phone. Summer's name on the screen.

A smile automatically spread over my face. She'd called me every night we'd been at home in between shooting seasons—unlike Noah and Liana, we didn't have any siblings, so we'd joked that we were each other's sisters. The two of us talked for hours, trading funny stories of our weird experiences now that we were in the limelight. We'd taken off so fast. In the weeks leading up to the first episode's premiere, Atlas had run a spot with Amber Nielson, star of *Girl Powers* (about a teenage girl who could do magic), conjuring up a torch and passing it to us. The day she'd come to film it with us, we'd all been awed. She was the biggest star on the channel! I used to watch her show with the kid I babysat! Amber was nice enough to us, if distracted. Of course, Atlas had pulled the ad when she got caught doing coke. Still, we'd debuted to massive numbers and had only grown from there.

I flipped the phone open. "I'm glad you called because I have to tell you, a girl just screamed so loud when she saw me that I think my eardrum burst."

She made a hiccup noise—not her usual laugh. But I barely noticed because my eyes had skipped down below the "Liana" section, drawn to the "Mostly Cs—Kat" description: *We know, nobody wants to be Kat. But you are, so you've got a choice: embrace your inner villain, or try to be a better person so that the next time you take this quiz, you get Summer instead.*

It's amazing how the smallest negative thing can ruin the biggest good. A drop of food coloring tints an entire glass of water. Taints it. Suddenly, all I could think of was the girl's question—"Are the others here too?" I was the consolation prize. She was excited to see me, yes, but she'd rather have seen *them*. Because nobody wants to be Kat.

Summer made that weird hiccup noise again as I frowned down at the page. "My dad died."

I forgot all about the stupid quiz. Mr. Wright, with his booming voice, who had made me understand the definition of the word "hearty," couldn't just be gone. He was supposed to be there on set when we got back for season two, as always, on our side, cheering us on. "What? How?"

"Car accident," she managed to get out, her voice made small and ragged by grief. "He was coming home late from a bar, driving too fast in the dark."

My own inadequacy paralyzed me. How do you even begin to comfort a person when the worst thing has happened to them? "It's going to be okay," I said, just a stupid nineteen-year-old who'd never had to deal with something like this. "He's in a better place." (I didn't even really believe in God, but Summer did, so I thought I was supposed to say that.)

"I have to go," Summer said. "I should call the others. But can you come to the service?"

· · · · · · · ·

All of us went—me, Noah, and Liana. Michael, in a dark suit so different from the oversized T-shirts he wore when he was commanding the set. Even Mr. Atlas was there, sitting quietly in a pew to pay his respects. Summer, a shell of herself, stood next to a petite Latina woman wearing large sunglasses to hide her eyes. "This is my mom, Lupe," she said to me when I came over to give her a hug, and Lupe shook my hand stiffly.

"Thank you for coming," she said in a lightly accented voice.

It was funny, for all that Summer's dad had dominated the first season with his loud laugh and his constant looking out for Summer's interests, Summer had hardly ever talked about her mom. I'd just assumed she was as lily-white as Summer's dad.

On Summer's other side, a blandly handsome boy in a suit tugged at his shirt collar, uncomfortable. So this was Lucas, the boyfriend from back home. Noah introduced himself, offering his hand, and the two of them shook a little too heartily, sizing each other up.

The church was stifling, the air heavy with perfume and perspiration. Summer came to the front and sang "Danny Boy," tremulous but determined, and the sounds of weeping rose around me. As a pastor offered a long sermon and Mr. Wright's brother delivered a eulogy, I longed for fresh air and daylight.

But when we left the church, people had gathered outside. Paparazzi, about five or six of them. They swarmed toward us, toward

Summer, their cameras clicking in a mad frenzy, some of them shouting her name, asking for quotes about her father, if she was going to need to take time off from the show. Summer shied back, like an animal escaping a kick. Her boyfriend furrowed his face in confusion. Noah jumped in front of Summer to block her from the cameras' view.

Paparazzi surround you on three sides, though, so that when you try to turn away from them, someone else can get the photo. They spread out, working together like a sinister, strategic army. Liana and I looked at each other, a realization coming over both of us. At a certain point, your fame grew so large that you couldn't turn it off when you wanted to. That tipping point was on the horizon for us. Maybe it had already tipped over for Summer. I welcomed it in the fun moments, like when that fan screamed at me in Walmart. Would I be willing to take it in the bad moments too, moments as low as this one? Yes, I decided as the cameras clicked away, it was a fair trade, to give up privacy for the chance to do something you loved. We'd stick together and protect one another, and it would all be more than worth it. Liana and I stepped forward and took Summer's other two sides, the sides that Noah couldn't block. If the paparazzi were an army, we could be one too.

There was some discussion of postponing our start date for filming the second season so that Summer had time to grieve. But although Summer had expressed a preference for that, the execs didn't want to wait. We had a strict release schedule, and we'd managed something so rare: momentum. If we took too much time off, we risked letting that die.

"It's important to grieve," Michael said, explaining the predicament to me as we ate finger sandwiches in the corner at the wake. "But you also don't want to let your other responsibilities go, and then be saddled with regret on top of the grief."

"You really think people would stop caring about the show?"

He nodded darkly. "Or, if she insists on too much time, the network might do something really dumb and decide to replace her."

The show couldn't work without Summer. The rest of us would be heartbroken to lose her. "They wouldn't," I said uncertainly.

"The network is a fickle god," he said, and shoved the rest of his sandwich into his mouth. Then he fixed me in his gaze, like he was seeing me for the first time. "She trusts you. I bet she'd listen, if you tried to save her from herself."

The next time Summer and I talked on the phone, a couple days later, I asked her how she was doing.

"It's been a really bad week." Her voice caught and she cleared her throat. "I, um . . ."

"Maybe what you need is a distraction."

"You think so?" she asked. She sounded like a child on the other end of the line. "Like, maybe you and Liana could come out here and stay over for a bit? I have a trundle—"

"Yeah. And then it could really help to get back to work. You know, where we can all be together, making something." No response from her. "Michael was saying it would suck if people lost interest in the show, and we didn't get to keep doing it." She let out a quiet, resigned sigh.

We were back on set a week later.

. . . .

Liana and I tried to help Summer with movie nights and slumber parties in my apartment. She'd smile vacantly at us. She was vacant a lot during that first week back, unable to remember more complicated choreography, leaving her trailer door unlocked.

Once, I came to get her in her trailer, and there was a bunch of tulips on the chair. "Who are those from?" I asked.

"I have no idea," she said, picking them up, tracing the flowers with her thumb, tears welling in her eyes.

She forgot her lines. She forgot to hit her marks. It got so bad that word traveled to the higher-ups. One day, before we started filming, Michael walked over to where Liana, Summer, and I were stretching in the corner.

"Mr. Atlas sent a present over for you," he said to Summer. "He wants you to know how much the network values you." Liana nudged me, and we both turned to watch as Michael pulled out a journal with a soft seafoam-green cover, the word SUMMER embossed on it. It was gorgeous. And more than that, the *effort* Mr. Atlas had gone to—picking it out, getting her name on it— despite being a busy man. (Looking back at it now, I'm sure he had an assistant do this for him. But at the time, I was convinced that he, the head of one of the most important networks in the world, had taken the better part of a day just to get Summer a gift.)

Michael was still talking, saying that he was the one who'd recommended something like this for Summer. Writing could heal, and they all wanted her to heal very badly. I barely heard him. I was peering over Summer's shoulder as she opened the front page of the journal to reveal an inscription from Mr. Atlas: *To our brightest star.*

Liana and I stared as Summer closed the notebook back up and hugged it to her chest, all of us unaware of the disaster it would bring.

Dear Diary,

I guess I never really "got" the whole idea of writing down your feelings instead of just feeling them. But maybe I've been feeling mine a little too much recently. Michael gave me this yesterday, from Mr. Atlas, although of course Michael tried to take credit for it too, with a big long speech about the importance of writing, the "healing powers" of it, where he made sure to throw in a few references to his own incredibly important writing, just look at how him writing "The Daydreams" has healed so many people from the wounds of 9/11, etc. . . . Sorry, I'm being a little mean. This is a nice gift. I think Kat and Liana were jealous, but I'd happily trade them a journal for a father.

   Anyway, I think I'm supposed to write about Dad dying, but I don't know what to say about it except that I didn't know it was possible to feel this sad. There's a big black hole at the center of my universe where there used to be a sun. Mom asked me if I wanted to quit the show, but that would be like Dad dying all over again, if I just gave up on something he was so happy about. He was the one who always thought that I was worthy of being a star. He knew it ever since I got that first solo in the children's choir at church, when I was five years old. Mom let Dad take the reins on going with me to auditions, showing up at rehearsals, etc. . . . It's not that she didn't believe in me. More like she was worried about me getting hurt. And besides, Dad said when I used to get upset about it, it was better to have her stay home anyway, because maybe it would hurt me to not be entirely "all-American," whatever the heck that means. Okay, fine. I know what that means. (Mom used to speak Spanish to me when I was little. And then after I got that solo in the children's choir, Dad told her that it was confusing me too much. He was the one who told me I should think about dyeing my hair blond too, after I wore a blond wig for one of the community plays. That the color just looked better on me. People <u>did</u> look at me longer and smile at me more afterward, and I started getting more callbacks, even if I thought that I looked weird. Now I'm used to it, though, and think it would be strange to go back to brown. I guess you can get used to anything. I don't know if that's comforting or terrifying.)

I was tempted to quit the show like Mom suggested when that crowd of greasy men surrounded us outside the church after the funeral, and during that next week when I was feeling so bad, and nothing I tried made me feel any better, and everyone from the show was saying that if they had to wait for me much longer, it was going to ruin production. I was like, maybe this all isn't worth it. Maybe I should just go back to being a normal person, let them cast some other girl while I finish up school and marry Lucas. Dad liked Lucas.

But Dad liked "The Daydreams" more. Besides, how could I leave Kat and Liana? (Even though, ugh, Kat has been really annoying, like just telling me it's all going to be okay whenever I try to talk about all this and looking so uncomfortable that I change the subject. Fine, then, I won't talk to her.) And Noah. I don't know if he's changed or I've changed. Well no, that's not true, I know I've changed. Now I'm a girl without a father. But I'm noticing things about him that I never saw before. Did you know that he has a freckle behind his ear, in the spot where you might give someone a hickey? Did you know . . . who am I asking? You're a journal. Sorry to Michael, but this feels a little stupid.

Nine

· · · · · ·

2018

When I wake up the morning of our first day back, in a hotel room that Atlas has booked me for the next month, I throw up from nerves.

Our first order of business isn't a rehearsal, but a meet and greet with the press, a clear signal of Atlas's priorities with this reboot. Nobody expects this show to be a work of art. They expect to generate headlines.

We're to meet in a greenroom adjacent to where the press has gathered. We'll say our hellos—me, Liana, Summer, Noah, and Michael—and then go face the crowd of journalists and photographers together, a united front.

When I arrive, Michael is already there. Our creator. Saying it that way makes it sound like he *made* us, which I suppose he did. (And ruined us too?) "Kat," he says, coming over to greet me, schlubbier than ever in one of his trademark oversized T-shirts (this one printed with an old classic movie poster on it), his hair shaggy, his bulky frame a little creakier than it was thirteen years ago. Do I hug him, or shake his hand? We never had a close relationship—I was so paralyzed by wanting to win his favor that I couldn't pal around with him like Noah did. I'm almost as old now as he was when he created the show, and I work with middle-aged rich guys all the time, but still, as he walks toward me, I seize up with nerves, then choose the handshake.

"By the way," I say, pumping his hand, "offscreen I go by Katherine now."

"Mm," he grunts, then indicates a videographer hovering behind him. "James is capturing some behind-the-scenes footage we can release, so look alive." Well, you know what they say: when you're about to awkwardly and terrifyingly reunite with the people who once meant the world to you, why not throw a videographer into the mix? I nod at James as Michael goes on. "Good guy. We work together on *Disaster Ship*. Have you watched it?"

"Oh yeah, congratulations on all the success," I say, to disguise the fact that I've had zero interest in checking out Michael's latest show, about a group of kids whose parents work on a cruise ship, and the shenanigans they get up to on the boat. It's not a phenomenon like *The Daydreams*, but it's been running for a totally respectable three seasons on a streaming service. In fact, "totally respectable" describes the whole career he's managed to build since *The Daydreams*. I wonder, though, how much time he's spent blaming Summer for things. How much more he believes he could have achieved if not for her.

"Grab yourself a coffee or a snack," Michael says, indicating a craft services table. "The press is already arriving, so we'll head out there as soon as everyone else gets here." He turns to an assistant, discussing logistics.

I pour myself a cup of coffee, too agitated to eat anything, then notice that craft services set out this brand of flavored almonds that Miheer swears by, even though *I* swear by the fact that they taste like feet. I text him a picture. Apparently, someone on our production team shares your terrible taste.

Hey! he texts back immediately, and my shoulders relax in relief. We left things in a weird place at the airport, but we're going to be fine. Eat some in my honor.

KAT: Absolutely not.

Good luck today! he texts, then a moment later: Wait no, break a leg? Do people say that for rehearsals?

I'm smiling down at his message when Liana emerges from a door on the other side of the greenroom—a bathroom—and gasps at the sight of me. She strides over, opening her arms for a hug. "Kat!" she says, and clutches me tight. I'm unprepared for the level of affection and the odd angle at which she's come in, and I freeze while trying not to spill my coffee. Liana was the only one with whom I kept in touch in the months after the live show, the two of us on the phone checking in, until it became too painful to talk about how much we'd lost and we drifted apart. She steps back, holding me by the shoulders. Her face looks like it's been stretched since I last saw her, her round young cheeks giving way to something contoured and sharp. A natural byproduct of time and growing up? Or is it due more to plastic surgery and an unforgiving workout regimen? Liana has always applied herself studiously to whatever she's pursuing, and it seems that she's been very studious indeed about being somebody's hot wife. Despite the change in her, it's good to see her again, to feel her hands on my shoulders. My throat tingles. For a moment, we just look at each other, overcome. I picture the two of us clasping hands and fleeing the room, posting up at the nearest bar and talking for hours.

Then she looks away. "That was awkward. I came at you like a velociraptor." She holds her hands up like claws and makes a funny face.

I laugh. "Yeah, not the smoothest of hugs."

"Should we . . ." she begins, then makes the decision. "Yes, let's do it again." She indicates James the videographer, who has been capturing the moment.

"Wait, seriously?" I ask.

"You really want the whole world to watch that weird-ass hug?"

"Oh God," I say. "Fine." So I put my coffee down, plaster on a smile, and we throw our arms around each other, embracing like someone's just come home from the war. Well, I guess it's good to dust off the old acting chops before diving back into rehearsal.

"Holy shit," a voice says, and everyone's attention turns, because Noah Gideon has entered the room.

Back in the day, he would have bounded over to us, a gangly, enthusiastic puppy of a boy who ran toward the world, eager to see what it might offer. Now, however, he leans in the doorway, a grin spreading over his face at the sight of me and Liana.

"Look at you guys," he says, shaking his head, his arms folded over his chest. He wears a tight gray sweater, a close-cropped beard (just this side of scruff) glinting on his cheeks and giving him a grown-up air. He's . . . rooted. He no longer needs to run toward the world. It comes to him.

The golden boy has become a golden man, and he gleams, but I will not let his shine blind me again. Now I know his secret: that he's perfectly aware of his own shine, and he wields it purposefully. He might look at me like I'm the only person in the room, but then he'll turn around and look at someone else the exact same way, and I'm not the lovesick girl I once was, hanging around him hoping for scraps. Miheer feeds me whole meals. (Literally— he's an excellent cook.)

Still, there's something about your first love. Some part of you, the part that longs for who you used to be, will always care too much about them. They will always be . . . charged, if you are lucky or unlucky enough to encounter them again.

And so, when Noah holds his arms open, I walk into them. It's involuntary, this walking forward. He lifts me up a few inches off the ground—God, he is annoyingly strong, his chest solid and broad beneath his stupid tight sweater—then turns to Liana.

"Careful, no lifting!" She indicates her short skirt.

He holds up his hands in mock surrender, giving her a kiss on the cheek instead. Liana accepts it calmly—Noah's powers never particularly undid her, and especially not now that she's married to a superstar athlete—but I catch a glimpse of Michael's young assistant staring, her hand flitting up to her own cheek in a sub-conscious wish that Noah might turn and kiss her next. "I have an important question for you," Noah asks Liana. "When will your husband be coming to set, and can I have his autograph?"

"Oh, he can't wait to visit. He wishes he could be here the whole time, but with training and the season, you know how it is," she says, so smoothly that it sounds rehearsed. She blinks. "Actually, let's take a picture for him!" Whipping out her phone, she takes a selfie of the three of us together. As we all smile, I place something that's been bothering me. When we were young, Liana had a re-freshing bluntness to her. She put herself out there, and spoke her mind, and sure, maybe it rubbed people the wrong way, but I loved it. Now, though, she feels artificial, like one of those beautiful house-plants you admire from a distance, but whose leaves turn out to be plastic.

"Sorry to hear about you and Cassie," Liana says to Noah as she scrolls through the photos she took, texting one to Javier.

"Thanks," he says. Noah's ex Cassie Mueller is a sort of girl-about-town mainly known for her famous father, a director who has won every award in the world. Cassie dabbles in creativity in the way that children of famous people do—publishing a book of confessional essays, getting into photography—and she's fine. But if she were some random girl from South Dakota, no one would be giving her gallery space.

"So you're on the prowl again, huh?" Liana continues, only half paying attention. Now, she's putting the photo of us on her Instagram, typing some caption that reads BFFS REUNITING as she barely looks at us.

"The women of the world better watch out," I say, my voice as dry as a desert.

Michael calls Liana over for something, and the videographer turns toward them.

"Hey." Noah brushes his hand against mine and lowers his voice, keeping a casual look on his face. "I know the last time we hung out was . . ." I wait, silent, raising the eyebrow, making him say it. "Not great. But friends again?"

We had thirteen years to be friends again. But he never bothered to reach out to apologize or even just to talk. In the meantime, he was happy enough to laugh when interviewers said something cutting about the show. Or about one of us.

I force my lips into a smile that doesn't reach my eyes. "Sure. Friends."

But I wonder: How beneficial is it for him to be buddy-buddy? Sure, he got suckered into this reunion, but it can't hurt his reputation to have the world see him palling around with us. If we don't seem to blame him for how he acted in the aftermath, nobody else can either.

We all catch up for another ten minutes or so, a growing awareness hitting us—Summer isn't here yet.

Finally, Michael approaches. "Anyone heard from Summer?"

he asks, and we shake our heads. He smirks, an unpleasant twist of his mouth. "Should we take bets on whether or not she shows?"

Beside me, Liana looks down at the floor. Noah smiles, but his leg jiggles, ever so subtly, as he taps his foot.

An assistant anxiously flutters in from the pressroom. "They're asking if something's wrong," she says to Michael in a low voice.

"Dammit," he says, too loudly, and then, rubbing his eyes: "I swear to God, if she ruins this reunion too . . ."

"She's going to be here," I say. And as if my words have summoned her, the door swings open, and she appears.

"Hi!" she calls out, and I blink, surprised. She looks different than she did a month ago, when she came down to DC to woo me. Her hair is full and freshly dyed, her nails manicured, her makeup expertly applied. Dressed in a sweet, cornflower-blue sundress, she gives off . . . well, I wouldn't go so far as to call it a *healthy* glow, but it feels healthy compared to what it was before, like she gave up alcohol and started jogging. She's clearly spent the intervening month working as hard as possible to transform herself back to who she was the first time we were all together, a sweet little innocent. But she can't disguise the rasp in her voice, the history that hangs over her like a storm cloud.

It is really, really strange.

She doesn't apologize for her lateness, just shyly enters the room and hugs me tight. She grabs Liana's hands, and Liana's breath catches before she switches on her big fake smile for the camera and says, "It's amazing to see you!"

"We're going to have so much fun," Summer says. As she stares into our eyes, it doesn't feel like she's looking at us so much as purposefully not looking elsewhere.

Beside me, Noah clears his throat. For just a moment, Summer's smile wavers. Then she turns to him.

In the moment when their eyes meet, it's like they want to either rip each other apart or rip each other's clothes off. If this reunion were happening in private, maybe they'd pick one and have at it. But now they're caught in the camera's lens, spotlighted by the gazes of everyone in the room. So instead, seeming not to breathe, Noah inclines his head toward her. "Summer," he says.

"Hi, you," she says. She reaches out and touches him, her fingers just grazing the bare skin of his forearm where he's rolled up the sleeve of his sweater. "Congratulations. You've done so well."

He cannot say it back. We all know it. His Adam's apple pulses. "It's great to see you."

"I want you to know that I watched *Woodlands*," she continues, and he stiffens as though worried about her judgment. He doesn't need to be. Everyone, apparently, loves *Woodlands*, a melancholy animated adventure movie that Noah wrote (about chipmunks or something, I don't know, I've never seen it). It won for best animated film at that year's Oscars and nabbed Noah a surprise nomination for best original screenplay. I once thought that the sun shone out of Noah's ass, but even I didn't realize he had that in him. The movie's success changed Noah from famous to respected. No one could sniff that he was just a pretty face after that.

"It was beautiful," Summer says, and something shifts in Noah's expression.

Their eyes stay locked together for another second, a second that seems to last years. Crops grow and wither, cities rise and fall. The rest of the room begins to titter about *Woodlands*. ("Oh yes, it was *so* great." "I cried my eyes out, but also felt strangely uplifted?")

"Yeah, yeah," Michael cuts in. "We all think *Woodlands* is a fucking masterpiece. Now, Summer, are you ready to go charm the press?"

She finally pulls her eyes away from Noah. "Of course," she

says. Her tone is light, but her neck has flushed a rosy pink. The assistants start shepherding us toward the door. I sneak a glance back at Noah. He's smiling along with everyone else, but the golden hair on his arm, where Summer touched him, stands up among raised bumps of gooseflesh, the sign of someone who has just seen a ghost.

· · · · · · ·

The noise of the pressroom slams into us as we take our seats. Michael gives a quick prepared speech about how we're excited to be back, and then it's off to the races, hands shooting into the air, cameras clicking.

What is it like to see one another again after all this time? ("It feels like a family reunion," Liana says, which is technically true if your family is estranged.) Can Noah tell the crowd anything about his next project? ("When I'm allowed to talk about it, you'll be the first to know," he replies, shooting the reporter his charming smile, leaning toward her as if they're in private conversation. She flushes magenta.)

Michael calls on a woman in the front row who has a self-satisfied look about her, and she stands. "So we all remember how things ended here. And while I'm sure everyone's excited to be back, how will you ensure that what happened last time doesn't happen again?"

When Michael's uncomfortable, his first instinct is to be snide. Sure enough, he leans toward the microphone and says, "Don't worry, we're making sure that the costumes this time are much more complicated to take off." A few of the reporters laugh. I sneak a glance at Summer, who has fixed a smile to her face as if she's in on the joke.

"Nobody's keeping any journals this time around, are they?" the next reporter asks.

"Not me," Summer says. "I haven't gone within six feet of a journal in the last decade."

"And why were you all late today?" someone else asks, relentless. "Not the best foot to start off on, is it? Is there drama behind the scenes already?" The reporters all stare at Summer. She's the unstable one, so she must be the reason for the delay. Her smile wavers. I don't think she was prepared for this onslaught. God, it's like we're all making her do penance.

Before anyone else can say anything, I jump in. "I was stuck in traffic. You move away from LA and forget that the roads here are actual hell."

The reporters nod in sympathy, and for a moment everyone in the room is locked in solidarity, our mutual hatred of the LA traffic bonding us together. Then a man in the third row rises to his feet.

"Seriously though," he says. "Live shows can go wrong in the best of circumstances. Given the track record here, did you all consider doing a pretaped special instead?"

It's a legitimate question. I couldn't believe it when I heard we'd be going live again. But apparently Atlas did some internal polling and found that viewers were far less excited about a pretaped special. They wanted the excitement of live television, and the danger too.

"Well, you've got to love that built-in eight-second delay we've got nowadays," Michael begins.

Summer blanches, and I register that Liana's sneaking glances at her too. Quickly, smoothly, Liana draws the attention to herself. "Look, we were kids back then," she says. "You can be as skeptical as you want, but the fact is that kids do all kinds of stupid things, especially kids in the spotlight. Now we're older. We might not look it, but it's true." She fluffs her hair and bats her eyelashes half jokingly, then grows serious. "We're wiser too. We know what the fans want, and we're going to give that to them, because who are we without them?" She delivers her speech very stirringly. I wonder if she prepared this, just like her line about Javier. "I trust my castmates to be professionals. We all trust each other, don't we?"

We all hasten to smile and nod, and I wonder if anyone else's heart feels like it's thumping so hard it might tear out of their chest. Because while I love them and hate them and I've missed them so very much, I don't trust them. Not at all.

Topic: *The Daydreams*
Summer/Noah
Title: Dare to Fly
By: WordyNerdyGirl882
Rating: Mature

**Hey guys! Since we didn't get to see this, I'm writing how I think the show should have ended. I know that this is a bit of a slow burn, but that's just like Summer and Noah's relationship on the show, lol! Let me know if you enjoy, and I'll keep writing!

CHAPTER ONE

Summer sat in the school music room on the afternoon of high school graduation. She sighed and looked at her reflection in the window. Even though she was so pretty, she didn't have a boyfriend. Liana said she was too picky. But she couldn't help what her heart yearned for—the one boy she'd couldn't have.

Noah. She could see his reflection in the window too, staring at her like he never wanted to look away. But that must be her imagination. Kat had told her that he didn't like her like that, and that if she tried to date him, it would definitely ruin the band.

But then he tapped her shoulder. She wasn't imagining him after all! Her heart leapt.

"Noah!" she cried. "What are you doing here?"

Noah couldn't stop himself from smiling. Summer looked so beautiful when she was surprised. They were about to leave high school, and if he never told her how he felt, he'd hate himself for the rest of his life.

He sat down next to her on the piano bench. "We've had so many important moments in this room rehearsing for *The Daydreams*, haven't we?"

She smiled sadly and pressed a few notes on the piano. "I guess that's over now."

"Then let's make this last moment the most important of all," he said, and kissed her.

As she felt Noah's warm lips on hers, Summer couldn't believe that this was finally happening! His eager mouth felt even better than she'd imagined it would. Their tongues met, slipping together, until she pulled back in disbelief. "Wait, I thought you didn't feel that way about me!"

"I've wanted to do that ever since I met you. Summer . . . I love you."

She gasped and threw her arms around his neck. "Oh Noah, I love you too."

He kissed her again, harder this time. He would make her his own right here on this piano bench. She pulled his shirt up to show his six-pack abs, which were very tan and sexy.

At the sound of loud footsteps outside the door, they pulled apart. Mr. Talbot, the music teacher, walked into the room. "Oh, hello! I'm just looking for my clarinet! Shouldn't you be getting ready for the graduation ceremony?"

As Mr. Talbot gave them an expectant look, Summer and Noah walked out of the music room, joining the crowd of other students in the hallway. But before they parted ways, Noah touched her hand, and whispered in her ear, "I'm not done with you yet . . ."

To be continued . . .

COMMENTS:

DREAMSCOMETRUE91: CRYING. I can't believe we're never going to get to see this!!!!

MRSNOAHGIDEON7: I don't know how u can even write something like this when Summer's a bitch slut who betrayed Noah's true love, it's like did you even read the horrible things she wrote about him?? Anyways I hope he forgets all about her because there are a lot of girls out there who would never break his heart and maybe he should give us a chance instead.

LIFESLIKETHISUHHUH: Write the next chapter right now. I need them to have sex.

Ten

· · · · · · ·

2004

Looking back at it, New York was where we really began to frac-ture.

A few months into filming the second season, Atlas flew us out to the city for a story line about us auditioning for a Broadway show. In the episode, a casting director stumbled upon us singing along with a busker in Central Park and begged us to come into his office. Despite being offered roles, we decided to stay in high school and reconsider becoming Broadway stars *after* graduation. I swear, the wish fulfillment in *The Daydreams* gave so many kids the wrong idea about how easy it was to become a star. There must have been a generation of tweens bursting out into song in public, desperately looking around to see if anyone would offer them a record deal.

It was an astronomical expense to move filming all the way across the country for just one episode, but we were worth it. Mr. Atlas had told Michael that *The Daydreams* was the company's most important show, and now Michael was coming up with all sorts of new ideas: maybe we should do a live season-two finale! He'd started in the theater world, and there was nothing like the adrenaline you got from performing in front of an audience! He had another idea too, one so big that he couldn't even tell us about it, but he promised it would change our lives if it went through.

Our time in New York began well. When I heard what our first stop would be, my legs almost collapsed under me: we were guesting on *TRL*. *The TRL*, on MTV. On so many dreary afternoons back home, I'd comforted myself by watching my favorite celebrities visit the Times Square studio and calling in to vote for my favorite music videos in the countdown.

And now we were walking out into the studio in a line, clutching microphones in our hands, tottering in high heels. Had my own idols stepped exactly where I was stepping? The fans lucky enough to be seated in the studio screamed their heads off. The VJ told us to go over to the big window and look outside. "Feel the love!" he said. Down on the street, among the glowing billboards and Planet Hollywood, more fans stood behind a barricade, holding signs and waving up at us.

I *did* feel the love, a gigantic ball of it bouncing in all directions, toward me and from me. Love for the fans, and love for Summer, Noah, and Liana. We knew exactly how to play off one another in the interview questions. We giddily held hands as the VJ played a snippet from an upcoming episode. In the clip, our band had been invited to perform at senior prom, so we got to go even though we were only juniors. I'd convinced Summer and Liana that we needed to wear simple matching dresses for "band unity," and then showed up in a spotlight-hogging ball gown. The fans in the *TRL* studio squealed as, on the screen, Noah told Summer that she'd look amazing even if she showed up in a paper bag. They laughed as my ball gown got tangled in microphone cords and I tripped right before I was supposed to start singing, leaving Summer to take the solo. (And Liana was there too.) They bounced along to the chorus of the song, which we sang in four-part harmony:

It's the night of your life, so really live it!
The night of your life, so go on, give it
Aaaaaaall that you've got
Come on, take your shot
It's the night of your life!

And it didn't matter that I'd never been to prom and never would go, because being in this studio with my three favorite people put school dances to shame. I felt sorry for anyone who thought that prom was the night of their life, because our nights were just going to get better and better.

And we could start now. "What should we do with the evening?" I asked as we got into the elevator down to the street after the taping was complete.

"*Wicked*," Liana said. "We must see *Wicked*."

"Or, hear me out," Noah said, "we go to a Yankees game and boo them." The rest of us looked at him in confusion. "Don't worry, I brought enough Red Sox gear for all of us."

"No," Liana said.

"What if," Summer began quietly, "we wandered around Times Square?"

"It's so touristy," I said.

"We're right here. We could see the Naked Cowboy and the M&M's store—"

"I've done it on field trips, and it sucks, I promise you."

"My dad always said it was really fun," she said.

The rest of us exchanged glances, chastened. "Yeah, let's do Times Square," Noah said.

So against the advice of our handlers, we stepped out onto the street and walked right into our fans.

From the studio above, the crush of them had been thrilling. Screaming fans plus distance equals perfection. But a hundred people yelling your name straight into your ear, trying to touch you, is different. The excitement, the novelty, the affirmation all crumbled into anxiety.

"Smile and wave," Liana said, plastering on a grin, so we followed suit, then attempted to push our way into the throng.

We could barely even see through the wall of preteen girls holding signs reading MARRY ME NOAH or wearing their hair in the same style that Summer wore it during one popular episode. Flashes from a hundred disposable cameras popped in my vision, like we'd gotten too close to a fireworks show. Even as I tried to stay grateful, to remind myself that this was what we wanted, claustrophobia took over.

"Retreat?" Noah whispered. We backed away, still smiling and waving, and took refuge inside. They ordered a car to come pick us up. No *Wicked* or Yankees or M&M's store or the multiple museums that I wanted to see. We went back to our hotel instead.

We huddled in my room, a strange ambivalence overtaking us. We were so incredibly lucky. And also, what had we given up? Liana pulled out a bottle of vodka—she was twenty-one now, which was a game changer—and we all passed it around, even Summer.

I looked at my friends. Summer staring into space. Noah and Liana both texting on their flip phones. If this had been the first season, Summer would have sweetly reminded us to look on the bright side. But now, she was quiet, so I stepped into her role.

"Okay, this is ridiculous," I said. "We can still have fun tonight. We're in a swanky suite with our best friends. Like, look at this room!" I gestured at the sumptuous curtains, the king-sized bed. Whenever I'd gone on vacation with my family growing up, we'd stayed in motels; or in the guest room at my grandparents' house; or one time, when we were *really* splurging, a Marriott.

"I actually have to . . ." Noah held up his cell phone, a sheepish look on his face. "Michael invited me to go out with him and some of the writers."

"Really?" asked Liana. "What are you guys going to talk about?"

"Dude stuff?" I teased, even as jealousy simmered. He was so lucky to be invited. Not that I actually wanted to hang out with Michael. But I wanted to be asked.

"He said that if all of us came, it would attract too much attention," Noah went on. "And you can't really say no to Michael, you know?"

"Fine, abandon us," Liana said. "We'll have a girls' night."

As Noah walked out the door, Liana put on "Defying Gravity," and the three of us sang along, trying to outbelt one another while pretending we didn't care who did it best.

But within an hour, Liana was gone too—she'd been texting with one of the chorus boys for a couple of weeks now, and he invited her down to his room. "Goodbye, ladies," she said to us, grinning with anticipation. "I'm going to get my body worshipped like I deserve!"

So it was just me and Summer. Well, that was more than fine. She brought out her heavy brick of a laptop and scooted next to me on the bed, resting her head against my shoulder, her hair tickling my skin. "What do you want to do?"

An idea hit me. "Let's go into a *Daydreams* chat room."

We created a fake AIM account and I logged us in. A/S/L? a user asked almost immediately.

I contemplated our actual age, sex, and location, and then, to make Summer laugh, typed 27/m/Alaska. We started writing silly, ridiculous things to the fans who didn't know it was us on the other end of the screen, egging each other on to write the wackiest stuff. Two famous girls, in the greatest city in the world, talking to strangers on AIM. Despite the turn the night had taken, I was incandescently happy.

What would you do if you ever actually met them in real life?? I typed in. The flood of responses came quickly.

Declare my undying love!

Sing for them so that they'd get me on the show too!!

Depends on when, someone typed, and sent a link.

"What does that mean?" Summer asked, so I clicked the URL.

A clock spread across the screen, big numbers counting down to something: three weeks, two days, five hours, seventeen minutes, and seconds ticking away as we stared at them, uncomprehending. Then: "Oh," Summer said. It came out of her less as an articulated word, more like she'd been punched in the stomach as we registered the pictures of her all over the site. Three weeks, two days, five hours, seventeen minutes, and a certain number of seconds until she turned eighteen.

"Close out of it," she said, but I kept looking. The most prominent picture on the site was one from that pervy *Vanity Fair* interview she'd done. She was pulling her skirt up to reveal a gleaming stretch of thigh, an innocent *oops!* look on her face as she registered the camera flash.

Underneath the picture, more text from whoever had created the website:

If you can't wait, you can always go for the knockoff version. Kat Whitley turned 18 last year. Put a bag over her head and use your imagination.

Summer closed the laptop sharply, nearly catching my fingers under its lid. "People can be disgusting," she said, as if it had never occurred to her before.

If only Liana had still been there. *Fuck men*, she would've declared. *Or maybe we should never fuck them again. Boycott?* Even Noah, acting all chivalrous and indignant on our behalf, might have changed things. But as it was, we were just two girls sent out into the world without any armor, and the only enemy we could see was each other.

"I can't believe everyone's making such a big deal about that picture," she said, and suddenly her whole naive act felt cloying.

"Oh, come on," I said, tasting bile in my throat.

"What?"

"You're, like, lifting your skirt up. Of course it's a big deal."

She stared at me. "I was readjusting it. I didn't know they were going to take a picture."

She could have stopped it if she really wanted to, though, I thought. Demanded final approval over all printed images. I shrugged. "Maybe you should've been more careful."

Heat rose in her cheeks. "There's a lot going on when you're the center of a photo shoot. But I guess you wouldn't know." She flinched as the words came out, startling herself with her own cruelty. We looked at each other for a moment, not saying anything, and then she stood up and shut herself in the bathroom.

Faint sounds came from behind the door, so low that I could barely decipher them. Crying, maybe? I crawled underneath the covers, pulling them up over my chin, half wanting to apologize and half wanting to slap her. I tried to lose myself in sleep, but when I closed my eyes, I only saw myself next to Summer, her perfect and radiant, me grotesque. The knockoff version. *Put a bag over her head.*

A little while later, she came into bed beside me, nestling, the big spoon to my little one (even as a voice in my head whispered that *I* was the big one, she was delicate). "I didn't mean it," she whispered. "Do you want me to go back to my room?"

I shook my head. "Stay here." She wrapped her arms around me more tightly, and somehow, eventually, we fell into an uneasy sleep.

· · · · · · · ·

In the morning, we pretended that nothing had happened, and threw ourselves into filming. Then, three days before we were going to head back to Los Angeles, Michael had some important meeting come up. We were ahead of schedule anyway, so we wrapped early for the day. Noah chatted up a production assistant, touching her arm and turning her all giggly, then returned to us with her car keys in hand. "We're going hiking," he informed us as she waved goodbye, probably now convinced they'd be marrying in the spring.

We sped upstate, the leaves on the trees deep gold and burgundy. Summer sat in the front passenger seat, next to Noah at the wheel. It wasn't even a question. Liana and I were the second-class citizens of our Fearsome Foursome, so we would ride in the back even though Liana had the best music taste and should have been in charge of the radio. Summer just turned it to a generic pop station. An Usher song ended, and the familiar chords to one of our songs began. "Oh God, change it," Noah said.

"Keep it on!" Liana said. She sang along, doing all our parts in parodies of our voices. *"You gotta follow that dream,"* she crooned in a low voice, squinting like Noah did sometimes when he was getting really into the music, then turning her voice all breathy and sweet when Summer's solo came. She made a stank face for my line and tossed her hair proudly when her own came up. It struck me then how talented she was, how effortlessly she controlled her voice. The performance poured out of her, and you got the sense that she could've gone on forever, even though for me to do something like that, I would've had to practice very hard.

"Give me a damn soliloquy, Michael," she shouted up at the sky when the song was done, over the sound of our applause. Most of the time on the show, we sang songs that were happening in the "real world," performing at talent shows, auditions, and so on. But every once in a while, Michael broke from established reality and went full-on musical theater, doing things like giving Summer a song to sing about her hopes and dreams while she walked down the school hallway unnoticed, or me a big showcase number in a shopping mall as I tried on clothes. Sure, these songs didn't quite make sense in the world of the show, but we (and the audience) loved the chance to get inside our characters' heads. Among ourselves, we'd started half jokingly calling these solos "soliloquies," a dramatic term to distinguish how special they were. Needless to say, Liana had never gotten one. She'd barely even gotten any lines in the songs we sang with the band. Michael was the biggest idiot in the world for relegating her to backup. At least she had a whole solo verse in the scene we were filming tomorrow, where we all joined in with a busker on the subway. She'd been practicing all week, and I knew she'd knock it out of the park.

Noah parked at a trailhead, a mountain looming up before us, hardly any other cars in sight on this random weekday.

We were all dressed in various states of readiness for a trek. I wore my workout clothes. Ever since reading the "bag over her head" comment, I'd gotten up early each morning to run on the treadmill in the hotel gym, hurtling myself forward as my breath grew ragged, determined not to give anyone more ammunition in comparing me unfavorably to Summer. Liana wore a velour tracksuit with the word **Angel** emblazoned on her ass; Summer was in pajama pants with a pattern of little purple flowers; and Noah had on athletic shorts even though it was fifty-five degrees out, that crazy boy.

He bounced up and down a few times on the balls of his feet, then put a casual arm around my shoulder. "You ready for this?" When he was excited, his blue eyes actually sparkled. I tried to relax my shoulder, to make it comfortable and unobtrusive so that maybe he'd just leave his arm there, holding on to me the whole way up the mountain. There were other boys on the show, boys who played temporary love interests or Noah's friends from the school soccer team, and sometimes they tried to invade our clique of four, but they never succeeded. They were lesser members of the species, paling in comparison to the boy we already had.

Noah pulled his arm away as he bounded over to look at the trail map, and I shivered. Then we set off, our feet crunching over dead leaves, Noah pointing out the different types of trees and birds around us.

"You know a lot," Liana said.

"I used to think I was going to grow up to be a park ranger," Noah said, laughing. Noah and I were alike in this way: we'd lived as normal kids for a while, unlike Summer and Liana, who had been pursuing stardom for as long as they could remember. We understood each other!

The trail turned steeper. Within a few minutes, I was panting. Soon after that, Liana paused. "Shit, hold on a minute," she said, fiddling with her sock. "I think I have a blister." I turned around to help her examine it.

Summer's jaw was set, determined. "I'm cold, so I'm going to keep going."

"You shouldn't go alone," Noah said to her, then turned to us. "Meet you at the top?" Without waiting for an answer, he followed after Summer, the two of them disappearing into the trees ahead.

Liana rolled her eyes at me. "Thanks for waiting, guys," she said.

I snorted. "Very considerate."

We trudged on, slowly. "What do you think it is about Summer," Liana said after a moment, "that makes people do things for her all the time? Like yeah, she's pretty. But find me a girl on this show who *isn't* pretty. And not to be mean, but I have a better voice, and you're just as good of an actor."

"Well, I don't know if that's true," I said. If I found out that, up ahead of us, Summer and Noah were discussing the failings of Liana and me, I'd be devastated. Still, a small part of me buzzed with relief that I wasn't the only one who had thought these things.

"I'm not trying to be a bitch," Liana said. "I love her. And she's going through a really hard time right now. But you know what I mean."

"Yeah," I said. "I guess I feel like, if we were going through something bad, would Mr. Atlas have given us a journal? Like, the most I'd get would be an awkward pat on the shoulder."

"Well, we're not his *brightest star.*" Liana laughed ruefully. "And she doesn't even care about it! She spilled some coffee on it the other day and was like 'oops,' and then tossed it into a drawer in her trailer."

The image of Summer blithely dropping the journal into some drawer pissed me off. It wasn't special to her, this thing that the head of the network had taken such time and energy to procure, because people gave her whatever she wanted all the time. I surrendered to the relief, the catharsis, of secret shit-talking. "She is really entitled sometimes. I don't know if she's aware of it, but she is."

"Yeah! It's like she needs every guy to be in love with her even though she has a totally cute boyfriend at home." I actually didn't think Lucas was that attractive. He had all the disparate features to be cute—blond hair, blue eyes, muscular arms—but somehow they all added up to less than the sum of his parts. Still, he seemed like the kind of person who *should* be cute, so everyone had just decided that he was. (Noah, on the other hand, was greater than the sum of his parts. His smile; his friendliness; how his eye contact hit you like a spotlight, making you feel like the most special girl in the world, tied everything together.) Anyway, I'd never gotten much of a sense of Lucas's personality and didn't understand Summer's devotion to him. She claimed that she loved him. One time, she even said that she'd probably marry him someday, but in all of our heart-to-hearts, she'd never really said why.

"Like," Liana went on, "I think that Noah could be into you"—my heart fluttered here—"or into me." The fluttering stopped a bit. "But she's always got to monopolize his attention and flirt with him even though she's already taken!"

We reached the final ascent to the top, a straight-up scramble. Going ahead of Liana, I grabbed at a tree root to hoist myself up, then pushed through a few more feet of sharp turns and dense trees before coming out into a clearing, a vast expanse of sky overlooking a valley below us. But the magnificent valley view wasn't what caught my eye.

Summer and Noah stood maybe ten feet in front of me, next to each other, facing the vista. The wind, loud enough to cover up the sounds of my arrival, ruffled Noah's hair, and whipped Summer's long strands around. But amid all that wild motion, their bodies had a charged stillness, their shoulders rising and falling ever so slightly, their hands at their sides so close that they almost touched.

Slowly, Noah moved his hand closer and closer, until he intertwined his fingers with Summer's. This was not a casual touch, like the arm he'd slung around me. Though they looked out at the view, all their energy seemed to be in their clasped hands. Noah lifted Summer's hand up and held it against his chest, and finally she turned her head toward his, shivering, whether from the cold or something else, I couldn't tell. He said something to her, so quietly I couldn't hear it, but even from here I could tell that he had none of the suave charm he usually deployed so easily. She stared up into his eyes.

Liana crashed into the clearing behind me, and Summer and Noah startled apart.

"Why the hell would you do this to us, Noah?" Liana yelled, only half jokingly staggering around the clearing. "My foot will never be the same!"

"Poor Liana," he said, clearing his throat, recovering himself. "Need me to carry you down the mountain?"

"That seems only fair," she said in a mock-regal manner.

I snuck a glance at Summer as Noah rushed Liana, pretending that he was going to throw her over his shoulder and carry her down that way. Summer wasn't looking at them but down at her hand, a strange expression on her face, her eyes glistening. With tears, or just from the sting of the wind? She shook herself, swiped at her eyes, and looked at me. "Did you see the view?" she asked. "Come look!"

· · · · · · ·

On our way back down, Summer and Noah took the lead again, stepping fast and light while Liana and I tried not to slip down the slopes, the two of us concentrating too hard to participate much in the conversation. A brownish-gray bird flew across our path, settling in a branch and letting out a low call. "What's that one?" Summer asked Noah.

"A mourning dove," Noah said.

"It's beautiful," she said, studying it. "Funny, that it's out in the afternoon."

"Not morning like early in the day," Noah said, looking at her like she had just made the most adorable mistake. "Mourning with a *u*."

"Oh, duh," she said. She walked in silence for a moment, then continued. "It would be funny if there was one of them who didn't understand that she was supposed to be sad, you know? Who was like, 'It's morning, doves, and time to seize the day!'"

"Yeah," he said. "And there was one who was always trying to explain it to her." He made his voice gruffer. "Like, 'No, there's a *u*!'"

"There's a me? Thank you!" Summer said.

They continued like that down the mountain and into the parking lot, bantering about these imaginary birds as the light waned around us, until finally, to get them off the topic, Liana said, "We should go out tonight." She pulled out her Razr as we drove toward the city. "This guy I filmed a pilot with told me about a cool club where he does drag sometimes. It's not like any preteens will be there to recognize us."

So, still in our hiking clothes, we went to a club in the East Village, Liana flirting with the bouncer to distract him while the rest of us slipped inside.

On a small stage, a drag queen in a feather boa was lip-syncing to a Barbra Streisand song while a few others waited their turn. Liana beelined for the bar to order us all drinks while Summer, Noah, and I looked around in wonder, laughing a bit nervously. None of us had ever been to a club like this before, this place with red tabletops, people in glittering outfits and towering high heels. I'd never met a drag queen, just watched Patrick Swayze in *To Wong Foo, Thanks for Everything! Julie Newmar*. Sure, I was a TV star, but I wasn't nearly cool enough to be here.

One of the queens—electric-blue eye shadow, hair piled high— glanced at me, then looked away, then glanced again. "Holy shit, girls," she said to her two companions, and I braced myself. They'd seen that I was underage. That, or they were going to kick me out for daring to show up in my workout clothes. But instead, she gave me an incandescent smile. "It's The Bitch!"

"What?" I asked as the three of them flocked to me.

"You're from *The Daydreams*, right? Zsa Zsa Galore—she's not here tonight, she's going to die of jealousy that she missed this— she did one of your songs."

"The 'I Deserve It All' one!"

"And we were all obsessed, so now we watch your show."

"Thank you so much," Summer said beside me, and they registered her and Noah.

"The sweethearts came too!" the first queen said. "Precious." Then, they all turned back to me. "Do the eyebrow."

"And say the line from the song. The 'tragic' one!"

Their attention was intoxicating. I tossed my head, raised my eyebrow, and recited, "That's not magic, it's just tragic!"

They clutched me by my shoulders, complimenting me, calling over their friends, and as I fell into their spotlight, I knew what it was to be Summer or Noah. Was this how I would feel all the time if that woman at my audition had stuck to her original instinct and sent me in to read for the lead, if I'd gotten Summer's role along with everything that came with it?

I lost track of the others, swept up in the rush of attention, becoming instant best friends with every new drag queen I was introduced to. They pressed shots of vodka and tequila into my hands. Eventually, they brought me up onstage, stuck a microphone in my hand, and draped a boa around my shoulders. Two of them flanked me, singing backup, and we did "I Deserve It All," my big soliloquy from the first season, and I was shining, sparkling, preening, and posing, my future limitless and ever so exciting. I hurtled toward the applause, applause that, for once, would only be for me.

Right as we were entering the final chorus, a commotion started in the audience. I squinted into the light, thrown off. Someone had climbed up on a table, singing along, while a couple of other people attempted to coax her down so that she didn't hurt herself. It was Summer, drunk, apparently not content to let me have the spotlight for even one night. The attention turned to her, some of the club's patrons pulling out their new camera phones to take pictures as Noah gently tried to get her back down on the floor. "Stop," Liana was saying to the picture takers. "Don't!"

For a moment I stayed up on the stage, so close to the big finish I was supposed to have, but no one was listening now. So I plunged into the throng, coming to Noah's side. "Summer," I yelled. "Get down!"

"Or you come up!"

"You're embarrassing yourself."

Her mouth opened in a little O of offense. "Not embarrassing. We're having fun!"

"I think it's time to head home," Noah said to her. "It's been a big day, let's get some sleep. You know?" She stared at him, then nodded, and allowed him to take her hands and start helping her down.

Liana leaned in toward the rest of us as Summer stumbled into Noah's chest and stayed there. "Shit, this guy was just saying that there are policemen coming in to check about underage patrons."

"We're TV stars. They wouldn't arrest us, right?" I asked.

"But if it gets out to the paparazzi . . ." Liana said. "And everybody is taking pictures! What the hell do we do?"

"You take care of Summer," Noah said to me and Liana, pulling out his phone. "I'll be right back." Summer resisted letting go of his arm. "Right back," he repeated to her, with such tenderness in his voice as he extricated himself.

"Did I mess up?" she asked him. "Do you not think it anymore?"

I had no idea what she was talking about, but Noah just shook his head. "I'll always think it. Now stay here."

So she curled into me as the crowd pulsed around us. "Sorry," she mumbled. I resented her so much. I wanted her stupid frail body off me.

Noah returned a few minutes later. "Okay, Michael's sending his assistant over to get the contact information for everyone who took pictures."

"You told Michael what was going on?" Liana asked, her eyebrows rocketing up her forehead. *Shit, shit, shit.*

Noah furrowed his brow, confused by our reaction. "Well,

yeah. And he said that bars usually have a back entrance, so we should go out there right now and he'll send a car for us."

We took Michael's direction well. We'd had plenty of practice.

. . . .

"Why the hell would you even go there in the first place?" Michael asked as we sat in a row on the bed in his hotel room, in various states of sobering up. "Whose idea was it?"

Summer, still not fully in control of herself, glanced at Liana, then immediately glanced away. But that was enough for Michael. He zeroed in. "You're the oldest. You should be the most responsible."

"I'm sorry," Liana said. "I didn't realize it would turn into a whole thing."

"It was just reckless and stupid—"

"You took Noah out to a strip club the other night! How is this—" She cut herself off as Michael stared daggers at her. Then he turned to Summer.

"You're taking the second verse tomorrow."

"What?" Liana asked, her mouth opening in outrage.

"If your judgment is that poor, why should I trust you with a solo?" He pressed a finger to his temple, calming himself. "Anyways, we'll get tonight taken care of. You're all lucky that I'd already finished my meeting with Mr. Atlas when you called. Hopefully he'll never have to find out."

"Meeting with Mr. Atlas?" Noah asked, and for the first time I registered that Michael was spruced up, his face clean-shaven, in an actual button-down shirt instead of one of his sloppy tees. A bottle of champagne chilled in a bucket on his bedside table.

"Yes. I was going to call you all in here anyway with some news." He grabbed the bottle and indicated that we should each take a paper cup from a stack next to the bucket. "I shouldn't give this to you after the shit you pulled tonight, but, well . . ." A smile broke over his face. "We're not going to be filming a season three after this."

Any remaining tipsiness we were feeling disappeared as we blinked, dismayed. A cancellation didn't make any sense. We were popular, the highest-rated show on the network by far. "Why are you smiling?" Liana asked, her voice thick from the combined shock of this and her punishment.

"We're holding off on season three because, first, there's going to be a movie!" Michael yelled, and let the cork fly.

Liana gasped, almost dropping her paper cup.

"*What?*" I yelled.

Oh my God, the *money* this would mean. We'd all signed a TV contract before we knew how big this show would get, locking ourselves in at a rate that seemed exciting at the time but that had started to feel low, given how much we were clearly making the network. Movie money was a whole other ballpark. We'd get a chance to negotiate a share of the profits. I could buy myself a nice apartment, maybe even a house, and make it a real home, filled with things that felt like mine. Or maybe Summer or Liana would want to live with me, and we could rent ourselves some palatial mansion in the Hollywood Hills. I could give my mom money to go back to school like she always talked about, and maybe she'd finally feel satisfied with her life. (Maybe too, if she could go back to school, she'd stop being upset with me for not finishing it.)

"No way," Summer said. "No way!"

Michael smiled the indulgent smile he liked to give us sometimes to remind us that he was much older and wiser. "*Yes* way," he said, aping Summer's tone.

And then we were all hugging and screaming.

"Now listen up," Michael said as he poured champagne into all of our cups. "There's two ways this could go. I'm pushing Mr. Atlas toward the big-screen version. We're talking worldwide distribution, where they see your faces in China, they dub you into French. I already know what the plot will be. The summer after high school graduation, when you go on a Euro tour! So the season-two finale will be your graduation, and we'll finally give those fans a Summer and Noah kiss to send them all flocking to the movie theaters."

Summer's and Noah's faces both turned pink. "That's a good idea," Noah said.

Michael held up a finger. "But there's another way too. This season doesn't go like we want it to, you all keep pulling stupid shit like tonight, Mr. Atlas will just dump it on the channel as a made-for-TV movie. So focus on the work and on being perfect little Atlas stars at least until all the contracts are set and signed. I don't want anyone here doing anything in the next few months to mess this up."

"Of course," Summer said. "We'll be good."

But we were teenagers and we were famous. And famous teenagers can stay out of trouble for only so long.

SUMMER WRIGHT GETS
TOO HOT TO HANDLE

Since her father's tragic death, *Daydreams* star SUMMER WRIGHT has been photographed spending more time with her mother, Lupe Wright, and some fans have been surprised by what they see. Summer plays the blond, all-American girl next door like a natural. But maybe she's a better actress than we all thought, because her mom is from the other side of the border. And we're not talking Canada. *¡Ay, caramba!*

"Oh, Summer's definitely not a natural blonde," a childhood friend tells us. "I was really surprised when I saw all the *Daydreams* stuff, because it felt like she was hiding her mom or something. Maybe she thought it would help her get ahead, but it feels pretty gross to me."

Now that her father is gone, Summer's embracing her spicier side. Just look at these photos of her out shopping in a crop top that's a little too *caliente!* Let's hope that the younger, more innocent *Daydreams* fans don't see, and start demanding crop tops of their very own.

Over here at Popslop, we're just concerned for her. And we can't help wondering . . . if Summer lied about this, what else is she hiding?

Eleven

. . . .

2018

After our time with the press, we are ushered into another room, a large, bright one with a long rectangular table, for a read-through of the script. The scents of lemon and bleach hang in the air.

There are more old familiar faces here: actors who played supporting roles like our band teacher or Summer's annoying little brother, our choreographer and music director from way back in the day. We're all greeting one another when Mr. Atlas walks in, and the temperature of the room seems to drop five degrees.

In a freshly ironed gray suit, he's the most mild-mannered boogeyman I've ever seen. Cordial but ruthless, the rumors always said, the type of man to cut you loose in a second if you tarnished the clean-cut Atlas brand. He was a perfect gentleman to us, yet we lived in fear of his disapproval. He never shouted, but also, in all the read-throughs he came to, I never once saw him laugh. He just watched us all with a look of furrowed concentration, then started a round of polite clapping at the end. Funny that he made the decisions about Atlas's programming when he didn't display any outward enjoyment from watching it. He was the richest and most powerful man I had ever met.

He still is, probably, despite the fact that the Atlas network is no longer must-see TV. Its wholesome content doesn't captivate quite like it used to, and the company's attempts at diverse programming have been clunky (for example, the TV show about a Black teenage girl that was created and run by . . . a white man). Instead, Atlas has been cleaning up on the film side—they've gone into coproducing superhero movies, setting the internet abuzz with casting rumors each time they announce a new project. Their latest is Snow Leopard, whose superpowers are that he's very fast and can stay warm in the cold, aka he runs shirtless in the snow.

The past thirteen years have added a slight stoop to Mr. Atlas's shoulders—he must be in his sixties now—and his salt-and-pepper hair has gone entirely white. Our spines automatically stiffen as he walks toward us—*best behavior now, children!*—and he shakes all of our hands in succession, with a thoughtful word for each of us. "I heard you went to law school," he says to me. "Good for you." To Liana: "I enjoy watching your husband play. He's very talented." To Summer: "You look well." He avoids her eyes, though, as if in distaste. And then, to Noah, with a hint of a smile: "What a pleasure to be working together again."

An assistant passes out bound copies of the script, which Michael wrote himself, not bothering with a writers' room. None of us have seen it yet, just heard the general outline—that it takes place at our ten-year high school reunion.

We flip to the first page and begin. The show opens with the chorus, then Liana and I enter, then Noah. My character has become a bitchy record label exec, clad in power suits, very corporate. (Hm, I wonder where Michael got that idea?) Liana talks all about her husband, orbiting him now instead of her best friends, even though the joke is that he's a nobody, so bland that none of us can remember his name. Noah's a drama teacher, shaping the minds of tomorrow. But where is Summer?

We turn the page. Here's her entrance. She takes a breath and reads the line. "Hello, party people!"

I dig my nails into my thigh under the table as it sinks in: Michael has written her character to be a hot mess. In an Atlas-approved way, of course, with veiled illusions to having spent time "trying to find herself," no career of which to speak. She's not getting drunk at the reunion. She's downing so many cups of the punch that she gets a "sugar high," tries to climb up on the stage where the band used to perform, falls off, and bonks her head.

She reads it haltingly, trying to be game. We *all* read haltingly. Our chemistry is off. You need to trust your scene partners to make anything good. Instead, we don't know when to look at one another, how to trade lines of dialogue with a natural rhythm. There's no easy rapport, just stilted, awkward talk.

At least things get better for Summer's character after the head bonk because it knocks her out, providing the excuse for a long fantasy sequence inside her head set back in the old days, a remix of our more famous numbers. When she wakes back up, she "reforms," apologizes for causing such a commotion, we all hug, and then we do an epic finale song and dance. No big solos for Liana. I look over to see if she's pissed. Sure enough, a frown tugs at her mouth as she flips back through the pages of the script, though her expression isn't quite anger. It's almost like . . . despair? That seems a bridge too far. Maybe I'm imagining things.

Michael's eyes dart around the room, trying to see everyone's reactions to this thing he has made, from which he has pulled liberally from our lives. (Liana quickly rearranges her face back into a smile.) Maybe he was in a time crunch to churn something out and didn't have a chance to get creative. Or maybe he wanted to keep blurring the lines like he used to.

After the script is finished, Mr. Atlas leads the polite applause as usual, speaks quietly to Michael for a moment, and then leaves to go to the next important event on his docket. An assistant comes into the room. "Noah has to go in a few minutes," she says to Michael. "Another commitment."

"Right, of course," he says before he's distracted by compliments, people praising him in that Hollywood way where everyone is so enthusiastic about things that are just fine. Because hearing it aloud confirms that it *is* just fine, nothing more. An excuse to walk down memory lane, with a little extra dose of demeaning Summer.

And that's the best-case scenario, if we can figure out how to recapture a modicum of our chemistry. For the first time, I realize that the worst outcome for Summer is not this reunion failing to happen. Worse is if it does happen, and it's bad. Another embarrassment added to her long list of them.

As if she's got the same realization ringing in her brain, Summer sits quietly, her forehead furrowed as one of the supporting actors tries to compliment her. ("Wow, you're still so good, I didn't realize you would be!")

My phone buzzes with a text from Miheer. **How's it all going?**

> KAT: Welp, I've seen the script and it has potential . . .
> to be incredibly humiliating.

He sends back a frowny face.

So, okay. I'll work my ass off to play my part as well as possible. We'll all have to work our asses off, commit hard, and then maybe we can at least hit "mediocre" if not "amazing." Serve up some serviceable nostalgia, which might prompt a producer to give Summer a chance in a better project, and then—

"Did you forget the kiss?" Summer asks, and the room falls silent at her voice. "Between me and Noah?" She's still talking sweetly, blinking her wide eyes.

"Well, no," Michael begins. "You have a nice hug moment."

"Oh, I just thought that the fans would want it."

"Sure, but—"

"I think if it's a tenth high school reunion, we would at least kiss." The sweet facade begins to rupture, just a bit. "Realistically, we'd get drunk and hook up in the bathroom."

Noah laughs, almost involuntarily, then clears his throat, as others around the circle exchange raised eyebrows.

She smiles at him. "Kidding. I know Atlas hasn't gotten comfortable with bathroom sex just yet. But a kiss at least." She turns to the wider room, asking as if it's an innocent question, "Or is something wrong? It's not embarrassing for him to have to kiss me, is it?"

Michael flushes, because that *is* the reason. A big shiny star like Noah kissing a mess like Summer—does it tarnish his shine? Everyone in the room seems to realize this too as Summer says it. It was a vague feeling, and she's made it into something solid.

"Of course not," Michael says to Summer. "We can turn the hug into a kiss if everyone feels comfortable with that."

A shifting in the room. What he means is if Noah feels comfortable. And how is Noah supposed to say no in the midst of all these people? He kisses his costars in movies all the time now. Why would Summer be any different? It's only a kiss. Still, it feels so much bigger.

I sneak a glance at Liana. Her mouth hangs slightly open, her eyes darting back and forth between Summer and Noah as the rest of the room is frozen in awkwardness. Liana always loved drama, was the first one among us to fall head over heels for reality TV.

"Definitely," Noah says, as if he'd reached the same conclusion himself. "We should give the fans what they want."

Summer ducks her head, but still, I see it before she swallows it down: a smile of triumph.

When Noah touches me, I start to question everything I thought about sex. It never seemed like a big deal to me that I hadn't had it yet. But now . . . we aren't in a relationship or anything, but I feel all tingly when he smiles at me. I get red when he brushes his arm against mine. If he tried to do something more, I would not say no.

The other night, I touched myself thinking about him. I've never really thought about specific people before when I did it. More like . . . situations, maybe? Scenes from movies where a man wants a woman so badly they just do it right then and there, no matter the consequences. Or I'd read stories on Open Diary on the computer in the living room when nobody was home, but I wasn't imagining people's faces or anything, just paying attention to the words.

But the other day he'd been especially jokey with me during filming, picking me up and spinning me around the way he does to all of us. And when I went back to my trailer for a break, I kept seeing him in my mind, the way his face cracks open when he smiles, the way his hair glints in the light, the way he looks at me sometimes like I'm the only girl he's ever seen, and without really making the decision to do it, suddenly I was touching myself and it was the best it's ever felt.

I've been doing it since I was thirteen, maybe, and for a while, I felt so ashamed about it. None of the girls I knew ever mentioned it, so I assumed they didn't, and I was a pervert.

Liana talks about it with us all the time though. She's always all "How are you supposed to let anybody else love your body if you don't love it yourself?" So I don't feel like as much of a freak anymore, even if I would die before talking about it all the time like Liana does. She's really open about that stuff, because she's kind of a slut.

Twelve

· · · · · · ·

2018

When I arrive for rehearsal the next morning, Michael is consulting with Kyle, his reedy, nervous-looking assistant director. Otherwise, the room is empty. "Ah, Kat," Michael says. "Go head over to wardrobe."

I pause. "We're not jumping into rehearsal?"

"Later. But first, I need you all to fix your chemistry problem. A little birdie told me that you just went your separate ways last night after the read-through, so today, you girls get to do your costume fittings in a big happy group."

"And Noah?"

"You want to try on clothes with Noah?"

"No! I have a very serious boyfriend." A pre-fiancé, one could even say! "I meant—"

He shoots me a look that says he pities me for my stupidity. "Noah's an in-demand guy, okay? He has important things to do." Right. Noah's a big-deal star who got sucked into spending a month with three people who don't matter to him, and he's going to devote as little energy to this as possible. I have important things I should be doing too—working on multimillion-dollar deals, flying back to Miheer and proposing to *him*, but—

"Put that eyebrow down," Michael continues. "And go have some fun trying on outfits together."

Anyone who thinks that trying on outfits is fun has never done wardrobe fittings with Harriet, our costume designer. A tall, pinched-faced woman in her late thirties back in 2004, she had a habit of making the exact kind of passive-aggressive remark about your body that could send you into a shame spiral for days. "Have you been bored on set?" she'd ask, squinting at my thighs in the capris she'd picked out for me. "Because there are more productive ways to fill your time than hanging around craft services."

I wonder if Harriet got off on shaming young women. By all accounts, she was always exceedingly complimentary of Noah, who had no idea why Summer, Liana, and I grimaced when a new costume fitting was scheduled. Or maybe she felt she was doing us a service, pressuring us to be as thin as possible. She wanted to spare us from the mocking of the world, to save us from ourselves. Maybe it was pity, rather than malice. I'm not sure which is worse.

Here's the thing about Harriet, though—she was brilliant. She dressed us all so *clearly*, so you knew just by looking at us exactly who our characters were supposed to be. The sundresses she gave Summer were to die for, soft and virginal. Liana got the "fun" clothes—the dresses over boot-cut jeans, the newsboy caps—so that her character suddenly had more of a personality than the script ever gave her. One glance at my plaid skirts, and it was clear that I was a rich bitch who believed she deserved everything she wanted.

In the second season, Harriet knew exactly where the line was between sweet and sexy, and she tiptoed right up to it. Summer's shirts got a bit tighter, her skirts a bit shorter, but never enough for anyone to complain about it.

There was only one time when Harriet may have crossed the

line. During a plotline when I caused such a big fight between Noah and Summer that he temporarily left the band, the three of us girls had a number together. Harriet designed matching dresses in different colors, made of bright neon pleather with little cutouts at our waists. Remember Ginger Spice's Union Jack dress? Britney Spears's red bodysuit in "Oops! . . . I Did It Again"? These dresses had some of the same appeal. They were very tight, but also high necked, so maybe that's how Harriet got them approved. Our most conservative viewers stirred up outrage. But that episode ended up being one of our highest-rated ever. That spring, collections inspired by the dresses sold out at stores across the country. Harriet was quite smug about it all.

Harriet has come back for the reunion just like the rest of us. But this time, I'm not going to let her get to me. I walk into the fitting room with my head held high.

Liana's there already, sipping a brightly colored juice, talking about Javier in response to a question Harriet has asked. "—wishes he could be here the whole time," she is saying. "But with training and the season, you know how it is." Wait, are those the exact same words she used yesterday with me and Noah?

Harriet clocks my entrance. "Kat," she says, and kisses my cheek. Her wispy hair is dyed burgundy. "Have I got some bitchy power suits for you." I see from the costume rack that I'll just being wearing flashier versions of what I normally wear to work. Harriet sweeps her eyes over me and purses her lips. "Are you sure you sent me your correct sizes? You look larger than your measurements."

She's wasting no time, I see. Luckily, at that moment, Summer rolls in, a gigantic milky coffee in her hand, the size of a Big Gulp, and Harriet turns her attention to her. "Oh, here you are," she says. "I've worried about you over the years."

How are you supposed to respond when people say things like that to you? Summer's evidently had lots of practice, because she gives a small nod. "Thank you. I'm doing better now."

"Good, good," Harriet says, leaving a moment of silence for the death of Summer's promising youth. Then she claps her hands. "Let's start with you trying on these." She pulls aside a curtain to reveal a rack of familiar color-coordinated dresses. Oh. Fuck.

The fantasy sequence remix includes our old girl-group number. And now the iconic cutout dresses we wore for it hang on a rack in front of us.

"I thought we weren't going to wear these since it's a medley," I say, treading carefully. "There's no time to change into them, right?"

"You're going to wear them the whole medley," Harriet says. "Michael and I discussed it."

I eye them, unconvinced, then see that Summer is making a similar expression. Liana isn't even looking—she's posting some Story to Instagram on her phone. ("All right, team," she says into it. "It's time to play dress-up. Luckily, ever since I started drinking FeelTrue juices, I love my body. Now, trying on clothes is one of my favorite activities." She swings the camera our way briefly. "Especially when I'm with my girls!")

"Well, go on," Harriet says. "I do have other things to do with my life."

She ushers us into makeshift changing rooms, separated from one another by curtains she's hung from the ceiling. I wriggle into the dress, the fabric cold and sticky against my skin, then suck in my stomach and use all my strength to tug the zipper up. Harriet never puts mirrors in these makeshift rooms. You have to emerge into the main area to see what you look like, which means that Harriet always gets to see too. She makes all the decisions.

Still, I look down the length of my body, and even without a mirror I can tell that this dress is a disaster. My heart plummets into my stomach. The pleather is stretched to its limit across my thighs. I take a tentative step, and it scrunches and wrinkles. If I do any dance moves at all, this dress is going to slowly but surely ride up and expose my ass. The cutouts dig into my skin like fingers, pinching the area between my hip bone and my ribs so that flab spills out.

I have made peace with my body not looking like it once did. It's a function of time and age, yes, but also happiness. Screw the Hollywood beauty standards that told me I was an unlovable sack of garbage if I didn't have a thigh gap. Miheer thinks I'm sexy. *I think I'm sexy!*

I tell myself these things because in this moment, I do not believe them anymore. God, Harriet is going to rip me to shreds the moment I step out. I can already hear her saying, *If I were going to be on camera again, I might prepare better.* Panic rises in my throat.

"You ready?" Harriet asks.

"Um, just a minute," Summer says.

"Almost," Liana calls.

"Kat?" Harriet pulls aside the curtain without warning and appraises me. Her mouth curls. "Oh dear. Come out here and I'll see what we can do about this," she says.

She guides me by the shoulders to the mirror, where I get the full, unwelcome view. As I take myself in, I'd like nothing more than to hop on a plane back to my normal life, because I've made a huge mistake.

Five months after our live finale, this terrible blog called Popslop published some pictures of me in New York City. I'd gone back to live with my mom, mostly sitting on the couch and eating chips all day, saddled with sadness and debt, too depressed to make plans for the future. My mom had dragged me into the city for a girls' day, hoping to shake some life back into me, and I was eating a slice of pizza in sweatpants on the corner when paparazzi took the photos. Popslop ripped me apart—*Kat Whitley's not living in a daydream anymore. Looks like she's living in a pizza parlor instead!* I fell even further into the hole after that. It took me months to climb out, to decide to ignore the critics and apply for colleges in Canada and the UK, somewhere I could introduce myself as Katherine, not Kat, and be anonymous.

And now I've decided to get back on television in front of millions of viewers and open myself up to all that criticism again. I picture the male partners at my law firm watching me in this dress and deciding that I lack the gravitas to move forward at work. I imagine Miheer, embarrassed for me, and is there any worse feeling than knowing that the people who love you feel sorry for you? I could very well be blowing up both my career and my relationship just to assuage some sense of guilt, to vaguely "make things right." Would Atlas sue me for breach of contract if I left right now, or would they decide the bad publicity wasn't worth it?

Then, Summer pulls aside her curtain, and steps out. We lock eyes. A laugh, quick and violent, almost like a grunt, escapes from her, and my first reaction is defensive—she's laughing at me. But as I take her in, I realize she's laughing at the situation. Because she looks absolutely terrible in this outfit too. Unlike me, she's gaunt in it, practically wasted away, although with stretch marks and sprays of cellulite visible on her thighs.

And then it hits me: Of course she looks bad. Of course *we* do! These dresses were made for teenagers, and we're not teens anymore.

"So clearly these are . . ." I begin.

"Horrible?" Summer asks, beginning to giggle in earnest.

"I was going to say 'an abomination,' but 'horrible' works too."

Harriet gives a little offended *tsk*. "I spent a lot of time on these," she says.

"I'm sorry, Harriet. They're very well-made," Summer says.

"It's just impossible for this dress to look good on a woman in her thirties," I say.

At that moment, Liana pulls her curtain aside and steps out. Summer and I stare at her, then back at each other, and suddenly, something melts. We're laughing again, but this time it's a helpless, all-consuming cackle, the kind of laugh that you couldn't stop even if you tried.

Because sculpted, ultra-fit Liana rocks this dress *better* than she did the first time around. I mean, she looks ridiculous. She's a grown woman in this day and age wearing a bright blue pleather dress with cutouts. But somehow it works.

"What?" Liana asks.

"Jesus Christ, Liana," I say, my stomach hurting.

"What's so funny?"

"Okay, we get it," I wheeze. "You're professionally hot now."

"I work out . . ." she says.

"Look at this," Summer says, and steers all three of us to the mirror, placing Liana in the center. These costumes fit like something out of Goldilocks—too big, too small, just right. "Can you imagine the three of us going on live television like this?"

Liana stares at our reflections for a long, silent moment as Summer and I wipe tears from our eyes. Then, she bursts into laughter too.

"Yeah, this is not good," she says.

"Why would one ever make a dress with cutouts on either side of the waist?" I ask.

"Because they're a monster," Summer says, and then, over her shoulder, "Not you, Harriet. I mean whoever came up with the concept."

"Watch this," I say, and do a step-touch from side to side. "Watch the hemline as it makes its way into my ass crack."

Summer crouches down, close to me, and pretends to study intently as the pleather squeaks up my skin. "Wow," she says, in a fake awed tone. "It's like watching a curtain go up."

"Showtime!" Liana says.

"Beautiful metaphor, yes," I say. "This show is not appropriate for children."

"Don't worry," Liana says, faux serious. "I've figured out a solution. We simply add a 'pull down the fabric' shimmy to the choreography." She warbles the song and spins from side to side, then shakes her shoulders while desperately tugging the dress back down. "This'll work great."

I'm laughing harder than I've laughed in years, and dammit, maybe Michael was right about how to fix our chemistry problem, because somehow the strangeness among the three of us has slipped away, leaving only the kind of intimacy where you're laughing so hard with other people that you're all on the verge of pissing yourselves.

"We need you to wear them," Harriet says. "It's already been decided."

"Please, I am begging you," I say. "You cannot send us out there looking like this."

"Well," Summer says, "You can send Liana."

"I'm not wearing this without you two," Liana says.

"Fine," Harriet says. "I will go talk to Michael." She storms out of the room, leaving us breathless with laughter and just a little bit abashed.

"We need to calm down or I'm going to shit myself," Liana says.

"No, that would ruin the dress!" Summer says, then taps a conspiratorial finger to her mouth. "Actually . . ."

"Wait, *shit* yourself?" I ask. "I was just worried about piss."

"These stupid juices I'm supposed to post about have a lot of fiber in them," Liana says, which sets us all off one more time.

"The problem," I say, as I wipe my eyes again, "is that I don't think Harriet comprehends that you can be worthy of love if you eat carbs." Liana lets out a laugh, so I keep going. "How wild, that Javier would still love Liana even if she didn't look like an absolute fox in this dress! What a concept, that it's possible to be happy being who you actually are, instead of obsessing about workouts and green juice like some brainwashed—"

I catch a glimpse of Liana's stormy face, any trace of her laughter gone. "Sorry. Your juice looks great. I didn't mean to imply—"

"That I'm a brainwashed Stepford Wife?" she shoots back in a withering tone. "Believe it or not, it is possible to be happy and take care of yourself at the same time." She retreats to her makeshift dressing room, leaving silence in her wake.

Summer grimaces at me. And just like that, the spell is broken, and the strangeness has returned.

Thirteen

· · · · · · ·

2004

One weekend, Liana got us invited to a party in the Hollywood Hills thrown by another Atlas actor, Trevor. He had been the male lead on *Girl Powers* opposite Amber Nielson. *Girl Powers* had since been canceled, but Trevor had landed on his feet, starring in a teen comedy that was set to come out in a few months. I wasn't sure if we should go to the party after the warning Michael had given us.

"It's going to be a bunch of Atlas stars. How raunchy could it be?" Liana asked. "We'll probably stand around learning choreography."

Summer couldn't come with us. Popslop, that terrible, scathing new blog that had started gaining traction in recent months (reporting on things so much more immediately than the tabloids and weekly magazines we'd gotten used to) had accused her of "hiding" her mother. Instead of dismissing the article as racist BS, she had to invite a reporter home to watch her and Lupe make tamales, to show that she wasn't "ashamed of her heritage." She'd hardly ever made tamales growing up, she told me. Her mom only spoke Spanish on the phone with her family back home, so Summer barely knew a word of it, but she was trying to study up now.

Besides, the time at home would be a good chance to hang out with her boyfriend. He'd been feeling neglected. Poor Lucas.

I wasn't exactly devastated at the prospect of a night without Summer. Liana's words from our hike, that she thought Noah could be into me if Summer weren't always monopolizing his attention, had been ringing in my ears. I even went out and bought a new dress, spending far too much on a shimmering gold thing with spaghetti straps and a short skirt. (Whatever. I'd have movie money soon!)

I straightened my hair and spent half an hour putting on makeup. On the show, I was never supposed to be too pretty. It was a joke, each time I tried to woo Noah for myself. Every episode, my character got to reach the heights of bitchiness, yes, but then to make up for that, I needed to be humiliated in some way—zapping myself while attempting to sabotage Summer's sound equipment, or getting smacked in the face with cold pizza at a cafeteria food fight. But the girl I saw in the mirror that night—her long dark hair shining, her eyes smoky—looked like she could be someone for whom good things happened.

Liana drove us to the party, picking up Noah first and then me. She wolf-whistled as I walked to the car. "Okay, someone's trying to get a boyfriend!"

"Damn, you look nice," Noah said, grinning, and I tried not to blush too much.

"Oh, this old thing?" I said, twirling around for their admiration.

When we arrived, a girl—either an official assistant, or a friend so bowled over by Trevor's charisma that she was willing to do all sorts of tasks for him—checked our names off a guest list before letting us inside.

Trevor came to greet us, shirtless and wearing a baseball cap. "Welcome, my dudes!" he said, showing us around his place. It wasn't huge, but it was decked out, with maybe twenty to thirty people milling around. The living room had floor-to-ceiling windows looking over the hills, and a sliding door that led to a deck with a pool. I recognized other actors who had been on Atlas TV shows past and present getting drunk off their asses, and doing a few other things too. Liana had been wrong about the nature of this party. Trevor noticed the look on my face. "Take it from a pro. This is the secret to having a good time as an Atlas star," he said, draping an arm around Liana. "Just party at a private home, where there won't be any snitches or paparazzi."

He took us into his kitchen and poured us strong rum and Cokes, then turned away from me and Noah to talk to Liana, who was batting her eyes at him. (I wasn't the only one hoping to make something happen tonight.) Noah and I stuck close together as we sucked down our drinks and began to explore, looking at the framed posters Trevor had of himself, at his pitiful excuse for a bookshelf.

"Is his book collection entirely self-help and biographies of Marlon Brando?" Noah asked me.

"Hey," I said. "Maybe he keeps his Steinbeck up by his bed."

"I dare you to ask Trevor what he thinks about the themes in *Of Mice and Men*."

We were the upstarts of the party, simultaneously Atlas's biggest stars and the most naive people there. Other actors kept trying to share their wisdom with us, then slipping in a request for us to pass their name along to our director, if he was ever looking for guest stars. So many of the people here who weren't on Atlas shows anymore were fading into obscurity. Well, *we'd* be different.

After my second drink, I desperately needed to pee. The bathroom door was unlocked, but someone else was already in there, a girl a couple of years older than me, wiping her nose.

"Oh, sorry!" I said, starting to back out. Then I recognized her. Amber Nielson. After she'd been let go from *Girl Powers* because of that cocaine picture, she'd apologized profusely in the press, claiming it had been a onetime mistake, but judging by the baggie of powder she held in her hand, it wasn't so onetime after all. The Amber in front of me bore little resemblance to the perky girl I'd watched on the TV screen when I was babysitting (strange to realize that some teen girl somewhere was babysitting a kid and watching *me*, and that I would never have to babysit again), or to the girl I'd gotten to meet briefly when we filmed a promo with her. Her mascara had bled down underneath her eyes; her long red hair had been flat-ironed within an inch of its life; and her skirt hung so loose around her waist, it was exposing the top of her thong in a way that I didn't think was intentional.

She squinted at me. "Hey, Kat from *The Daydreams*!" She held up the baggie. "You want to join?" Her voice was pack-a-day raspy.

"I'm okay, but thank you," I said.

"Probably smart." She widened her eyes, as if telling me a spooky story around a campfire. "If you don't toe the line, you might end up like me."

"I'm sorry about what happened," I said. "That really sucks."

"Yeah," she said, studying herself in the mirror, pushing her hair around like she couldn't decide where to part it. "The shittiest thing is that everyone was doing crazy stuff, but of course Mr. Atlas only knew about me, so I'm the sacrificial lamb." She met my eyes in the mirror. The cocaine had made her decide I was her temporary new best friend, or maybe she told her Atlas woes to everyone she met. "You don't want to get that man mad at you. He's like this unforgiving god. Step out of line one time and he'll cut you loose, as if you didn't spend your teenage years putting money in his pockets."

"Cold," I said.

"As ice. It's like he's not only angry that you caused controversy, but personally offended that you'd be a bad girl when he gave you every opportunity." She stopped futzing with her hair, seemingly satisfied, and pulled lip gloss out of her pocket. "Anyways, screw him. And screw my castmates. They're the ones who sold me out, I bet you anything. I thought we were friends, but you've got to watch your back. Somebody always has to go down. Just a little warning for you."

"Then why are you here at Trevor's party with all of them?"

"Trevor has the best coke." She smacked her lips together, ran her finger along their edge to keep the gloss in line. "I'm going back out there. Good luck, newbie."

She hugged me, then looked at me again before she walked out the door. "It's funny," she said. "You're way hotter than you seem on the show."

I texted Summer while I peed, still getting used to my new Nokia and the exhilarating access it gave me. Just had the STRANGEST encounter with Amber from Girl Powers. We need to discuss!

She wrote back quickly: I cannot wait!!! Ughhh I miss you. Is it weird that I'm sad you all are having even one night without me? :) :)

I smiled. Very weird, you freak.

SUMMER: This interview is awkward. They keep expecting me and my mom to speak in Spanish. I know like ten words, and she is so uncomfortable.

When I came back out, I passed Liana and Trevor making out in a corner. Good for her. Noah was out by the pool, chugging a beer while a couple of adoring girls oohed and aahed over it. He threw the can down and slung a triumphant arm around one of the girls, then noticed me and bounded over, leaving the hangers-on without so much as a goodbye. I'd never seen him drunk like this before. It gave him even more puppylike energy than usual. "You were gone for so long!" he said, picking me up and spinning me around. He put me down and indicated the pool. "We should swim! It's nuts that here we are, at a party, and the weather is perfect, but nobody's getting in the water." He said it with the hint of a Boston accent, losing some of the control he normally exerted to make himself sound like he could have come from anywhere.

"In the wahdda?" I teased. "Okay, Mr. Boston."

"I'm not ashamed! I think we should get in the wahdda and it will be wicked fun. The other day, some of the studio guys took me to a restaurant, and there was a pool right in the middle of it, and nobody was going in." He held me by the shoulders, his face sincere, as if trying to make me laugh with how seriously he was taking this. "The pool was just for decoration."

"That's tragic."

"I know! Can you imagine getting so used to living in Hollywood that you don't even take the opportunity to swim in a pool when you have it?" His face was still earnest. I'd thought he was trying to make me laugh, but maybe I was wrong. "I don't ever want to become the kind of guy who gets used to things. You know?" He took my hand and squeezed it, staring deep into my eyes. "We can't let Hollywood deaden us to pools, Kat. We just can't."

I couldn't help myself. A laugh slipped out. "No, you're right."

"Sorry," he said, and dropped my hand, shaking himself out of whatever had come over him, a sheepish grin on his face. "So come on, let's swim."

"We don't have bathing suits!"

"That's what underwear is for." He lifted his shirt over his head and pulled his shorts off so that he was standing in the moonlight in his boxers. I tried not to stare too obviously, even though my instinct was to run my fingers all over his chest, memorizing each freckle and muscle. Then, he leapt into the water, coming up for air grinning and shivering, a boy who had such a lust for life that it bent to his whim. "You coming in?"

"I want to, but . . ." I cursed the decision I'd made earlier in the night, trying on this dress with its low back and thin straps. "I'm not wearing a bra."

"Oh," he said, pushing his hair out of his eyes as little droplets of water glided down his skin. "Damn." He looked so disappointed, and a strange joy rose up in me. *I* was causing his disappointment, and I had the power to fix it too.

I was a star, and stars were bold. So, not letting myself think it through too fully, I lifted the dress over my head and jumped half-naked into the pool.

"Holy shit," Noah said, laughing in disbelief. "You're wild!"

"What are you going to do about it?" I asked, and he splashed me, so I splashed him back, and we wrestled in the water like rough-housing children, diving below the surface, grabbing at each other's ankles. On the lip of the pool, water puddled around my delicate dress. The fabric would be ruined by the chlorine, but it was a worthwhile sacrifice.

We floated next to each other, looking up at the faint stars above us, the noises of the others at the party muffled compared to the drumbeat of my heart. My arm brushed against his, and I felt a rippling through my body that had nothing to do with the water. I turned my head to look at him. His eyes lingered on my breasts for a moment before he pulled them away—trying to be a gentleman!— and looked straight up, suddenly interested in identifying constellations among the city smog.

"What?" I asked, my voice low, luring.

"Nothing," he said.

"Tell me what you're thinking about." If something was going to happen between us, now was the moment.

"Just that . . . don't you wish Summer was here?"

All at once, the water around me felt very cold. I had humiliated myself just like my character. This fit into the list seamlessly: Kat trips off the stage, Kat gets smacked in the face with pizza, Kat jumps into a pool topless with a boy and he still doesn't want her.

"I can't believe the show never lets her be funny," he was saying. "She's *so* funny! I mean, she's beautiful too, so I get why they focus on that, but you know, she talks about how watching sitcoms has been such a good distraction since her dad died, and how she wishes she could make people laugh like that, and I really think she *could* if they gave her a chance."

I folded my arms over my chest, a mummy in its sarcophagus. She'd never told me any of this, and I was her best friend. For the first time I wondered how much Summer and Noah hung out without me and Liana there, going over to each other's trailers or grabbing a coffee from the shop on the lot, or maybe even Summer calling him to talk at night, something she'd largely stopped doing with me.

The truth hit me then: If Summer lost someone else she loved, I would no longer be her first call. She had sweetly, quietly switched me out for Noah, and I'd had no idea.

He loved Summer, not me, and the worst part was that I understood. It wasn't that I didn't want her here. I missed her too.

But I wanted her here in a different kind of world, a world where she and Noah focused on me instead of each other. A world where I was the favorite person, the first choice.

When you're young, and you love someone, want to be them, and resent them all at the same time, it's hard to step back and separate out those different feelings. They just become one big swirl of emotion, and it's easy enough to label it as hate.

Fourteen

· · · · · · ·

2018

In a TV show, here's where the montage would be, as we throw ourselves into rehearsals and our first week back slips by. I say "rehearsals," but really, this first week is a boot camp.

Picture me learning how to sing, act, and dance again after more than a decade of letting those abilities decay. Here I am in a T-shirt and yoga pants, attempting a fast-paced combination that our choreographer has put together—a spin, a leap, a series of movements where my hands and feet are somehow supposed to do wildly different things at the same time. "Maybe we should simplify," the choreographer says the second time I nearly smack myself in the face. I insist on trying again and again, working on it in front of the bathroom mirror during my lunch break, giving myself the devastating eyebrow when I keep making the same mistakes. (It works, I feel chagrined.) Finally, *finally*, it clicks into place, and I ride on a wave of adrenaline until it comes time to learn the next difficult routine.

Picture me getting back to my room at night—though Liana, Summer, and I are all being put up at the same hotel, we do not carpool—utterly exhausted. The thing is, it's a good kind of exhaustion. At the end of the workday at home, I try to forget about my clients until I have to go into the office again. Here, I practice my dance moves while I brush my teeth and sing my songs in the shower. I'm exhausted, but also . . . I feel like I am waking up. Each night, I curl up in bed and call Miheer. Our texting continues to be jokey and fun and constant, but on the phone, his semi-proposal sits on the line with us like we're on a conference call, a hulking presence stifling our conversation. Plus, he always goes to bed earlier than I do, and now we've got a three-hour time difference to contend with. Still, we try valiantly to talk. I pump him for details about his projects at work, what new dishes he's learning to cook, which of our friends he's hanging out with. "How's the bad script?" he asks me. "Getting any better?" I tell him that it's not, but I *have* relearned how to do a pirouette, and then I explain to him what a pirouette is. "And how is it with the others?" It's a little weird but pleasant enough, I say, because it feels too raw to try to put the truth into words.

Picture Liana with that bright shiny hardness to her that I cannot get through. Her social media trumpets how glorious it is to be back with old friends, yet she spends her rehearsal breaks posting pictures or taking calls from Javier, during which she moves far away from the rest of us for privacy. In my more reasonable moments, I think that she's become one of those women who get so deep into a relationship, they forget how to hang out with anyone besides their One True Love. In my more paranoid moments, I worry that she's keeping her distance from me because she suspects what I did back then.

Picture Noah constantly flitting off to other commitments. He deploys his charm until everyone in the room is eating out of the palm of his hand, and then his assistant comes in to play the bad guy, shepherding him off to vague "magazine shoots" and "interviews." He's cagey on the details. Maybe the truth is that he's just going home to relax, or wining and dining various supermodels. Maybe he thinks he can simply slot on in while the rest of us work our asses off. We're lucky just to have him, and that's what we should tell anyone who asks. (*What a great guy! So kind of him to bother stopping by!*) "Don't give me that look," Michael says to me one afternoon, after I return from lunch to hear that Noah has skipped out on the rest of the day. "He's been a working actor the last thirteen years. He doesn't need to relearn how to do all this like the rest of you." So that's fun.

And picture Summer still doing her odd innocent act. Production assistants seek her out as a curiosity, pressing her for scandalous details about the most famous men she's hooked up with or her stint on that reality show where a bunch of washed-up stars were supposed to live in a house together for six months. (They lasted only one.) She blinks at them and answers in bland platitudes, seemingly unbothered.

But one day, during a break, I see her falter. A bunch of us are out on the lot, basking in the sunshine. Summer's talking with a supporting actor from the first time around who played one of our kooky teachers. Nice old Scotty, who always reaches out at Christmas with a big group email. They don't notice me as I pass behind them.

"So you really have no idea who leaked it to the press?" Scotty asks her, and my throat constricts.

Because they're talking about the journal. The beautiful seafoam one that Mr. Atlas bought for Summer, blank pages ready to be filled with one's most private thoughts.

The journal that ended up all over the news and the gossip blogs, those pages splayed open for the world to dissect.

I stop moving, almost stop breathing, as I wait to hear what Summer says.

She shakes her head. "I was so bad about locking my trailer in those days. Someone must have come in and taken it."

"What kind of a monster . . ." he begins. "Well, I'm sorry."

"Thank you." She gives him a smile then, a more genuine one, and he puts his hand on her shoulder in a comforting way.

"And let me just say, if you ever want to re-create anything you wrote in it, I can be discreet."

She rears back in surprise, his hand still locked on her shoulder, no longer comforting, just lecherous. Entitled. "Oh, no. Thank you."

"Hey, it's okay, I know you like to have a good time, and I do too. So if you change your mind, you know where to find me." He squeezes her upper arm as she stiffens, and then he saunters off.

She stares straight ahead, a vein in her throat pulsing. Then her eyes lock on mine as she catches me watching her. "What?" she snaps. The memory bubbles up in my mind, in my chest: the quiet click as I opened her trailer door, my heart pounding as I searched her drawers, my fingers scrabbling, closing around that soft sea-foam cover. For one reckless moment I think about confessing everything, begging for her forgiveness. But I can't. I can't say anything at all.

She looks at me for a moment longer, then sniffs, and walks back into rehearsal. But the stench of the journal is inescapable. It clings to her now, just as it has over the past thirteen years. And I stand there in the studio lot, stomach sinking.

Because I'm the one who did that to her.

FIONA SAVAGE-FUNE: Hello, and welcome to NPR's *Crosstalk*, tackling the issues of the day with people who disagree. I'm your host, Fiona Savage-Fune. Today I am joined by Carol Donaldson from *The Family TV Guide* and Mai Rodriguez from *The Femi-Gist*. Welcome to you both.

CAROL DONALDSON: Thank you, Fiona.

MAI RODRIGUEZ: Pleasure to be here.

FIONA SAVAGE-FUNE: Our topic today is decency standards in media. We're all aware of the recent outcry that resulted when the stars of a popular Atlas show appeared onscreen in costumes some viewers found inappropriate. Carol, you were one of the most outspoken voices in the backlash.

CAROL DONALDSON: It's about the health of our children. My preteen and I watched the first season of *The Daydreams* together, and it taught lovely lessons about friendship, teamwork, and the importance of emotional connections instead of physical ones. Summer Wright's character even wears a purity ring, a subtle costuming choice that opened up a valuable conversation for the two of us. But I worry that was all a gateway drug to a second season full of boundary pushing and lust.

MAI RODRIGUEZ: The leads haven't even kissed yet, Carol.

CAROL DONALDSON: But the tension between them is palpable! And it's confusing my preteen. I found her fondling the poster of Noah Gideon in her room the other day.

MAI RODRIGUEZ: Look, the real problem isn't what's happening onscreen. It's what's happening off. In my opinion, Atlas destroys teenage girls for our entertainment. The company discards its stars when they show any sign of acting like the adults they've grown into. The rate of former stars in rehab is, frankly, staggering. Surely you've seen the video of Amber Nielson, on a drug of some kind, being mobbed by the paparazzi.

FIONA SAVAGE-FUNE: Let's roll the clip.

AUDIO OF AMBER NIELSON: Do you . . . no, listen. Do you believe in alternate universes? I bet there's a universe where I never did an Atlas show, and I'm actually happy.

MAI RODRIGUEZ: We at *The Femi-Gist* have been reaching out to the network head, Gerald Atlas, asking how he's going to start taking better care of his stars, but he refuses to speak with us.

CAROL DONALDSON: I don't see what this has to do with the subject at hand.

MAI RODRIGUEZ: The real indecency is Atlas's behavior! Star after star is self-destructing in the public eye while we gleefully gobble up the mess these young women have made.

FIONA SAVAGE-FUNE: Mm, and it's always the young women, isn't it?

MAI RODRIGUEZ: Exactly. But we can fight back. The power of the consumer, Fiona. If the network doesn't take real steps to redress this issue, it's time to change the channel.

Fifteen

· · · · · · ·

2018

I return to rehearsal trying to shake off the interaction about Summer's journal that I witnessed in the lot. For a little while, I almost manage to. We're relearning the music for our finale song, the four of us standing around the piano singing in harmony. It feels close to natural. And then, like clockwork, Noah's assistant bustles over to Michael and whispers in his ear.

"Pause," Michael says. "Okay, Noah has to go."

"Damn, right now?" Liana asks.

"Sorry, guys," Noah says, holding up his hands, a suave smile on his face. "Wish I could stay, but duty calls." Summer bites her lip, her disappointment clear.

I'm livid. How the hell is Summer supposed to get the redemption she craves when Noah isn't taking this seriously?

As Noah swaggers toward the door, Michael flips through his script. "Let's focus on the Summer and Liana scene on page thirty-two for the rest of the afternoon," he begins.

"Can I go?" I cut in.

"Sure, fine, whatever," he says, and I'm out of there like a shot, charging after Noah into the parking lot.

"Hey!" I call as he reaches his car, and he turns in surprise.

"Hey," he says. "Sorry, I'm a little late for—"

"I know you're fancier than we are now, but this running-out-of-rehearsal shtick is getting old." I can't stop now that I've started. "We're all *here*. We gave things up to do this! I threw a bomb into my life, and you can't even be bothered to pretend it's a top priority for you? What the hell else is so important?"

"I . . ." he starts, then glances at his watch. He's still just going to leave. Of course. What an avoidant piece of—

"You want to come with me?" he asks, opening the passenger-side door.

. . . .

In the car, Noah says, "They'll probably make you sign a nondisclosure agreement when we get there, but I'm just going to go ahead and tell you now." He stares straight ahead at the road. "I'm going to be Snow Leopard." He's trying to be cool about it, but the corners of his mouth fight him, bursting into an untamed smile.

I refuse to be awed. "Oh. Congrats." But this is huge news. Comic fans love Snow Leopard, and he's never gotten a movie before due to copyright issues that have recently been resolved. Ever since the development announcement dropped, the internet has exploded into fantasy casting frenzies. Noah has been mentioned, but so have the various Chrises, a wide crop of studly Brits, and pretty much anyone else with name recognition and a six-pack. If I found it hard to avoid Noah in the news before, it'll be impossible now.

I keep my voice casual. "Everyone in the world is going to know who you are. Are you nervous?"

"Well *now* I am, thanks a lot." He turns off the freeway, navigating us down narrow side streets. "I wasn't sure if I should take it at first."

"You get one Oscar nomination and suddenly you're too high-brow for superheroes?"

"From now on, I only do art house Westerns about tortured cowboys." He shakes his head. "Nah, I can't do any more Westerns. Horses hate me."

I swing my head to look at him. "What? No."

"It's true. I did one Western, and I tried to ride three different horses, and they all kept attempting to throw me."

"What did you do to them?" I ask, giggling a bit in spite of myself.

"Nothing! Maybe they could sense that I cared too much?"

"Did you get a fourth horse?"

He shakes his head. "The producers had to bring in a body double and CGI my face on. The shame, I carry it with me."

"And that's why you weren't sure if you should do *Snow Leopard*. Because of all the horses on the tundra."

He grins and gives my shoulder a friendly shove. "No, because of what you said before. It's life changing. You're signing up to be part of this huge machine. But hey, don't say no to things just because they scare you, right?"

"Unless they scare you for good reason." I start to laugh, then press my hand over my mouth. "Like horses."

He shakes his head and says quietly, "I think I would be out of my mind to turn this opportunity down." For a moment he seems almost hesitant, as if he's convincing himself. Yeah right. He's spent his whole career doing what he needed to make it to the top, chumming it up with the right people, leaving the wrong people behind without a second glance. What inconvenient timing for him, that those people he left behind have come back into his life right as he's reached the apex. Well, all he has to do is make it through a few more weeks with us, and then he can go hang out with the other superstars at his level.

"So that's why you've been MIA?" I ask. "You've started working already?"

"We're filming a big announcement featurette," he says. "Atlas is going to air it during the commercials of our live show." No pressure.

Noah turns off and parks outside of a gray brick building, an anonymous, largely windowless structure that gives no clue about what lies inside. I follow him to the door. "Today, they want to document my 'transformation,'" he says, swinging it open to reveal a gym, mats on the floor, rows of gleaming equipment. Nobody's working out, though. Instead, the space is full of crew members. "We're filming a personal training session."

A frowning man spots me. "Noah! Who is this? She's not on the approved list!"

"She's a friend," Noah replies, slinging an arm around me. "She won't tell anyone."

The man snaps his fingers at an assistant. A nondisclosure agreement materializes in my hands while Noah is whisked over to a makeup artist. She starts dusting him in foundation and powder. Won't he just immediately sweat it off again? She signals for him to take his shirt off. "Not even going to buy me dinner first?" he asks with a wink, making her blush as he lifts it over his head. I try to keep my mouth from falling open. I knew Noah was ripped. He's a movie star. But his chest right now is next-level. Forget a six-pack. He's got at least eight abs. Honestly, it's tipped past attractive and toward cartoonish, like he's turning from flesh and bone into a plastic action figure.

The makeup artist pulls out a bottle and spritzes him with water to make him look just the right amount of sweaty—the kind where he glistens, where you'd still want to run your fingers up and down his body instead of telling him to take a shower. She steps back, squints at him (a thought bubble reading *Stop ogling him and focus!* practically appearing over her head), and then brings out the baby oil. Noah stands stoically as she pats his chest with a weird wet thwacking sound. I stifle a laugh.

The shoot director leans over to the woman next to him, who seems to be an Atlas emissary. "Should we lose the beard?" he asks her as they both watch Noah's baby oil slathering.

"Mm," the woman says, her tone so serious, it's like he just asked if they should declare war on a neighboring nation. "If Snow Leopard has self-warming powers, we should have as much of his skin exposed to the elements as possible. And that includes face skin."

"Exactly. Same page." The director strides over to Noah and the makeup artist. "All right, we're going to shave the beard real quick."

"Oh." Noah blinks. "Sure." He scratches his scruff. "But don't you think it helps make Snow Leopard feel more rugged?"

"Oh, you look *very* rugged with it," the director replies.

"Like you're ready to go chop down some trees," the Atlas emissary chimes in.

"But I think what we want here is *sleek*."

"And Snow Leopard would actually leave trees alone because he respects the natural world."

Noah clears his throat as the makeup artist pulls out a razor. "Gotcha."

As he is shorn, Noah looks up to the ceiling, keeping his face blank. The makeup artist turns Noah's head in my direction, and he catches me watching him. For a moment, there is something unguarded in his eyes. Then, quickly, he winks, as if to say, *What a ridiculous profession, huh?*

Once he's been sufficiently cleaned and dusted, his physical trainer—a tattooed, top-heavy dude named Xander—steps up, ready to at least pretend like he's putting Noah through some paces. Noah does mountain climbers, a cameraman getting up close to capture the one bead of sweat rolling down his hairless face. He lifts some weights, grunting performatively. "We can highlight that bicep more in post, right?" one crew member asks another, who nods.

As the camera runs up and down his tanned thighs, pushes in on his abs, I wonder if he's feeling at all dehumanized. The footage I see on a monitor in front of me feels *hungry*, the way that so much footage of Summer felt over the years.

The crew gets what they need and starts to pack up. I pick up my bag, assuming we'll head out. But Noah shakes his head. "Now it's time for the actual workout," he says.

"I'm not going to sit here and watch you lift," I say, annoyed.

"I know. You're joining in."

"Absolutely not," I say.

"You're in the right outfit," he says, indicating the workout clothes I wore to rehearsal. "Keep me company. It'll be fun."

I stare daggers at him.

"Kat! Kat! Kat!" he chants, getting some of the assistants and his trainer to join with him.

I throw up my hands. "Fine," I say. "But it's Katherine now."

Xander proceeds to work me harder than I've ever been worked in my life. No wonder Noah's developed abs of steel. I'm worried that my heart will give out, or that I will slip on the puddle of sweat I've shed and give myself a concussion. It's agony.

"I will murder you," I say to Noah, with the last bits of breath I have as Xander makes us do burpees.

"I think Xander's going to beat you to it," he huffs back.

When the workout finally ends, I lie on the ground, Noah collapsed next to me, both of us dizzy with relief that we survived. We straggle out of the building, laughing about how sore we're going to be tomorrow. Noah rubs his cheek absentmindedly, then rubs it again.

"Missing your beard?" I tease. "You can always grow it back."

"Sure, in ten years when Snow Leopard sacrifices himself for the next generation of superheroes, maybe I will once again grow a small beard."

"I'm sorry, is that a note of self-pity I hear? It's hard being a movie star?"

"Yes." He pouts his lip, then breaks into a grin. "How insufferable am I? Nah, it's all good. Feel how smooth my face is."

He takes my hand and holds it to his cheek, and yes, with the combination of the shave and the sweat and the oil, his skin is incredibly soft. Warm too. For just a moment, he's the teenage Noah again, untouched by time, and I'm the girl who would have done anything for him.

No, dammit, I'm not here to fall back into his shiny mantrap. I yank my hand away and keep walking to the car. Then I stop, whirling to face him directly. "I'm still pissed at you, you know. Just because you took me along today, just because you're going to be a superhero, doesn't mean you can keep being careless with *The Daydreams*." Back in the day, Noah had a signature look, the lazy smile up from underneath his eyebrows. It made it seem like he was really *seeing* you. Now, he stares at me with a slight squint to his eyes, a little wrinkle in his forehead. Apparently, his new signature look is him really *listening.* It's infuriating. Unless it's genuine.

"We need you," I finish, and after a moment, he nods. I think I see relief in his expression, maybe relief that this is all I'm pissed about.

"You're right," he says. "I'll talk to Atlas and see what I can do."

Sixteen

· · · · · · ·

2005

The world may have been deprived of a Summer and Noah kiss, but I got to see it happen so much I got sick of it, once we started rehearsing for the live season-two finale.

The first time that Michael led them through the kiss rehearsal, they were tentative about it, shy smiles on their faces that they were trying to hide, Noah's foot tapping anxiously. The actual live show would take place on a big stage, with fireworks set to go off over the theater at the end of our last number, but for now we were in a rehearsal room with fluorescent lighting on the studio lot, just some teenagers in sweatpants and no makeup and sprinkles of acne on our cheeks, like we could've been rehearsing for our high school's musical. Liana and I sat on the sidelines, ready for our entrances.

"So," Michael said. "You'll say your lines, and then, Summer, you'll step forward and kiss Noah. Noah, you'll react like you've won the goddamn lottery, okay?"

They nodded and began, a blush rising on Summer's cheeks.

"I'm going to miss the band," she said. "But more than that, I'm going to miss you."

"You are?" Noah asked.

"Because I . . . well, I . . ."

It felt like everyone in the room was holding their breath as Summer stepped forward. There was a dull, heavy weight in my stomach. I wanted the kiss to be awkward, disappointing.

And it *was*. Summer didn't know where to put her hands. Noah was wooden. The awareness that they were surrounded by other people seemed to hang over them, a self-consciousness to their movements. They pressed together for a moment, then stepped apart, Noah rubbing the back of his neck, Summer biting her lip. I felt a strange spark of satisfaction. Take that, creepy men on the internet—Summer was a bad kisser!

"Can we try that again?" Summer asked.

"I think you should," Michael said.

"Sorry, just a lot of pressure!" Summer said.

"Why, because this is the kiss that millions of tweens have been dreaming about?"

"Something like that," Noah said.

"Imagine the two of you are alone, okay?"

"Okay," Noah said, shaking out his shoulders. He and Summer looked at each other and, so quickly I almost missed it, she crossed her eyes and stuck out her tongue. A snort escaped him, which made her laugh too.

"Okay," she said, and recited her lines again, then stepped in to him.

This time, it was one of those kisses where the rest of the world falls away, a kiss where two people feel something entirely new and come home at the same time. You could practically hear the music swelling, even though nobody was playing the instrumental underscoring yet. He slid his hand up her back, pulling her in. She arched up on her tiptoes, tangling her fingers in his hair.

"That's a lot better," Michael said, and they broke apart, a little gasp escaping Summer.

I wanted, just once in my life, for someone to kiss me like that, with such focus, such desire. And I wanted, just once, to kiss someone like that too. Not because they were around, not because I felt like I should. But because something voracious inside of me wouldn't be satisfied until I'd pressed myself against them.

We rehearsed it again and again, adding in the instrumental, trying to time out Liana's entrance and then mine. Each time, the kiss grew more passionate, more assured. Hornier. It wasn't one of those kisses where the music gently swelled anymore, unless the music was "Let's Get It On."

"Guys," Michael said. "You can't eat each other's faces at your leisure. We need to time it with Liana."

"Sorry!" Summer said.

"Liana, Kat, you guys ready to go?"

We jumped to our feet.

"Oh," Liana muttered. "So we're not going to sit around all day and watch them make out?"

"Strange," I whispered back. "I thought that was our purpose."

· · · · · · ·

That night, at the end of rehearsal, I had a wardrobe fitting with Harriet. I stood there while she stuck pins into my outfit, complaining about some talking-to she'd gotten from Michael, about how she'd added cutouts to those sexy dresses at the last minute without his approval.

"And the little bit of controversy is helping you all out, isn't it? But he's so terrified of Mr. Atlas being angry that he has to dress me down anyway," she said. She stared at me and clucked to herself. "I guess I could cinch this, try to give you more of a waist."

I looked straight ahead at a picture on Harriet's desk, Harriet with her daughter, a girl in her early teens. Harriet had brought her to set once and introduced her to us, and the girl had been so starstruck she had forgotten how to talk. If Harriet was this awful to us, I couldn't imagine how big a complex that girl was going to develop.

"Michael could never do my job, but I bet I could learn to do his," Harriet went on.

Because I had a bitchy face and played the mean girl role so well, people had started coming to me to share their own hidden bitchiness. I was constantly hearing about someone's feud with somebody else. I knew exactly who hated whom, and why. People wanted me to listen, to join in, so that they could walk away feeling like I had taken their confession. I heard people turn on the friends who they seemed to love, mercilessly flay their husbands and wives, shit-talk the scene partners that they told the press were "just like family!" Could you trust anyone to care about you as much as they said they did? Or was everyone secretly hating everyone else behind their backs? I absolved them and absorbed, studying all the ways one could be a bitch, putting it into my performance. But I wasn't one myself. I was good; I was kind.

"I'm sure you could do his job just fine," I said. "Maybe you'd run rehearsals more efficiently, and we wouldn't have to spend hours watching Summer and Noah suck face." Well, I was good and kind most of the time.

She looked at me then. "Chemistry is a funny thing, isn't it? What Summer and Noah have . . ." She shook her head. "It's like the dresses I made."

"What do you mean?"

"It hasn't crossed a line, exactly, but it's dancing right on it. Move a little bit one way, and it's safe, boring. Move a little bit the other way, and it's inappropriate. People can't stop watching, because what if it crosses over to the other side?"

When I left the wardrobe room, heading back toward my trailer, I stopped short at the sight of two figures ahead of me in the dark. Summer and Noah, standing close to each other, talking quietly in the balmy evening air. Almost as if Harriet's comment had summoned them into being. I inched closer to hear what they were saying, stepping into the shadows between trailers. "You feel it too," he was saying, reaching out to take hold of her arm. "I know you do."

"Noah . . ." she said, but she didn't pull her arm away.

"And I don't care about the sex! If you're worried 'cause I've done it before, I think it's cool that you're waiting," he fumbled. I'd never heard him talk like this before, his words so choppy and desperate. "I admire you for it. Like, maybe I like you even *more* because of it." In the dark, I rolled my eyes.

"You do?" Summer asked.

"Yeah! I want you to know that I really respect you. And then, if we ever do . . . it will be more special. I just want to know that we're each other's, not anyone else's. Be with me."

For a long moment, Summer said nothing. Then she flung herself into his arms. "I want to," she said. "I'm going to end things with Lucas."

Noah let out a laugh of pure joy and stroked her face. She ran her hands through his hair. He leaned in to kiss her, but she stopped him.

"I just need a few weeks, okay? I don't want our breakup to become the big story right before the live show. He'll be upset, and so will our friends from home, and I'm worried someone could go to the paparazzi trying to make some stupid controversy. You saw what happened with people from school who didn't like me talking to the press about my mom. Let's get through the show, sign the movie contract, and we'll be safe. Can you give me that?"

"Of course I can," he said, tightening his arms around her, leaning in to kiss her, a private kiss this time, hungrier and longer. I was stuck in place as they kept touching each other, their breathing soft and fast, knowing that I should leave, not wanting to witness what was happening and yet unable to look away as Noah slipped his hand underneath her skirt. Summer let out a moan, then pushed his hand away.

"Stop," she said. "Not yet."

"Okay. Okay, right."

"I'm scared," she said. "This . . . it scares me. I think we might try it and drive each other crazy within three weeks, and then everything will get so awkward."

"But you still want to try?"

"I do."

"You and me," he said, "we're going to take over the world."

A golf cart sounded in the distance, and they stepped apart as it approached. A production assistant was driving, Mr. Atlas in the seat beside him, making his rounds of the studio lot, going from set to set to pronounce his judgment, to decide who would continue to make the show that had become their whole world and who would not. He tipped his hat to Summer and Noah as he passed, and they waved innocently at him.

"Hey, guys," I called, stepping into the lamppost light. "What are you up to?"

"Just talking through a scene," Summer said.

"Yeah?" I asked, raising my eyebrow.

"Yeah, but I think we're done now." She gazed back at me, a placid look on her face, as if she hadn't just been whispering desperate things with Noah in the dark. He had no such chill, his face burning red even in the dim light, a dopey smile coming onto his features despite his attempts to fight it. Summer, though, lied as if she believed what she was saying, or as if it came naturally. As if she lied all the time.

SECRET ROMANCE?

Sources say that **Summer Wright** and **Noah Gideon** are finally getting the kiss that fans have always wanted, and they are a little too excited about it. Apparently, rehearsals for the live finale (tune in to the Atlas Channel next Wednesday, 8 p.m. ET) have been getting hot and heavy! "Summer's supposed to be a role model," one source says, "but she's basically cheating on her boyfriend in front of a room full of people. I wouldn't be surprised if there's more going on between Summer and Noah behind the scenes."

Seventeen

· · · · · · ·

2018

The morning after my surprise physical training with Noah, I can barely move my arms. Still, fortified with coffee and Advil, I drag myself into rehearsal. Michael starts out by going over the agenda. "And Noah has to duck out early, so we'll—"

"Actually," Noah says, raising his hand, "I'm fine to stay." Michael raises his eyebrows in surprise. "I pushed my other commitment to a different time." Noah leans over to me and says, under his breath, "Who needs sleep?" I give him the briefest of smiles, the smallest bit of credit.

So, later in the afternoon, while Liana and I sit in the corner and try to memorize our lines, Noah and Summer go to the piano to relearn their duet. This was the first song the two of them ever sang together, the song that brought the house down at our school talent show.

They stand a foot apart, and somehow the negative space between them crackles, like if either of them attempts to move closer, an invisible electric fence will shock them.

Still, Noah shoots a devil-may-care grin at the pianist as if he hasn't even noticed the crackling, while Summer starts them off. *"There are people who sleepwalk through all of their days."*

"*Who say the word 'no,'*" Noah sings, "*in a million ways.*" The melody leaps up half an octave for the word "million" and seems to take Noah by surprise, because his voice doesn't quite make it, coming in flat and low. He laughs and clears his throat. "Whew, sorry about that."

My first, ungenerous thought is a screw-you to Michael. Noah needs to practice after all! He might be the only one of us still getting work, but he's not some God of Talent among the plebians.

The pianist takes it back to the beginning, and Summer sings her line with her eyes glued to the sheet music. Noah's still grinning but, this time, he thinks too hard about the note and overshoots it. He shakes his head quickly, then tries again, and his voice cracks with a quick pop, like he's an adolescent boy going through changes. The sheet music he's holding trembles, ever so slightly, in his hands. Could the golden man actually be nervous?

Liana has been staring at her phone (texting lovey-dovey things to Javier, no doubt), but now she puts it down, watching Noah too. She and I exchange a glance.

I think about Noah trying to ride three different horses on set until he had to give up in shame. He's getting in his head about this note. And the thing about getting in your head? It only happens when you actually care about something.

"Sorry," he says to Summer quietly.

"It's okay," Summer says. Poker-faced, looking down at her music, she goes on, in a voice that I just manage to overhear, "We're all trying to recapture our teenage selves. You just went too far back and recaptured puberty."

He lets out a startled bark of a laugh. "I'm having flashbacks to one terrible month in eighth grade."

"Poor little Noah." Summer bites her lip and says, in a casual tone, "You know, I've always liked your line better than mine."

He turns his head to look at her. "The 'million ways' part? It's better in a girl's range. So I'd switch, if you wanted to."

"Yeah?" Noah asks. "Okay, let's try that."

They start again, with Noah taking the first part, and this time, they do it seamlessly. Summer doesn't say anything, doesn't turn to look at him, but the skin around her eyes crinkles. She's pleased with herself. As they continue singing straight through, alternating vocal lines on the rest of the verse (*I worried that I might be one of their kind, but now you're here, and it's all so clear*), Summer moves half a foot closer to Noah, crossing that invisible electric fence between them right as they leap into the chorus:

> *That I'm meant to dance and I'm meant to shout*
> *I'm meant to know what they're talking about*
> *In poetry and songs*
> *I'm so glad I was wrong*
> *'Cause you're meant to laugh and you're meant to sway*
> *Please take my hand and don't go away*
> *Meant to be, here with me*
> *You're here with me.*

If you'd put Noah in a song with Liana back in the day, he would've disappeared. But he and Summer were always so evenly matched when it came to vocals.

Now, voices just a little rusty, they complement each other as well as they always did. Listening to them, you can almost pretend they're still evenly matched in other ways too, the ways that matter: credibility, stability, happiness. The illusion of that seems to intoxicate Summer. Her eyes flit up from the sheet music to Noah's face and back down again. Her body leans a little closer to his as the music director gives them notes and has them try again. Noah sneaks a couple of glances at her too. I can't quite read his gaze. Puzzlement, maybe, like he's trying to square the woman in the tabloids with the one standing next to him. In Summer's, though . . . Summer looks hungry. Like she'd devour every smile he sent her way, every laugh she pulled out of him, and only want more.

Oh God, if she falls for him, he's going to break her fucking heart.

Eighteen

. . . .

2005

The day after that *Us Weekly* article insinuating a secret romance between Summer and Noah came out, we were putting on a full run-through for a small group of producers and invited guests. The important people gathered. Mr. Atlas settled in his seat, leafing through a binder of press clippings an assistant had collected for him while he waited for us to start. I snuck a peek over at them. **Amber Nielson's Downward Spiral!** one headline read. **Which Atlas Star Is Next?** Another was an editorial from *The Femi-Gist*: **Atlas: Destroyer of Girls?**

Among the important people, one seemed out of place: Summer's boyfriend, Lucas.

"Why is he here?" Liana asked Summer as the three of us sat on the ground and stretched in the corner of the rehearsal room.

"Oh goodness," she said, leaning forward to grab her toes, her hair falling into her face. "He's being paranoid, so I told him he could come today."

He looked around the room, sulky, seething, as we took our

places. I preferred not to be so obvious about my jealousy. I kept it hidden, dealt with it in other ways. Being in everyone's faces about it made you look like a fool, a vulnerable one too.

The run-through went well, especially for a group that was used to having multiple takes to get things right. The number where I had the lead vocals prompted snorts of laughter from the audience. Even, I saw out of the corner of my eye, a slight smile from Mr. Atlas himself. But when it came time for Summer and Noah to do their kiss, she approached him tentatively, like their awkward first attempt all over again, before pecking him on the lips. In the audience, Lucas audibly scoffed. Noah stepped back from the kiss, his forehead furrowed, his eyes flitting to Lucas in the corner, but carried on with the rest of the scene as normal, and we made it through the remaining five minutes to the end.

Afterward, we caught our breath in preparation to rehearse the problem spots that the run-through had laid bare like a black light. Mr. Atlas came around and congratulated us all individually. "Quite funny," he said to me, and to Liana, "Very nice enthusiasm."

He gave Summer a paternal smile. "Really something special happening here," he said to her. "I'm proud to see how you've grown in this role, and how you've overcome the setbacks I know you had to face."

She clasped her hands to her chest and thanked him.

Then he cleared his throat. "And you girls are all . . . doing all right? Feeling well?" he asked. And for just one second, the powerful gentleman of whom we were all afraid seemed a tiny bit afraid of us. The company couldn't take another Amber, another downward spiral, right now.

We all nodded and smiled. "Good, good," he said, and went to Michael in the corner to discuss his most pressing thoughts. Summer walked to Lucas's side and let him compliment her performance while she acted all modest about it. Liana nudged me, and we both looked over as Noah approached them.

"Yeah," Noah said. "You did great, Summer. Even though it was hard, 'cause some of the audience members were really distracting."

"I wasn't distracted," Summer said, working to keep the trepidation out of her voice, but not entirely succeeding. "Except that it's scary to do it in front of the head of the network."

"Right," Noah said, and flicked his eyes to Lucas. He was going for a look of cool disdain, but he cared too much to achieve it.

"Hey, man," Lucas said. "I was just sitting there watching. Not my fault if I make you uncomfortable."

"Why would you make me uncomfortable?"

"Let's let it go," Lucas said, shaking his head, a model of restraint. He put his arm around Summer's shoulders.

"Anyways," Summer began.

Noah interrupted her, staring daggers at Lucas. "No, really, why?"

"'Cause you're jealous of me. Obviously."

Noah smirked. "I'm jealous of *you*? I'm about to be a movie star. What are you doing with your life?"

"Yeah, a movie star to twelve-year-old girls. Real cool."

They began to enact a sort of absurd peacocking, puffing up their chests as they walked closer and closer to each other. Perhaps they thought they looked like *men*. Really, they seemed like little boys.

Liana grabbed my hand tight. "Oh, it is going down!" she whispered in my ear.

"You know why you're jealous," Lucas said.

"Guys," Summer said, her voice rising. "Stop." In their corner, Mr. Atlas and Michael turned to watch the scene.

"Of your lame job and your crappy car?"

"No. Because I have Summer, and you don't."

"Are you sure about that?" Noah asked. Lucas's face twisted. He stepped forward and shoved Noah, who stumbled back and then lunged forward, intent on retaliation, as a gasp went up from the extras.

"Stop!" Summer yelled, stepping in between them. They broke apart, neither one of them wanting to hurt her.

"What the heck, Noah!" she hissed at him. "What is wrong with you?"

"Get out of the way, Sum," Lucas said.

"Gentlemen," Mr. Atlas said, his mouth in a tight straight line. His voice was quiet as always, and yet the room fell silent, even the fighting boys turning to listen. "I own this room. In fact, I own this entire lot, and I abhor violence on my sets. So if you must beat each other up, you're going to have to take this dispute to someone else's property." He looked at Lucas. "And I'd ask you not to hit him in the face. I have a lot of money riding on it looking good on TV next week."

Noah stared down at the floor, mumbling an apology.

Summer took Lucas's arm. "Let's go for a walk." She didn't even look back at Noah as she left.

Noah, a broken expression on his face, stared after them as Michael and Mr. Atlas came to his side. "Sorry," he said. "I didn't mean to . . . he's just such a . . ."

"Look, we've all wanted to punch a meathead in the face," Michael said. Mr. Atlas inclined his head in a small nod, though the idea of him punching anybody seemed laughable. (Either he would never resort to violence, too far above it, or he'd already ordered his minions to drop multiple bodies in a river somewhere without ever dirtying his own hands. I really couldn't tell which one.)

"Don't let him antagonize you." Michael clapped Noah on the shoulder. "He's small potatoes. You're a star."

It's strange how easily your feelings about someone can be undone. I've spent so much time holding up Noah as this perfect guy who could do no wrong. But now I see that he's human like everyone else. And sometimes, he's really fucking annoying. Shall I count the ways? Why not!

Number one: He's selfish. The only thing that matters to him is what he wants, and he doesn't bother to think about how that might make other people feel.

Number two: He pretends he's super caring. He does that soulful look at you when you're talking so that you feel so special, but is he even really listening? Or is he just focused on how attractively he's furrowing his face? I always thought, "Oh, Noah's a normal guy who isn't an attention-seeking narcissist like so many other celebrities, he's just so cute and wonderful that everyone else decided he should be famous!" But actually, he totally does sees himself as THE STAR, as the hero, when sometimes he should realize that not every single thing is about him. He's not the only man in existence. I mean, who even says stuff like "You and me, we're going to take over the world"? And then fighting with Lucas in front of everyone?? Which leads me to . . .

Number three: His macho act, like he needs to prove that he's a Big Man even though he's on a stupid show for preteen girls. He probably thought he looked cool, fighting like that, but really, he looked pathetic. If the girls who love him so much had watched it, I bet a lot of them would have taken down their Noah posters.

Anyways, he's pissing me off, and I see him in a new light. Obviously I'm going to keep treating him the way I always do. I don't want to be on this stupid show forever. I'm a better actress than people give me credit for, and I can go on to bigger things, but only if I play my cards right, do this movie, and knock everyone's socks off. (Ugh, how many clichés did I just use in one sentence?) The last thing I want to do is make more drama. I'll keep adoringly listening to his stories. But now I know.

Nineteen

. . . .

2018

That night, I stretch out in bed and dial Miheer's number for our usual call. He sounds strange when he answers the phone.

"You all right?" I ask. "Just tired?"

"I, uh, read an article about you." He texts it to me, and I put him on speaker as I pull it up.

Under the headline **Noah Gideon Moving On?** there's a series of photos: me and Noah exiting the gym. In the first one, we're laughing. In the others, we're gazing at each other, him holding my hand to his cheek.

"Oh God," I say. I forgot how much it sucks to be followed around by paparazzi. Somehow those talented, merciless vultures captured that one brief moment when an old feeling reignited, before I poured my cold, cold hatred all over the spark. "What's happening in these photos is that I was calling Noah out on being a dick. Because that's what I think he is."

"I don't mean to be a jealous jerk. It's just, well, he's a movie star."

"And you're working to protect the environment, which in my mind is way sexier."

"Thanks," he says. "But you're sort of . . . glowing."

"We'd gone to the gym. The glow is perspiration."

He half laughs but then is silent for a moment. "It's more than that, though. You're lit up in a different way than you are at home."

I study the photo. He's right. "If that's true, it's not because of Noah. It's because . . ." Stumbling, I fall into a realization. "I'm engaged here in a different way than I am at work." Hmm, "engaged" was probably not the smartest word choice. "It's been an interesting break from the law firm stress, I suppose."

"Interesting in that . . . Wait, you're not having second thoughts about the firm, are you?"

"No, of course not!" I've been checking in with Irene every few days, answering questions that have come up from clients who don't want to work with anyone but me. And there's something I love in that too, in being viewed as competent, a decision-maker, more than just a body performing at the whims of others.

"Okay," he says.

"Also, I'm in LA, where you're obligated to eat a lot of seeds and spirulina and shit. Maybe that's making me look more radiant."

This time his laugh is full. "Of course, the official foods of Los Angeles. Sorry to be insecure about this. Believe it or not, I'm not used to dating celebrities."

"I hardly think I count as a celebrity. And please don't apologize. *I'm* sorry."

After we hang up, I log into my work email, intending to check in with Irene. I can't let myself get sucked too far into this *Daydreams* world when the real world waits for me at home.

But I already have an email from her waiting:

Dear Katherine,

This tabloid article about you caused quite a stir at work this afternoon. I'm sure it's a gross distortion of the truth, and that's what I told everyone. But you should know that these sorts of stories are not good for the firm's reputation, or for yours. Don't give the men who work with you an excuse to withdraw their respect, especially not when you're so close to making partner. If there's anything else you can do from afar to demonstrate your commitment, I'd advise you to consider it.

Shit. I rub my eyes, thinking. I'd given myself an extra day in Los Angeles on the back end to decompress. Now, I rebook my flight home to a red-eye leaving right after the finale. I reply to Irene with the update, along with an offer to pick up some remote work, and my gratitude to her for looking out for me. I pray that that's enough.

After that, falling asleep is futile. Kicking the sheets around, I wish I could turn over and nuzzle Miheer, that we could pull off our pajamas and do something that we do very well together. I miss him. I worry that both he and my partner prospects are slipping away. And on top of that, I think I'm lonely.

I wasn't expecting to come back and have everything magically feel like it did our first season together. But this awkwardness, this sense that everyone has their own strange agenda they're not sharing, the paranoia and guilt that clog my throat whenever I look too hard at Summer . . . it's getting to me.

I turn on the light and reach for my phone, scrolling through social media. My agent forced me to get an Instagram account at the beginning of this, assigning her assistant to run it. A few times a week, the assistant texts me a photo and a caption for my approval,

I text back a thumbs-up, and she puts them online. My account is following the whole *Daydreams* crew. Summer posts rarely now, often with some cryptic caption. Noah has been allowed to stay off Instagram, that lucky bastard—he's famous enough that forgoing social media only makes people more interested in him. Liana posts all the time: highly filtered selfies, influencer product promotions, pictures of her and her husband staring longingly into each other's eyes, and now a whole alternate-universe narrative of our new *Daydreams* adventure where we've fallen right back into being the best of friends. I stare at a selfie she posted of the two of us making funny faces at the camera, a longing pinging inside of me for a world in which we actually are having that much fun together.

She posts a new photo while I'm still staring at her page. Her, in her hotel bathrobe and a bold red lipstick, making sexy eyes at the mirror. The caption is Loving the work but missing my boo!

I like it, pause, then message her: I see you're still awake too.

After a moment she responds. Lol. My body is tired but I can't fall asleep.

Same. Taking a deep breath, I continue. Want to come to my room and raid the minibar?

Three dots appear, then disappear. She's going to say no. Then: Room #?

She knocks on my door ten minutes later, having traded her bathrobe for a maxidress and a sweater. Perhaps I should have put on real clothes too, instead of the boxer shorts and oversized T-shirt I was wearing in bed.

"Welcome to my home," I say in a mock-formal tone.

"It's gorgeous," she says, holding a hand to her heart as she pretends to take it all in. "It looks a lot like mine."

"Funny, that," I say, then crouch down at the minibar. "Okay, what should we drink on Atlas's dime?"

She stretches out in the suite's armchair, in a posture that mimics ease without actually achieving it. "Surprise me."

I twist the cap off a small bottle of whiskey, then pour it into the hotel's provided coffee mugs, handing her one. "Hey, I wanted to apologize about what I said the other day, at the costume fitting. I hope you know I didn't mean—"

"I was an asshole too." She takes a gulp and then, staring nonchalantly down at the mug, asks, "So how do you think Summer's doing?"

"Well. Her dancing is great, even if her voice sounds a little different—"

She leans forward, her tone suddenly urgent. "No, I mean, like, mentally. Emotionally."

"Ah. I can't tell."

"I was honestly expecting her to be . . . chaos. Like a walking, talking drama machine, but she seems more stable, right?"

"I think so."

"Yeah, she's doing okay." We both let out a sigh of semi-relief that we've been holding in for over a decade. "I'm glad," she says. "She is *totally* flirting with Noah, though."

"So I'm not the only one who noticed!"

"I'm like, 'Girl, chill.' Also, you can't play those tricks on him again! Not after he and everybody else read your journal!"

"Maybe they're not tricks. I just hope she doesn't think that he can be the answer to her problems." I down the rest of the whiskey in my mug and open up another bottle from the minibar.

"So, what's really going on?" she asks, watching me. "Why are you messaging me for company at midnight?"

In her hard, shiny wall, she's cracking open a window. I step toward it. "Long distance is hard. You're basically a relationship expert, you got any tips?"

"All the usual ones. Open communication and sending lots of nudes."

"I'm too scared to do anything like that after how everyone lost their shit over what happened with the finale."

"Yeah," she says, and we lapse into silence for a moment. "You ever wish we'd gotten famous just, like, seven years later? The world was kinder to girls seven years later."

"Those kids on Atlas now don't know how good they have it," I say.

"Screw them." She smiles at me, and we sit together for a little while, not saying anything, almost comfortable.

I lean forward. "How did you know that you were ready to marry Javier?"

"A magazine offered us a bunch of money for exclusive engagement photos, and I wanted a new car."

I stare at her.

"I'm kidding," she says, and fiddles with her wedding ring, a gigantic rock. "I don't know. I loved him. Being with him was the most exciting thing in my life." She watches her diamond sparkle. "I was bored, bored, bored, and then when we were together, I couldn't catch my breath."

"That's funny."

"Why?"

"It was the opposite for me and Miheer. We were in the same study group in law school. We didn't date until we were both living in DC later, but that's how we met. I was so stressed all the time, and then at some point I realized that, whenever he and I were studying together, or just talking on our breaks, or when he smiled at me . . . those were the only times I *could* catch my breath."

"What's he like?" she asks, so I tell her all about how quietly smart he is, how I'd known him a whole semester before one of his other friends dropped that he'd done a Fulbright. How if he'd wanted to go into the private sector, he'd probably be astoundingly rich by now, but instead he wanted to work in the nonsexy, nonlucrative world of land conservation. How he has this doofy giggle that comes out when something really funny takes him by surprise, and it always makes me crack up too. How he just . . . watches out for the people he loves. (As opposed to Noah, who watches out for himself. Although, to be fair, kudos to him for telling the *Snow Leopard* people to wait while he shows up for us.) (I don't say any of this part out loud.)

"Miheer will probably be the best dad. Kids follow him around like he's the Pied Piper." Liana cocks her head, truly paying attention to me, and somehow we are kind of connecting, so I charge ahead. "Although that's a whole other can of worms. His dad was pretty old by the time Miheer was born, and died when he was in his twenties, so Miheer would like to start talking about kids soon, but if I want to try for partner, especially after taking time off to do this reunion . . ." I wave my hand through the air.

"It's a big step," Liana says.

"You seem to be doing a good job of saying, 'Screw the pressure, we'll do it on our own time!' It must be awful, with all those magazines and their stupid headlines."

She holds her coffee mug tight, staring down into it. "We are trying, actually. We have been for a while."

And I've put my foot in my mouth again. "I am so sorry."

She gives me that *stop being an idiot* look that I've missed in this new, manicured version of her. "It's okay. I've been doing a good job of making it seem like we're so busy and fabulous we haven't gotten around to it." She shakes her head. "Remember being a teenager, and being so terrified of getting pregnant? Well, maybe not, I guess you weren't running around having as much sex as I was." She shakes her head. "Not *kind of a slut* like me."

"I'm sorry it's been difficult."

"We'll keep trying."

"I'm here if you want to talk about any of it."

"Thanks." She seems for a moment like she's about to say more, but purses her lips and stands up. "I should go to bed, rest up for rehearsal tomorrow. I'm feeling much more relaxed now, this was helpful." She gives me a quick hug, still tight and forced feeling, but a little bit better. Then, she is gone.

Twenty

. . . .

2005

I wasn't Summer's first call when something bad happened any-more, but she was mine.

As we hurtled toward the live show, I found out that my dad was getting remarried. On the phone, my mother was bereft, more than I would have expected given how much they'd screamed at each other.

"He's replacing us with a younger, shinier model," she said, sniffling, then caught herself. "I shouldn't have said that. He's not replacing you. He loves you very much."

"You guys fought all the time. You don't *like* him."

"I just wish he'd been sad about it a little longer." She was si-lent for a moment. "I miss you."

I pictured my father with a younger, prettier family. Shaken by her emotion, I wanted to tell her that I understood the kind of rejection she felt. Instead, I said, "We're doing a movie. There's going to be a lot of money. You always said you wished you could go back to school. I could . . . I could pay for that."

"Honey," she said, the word thick with emotion. "That's so kind. But you should use the money for your own schooling."

"There will be sequels," I said. "There will be more money."

"Well," she said, and I could hear the smile in her voice break-ing through the tears. "Maybe I'll order some brochures, just in case."

As soon as I called Summer and told her what had happened, she asked me where I wanted to meet and when (the entrance to the lot, ten minutes) and if she should bring Liana too (yes).

"I want to buy a car," I said when the two of them released me from their hugs. "A fancy one." I'd been driving around a solid car befitting a mom in the suburbs because it was what Atlas had got-ten for me when I first came out.

But now I wanted something *flashy*. Something that, as I drove, would make people turn their heads.

So the three of us hopped in a taxi over to the car dealership. Liana peppered the salesman with questions to make sure that I was getting a good deal. Summer smiled politely at the various customers who came over and tried to impress her. We looked at car after car in a sensible price range, and nothing felt right.

The salesman eyed us, then said, "I do have one more option." He brought us over to a red BMW convertible. Our mouths fell open. It didn't even matter that the price tag was $40,000. I handed over my credit card.

We hopped in, Liana rushing over to the passenger's seat, Sum-mer good-naturedly climbing into the back, and I immediately put the top down. We blasted pop music, our hair streaming in the wind, whooping as we flew down the highways, our resentments whooshing out, left far behind us. And as we drove, it was enough. No, *more* than enough, to be young and promising and happy with them.

"I'm hungry," Summer yelled. I was always hungry now. "Want to get fast food?"

"Mickey D's!" Liana chanted. "Mickey D's!"

I couldn't eat a huge, greasy meal like that, especially not so close to the live show. (*Put a bag over her head.*) But maybe I could allow myself a few fries.

We pulled into the drive-through in a playful mood, still high on one another. I put on an old-school movie star affectation to answer the crackly voice asking what we wanted. "Yes, darling, I'll have one Coca-Cola of the diet variety."

Summer leaned forward and did a passable Katharine Hepburn impression, though her bursts of laughter kept breaking it up. "A large order of fries and a burger would be absolutely swell, please."

"Hello, pussycat," Liana drawled. "Give me your finest chicken tenders."

We were all still laughing when we rounded the corner to the pickup window and saw the paparazzi. "Evening, gentlemen," Liana said, flashing them a smile as I paid, waiting for the woman at the window to bag up our order. There were only a few guys. So what, they'd capture us having a wholesome time eating fast food?

"What are you all ordering?" one of them asked, conversational, his camera clicking away.

"Just some dinner," I said.

"You having fun?" asked another as he recorded us. He spoke in an indulgent tone, like a proud father taking a home video.

"Of course," Liana said, draping her arm around me. "I love these girls." The woman behind the window was distracted by the presence of the cameras, waving and mugging at them instead of getting our ketchup.

"Summer, over here!" Summer smiled brightly. "Are you and Noah having a secret romance?" the third guy shouted, a middle-aged dude who made his living from trying to determine whether two teenagers were having sex.

Her happy expression faltered as the woman at the window finally handed me the bag.

"Summer, what does your boyfriend think about that?" shouted the one who had been so fatherly before.

"Okay, time to go," I said.

Then, seemingly from out of nowhere, more men descended. It happened so quickly. Was there a fucking paparazzi dispatch? *Emergency alert, three young women eating fries on Melrose, all vehicles needed!*

They swarmed us like locusts, blocking us in so we couldn't drive forward. They'd had hours of practice at this, and they were all competing against one another for the perfect shot, the one that would make them a few thousand dollars. Or maybe they could provoke us into something that would make them much, much more. This was how they put food on the table, provided for their families. Briefly I wondered if any of them had once dreamed of photographing beautiful vistas, taking pictures that really mattered. Maybe they hated us like we hated them, hated the parasitic system that made them depend on us. But we depended on them too, right? We'd wanted this.

A guy came around to my side, between the car and the drive-through window, getting in my face. "Kat, you sure you should be eating that?" he asked, pointing to the carton of fries.

We were so exposed, so trapped. "Put the top up," I said to Liana as I attempted to reverse. But—God, there were more of them behind us too. Liana frantically looked around for the roof button, jabbing at it as, in the back seat, Summer shrank away from the cameras.

The men came closer. There was a scraping sound, like nails on a chalkboard, against the side of the car: somebody's belt buckle, ripping jagged little lines across the new red paint of the metal I'd just spent far too much money on. The men pounded on the windows, shouting at us to look their way, to roll down the window and talk to them a little bit. To give them a smile like nice girls.

Summer whimpered. "These dudes are crazy," Liana said.

A dull thudding of fists came from the roof. Any moment, they might break through the canvas, their hands shooting down to grab us by the neck, to claim their ownership of us. What had I been thinking, buying myself a flashy car with a flimsy top? I should have bought myself a minivan. Or a tank.

The onslaught felt like that moment, driving through a thunderstorm, when you pull under an overpass and wait it out because if you keep pushing, something very bad could happen. But this wasn't some natural event, some opening of the heavens. These were men treating us like we owed them something just because we had dared to leave our homes for a Diet Coke.

"Summer, you okay?" Liana asked, and I looked back to see Summer shaking in the back seat, holding a sweatshirt over her head. I couldn't see her face, but her breath was coming out in sharp little gasps.

A thump on the hood grabbed my attention. One of the men was clambering up onto it, only inches away from the glass separating us. "Look over here, girls," he shouted, pressing right up against the windshield, angling his camera so he could capture all three of us.

I pressed the windshield washer nozzle button, squirting him with fluid, then turned on the wipers so that he had to move back. He wiped his face in shock, and then spat at me, "Bitch!"

Rage flooded into me, alongside the panic. "Fuck off," I snarled. I threw the car into drive and pressed down on the gas so that the men had no choice but to scatter out of the way. We moved forward slowly at first, then faster, and as I turned out of the parking lot and into the street, Liana rolled down the window and leaned out, giving the men the finger. We sped down the road again, like we had half an hour earlier, but this time we kept the top up. I didn't know if I'd ever put it down again.

. . . .

Michael called me and Liana into his office the next morning before rehearsal, both of us bleary-eyed but trying to hide our hangovers. She'd come and slept over after we dropped Summer back at her car, and we'd gotten exceedingly drunk to block out the memory of the drive-through. Michael made us sit down and pulled up a link on his computer. "Popslop posted some pictures of you at McDonald's yesterday," he said.

"It was pretty scary," I began, an idea starting to bud inside me. Michael was a real adult. He'd know what to do. Atlas had so many resources, and their job was to protect us, right? Maybe the company could release a statement of some kind asking the paparazzi to be gentler, reminding them that we were still young.

But Michael was frowning at us, not at the situation. There, on the Popslop website, splashed across the screen, was the headline **Daydreams or Nightmares? The Atlas Stars Stop Playing Nice!** Underneath, a picture of me and Liana in the front seat. We looked . . . unwell, our eyes bulging, my mouth gaping open, tendrils of spit clearly visible as I screamed at the man taking our picture. Behind us, Summer huddled under that sweatshirt, so you couldn't see her face, just her rigid shoulders. A second picture showed Liana flipping off the cameras in perfect detail.

"There's video too," Michael said, and played a clip of me yelling at the paparazzi to fuck off.

I hated Popslop with a fiery passion. Just a few months ago, we could expect news about us once a week, maybe, in the periodicals and tabloids. And there was limited space too, so only the bigger stories got play. But now, thanks to this terrible blog, footage went up almost immediately, the machine hungry for more and more of it.

"We're sorry," I said, my face growing hot. "They kind of attacked us."

"How do you think Mr. Atlas felt about this?" he asked.

"We didn't do anything wrong!" Liana said. "They scratched up Kat's new car. The roof is dented, and she *just* bought it!"

"You're supposed to ignore and not engage," Michael said. "Like Summer did."

"So we should all put sweatshirts over our heads and sit there while a bunch of men tear the car apart?" Liana shot back. "Someone had to get us out of there!"

"You certainly don't scream expletives at them!" he said. Then he pressed his fingers to his temple. "You guys are not essential, okay? People don't watch this show because of the two of you. Summer's the draw here. I could make this whole movie with just her and Noah. I don't *want* to—that's a pain in my ass—but if you keep pulling this kind of shit, eventually you're going to give me no choice."

My stomach dropped. I did not want to get kicked out of Eden. Also, I couldn't afford to, not after the purchases and promises I'd made. I blinked back tears, embarrassed, wanting more than anything for Michael not to see me crying, but these were not the kind of tears one could subtly wipe away. They closed off my throat, caused my nose to start running.

"Oh God, don't . . ." he said, sighing. "I just wish you guys could be more like Summer."

Liana's eyebrows shot up at that, but she pressed her lips together tightly.

"Take an hour and get yourselves together, and then be ready to work."

"We will, we promise," I choked out. "This show is the most important thing in the world to us."

"Start acting like it," he said, then stood up and ushered us out his door.

As we walked out into the sunlight and down the lot, Liana shook her head. "*Be more like Summer*," she said, fishing a tissue out of her bag and handing it to me. I blew my nose with a loud, unappealing honk, a melting-down mess as, beside me, Liana drew herself up taller with righteous fury. "Right, so let us take all the blame for the mess you created? There wouldn't have been so many paps there in the first place if she hadn't been with us. And we were trying to protect her!"

"This is so unfair."

Liana kicked at a pebble on the ground, sending it skidding down the lot. "Michael's right, though. I'm not essential. He hasn't even given me a solo, even though I would *rock* it. I know he was mad at me about the drag club, but I've apologized over and over again."

"Have you asked him about a song?"

"Of course I have! I think he won't give me one because he knows that people would see that I'm more talented than Summer, and that would throw off the whole fantasy world he's created where she's the star of the school and I don't matter."

"You do matter—"

"No, I'm the token. And because he's made sure that that's my only purpose, whenever he decides he's had enough, he can just get some other Black girl to come in and replace me, like Aunt Viv on *Fresh Prince*, and no one will care. Or maybe he doesn't need a Black girl anymore, now that Summer's all 'diverse' too."

I hugged her then, wrapping my arms around her as a golf cart drove by. She pulled back and straightened herself up. "And the shittiest part," she said, "is that Atlas has us locked in so tightly, I can't even audition for other things where I can be interesting. They own us until we've outgrown our usefulness to them."

"We should have Noah talk to him," I said. "Michael loves Noah. They have this, like, secret man code." Michael was always inviting Noah out with the guys now, telling him jokes, listening to his suggestions in rehearsal the way he never did with the rest of us.

"You think?"

"Yeah. I bet that, after the finale, when Michael's flying high on success, Noah could pull a star move and be like, 'I want Liana to have a solo in the movie.' No, not just a solo. We're getting you a *soliloquy*."

She stared at me, wary. "Would he even do it?"

"I'm sure. I can feel it out for you if you want."

"Yeah?" she asked. I nodded, certain that I was someone who did the right thing. I could be jealous, sure, but at the heart of it all, I was a really good friend. "Fine," Liana said. "I mean, yes. Yes, I'd honestly appreciate that more than anything in the world."

"Okay then. And I guess we should be really well-behaved for the foreseeable future."

I followed through on the first part of the plan. That afternoon on a rehearsal break, I mentioned it to Noah. "Dude, yes," he said. "I bet Michael doesn't even realize."

The "being well-behaved" part, however, lasted about two

days, until Trevor (with whom Liana had been casually hooking up) invited us to a private premiere party for his new movie.

"Trevor says that there are going to be actual movie stars there," Liana told me. We'd moved to rehearsing on the stage where we'd be doing the live show. Liana and I lounged in the rows of the chairs in the audience—two hundred seats, with a large open area in back for more audience to pack in. Up onstage, Summer was going through the motions of a solo song. "Apparently his costar's uncle is Denzel Washington, and he might show." Liana handed me a Twizzler from the pack she was eating, and I peeled the strings of it apart, chewing them one at a time, little tiny bites. If I took enough time to eat it, I could convince myself I'd had a full meal.

"We shouldn't."

"*Denzel. Washington.* If he met us and liked us, do you know how good it could be for our careers? We can't be on this show forever. Besides, I'm twenty-two years old, I should be allowed to leave my home and go to a party."

"We're supposed to be more like Summer, remember?"

She let out a frustrated grunt, and absentmindedly chewed on one of her nails. Up onstage, a spotlight hit Summer's hair, making it shine. She tilted her whole face up to the light, radiant. She was so clearly a girl on the cusp of something. Superstardom, maybe, or true love. Now, I know that the encroaching *something* heading her way wasn't any of those things. It was disaster.

Liana and I stared at her. "Or," Liana said, "we go, but we're careful. In and out, one drink, just to meet Denzel. And we make sure that Summer comes with us."

The thing about sex is that it's really not that special. You wait and wait for The One, and then one day you decide to just do it, and you're not a virgin anymore, and you don't feel all that different. I thought it would be Noah. For a while, I wanted it to be him. But Noah's not the only guy in the world, even though he might think he is.

We went out last night to a party, just us girls, doing this whole complicated plan to avoid the paparazzi. (Wigs, back doors, calling in a fake tip that we were going to be somewhere else across town.) Liana asked me if she should invite Noah and I said no. Denzel Washington was supposed to be there but he wasn't. Which, when I think about it now, of course Denzel Washington wasn't there. So we were kind of disappointed at first, but then we started drinking and having fun anyway. Even though Denzel wasn't there, it was in this cool private club where people knew to be discreet about things, so nobody minded that we were underage because we were on the guest list.

The three of us lost sight of each other as we got more into the party. I just wanted to dance and drink and not think about the pressure of the live show. I was dancing by myself and then there was a boy (a man? He was older, like late twenties maybe) who started dancing with me. He was cute, with curly dark hair, and he wanted me so bad, I could feel it as he pressed his hips up against me. We tried to talk but it was so loud. I don't know if he recognized me from the show. Sometimes it feels like everyone in the world knows who we are, but actually a lot of normal adults probably don't, because it's just a dumb show that's mostly supposed to be for preteens. This guy didn't say anything about "The Daydreams," just asked if I was having a good time, and then after we danced for a little while, if I wanted to go somewhere quieter so we could hear each other.

I've been trying so hard to live up to the whole annoying "be perfect Summer" thing, but it's exhausting. I wanted to not think for once, to follow the instinct in my body. To follow him out into the alley behind the club. So I did. And he didn't actually want to talk. He just pushed me up against the brick and kissed me, and I was in that perfect level of drunkenness where you know what you're doing but it doesn't feel like you're making any decisions, things just happen and you go with them. He grabbed my hand and put it inside his pants. And when he said he had a condom, I just went with that too.

It hurt a little. Maybe less than I'd expected because I was drunk. But it was exciting despite the pain. Like he and I were the only two people in the world who mattered for those few minutes when it was happening. And I didn't even know his name, knew I was never going to see him again, so in a way I felt like I was the only person who mattered in the world, until he shuddered and pulled out, and threw the condom on the ground.

"So," he said. "Do you want me to buy you a drink?"

"No, that's okay," I said, and went inside without looking back at him.

I didn't tell anyone that it happened, not even the girls. Definitely not Noah. My secret. It was so easy, the way it all happened. Maybe soon, I should make it happen again.

Twenty-One

. . . .

2018

When I roll up to the rehearsal studio with my coffee, a larger-than-normal crowd of paparazzi is waiting outside the building, squinting against the oppressive sunshine. We've only had a few each day, and now there must be fifteen or twenty of them.

What's going on? Has something old come out, a secret or scandal finally coming to light, well hidden for over a decade only to ruin lives and reputations now? My throat goes dry. They turn their cameras to me, their eyes glittering, their mouths opening, a frenzy beginning. This is it. Somehow, everyone knows about the journal. I'm frozen as they lunge forward, looking at me.

No, looking past me, at a man stepping out of a car. He's tall and tan, with arms so chiseled he could probably break a brick with his bare hands. That, or hit a baseball so that it soars over the fence with startling regularity. Javier Torres, Liana's husband, flashes a gleaming smile at the crowd, and my heart rate slows back down to something approaching normal. Thank God.

The energy from the paparazzi is different with Javier. They're generally happy to see us because we can help them make money, sure, but they aren't fans of what we do. With Javi, though, they want his picture *and* his autograph. "Over here!" they shout, in hopes that he'll give them a smile but maybe also a fist bump, a few lines of conversation.

He locks eyes with me and ambles over. "Kat, right?" Without warning, he hugs me and the cameras flash. He projects a sense of amiable stardom. Forget *aw shucks, who, me?* posturing. He knows how special he is.

We walk into the building together, passing the security guard, who gives me a sleepy nod, then visibly freaks out over Javier.

When Javier walks into the rehearsal room, Liana does a double take at the sight of him, blinking in disbelief for a second before letting out a scream. "What are you doing here?"

"Wanted to come surprise my beautiful wife," he says, and she flings her arms around him. But I notice that the hug looks as strange as it did the first time she hugged me. He's stiff too, both of them performing for the rest of us, or maybe for each other.

"Holy shit," Noah yells. He runs over, like a fanboy, and it's kind of cute to see him having the reaction so many people do when they encounter him. Turns out we're all still capable of getting starstruck.

"Hey, man," Javi says.

Summer hangs back, smiling blandly, unimpressed.

"I know you probably want to hang out with your wife," Noah says to Javier. "But also, would you like to hang out with me?"

"Easy there, Noah," Liana says. "You trying to steal my man?"

"I am, sorry," Noah says, grinning.

"Okay, okay," Michael says, a gigantic cup of Diet Coke in his hand. He's not a sports guy, so he's not losing his mind like so many others right now. "It's nice to have you here, Javier, but let's do the fucking scene, shall we?" Javier sits down in a chair an assistant has conjured up for him.

Today, for the first time, we're rehearsing the part where Summer "has too much sugar" and falls off the stage, bonking her head. This pratfall is a convenient excuse for the fantasy sequence, and also a strange direction for her character. Back in the day, *I* was the one whose character needed to be embarrassed or cut down to size. Summer could have her Everygirl awkward moments and vulnerabilities, but through it all, her character was supposed to remain aspirational. Now, Michael is basically asking her to play drunk (or high), and it doesn't fit, not in this setting. We've all seen her that way, sure, but in grainy tabloid videos or strange Instagram posts that later get deleted. Summer the Real-Life Mess doesn't square with Summer the *Daydreams* character, but Michael sure is trying. This hasn't been an issue when we've been learning the songs and the dances, most of which take place in the fantasy sequence anyway, and where Summer has chosen to play her character as she once was. And when she wakes up from her passed-out state, she "reforms" herself, so that hasn't been too much of an issue either.

But in the pre–head bonk scenes, Summer starts downing the Reunion Punch for no good reason, only to get a "sugar high" and spiral out of control. She climbs onto the stage where the band hired by the reunion committee is supposed to perform (they've been caught in a snowstorm, and haven't yet shown up), goes on some rant about the good old days, and then trips over an electrical cord.

The writing is lazy, but the scene could be a good comedic showcase in the right hands. But Summer's hands are most decidedly not right. Still, she puts down her script and starts to go through the motions, trying to be game.

"I'd slow down on the punch if I were you," I say in character, raising an eyebrow.

"You only live once!" she replies, pretending to guzzle from an empty glass we're using as a prop. She wipes her mouth. "Hey, how much sugar do you think there is in this?"

Liana squints at her own glass. "My husband's a scientist, you know. I bet he could tell you the exact glucose content or whatever!" Javier laughs, and Liana can't stop herself from looking over at him, pulled out of the moment.

"I don't think you need to be a scientist to know that it's a lot," Noah says.

Summer tosses her glass away and begins to clamber onto the "stage" (which is currently marked out by tape on the floor of our rehearsal room). "Remember when we used to perform on this?" she asks. "The glory days—"

"Stop," Michael says, and we all drop out of character. "This feels awkward. *You* feel awkward."

"Sorry," she says, rubbing her eyes. "I know. I can take it back."

We reset and try again, then another time. Summer's unwilling to admit defeat, but she's holding back, a stilted quality to her delivery. "Just . . ." Michael finally says. "Forget about being family friendly for a second. Throw caution to the wind, okay?"

This time, Summer goes for it. Watching her clamber onto the "stage," her face flushed, her eyes half-closed, I could swear that she's actually on something. "'Member when we used to—" she slurs, then hiccups. "Sorry, remember when we used to perform on this?" Around the room, everyone watching shifts, a few of the assistants laughing like they're supposed to, but it's uncomfortable, more like a snicker. "It was *sooooo* fun."

Noah has the next line, so I look at him, expecting the typical *uh-oh!* look that he's been putting on throughout the scene. Instead, his face is drawn. Sad. Next to him, Liana bites her lip. She looks over at Javier again, but now he's staring down at his phone, not paying attention.

"Noah!" Michael prompts.

"Sorry," Noah says, then snaps into character. "Yeah, almost as fun as sitting down, right?"

Summer pretends like she's going to climb down, then pratfalls, collapsing in a heap on the floor. It looks too realistic. I feel like I'm seeing her as she was in all the years we didn't speak, her as she has the potential to be again if this reunion doesn't work out the way she hopes. Where does Summer go, if this is a failure? What the hell does she do with the rest of her life?

"That was better," Michael says, and she lifts her head off the ground, brushing hair out of her face, to look at him.

"Really?" she asks, but her voice is thick, like she's on the verge of tears.

"Yeah," he says. The rest of us are silent. Amber from *Girl Powers* flashes into my mind. How the tabloids covered her first overdose with mockery. How they had to take the mockery out when they covered her second overdose, because that one killed her.

I never spoke up in rehearsals back in the day. Michael knew best, and I was just trying to stay in his good graces. But right now I feel like I do when I'm working with a client who has fixated on something that isn't going to happen. My job, which I've spent years doing, which I'm pretty damn good at, is to cut through the bullshit and get it done.

So the words just come out of my mouth. "This clearly isn't working." Everyone stops and looks at me, surprised. Michael frowns. "Summer never got out of control in the series. It doesn't fit."

"Kat, I don't have time to explain screenwriting to you right now," Michael says. "But this will work if you all commit to it."

"I'm just saying, what if it's more about her being nervous?" One of Summer's quirks in the early episodes was that she could get adorably shy, widening her eyes in fear when she got hit with a bout of stage fright.

"I don't know how that would work," Michael says.

"I could be drinking the punch too fast because I'm nervous about being around Noah again," Summer says.

"Yeah!" I say. "That's more the character, not this party girl who's all 'You only live once!' but an Everygirl who needs something to do with her hands."

"But then how do I bonk my head?" Summer asks, genuinely curious.

I hesitate. "Maybe you need to pee from all the punch," Liana says, her voice strangely husky. She clears her throat. "But it's so crowded that you can only get to the bathroom by cutting across the stage, where you get tangled in a cord."

The four of us actors contemplate it—not quite right, but better than what's there now.

"No," Michael says. "I don't like it."

"I understand why you wrote it the way you did," Summer says to him. "But I came back to play the character. I can do it, I've been working hard—"

"Who is the writer here?" Michael asks. "The last time I checked, it was me. Now, let's do it again, and, Summer, try it somewhere in between the two extremes you've been doing."

Summer, Liana, and I deflate, then reset.

Noah interrupts. "Michael, I actually think that they have a point."

Michael lets out an involuntary grunt of frustration. Because he *has* to listen to Noah. For all of Michael's big talk about how he's the writer, the fans aren't tuning in for him. He's got to keep his star happy.

"Fine," he says. "I'll take another look at it and *consider* a change." He stands abruptly. "We're almost at time anyway, so everyone can leave now, and we'll come back to this."

* * * * * * *

We all walk out of rehearsal together, the four of us plus Javier, who's saying something to Liana in a low voice about how they should go right back to the hotel (to get down and dirty as fast as they can, I assume). I check my phone: a text from Miheer asking how rehearsal is going. I start to respond, but get distracted because in front of me, Summer touches Noah's hand lightly. "Thank you, for what you did back there. I owe you. Dinner, maybe?"

He turns to look at her as we open the door to the parking lot, and the paparazzi roar hits us. Right, I forgot that Javier turned us into the hottest attraction in town. We all smile and wave.

"Liana and Javi, over here!"

"Liana and Javi, turn this way!"

Back in the day, hardly anyone ever shouted Liana's name. She's become far more famous with him than she ever was without. The two of them hold hands. Javier grins, but his eyes dart back and forth. Is he . . . nervous?

"Liana," a woman with a microphone shouts, pushing her way right up to the front of the fray. Liana leans over to her, ready to answer whatever question she has about how nice it is to reunite with her husband. "Do you have a comment about the fact that Javier's mistress is pregnant?"

Twenty-Two

. . . .

2018

As Liana blinks at the reporter, her face frozen in a mask of shock, Summer, Noah, and I turn to one another. I'm surprised (although am I *that* surprised? Clearly something was off), but there's no time to sit around wondering what the hell.

Javier steps forward, toward the press. "My wife and I ask that you give us some privacy at this time," he says, a canned response that comes out so smoothly, I'm sure he knew this was coming—if not right now, at least soon. Liana's expression is melting into something like fury, and the reporters are pressing forward, ready to devour her. Oh God, this betrayal must be a gut punch. But also, it's happening in the worst possible way for someone who prides herself on preparing. Liana practices and works hard and presents a certain image of herself. Right now, though, the world is watching the ground disappear from beneath her feet. These photos will be everywhere, and she's still in her rehearsal clothes, her forehead shiny, and she doesn't know what to say, and the cameras are going to revel in it.

"We've got to get her out of here," I say to Summer and Noah. "Right?"

"Yes," Summer says.

"You guys take her," Noah says into my ear. "I'll create a distraction." He strides forward into the center of the fray, toward Javier, stepping in front of Liana while Summer and I come up behind her. "Javier! What the hell, man?"

The cameras turn to Noah, and Summer grabs Liana's hand. "Come with us?" she asks, and Liana gives a dazed, grateful nod.

"I thought you were a good guy!" Noah continues, getting in Javier's face, although not actually touching him. "I respected you." The prospect of a brawl temporarily draws the focus of the crowd, allowing us to slip away. Thank you, Noah, for showboating. As we run toward my rental car, the dam breaks and a rush of hope floods me: that I have misjudged him, that he has changed. No time to think too much about that, though. There's a man with a camera leaning on my hood.

"My car instead," Summer says, and we switch directions, throw the doors of her car open, and speed off.

All is silent for a few minutes as we drive. In the back seat, Liana appears to be in shock. "Hey," I say gently. "You want to go back to the hotel?"

She gives a jerky shake of her head. "Javier knows which one it is. And if he goes, the paparazzi will follow."

"Okay, we'll figure something else out," I say, and Summer nods, putting on her blinker and going right instead of the usual left.

Liana begins to make a helpless sound, right on the border between laughter and tears. "You all really went for it," she says. "The two of you, practically throwing me over your shoulders to carry me away. Noah, screaming his head off at Javi."

"Well, yeah, we're here for you," I say, and she begins to cry in earnest. I awkwardly reach back and pat her knee as she curls up against the side of the car, mascara streaking down her cheeks.

Summer and I exchange glances. "Maybe we could find a place with a private room?" I ask. "Or, I don't know, a big park?"

But Summer already seems to have a destination in mind. She turns onto the freeway, clutching the steering wheel so hard that the knob of bone on her small wrist strains against her skin.

"Where are we going?" I ask her.

She swallows, staring straight ahead. "Home."

. . . .

A little over an hour later, Summer turns off the freeway, drives us through a small downtown area (boarded-up shops every few storefronts), and pulls into the driveway of an unassuming one-story house.

Her mouth set in a grim line, she opens the gate in the chain-link fence and walks across the dusty front yard, a gnarled lemon tree standing like a lonely sentry. "There should be . . ." she mutters, turning over a brightly painted ceramic lizard on the front step to reveal a key underneath.

"Well," she says as she unlocks the door to the place where she grew up, "come in."

The two things that strike me when I see the living room are (1) the hideous flowered couch, long and low, and (2) the extreme amount of family photos on the wall. They crowd around one another so that you can barely see the wallpaper beneath: Summer's parents at their wedding, holding each other tight. Summer's school photos through around when I first met her. Pictures of her in community theater productions, her hair long and dark. Her dad carrying her in a piggyback ride. Her mom holding her as a baby. But there's nothing more recent, as if everything that happened after *The Daydreams* started airing just disappeared into a void.

Summer is taking it all in, just like I am. She's been staying at the hotel too—it's much closer—and we've been working so hard that she probably hasn't had a chance to get out here for a visit yet.

Liana walks straight past us and face-plants onto the couch with a thud. "Oh God," she says, her voice muffled by the fabric. "That was not as comfortable as I thought it would be."

"Sorry," Summer says.

"Alcohol. Please."

"My mom's not a big drinker, but I'll check." Summer turns toward the kitchen, and I follow her.

"Where is your mom?" I ask as she walks straight to the pantry, rummaging through the canned goods and the sacks of flour until she finds a bottle of wine.

"Visiting her sister." Her voice is terse. Ever since we walked in the door here, her shoulders have been steadily creeping up toward her neck. She pours the bottle into three large cups for us, and I take a tentative sip. Oof, that is straight sugar.

Liana doesn't mind, though. She guzzles it as Summer and I sit on either side of her on the couch.

"Do you want to talk about it?" I ask, putting my hand on her knee. "You must be in shock."

Liana wipes her mouth. "I knew."

"What?"

She stands up and begins pacing the room as if she can outwalk her grief. "He promised me it wouldn't come out until after the reunion. That must be why he came today. She told him she was going to the press, and he wanted to be together for it. But I knew." Summer sinks against the back of the couch, watching Liana's frenetic movement.

"Since when?" I ask.

"Since . . . I don't know, he told me a couple weeks before

Noah did that interview?" She puts on an imitation of Javier's voice (which is actually quite good, she is so talented even in her lowest moments). "*I messed up, babe. I got so lonely for you out on the road.*" She stops in front of us, pressing her fingers into her temples. "I'm sure it's not the first time he slept with another woman, it's just the first time he knocked one up. Or maybe it's just the first time he knocked one up and wanted to keep it, since *I* can't give him a child." She looks over at Summer, her voice bitter and raw. "Right, on top of everything else, it seems I might be barren."

Summer picks at her split ends. "Having babies is overrated. They shit and cry and ruin your life. Or so I've heard."

Liana stares at her for a moment. We both do—this is the Summer who came to get me in DC, not the strangely naive version of herself she's been presenting in rehearsals. Then Liana bursts into more sobs, sinking down on the ground.

"Okay," I say, moving next to her and tentatively patting her back. "Do you need a good divorce lawyer? I can get you excellent recommendations." She sniffs but doesn't say anything, and I gape at her. "No. You're not staying with him, are you?"

"He thinks we should," she says. "We can *co-parent* with this woman. Because the two of us, we're a power couple. And while people will still be interested in him if we split up, no one will care about me anymore. He's doing me a"—she hiccups—"favor."

"People will still care about you too!" I say.

"I'll get one month of *you go, girl* coverage, and then everyone will forget about me." She shakes her head. "You don't understand what it's like. He isn't just my husband. He's my livelihood. I thought coming back here . . . maybe I could remind everyone that I exist separately from him, and that would help me figure out what to do." Ah, this explains all the overly enthusiastic Instagram posts, her despair that Michael made her character revolve around her husband. "But it's clearly not working. I'm going to quit the reunion."

"What? No!" I say, handing her a tissue. She honks her nose into it, crumples it onto the floor, and holds out her hands for another one.

"What's the point? I sing backup for you guys and have my whole thing be that I keep talking about my husband while everyone in the audience knows about my humiliation? No thank you, I'll pass!"

"We'll ask Michael to change the husband story line for you," I say.

"Michael won't do a single thing for me," she says. She is drained, exhausted, her face drawn. "Besides, I'm too sad."

Summer has stayed back this whole time, barely speaking, just watching. But now in one swift motion she comes off the couch and kneels in front of Liana, cupping Liana's face in her hands. "Stop that," she says. "You're not quitting because of this man. And you're not staying with him either."

"I don't know who I am if I'm not his wife," Liana says. Her voice is a quiet, bitter thing. "Besides just a laughingstock."

"Well, welcome to the laughingstock club."

"You're not . . ."

"Of course I am." Summer goes on. "I've had my heartbreak and bad decisions and embarrassing moments splashed across every magazine cover, and it's awful. Every person you talk to is waiting for you to break down in tears, wondering how you can show your face in public. Most of them think that you deserve every humiliation. *They* would never get themselves into such trouble. The nice ones tell themselves that you're so brave. But you're not brave. You don't want to show your face. You wish you could just crawl inside your bed. Not *into* bed, *inside*. You want to rip a hole in the mattress and live in it. But you pick yourself up and get back out there, because you don't have another option."

"I know who you are if you're not his wife," I say. "You're Liana Jackson, and you've always been the most talented one of all of us." I look to Summer. "No offense."

"None taken," she says to me, then turns back to Liana. "Don't let him take *this* from you, along with everything else."

Liana stares at Summer for a moment in silence. Then she leans forward and pulls Summer into her arms, a real hug, without any vanity or performance to it. Summer puts her arms around Liana too, and they clutch each other tight, until Liana turns her face to me. "Well, you get in here." So I do, the three of us smushing into one another, wet with Liana's tears and snot, a ball of women on the floor. I'm not sure who says it first. Maybe we all say it at the same time, and soon we're murmuring it over and over again: oh, how we've missed one another.

Twenty-Three

. . . .

2005

The final days leading up to the live show were fraught ones. Liana had gotten in trouble with Michael again after the Denzel Washington party, which she'd left with Trevor. He was driving them both back to his place when they got pulled over. Paparazzi showed up in time to snap photos of him blowing into a Breathalyzer, Liana by his side.

"I literally did nothing wrong!" she said to me and Summer in our dressing room as we took off our costumes after our last run-through. The rest of the day was a mix of things—working through notes, final wardrobe consultations with Harriet. And Liana had to go meet with Michael in his office for another talking-to. "Trevor said he was good to drive and I trusted him. *I* wasn't behind the wheel."

"Don't get defensive," Summer said in our dressing room. "Go in and apologize. Tell him Trevor lied to you. Michael's not going to do anything to you, not with the live show tomorrow."

Liana stared daggers at her. "Easy for you to say." She turned on her heel and walked out.

When I saw her later, she didn't want to talk about how it had gone. She just wanted to go home and go to bed. We all went home early that night and tried to sleep, shaky with nerves and anticipation.

The day of the live show dawned clear and warm. I woke up an hour before my alarm and lay in bed, my heart pounding. Sure, millions of people had watched me perform before, but today was different. There was no room for error, no calling "cut" and trying it again. I didn't want to screw things up. What if I was the one whose bad performance made Mr. Atlas decide that we weren't deserving of a theatrical release? Or, even worse, the one who got cut from the movie entirely, and had to watch its blockbuster success from afar?

I'd forgone dairy that whole week because it could mess with your vocal cords, and ate a banana for breakfast instead of my usual milk and cereal. I stretched for an hour, warming up my entire body. *You worry,* I told myself, *but it's going to go great.* Still, worst-case scenarios crashed through my head—me twisting an ankle during our choreography, me blanking on my lines. The actual worst-case scenario, the one that ended up happening, didn't even cross my mind.

Summer, Liana, and I sat quietly in a row during our hair and makeup, transforming into the shiniest versions of ourselves. The woman doing our hair flat ironed mine until it practically sizzled, then stuck a wig on Liana's head because she didn't know what to do with her. She barely touched Summer's hair, just brushed and spritzed it while murmuring compliments.

We talked in fragmented bits of conversation, unable to concentrate, our minds already out on that stage. About the celebration that Atlas had planned for us afterward, about who we knew in the audience. My parents had flown all the way across the country to be here after I bought their plane tickets (though I pointedly hadn't bought one for my dad's fiancée). Liana's had traveled from

Georgia along with her siblings and a bunch of her aunts and uncles.

"My mom's out there in the executive box," Summer said. "And Lucas."

"You gonna keep him away from Noah at the party?" Liana asked.

"That's the hope. I'll need you both to run interference." Summer and Noah had apparently made up after his fight with Lucas, though she had been more restrained about their kisses in rehearsal since, as if trying to throw us all off the scent. I wanted to ask her what was going on between them, but I didn't know if she'd tell me the truth. And besides, I wanted her to tell me without my having to ask. That was the sort of thing you were supposed to tell your friend. But now, maybe, I was just someone who was summoned to "run interference" without being trusted with the details of the story.

A production assistant poked her head in. "You all ready? It's time."

We congregated in a large greenroom backstage—the cast, Michael, wardrobe and makeup, assistants. A buzzing, jittery energy filled the room. What happened over the next hour had the potential to shoot us to the stars, or ruin us. Chorus members trembled. Assistants fumbled their clipboards. In the distance, a steady roar: the sound of our fans, ready to watch us, celebrate us, devour us.

"I know you might be nervous," Michael called out. "But I hope you're excited too. This is a chance to show everyone what you can do. Have one another's backs out there, and let's make this so undeniably good that Atlas has no choice but to fast-track us to the big screen."

A TV in the corner was tuned to *Entertainment Tonight* on mute.

They were doing some "preshow" coverage for us, as if we were the Oscars or the Super Bowl. Michael's gamble had paid off—doing this finale live meant we had gotten far more attention than if we'd done it the normal way.

Preteen girls standing inside the concert hall, wearing T-shirts with our faces on them, squealed and waved at the camera, braces twinkling on their teeth. But the preteen girls weren't the only ones there. The camera captured older teenagers unabashed in their fandom, lots of parents (some of whom were clearly bored, but plenty who looked as excited as their kids), and people in their twenties and thirties who didn't seem to have kids with them at all. We had grown so big so fast. Whatever else you might say about Michael, you couldn't deny his instincts. He'd known how to create a juggernaut.

Summer found Noah and took his hand. "You ready?" she asked. I thought about what Harriet had said about their chemistry. How the audience wanted it to be as strong as it could be without spilling over into something dangerous. Summer twined her fingers in Noah's, rubbing her thumb against his like they were two pieces of kindling, as if Summer were stoking a flame between them, one that was just the right size. Her purity ring glittered in the overhead light.

"I'm ready," Noah said, and reached up briefly to tuck her hair behind her ear. "We're going to be great." Somehow, the two of them were the only calm people in the room.

"Ten more minutes," our assistant director called out, voice shaky.

"It's looking good," Michael said to nobody in particular, trying to master his own unease. "I hear there's been a line of people almost a mile long, standing there in the sun all afternoon, just in the hopes that they can get in off the wait list."

An assistant ran into the room and whispered something in Michael's ear. Michael stared at him, uncomprehending for a moment. Then he gave a jerk of his head, and the assistant turned the volume on the TV up.

Everyone in the room turned at the unexpected noise. The show had returned from commercial to the two anchors in the TV studio, who both had solemn looks on their faces.

"Welcome back, everyone," the male anchor said. "We apologize for interrupting the preshow coverage, but we feel we have a duty to report on a new story about a scandal that might just rock *The Daydreams* just moments from the start of their live finale."

The female anchor nodded. "We can now confirm that the entertainment blog Popslop has gotten a hold of Summer Wright's private journal."

Twenty-Four

· · · · · · · ·

2018

Liana puts away the majority of the bottle of wine over the next couple of hours as we fill one another in on the last thirteen years of our lives. She keeps trying to pour me and Summer more, and I help out a bit despite the fact that it makes my teeth hurt. Summer declines the offer.

"Shit, I'm sorry," Liana says, her filter gone, her bluntness making its welcome return. "Is it a rehab thing?"

Summer shakes her head. "I never had a drinking problem. Just a coke problem. And occasionally an ecstasy problem. But I want to cut down on how much I'm drinking while I'm here. Trying to be professional. Don't worry about it."

"I've been worried a lot," Liana says, her eyes filling again. "Over the years."

"You could have reached out," Summer said.

"I know. I was so . . . upset about the movie deal, and once I got over that, it felt too late. You don't know how much I've kicked myself, how much I wish I could go back and do it all differently." She wipes her eyes and overenunciates to stop herself from slurring her words, making the sentiment extra emphatic. "I would've reached out right away." She shakes her head, then picks up the bottle, drinks the dregs, and wobbles to her feet. "I must get my beauty rest," she announces. "It's more important now than ever."

"We can sleep here?" I ask Summer, and she nods. So we each take one of Liana's arms and walk her to the bed in Summer's mom's room. Summer tucks her in gently, smoothing her hair. I shut off the light, and we tiptoe back out into the hallway.

"Should we crash too?" Summer asks, then catches me staring at her. "What?"

"Why aren't you being yourself in rehearsals?"

"I don't know what you mean." I raise my devastating eyebrow at her, and after a moment, she throws her hands into the air. "Fine. Maybe I'm trying to do a good job and be the person everyone liked before the journal ruined it all. Is that so bad?" I shake my head, and Summer loops her arm in mine, a bit of the old, easy physical intimacy coming back. She doesn't seem to notice that the mention of the journal has turned me wooden. She just rests her head on my shoulder. "Let's go to bed."

She leads me to the only other bedroom in the house. Hers. We open the door and step back in time.

It's straight out of the early 2000s. Pink walls, one with a small cross hanging on it. There's even a green fuzzy beanbag chair. A corkboard with photos stuck in it—my own young face smiles up at me. In the corner sits a twin bed with a frilly comforter. Summer bends down and pulls out a trundle.

I walk around, peering at Summer's bookshelf. There's a CD rack full of earnest pop sitting on it, and the wood is covered with stickers you'd get in teen magazines sometimes back then, stickers with pictures of celebrities on them. I spy Amber and Trevor from *Girl Powers*, plus the members of various boy bands you were contractually obligated to love as a thirteen-year-old girl.

"Your mom never wanted to move?" The whole house is so

small, worn, not the kind of place you'd expect the mother of a starlet to live.

"She wouldn't take money from me. And then rehab was expensive, so there was no money to give her anyway." Summer shrugs. "Besides, leaving here would be like losing my dad all over again. Their relationship was screwed up, but they loved each other so much."

"It's like a museum. She could give tours," I joke, but Summer doesn't laugh.

"'Step right up and see the bedroom of my greatest shame,'" she says in a low voice, sweeping her arm out. Everything is covered with a thin layer of dust. The cloying scents of expired Bath & Body Works products fill the room. The air feels thicker in here, or maybe it's hard to breathe for a different reason, because of the guilt and anxiety clogging up my throat.

Summer is trembling, as if she's freezing. Without looking at me, she says, "She's visiting her sister on purpose. I told her I was coming out for the reunion, and she conveniently scheduled a monthlong trip to Texas."

"I'm . . . I'm so sorry," I say, and she walks deeper into the room, staring up at the walls.

"She loves me. I know she does. She just can't quite bear to look at me. It's too hard to see the train wreck I became. She picks me up from rehab. I can always crash here if I really need to. But I don't think she's looked me in the eye since that journal came out."

When I'd come home after that disastrous finale, my mother had taken me back in with open arms. As she hugged me and I cried into her chest, I could feel the "I told you sos" pounding inside her. But she swallowed them down. She never reproached me or asked about the money I'd promised her for school. She told me to stay as long as I wanted.

"I just wish I could understand it," Summer says. "Why somebody wanted to sabotage me that badly. I think that's part of the reason I really can't let go. You can try and work so hard, and then someone comes along and . . ." She trails off.

From the back, if I squint, she still looks like the teenager who lived in this bedroom. But when she turns around, she is the grown woman I ruined. She pulls down the sleeves of her oversized sweatshirt and rubs her arms, trying to warm herself up. Goose bumps rise on her skinny legs, barely covered by her frayed jean shorts.

"I have to tell you something," I say.

She meets my eyes, one last moment of naivete. One last moment when she cares for me, maybe even loves me. But then she sees the expression on my face, and there's no going back now.

"Oh," she breathes, understanding settling over her. "You're the one who gave the journal to the press."

Twenty-Five

. . . .

2005

"Now, normally we wouldn't report on the contents of someone's private journal," the male *Entertainment Tonight* anchor said. "But given the level of hypocrisy, we do feel we have a duty to share it." Sure. More like they wanted to be the first TV show to break the story. Maybe they'd even coordinated with Popslop—traffic to the blog in exchange for an exclusive TV scoop.

The female co-anchor, chunky blond highlights gleaming under the studio lights, practically bounced with excitement, despite her solemn face. "Summer has quite an angelic reputation, but it turns out that the inside isn't so pure. This journal is full of trash talk about what she calls this 'stupid' show, and none of her costars are spared. A warning to any parents watching that some of the following language will get a bit naughty. According to Summer, Kat Whitley is 'annoying' and Liana Jackson is a 'slut.'"

People turned toward us to see our reactions. Liana swallowed hard. "What the hell, Summer?"

"I . . ." Summer said, stunned, grabbing on to a chair, her knuckles going white.

The male anchor went on. "But she saves her harshest words

for Noah Gideon. We'd been hoping that they'd couple up, and while Summer crushed on him at one point—cover your ears, kids, she talks about touching herself while thinking of him—she now seems to hate him, devoting an entire entry to listing all his faults."

"That's not true," Noah said. "This is bullshit. They're making it up!" He turned to Summer, desperate. "Right?"

"Right, I don't know what they're—"

"Apparently he's selfish, pathetic, and, in her own words, 'he should realize that not every single thing is about him. I mean, who even says [expletive] like "You and me, we're going to take over the world"'?"

"Honestly," the female anchor said, "I'm surprised she has this in her."

"How did they know I said that?" Noah asked, his voice low and quavering. "Did you tell people?"

"I didn't," Summer said. "I didn't tell anyone."

"But the biggest bombshell in here . . . despite all her claiming otherwise, she's not a virgin. Although publicly she talks about how 'special' sex should be, according to Popslop's scoop, and I quote, 'Just last week, she was doing it in an alley with some guy whose name she didn't bother to learn.'"

"I've got to say," the male anchor began, "you might be surprised, Erin, but I'm not. She talked a big game about being a role model, but you could tell there was something off—"

Michael let out a strangled noise, abruptly turned off the TV, and rounded on Summer, the room gone silent. "How the hell could you let this happen?"

Everyone was staring at Summer. No one looked at me as time slowed down and my heart clattered inside my chest. Voices in my head screamed at me to say something and also to run as far away as I could from this chain of events that I had set in motion.

I didn't leak Summer's journal. I wrote it.

. . . .

Summer used that journal one time and then threw it into a drawer to gather dust. Liana had told me as much on our hike. Not long after that, Summer and I were supposed to meet up at her trailer before going to get lunch. Right as I arrived, my flip phone dinged with a text from her. **Be there in 15!! Sorryyyyyy!**

I tried the trailer door—unlocked, as usual—and went inside. As I picked up a magazine from her table, my eyes landed on her dresser drawers. Heart thumping, I inched over and began to rifle through Summer's discarded things. I just wanted to hold the journal in my own hands, feel that beautiful cover, imagine for a moment that Mr. Atlas had deemed *me* worthy of a present like that.

The first drawer I opened was full of bobby pins, butterfly clips, and a sheaf of fan letters, sweet ones decorated with stars and hearts by little girls who loved her. The second drawer contained more fan letters. These ones were disturbing, from grown men with scratchy handwriting, some who stated that they would pay her for her virginity, others who promised to wait for her. Why had she kept them instead of immediately throwing them into the ocean? And yet a tiny voice in my head wondered why no leches had written to me.

I pushed the last of the letters aside, and there it was, that gorgeous green notebook. I ran my fingers over the smooth cover, tracing Summer's embossed name. I flipped it open, my throat tightening. *To our brightest star.* Only one entry, dated from over a month ago, the rest of the pages blank and full of possibility. God, even our handwriting was similar, just another thing that made me want to weep at the fact that I'd gotten so close to being her. I didn't plan on reading the entry, but then I saw my name. She'd called me annoying.

By the time Summer opened the door to her trailer, all smiles and apologies, the book was buried deep in my bag.

I started to use it as my own journal. Not too often. After all, I couldn't just fish it out whenever I felt like jotting down some thoughts. I only wrote in it in the privacy of my trailer or my apartment, bringing it out with the utmost secrecy. I didn't want anybody seeing me with it and mentioning it to Summer, though she probably wouldn't have cared much. She might have even gifted me the journal if I'd asked. She could be generous in many ways, giving freely of the things she didn't particularly want for herself, only hoarding what really mattered to her—attention and love, like she did with Noah, like she had at the club in New York City, where she couldn't even let me have one night when I took her place in the spotlight.

I didn't want her to give me something. I wanted to take something from her.

I would put it back if Summer ever mentioned that it was missing, rip out the pages I'd used, and slide it right back into her drawer. But she never noticed it was gone.

I didn't quite realize, at the time, how easy it would be for someone to read my entries and assume they'd been written by Summer. But the looping, graceful handwriting was close enough. And I didn't really mention Summer in my entries because of guilt, or because it didn't feel right to trash-talk her in her own journal. Or maybe it was because getting too deep into what it was like To Be Kat would have reminded me that the name on the cover wasn't mine, that I had taken something no one had wanted to give me. That I was not the brightest star in the journal's inscription after all. Anyway, I wrote about my feelings, my love for Noah and my disillusionment with him too, and somehow the specifics of who I was didn't come through. But the writing calmed me down, giving me a secret that wasn't hurting anyone.

Or wasn't supposed to, anyway. How the hell had it gotten to the press?

I thought back to the last time I'd written in there, the day after I'd lost my virginity at a bar because I needed to feel wanted and wild. I was hungover, spots of blood in my underwear all morning, sore and tender when I moved. And for the first time, I had broken my rule. I had to write in there immediately, to process the feelings and reassure myself that what I'd done was right. I'd snuck the journal into my messenger bag and written in our dressing room during my break, while Summer and Liana were busy rehearsing a part I wasn't in, furtive and hunched in my chair, so lost in my own thoughts that I hadn't heard the production assistant calling me to the stage. She came to the door looking for me, and I startled, shoving the journal back into my bag, then throwing the bag on a pile of our belongings in the corner. I'd been so distracted by preparations for the live show that I didn't think to check my bag for the journal when I got home.

Shit. I wasn't sure, in retrospect, if I'd even buckled my bag closed. The journal could have easily fallen out, lying there for whoever happened to pass through. The dressing room was just for me, Summer, and Liana. Supporting actors and chorus members had their own, not-as-fancy areas, and they didn't dare intrude. The men on set stayed away too. We were working for Atlas, and nobody wanted to get a reputation as a creep, someone who casually strolled into the dressing room of the teen stars, hoping to catch us while we were changing. (For all that Atlas put us through, at least the company did protect us in this way—other girls on other sets were not so lucky.) But still, plenty of people traveled into the room, from hair and makeup artists to wardrobe to the occasional production assistant sent to fetch whatever we'd accidentally left behind. Perhaps one of them had seen the soft green of the cover, Summer's name emblazoned on it, and decided to make some quick money. Someone working long hours for little pay, for whom a movie deal would not be life changing, but more of the same. For someone like that, the journal could be a gold mine, an opportunity to finally be able to rest, to escape dictatorial directors shouting orders at them, and fourteen-hour days, driving home at two in the morning only to turn around and come back into set at dawn. All it required to escape that life was ruining a teenage girl.

* * * * * * * *

I cursed my own stupidity, my carelessness. I opened my mouth to confess. And then Michael spoke again. "Mr. Atlas is going to nix the movie."

Oh God, I'd been so distracted by the various hurt feelings, by my shame, desperately trying to recall what exactly I'd written in there (when I was losing my virginity, it felt like I was using that man, but hearing the anchors talk about it, it felt like that man had been using me), that I hadn't even thought through all the consequences.

"Michael—" Summer began.

He turned to her, wild-eyed, and practically spat, "I should've known better than to stake my career on a mediocre teenage girl!"

She stepped back as if he'd slapped her. "I . . . I didn't write those things. I don't know how this happened, but it's not— I barely used that journal!" Summer turned to me and Liana to back her up. Liana turned her face away. Summer's eyes locked on mine.

If I spoke up right now, all of Michael's ire would turn to me. And I was expendable. He'd told me so. This was bad for Summer, yes, but we couldn't do the movie without her, if the movie was going to happen. Me, on the other hand . . . Michael would drop me from it in a heartbeat. I would truly be the villain, not just onscreen but in real life too, the girl who tried to screw with the star, and got what she deserved. I would watch my best friends ride off to bigger things without me while I, swamped with credit card debt and regret, told my parents that I couldn't give them what I'd promised. I needed to figure out how to defuse this situation, how to exonerate Summer without implicating myself. There had to be a way, but in the confusion of the moment, I couldn't *think*, couldn't stop the shock from scrambling my mind. A little voice, trained by months of listening to bitchy confessions, fought its way through the noise, quiet but strong, like Mr. Atlas whenever he spoke. *Everybody here is ultimately looking out for themselves*, it whispered. *Don't you be the one fool who sacrifices it all for someone else.*

So I just shook my head helplessly at Summer, as if I had no idea what was going on.

"I hate to interrupt, but we have to go out and start the show. Like, now," the assistant director said.

"Fuck!" Michael said, clearly in no mood to give a preshow pep talk. All of the actors shuffled nervously, unsure what to do.

So Harriet, of all people, stepped in, clapping her hands sternly, drawing everyone's focus to her. "Listen up. This is bad. But it might not be as bad as we think. Go out there and do the best show that you possibly can. Make it so good that Atlas can't cancel you. Summer, you do the best of anyone, okay? We'll sort this all out afterward."

God bless Harriet, I thought for the first time. This was the solution. We'd all do the best performances we'd ever done in our lives. After the show, once I'd gotten my story straight, I would talk to Michael. No, to Mr. Atlas! I'd tell him that I knew Summer hadn't written those things, that I'd seen her journal with only the first entry in it, and then it had disappeared somehow. (I'd leave out the part about writing the entries myself.) He terrified me, but I would face him for her. Liana and I could publicly vouch for Summer, say that we went to that party with her and she never went off into the alley with someone, that this was clearly a plot from some crazed fan or jealous PA to destroy an innocent girl. We'd get through this.

"Summer, it's going to be okay," I said, running to her side. But she looked through me, not even listening, pushing away my touch and heading for Noah, who was standing with a dazed expression, his chest heaving in and out. The crowd swelled around them, cutting them off from my sight, and I couldn't hear what either of them said.

"*Now,*" the assistant director called. Noah broke through the mass of people, hurtling out the door to his entrance spot, which was on the other side of the stage from the rest of us. Somehow, Summer, Liana, and I followed the crowd into the hallway that led toward our entrance. All the adrenaline, the sweaty bodies, felt almost violent, excitement turning to a sense of doom. In the crowd, a woman pushed through. Summer's mother. I didn't know how she'd gotten backstage, but she was barreling toward us. "That's my *daughter,*" she yelled at a man who tried to stop her.

"Mom," Summer cried, running to her for comfort. Lupe took

her into her arms for a moment. Then she held Summer out by her shoulders and slapped her across the face. At that, the security guard who had let her through stepped forward, pulling her away, protecting the star.

"You've broken my heart," Lupe said to Summer as the guard tugged her back. Her eyes flitted up toward the ceiling, heavenward. "I know you have broken your father's too."

Summer held her hand to her cheek, dazed, as the guard herded her mother out of the hallway, and the band began to play the opening music onstage. Summer's eyes were cloudy with confusion, rimmed with red.

"Hey," I said to her, and she startled, looking at me. It killed me to see the pain on her face. "Do the best show you can. We're going to fix this afterward, I promise you."

She nodded mutely at me and cleared her throat. She closed her eyes, taking a breath, her spine lengthening. Plastering on an innocent smile, she turned and ran into the light.

Twenty-Six

· · · · · · ·

2018

Now, I tell Summer the truth. "I didn't leak it. I took it from you and I wrote in it about myself." Her eyes are so big. All I can see in her face is those eyes, burning a hole into me. "I was careless and brought it to set, and some PA must have picked it up and decided to make money off it. I'm so sorry. I came back here to do whatever I can to make it up to you."

She turns her back, bracing herself against the desk in the corner, her shoulders tense.

"And I was going to talk to Mr. Atlas after the show and try to fix things for you, but . . ." Still, she is silent. "But that doesn't matter. I should have spoken up."

A couple of times over the years, I'd imagined this moment, and thought that maybe she'd laugh. *What a wild misunderstanding!* But that was never going to happen. I wait, and the noises of the house roar in my ears. "Say something. Scream at me. Slap me. I'm the reason everything got so screwed up for you. I'm the reason the whole world thought you'd lied about being a virgin—"

"I did lie about being a virgin," she says, so softly that at first I think I've misheard.

"What?"

She turns back to me, a muscle pulsing in her throat. Otherwise, she is deathly still. Her veins course not with blood, but with fury.

"I want you to sit the hell down," she says, "and listen to everything you did to me."

Twenty-Seven

· · · · · · ·

SUMMER'S SOLILOQUY

When I was a little girl, a normal girl, I dreamed about signing a big movie contract. Right afterward, I'd get all dressed up and go out to the fanciest dinner I could. I'd feast on bright red lobsters and dark chocolate cake, plus one of every single appetizer on the menu.

But when the big movie contract was in reach, and I wasn't so little and so normal, the thing I fantasized about doing the moment the ink dried was breaking up with Lucas.

I guess I've always liked telling myself stories. Here's how the Lucas one went, at first: He was the handsomest boy in church. I was the sweet, singing angel in the choir who captured his heart. We were going to live happily ever after. But then I had sex with him. It was in the week after my dad died, when I needed to feel something besides bad and I was furious with God for taking my father away. Once was enough to change everything. Even while Lucas and I were in the middle of it, I could feel the fairy tale disappearing.

As the show got bigger, he got angrier. Sometimes he'd yell

that I'd tempted him into sin and now I was going to forget him. How could he trust me when I was lying to everybody else about being pure? Maybe people deserved to know who I really was.

I told him he had nothing to worry about. Lying is just like swimming. The first time you do it, you open your mouth and think you'll drown. With enough practice, though, you don't even have to think anymore. Lucas was right not to trust me. I'd fallen in love with someone else, and I couldn't believe that I'd ever considered marrying Lucas when Noah existed in the world.

It started with the flowers that appeared like magic in my trailer after my dad died. They were yellow tulips, so bright when everything else had gone gray. Plenty of people had offered me things, from a journal to a shoulder to cry on, and it felt like they were all saying, *See what* I'm *doing for you? When you're the biggest star in the world, remember that I was here when you were only a star ascendant!* But these flowers didn't come with a note.

I tried to keep them alive as long as possible, moving them from surface to surface in my trailer so that they could drink up the perfect amount of sun. When they finally wilted beyond saving, I almost cried. But the next time I came back to my trailer, the tulips were gone, replaced by a vase of daisies. They were yellow too, my favorite color.

The flowers had both come on Tuesdays. So the third week, I doubled back after leaving my trailer just in time to see Noah disappearing inside, a cluster of sunflowers in his hand. And although it had all felt like a big mystery until that point, seeing him confirmed something I hadn't known I knew.

I called him that night. We'd talked on the phone before, but almost always in a conference call with you and Liana, or to discuss practical things. "I solved it," I said, when he picked up.

"I don't know what you're talking about," he said, and then the weirdest thing happened. You know how some people can picture stuff in their mind with a lot of detail? Like, you tell people to think of an apple, and some of them can see it down to the glistening water droplets on the skin? I'd never been one of those people—it was always only the idea of an apple, never the actual picture. But Noah spoke, and just hearing his voice, I could see his face like he was right there next to me.

"Thank you. The sunflowers are my favorites so far."

Enthusiasm rushed into his voice. "They're beautiful, aren't they? I can tell you the best way to keep them alive longer, but only if you're interested, 'cause I know you didn't exactly ask for them—"

"Tell me," I said, and we didn't hang up for another hour and a half.

The night we got back to LA after our New York trip, during which he'd told me on a mountaintop that I was the most amazing girl he'd ever met, I called him again. When he answered, I realized I didn't have an excuse to talk to him. He said my name, and I panicked, and then I said, "I was thinking about the birds!"

"The mourning doves? What about them?"

"Well." I paused. "What do you think would happen to the happy one if she ever experienced a truly bad thing?"

"What kind of bad thing?"

"Like . . . losing something she cared about. Do you think it would change her, deep down? Would it get rid of something beautiful, the hopeful, happy part inside of her?"

He considered this. I twisted the cord of the phone around my finger, lying back on my bed, imagining that he was in bed too.

"No," he said. "I think she could see the world more clearly without losing that important part of herself."

"You do?"

"Yeah. Maybe it'd be hard for a while, but that beautiful part in her would be strong enough that she'd come back to it." How soft was his comforter? What did his sheets smell like? Lucas's mom washed his sheets for him, once every two weeks. I bet Noah washed his sheets himself, maybe once every couple of months. He was a boy, but not a disgusting one, not the kind to go a whole *year* sleeping in crumb-filled sheets. If he had someone else sleeping in his bed too, he'd wash his sheets more often, to be considerate. I didn't like thinking about some other girl sleeping next to him.

"I think you're right," I said. "It's like . . . like there's a time to be sad, but there's also a time to be stupidly hopeful, despite the odds."

"Stupidly hopeful despite the odds," he repeated. "Yeah, there is."

We started talking almost every night, our phones pressed to our ears, him staying on with me until I fell asleep. He always waited, never falling asleep first. Would he wait for me in other ways too? Sometimes we talked more about the bird characters, making up a whole journey for them, but also, he listened to me when I talked about my dad. He didn't try to pretend that he understood what it felt like because his dog or grandpa had died, and he didn't say anything about how it was God's plan. He listened, and told me what he remembered about my dad—that he'd been so funny, this light in the room, and that I had that same kind of light, so it was like my dad was living on.

Everybody else saw us as the stars, and they were blinded by our shine. But because the two of us shone equally bright, it somehow canceled out, and we could see each other as we actually were.

Have you ever been in love like that, where it just feels . . . hallowed? Sometimes, when he drove somewhere without me, I'd be overwhelmed with anxiety. What if he died in a car accident, and I wasn't there next to him? But nothing could happen until we signed the movie contract. Because if Lucas found out, he might tell the press that I wasn't a virgin, and Michael had said that a scandal could ruin everything.

When I had sex with Noah, I knew it would feel like it was supposed to. I didn't think I'd be able to wait very long, but maybe that was okay. Sex could be a beautiful expression of love even if you weren't married. I argued it out in my mind: Our bodies were made by God. Therefore, in worshipping each other, we would also worship Him! It made perfect sense. How had I not seen it before?

Besides, we would get married someday. The paparazzi would try to force their way into the wedding. *People* and *Us Weekly* would offer us hundreds of thousands of dollars for exclusive pictures, but we wouldn't want that, because we wouldn't be doing it for the fortune or the fame. If we said no and closed the gates on them, though, they'd fly a helicopter above the ceremony and take what they wanted from above. Maybe we should just run away together, leaving the show and everyone else behind.

I almost told Noah the real reason I couldn't break up with Lucas one night. We'd been kissing all day in rehearsal, and I was on fire with longing for him. Afterward, in the lot, he pulled me aside in the darkness. "I can't . . . I'm sorry, but I can't stop thinking about you. And I know you feel the same way. Be with *me*."

Sometimes, I felt like we were so connected that he could read my thoughts, so I wasn't surprised that as soon as sex came into my mind, he started talking about it too.

"I think it's cool that you're waiting." His voice was halting, desperate even. "I admire you for it. Like, maybe I like you even *more* because of it."

Though it stung, it made sense. I'd been taught the lesson from the time I was small: boys don't like girls as much once they're tarnished. And Noah, even though he was the best of boys, was still a boy. Maybe I never had to tell him. I was a pretty good actress. I could pretend, when it finally happened, that it was my first time. In a way, it would be. The first time choosing to do it because of love, not sadness.

So I lied to Noah too. It was just like swimming.

. . . .

Backstage, before the live show, everyone else took deep breaths to deal with their preshow jitters, but I didn't need to. Then Michael had the assistant turn the TV volume up, and everything shattered.

When the reporters mentioned my journal, all I could remember was that I'd written something about my dad trying to whitewash me. Oh, no. Would this hurt his memory? I felt a tangle of confusion whenever I thought too much about it, but I knew he truly believed that everything he'd done was just to make things easier for me. I was already thinking about calling my agent to write a statement when the reporters said that I'd called Liana a slut.

Maybe I'd thought that a time or two, though looking back, it was out of jealousy. She could date who she wanted without it causing a national crisis. But I was certain I'd never written it down. I'd only written one entry. And as the reporters kept going, I felt like I was becoming . . . untethered from the world.

Because many of the thoughts in the journal *did* feel like mine. I had fantasized about Noah. And I had been angry with him after he got in that stupid fight with Lucas in front of everyone, a fight that had sent Lucas spiraling.

"What did he *mean*, 'Are you sure about that?'" Lucas had asked me that night, driving us home far too fast. (Did Noah ever worry, when I was in the car without him, that I'd die in an accident and he'd have to go on without me?) "Am I sure that I have you?"

"Please slow down," I said. "Please."

Abruptly, he swerved to the side of the dark back road we were on, turned the car off, and pounded his fist against the steering wheel. "I'm *not* sure, Sum!"

"No," I said, the dull thud of his fist making me flinch. This was a kind of fairy tale I hadn't read before, a fairy tale in reverse, where the handsome prince sheds his skin and transforms into a beast. "Noah's just, like, weirdly obsessed with me. And I don't want to do anything to set him off before the live show, because he could ruin it for all of us."

"Maybe it should be ruined. I don't like what this show is doing to you."

Alarm bells rang in my ears. I tried to speak to him as sweetly as possible, like the little girl he'd met in the church choir. "It's not just me, though. So many people are depending on this. Kat, Liana, everyone else who would be out of a job. I have to do it for them."

Still, he seethed. "You're such a good actress, how can I trust you? Do you know how much it sucks to have every magazine in the country talking about how your girlfriend is kissing some other guy?"

"Please, trust this," I said, and kissed him.

He stayed rigid for a moment. Then he groaned and breathed into my mouth, kissing me back, his tongue sour. He unbuckled his seat belt. He unbuckled mine.

I let him pull me into the back seat and fumble around and push himself inside me. I thought of it like getting a shot, taking a little bit of hurt in the short term to make life better for the future you. I performed for him, imagining he was Noah the whole time.

Standing in the greenroom, watching the TV anchors, I pressed my fingernails into the palms of my hands, like I had while Lucas was moving on top of me. There were details in the journal that I hadn't told anybody. Had I written in it in my sleep like somebody enchanted, rising from my bed and pouring out my half-truths, half-nightmares? No, someone was trying to sabotage me. They had been watching me, writing down a version of my life to sell to the press, and I had no idea why.

This is the terrifying thing about being famous, isn't it? You occupy people's minds even when you don't want to. You never really know all the people who are thinking about you at any given moment, wanting to possess you or ruin you.

Barely conscious of everyone's stares, the scandalized whispers, I pushed through the crowd to Noah's side, my hand seeking his, my heart pounding.

"Please, I need you to tell me none of it is true," he said, his blue eyes scared and searching mine.

"I didn't write those things, I promise you," I said as the crowd swelled around us and the assistant director called out that we had to start the show.

"But are they true?"

"No!" I squeezed his hand, hard. "I don't hate you." He was still looking at me, his face white and hurt, wanting to believe what I was saying. "I . . . I love you." I'd been holding it back, planning to wait until I was truly free to tell him. I liked the way it sounded, so I said it again. "I love you."

"You do?" he asked, hope peeking through his doubts.

"*That's* what's true. I think you're the love of my life."

"Now!" the assistant director was shouting.

"We can talk about it after the show. But please, trust me."

"I love you too," Noah said. "I love you so much." He gave me one last look, then ran off to places.

I floated toward my side of the stage almost in a fugue state. Nobody I passed seemed surprised. It was like they'd received confirmation of something they'd suspected all along. The slap from my mom, it set off a buzzing in my head. I had to put it in a tiny compartment inside of me, to open it up after the show was over. For now, all of these things were happening to Journal Summer, not Real-Life Summer.

Real-Life Summer hadn't lost Noah. So she was going to be okay.

I'd had my moments of impulsivity before, yes—from the harmless, like deciding that it would be fun to paint your entire apartment, to the stupid, like the night we went to the drag club and I was so happy I wasn't the center of attention for once that I'd overindulged and gotten far too drunk. But I'd learned over the course of these two seasons how to hold my real feelings at bay and smile for the cameras. So everything was going fine. My voice was clear and strong, the dance moves coming to me easily. The audience didn't know what had happened, not yet.

I ran offstage for a couple of minutes at one point when Noah was on for a solo number. A makeup artist freshened me up, avoiding eye contact, leaving as soon as the touch-ups were done. I noticed Mr. Atlas standing in the wings, staring at me. He must have heard everything, someone flocking into the VIP box to whisper the terrible news in his ear.

He'd hosted me and Noah for family dinners at his mansion, along with his wife and his sons, a couple of times now. I didn't tell you and Liana, because I knew how jealous you'd be. Your jealousy was always so guilt inducing, so obvious. But each time, he'd talked of grand plans for the future of the franchise, and of how proud he was of us, almost like he was trying to be a surrogate father. My own father would have trusted me about this, so maybe Mr. Atlas would too.

I ran to him. "Mr. Atlas, I don't know what you heard, but I didn't write those things, I swear. Someone took that journal from me after I wrote the first entry. They're making it all up."

His jaw clenched. It was dim where we stood, but a spotlight swept in an arc across the stage, its light bathing us for a few moments, and I shrank back at the expression on his normally placid face. Loathing. The depth of it terrified me. He looked away. Right, because he could barely look *at* me. Because he didn't believe me. Because nobody did but Noah.

"Just go out there and see if you can manage to keep your clothes on," he said, then walked away.

I ran back on for my own solo. So close now to the moment when this could all be over. The solo ended and Noah came back onstage, the show barreling toward the kiss and the final song. But something was strange. He wouldn't meet my eyes.

My fatal flaw, though, is that I always come back to hope. No matter how often the world laughs at me, no matter how often I screw up. Each time I go to rehab, I believe it will fix me. Each time I take a bump of coke, I believe I can do just one. Noah had led me back to hope after my father died, and so there on the stage, even though he was looking at a spot over my shoulder instead of at me, I believed that we were going to be okay.

On live television, stupidly hopeful despite the odds, I stepped forward to kiss him. And he turned away.

I landed against his chest with a thud. And in the moment before I peeled myself off him and tried to keep going, a series of thoughts collided in my mind.

First: confusion. I didn't know what had changed, only that he'd chosen the journal's version of the truth over mine. Well, was the journal's version so different? I *had* manipulated people, keeping them in the dark so that I could keep hold of the spotlight. I had broken my promise to God and failed to stay pure for Noah. Now, he was so repelled that he couldn't even pretend he wanted to touch me.

Next: all the other hurts I'd shoved into the box in my mind broke free. You and Liana not caring enough to stand up for me; Michael confirming that without my sweet virginal allure, I was no more talented than any random girl he might pluck from the chorus; Mr. Atlas making his disgust clear. And my mother. After I'd had sex with Lucas that first time, I'd run down to the basement and washed my sheets on the hottest possible setting while my mom was out of the house. I got down on my knees and prayed that she wouldn't come home before the cycle was done. She'd warned me that I was on a dangerous path, weeping over that *Vanity Fair* article with the picture of me adjusting my skirt, and I hadn't listened. She was never going to forgive me, was she?

Finally: rage. I'd been carrying this show on my shoulders, staying with a boy I hated for the movie deal, trying to walk the line so delicately. In another world, maybe I'd be in college, taking classes that interested me and rushing a sorority, but instead I'd been contorting and contorting myself. A normal person has some responsibility to their family and their friends and their bosses, and even that can feel like a lot of pressure. But I owed something to millions of people. I had women I'd never met before telling me that their little girl was in the hospital and that she was living for *me*, her hero, and I had better not disappoint her. I had you and the executives telling me that I couldn't take time off after my dad died because then we might get canceled and everyone would lose their jobs. I'd worked so hard to be the perfect girl everyone wanted me to be, somehow a role model for tweens and an object of desire to men and a nonthreatening friend to girls my own age and more and more and more, twenty different girls rolled into one.

But how many of these millions of people actually cared about my well-being? When it mattered, no one was coming to my defense. Nobody cared about me beyond what I could do for them.

Liana burst out onstage, you following her, the underscoring starting for the final number. "Guys! We don't have to break up the band after all! The Rome Music Festival had an unexpected opening, and they want us to fill it."

"Yeah," you said, rolling your eyes the way you always did when your character did something kind against your better judgment. You spoke with a strange, almost hyperactive fervor, though. "I had my dad pull some strings with the concert organizers. But you have to let me back in. That's part of the agreement."

"We wouldn't have it any other way," Noah said, forcing the words out.

"And I get to have the biggest solo."

"Well," I said, dazed, as the music swelled. "We can talk about that."

Noah launched into the first line of the song: "*When we all come together, there's nothing we can't do.*"

Me next, my voice a wisp of its usual self: "*It's not just me alone, it's me and you and you and you.*"

Then Liana: "*'Cause with your friends, life's not so tough.*"

And you: "*Try to fight it but they'll call your bluff.*"

All of us together: "*We know we've got each other from now on.*"

And then the chorus began, our backup dancers flooding onstage, Noah not reaching out his hand for mine like he usually did in this part of the choreography.

"See if you can manage to keep your clothes on," Mr. Atlas had said.

Well, screw him. Screw them all. If everyone was so ready for me to be a whore, I could show them a whore. All of this hand-wringing about my purity disguised a wish—people wanted me to mess up so they could say they'd always known I would. I'd been giving them all what they wanted for years now, so I would give them that too.

I knew our normal enthusiastic dance moves like the back of my hand, but those moves were for a version of me that had died. I stared down at my body, this body that had caused so much trouble, and then I began to run my hands up and down it. I wiggled my hips like I was at a club, the dirtiest girl on the dance floor. Since Noah wouldn't get near me, I turned to you. I rubbed myself against your side, punishment for you watching silently as Michael and my mother laid into me. You froze, just like some of the chorus members.

I sang in a breathy growl. Liana sang louder to try to cover it up, so I turned and started dancing with her too. Her reflex was to shove me away, and I stumbled, nearly falling to the ground. For a moment, it almost shook some sense into me. I squinted at the crowd, the fans murmuring in confusion. But then I saw Noah turn as if to walk offstage. He was just going to walk away from all of this.

So I picked myself back up and danced into the spotlight for the grand finale.

It made no sense that the world took such an interest in my body and what I did with it. It was just a body—a pretty one, sure, but still, only one in six billion. Maybe if people could see that, then the mystery would disappear and they would leave me the hell alone. I started unbuttoning my dress. I would take off all my clothes, show everybody everything right there in the harsh white light.

The cameras and Liana didn't give me a chance, though. The camera cut when I'd barely gotten my dress open. Liana tackled me to the ground right after I'd pulled my breast out, so that the horrified preteens and their eager fathers in the audience only got a quick flash of it. My head banged against the floor of the stage, and I bit the inside of my cheek. My mouth filled with the bitter tang of blood as someone from backstage threw a blanket over me to hide my body from view, like what they do with corpses.

The regret came after I was shuffled offstage, when I was pulled into a long meeting with my agent and Michael and Mr. Atlas and they made clear that *The Daydreams* was done. An assistant interrupted to tell us that, already, more men were coming forward and claiming they'd had sex with me too, men I'd spoken to one time at a party or never met at all. After my performance, nobody was going to believe any denials from me. So what was the point in even trying?

But still, there was one person I wanted to make understand. I ran across the studio lot in the dark toward Noah's trailer, my breath ragged. I'd apologize, tell him anything he wanted to know, do anything to fix this for us. I spun the story as I ran: He'd forgive me. We'd run off together and live in the woods, and nobody would bother us ever again.

Twenty feet away from his door, I practically collided with Liana in the dark. "What the hell," she said. "Summer? What are you doing?"

"Move, I have to talk to Noah."

She grabbed my arm, blocking my path. "What is *wrong* with you? Why did you have to—"

"Let go, I have to tell him." Tears sprang to my eyes. "Because he's the love of my life—"

Her face changed then. "Oh, no." She tried to hug me but I ducked out of her arms. "I . . . I wouldn't go in there if I were you. He's with someone."

I didn't realize it was possible to feel even worse than I already did. "What?"

"Some chorus girl," she said quietly. "I don't think you want to see that. But, Summer—"

No one would care that Noah was having sex tonight. No one would have cared if *Noah* had gone into an alley with a strange girl, because he'd always been free to do what he wanted. It was all well and good for him to judge me, but if we lived in a world where Noah was getting regular letters from middle-aged women begging for his virginity, where creepy reporters were always asking him about how pure he was, chipping away at his belief that he belonged to himself, would he have handled it any better? I loved him, but I doubted it. There was a chasm between us now, uncrossable.

I didn't wait to hear what else Liana had to say. I turned around and left, running toward a future of ridicule and regret, running toward the new managers who would bring out the worst version of a scared, scarred eighteen-year-old-girl, toward the substances that would help me forget the shimmering fairy tale that I'd almost managed to have. Running as far away from *The Daydreams* as I could get.

HERBIE: I'm here with Noah Gideon, the star of *The Daydreams*. Or, I should say, the former star of *The Daydreams*. I know you're here to talk about your new single, but, dude, that live show was epic.

NOAH: Yeah, it was . . . something.

HERBIE: Summer Wright just snaps and starts taking off her clothes like she's working the pole, not working for Atlas. So what's going through your head?

NOAH: I, uh, you know, I think I blacked out for a moment.

HERBIE: I bet you're far from the first guy to black out at the sight of Summer Wright's knockers.

NOAH: Hah, maybe.

HERBIE: Please tell me that she let you get in her pants before she went off the deep end.

NOAH: Sorry, Herbie, I don't kiss and tell.

HERBIE: Oh, look at that smug smile. You totally did. Listeners, you hear that? That is the voice of a man who had sex with Summer Wright. Tell us, was she as crazy in bed as she is in real life?

NOAH: *[Laughing]* Let's talk about my single before I get myself in trouble.

Twenty-Eight

· · · · · · ·

2018

My heart has broken for Summer roughly one million times over the last thirteen years. But now, as she finishes talking, it shatters fully, perhaps irreparably.

"I've never told all of that to anybody before," Summer says to me. "Nobody else could understand." I begin to reach for her, but she draws back, then points a furious finger at me. "Don't think that means that I forgive you!"

"I don't," I say, just so incredibly sad about everything. "I know you'll probably never be able to. I'll take whatever punishment you want to give me. But more than that, I want to help you with the reason you came back here. I'll support you, however I can, so you can do well in the show."

Her eyes slide away from mine, and the suspicion hits me. I think of the way she looks at Noah in rehearsals, searching, hungry. How she's always aware of where he is. "Wait. Is it all about redemption? Or did you also come back for Noah?"

"I also came back for Noah," she says. For a moment, I can see it happening: the two of them shedding the layers of resentment they've grown in the intervening decade and returning to each other as the golden kids they were. But in a hard voice, she continues. "To ruin his life the way he ruined mine."

I snort, before I realize that she's serious. "Because he turned away from you?" I ask. Sure, it was bad, and sure, he's been an ass in the years since. But screw it, over the past week, I've developed a hope that he was working to make things right just like I was. He's like a shitty hometown sports team. He disappoints me over and over, and yet some strange intrinsic loyalty means I can't stop rooting for him.

She gives me a disbelieving look. "Have you never watched *Woodlands*?"

"The movie he wrote? I've never seen any of his movies. I was trying to stay as far away from you all as possible."

"Oh," she says, and laughs a helpless, hollow laugh, one that looks like it could easily spill over into tears. She recovers, wipes her eyes, and starts marching out to the living room. "Well, come on."

The rest of the living room might be a bit old-fashioned, but Lupe's television is up-to-date. "My mom likes her programs," Summer says as she turns on the TV and scrolls through the list of available movies, pulling up *Woodlands* and pressing play. "Now, sit."

"It's almost midnight. Shouldn't we—"

"You're watching it."

A forest appears on the screen in an old-school animation style. The scene bursts to life with all the woodland creatures I saw in the ads that played on TV—some funny, chattery squirrels; a herd of dopey deer; a lumbering but kindhearted bear. A flock of birds flies around. The creatures exist in peaceful harmony as they prepare for the winter. I don't get why Summer seems so upset, why she watches it with her eyes narrowed.

And then a bird with big, bright eyes comes flying in to join the rest of the flock. "It's morning, doves," she cries. "And time to seize the day!"

"Holy shit," I say. "It's you."

She nods, grim.

We keep watching as a boy dove (voiced by Noah) flies down to meet the girl, trying to explain to her that they're *mourning* doves. She won't listen, staying cheerful and chipper, a bright light among the dour flock, no matter how many times the exasperated boy tries to explain it to her.

"Why would we be made to mourn when life is so exciting and beautiful?" she trills, flying in a loop-the-loop, arcing up toward the sky and skimming close to the ground, her face filled with glee. An older male bird, the father figure of the flock, shakes his head indulgently, telling the annoyed boy to let it go. She'll learn eventually.

Then, one day, tragedy strikes their woodland home. A storm blows through the peaceful village of creatures, destroying the provisions that they've made for the long, cold winter. All of the animal groups have their interweaving subplots, but the birds are the main focus. As the flock shelters from the terrible wind, the boy bird realizes that the girl is missing. She stayed out too long while the wind was changing, thinking it was a grand new adventure. When the father figure bird goes out to save her, he is crushed by a tree branch, right in front of the girl bird's eyes.

And in that moment, she changes. She finally "gets" what the boy has been trying to explain, that she's meant to mourn. The terrible wind carries her off, far from home, and she goes on a journey of danger and sadness, having her eyes opened to the world. Meanwhile, in the forest, the boy bird realizes that the only way to rebuild is to have hope like she did. He flies off to find her, to bring her home. Misadventures ensue, but ultimately, they are reunited—he helps save her, although she has also saved herself, and they return to the forest with the understanding that mourning is a part of life, but it's not all there is. There is a time to mourn but also a time to rejoice, and a time to be stupidly hopeful despite the odds against you. (I've heard that line before, "stupidly hopeful despite the odds," haven't I? Yes, I've seen it tattooed on people's arms, or made into pretty art on Instagram.) At the end, it's a brand-new spring dawn, and the birds take off into the sky, soaring above the budding trees, and I am full-on weeping on Summer's mom's lumpy couch.

Summer clicks off the TV in the middle of the closing credits, cutting off the beautiful original song Noah sang for the movie (some folksy, bluegrass-tinged anthem), and the room is silent except for my sniffles. Without saying anything, she goes to the kitchen, coming back with a glass of water in each hand. I take one and gulp from it, wiping my mouth.

"He gave you a happy ending," I say. This movie confirms for me that Noah did love Summer once, not just with a teenage boy's lust, but with a real understanding of her.

"But he didn't give me credit." Her voice is ragged, trembling with either rage or exhaustion or both. It's almost two a.m. now, the only light in the room coming from a digital clock on the mantel. "We came up with that whole bird story line together on our late-night phone calls. And that 'stupidly hopeful' line that became the quote of the movie, I said that to him. You know how many interviews he had to do about 'how he got his brilliant idea'? And it was always, 'Oh, my family used to go hiking when I was a kid, and in another life I'd be a forest ranger!' Not one single time did he mention me, or the fact that I said to him on the phone one night, 'Hey, maybe someday we could make this a movie.' You know where I was, while he was attending the Oscars? In rehab. He never called to ask my permission or if I'd like to voice her, or even to give me a heads-up. I had to see it during our 'community movie marathon,' where they showed us the movies nominated for awards that didn't involve drinking or drugs, because we couldn't go out to theaters and see them ourselves." She tugs at her hair, brittle strands of it coming off in her fingers. She flicks them onto the rug. "This movie is the reason everybody loves him. And it was my idea."

I reach for her hand. Her palm is clammy, unbending. She allows me to hold it, but she doesn't hold mine back. "I'm so sorry," I say to her. "About this, and about what I did. I'd do anything to go back and change it."

"You can't, though. None of us can go back, not really." She rests her head against the pillow on her side of the couch, her face angled up toward the ceiling, defeated and drained.

I lie back too, trying to think of what to say, but my head is heavy, my thoughts slow with exhaustion. I'm not sure when I begin to drift off, but at some point, I realize that Summer has tangled her legs in mine in the center of the couch. I'm only aware of it for a moment, and perhaps she's not aware of it at all, and soon we both surrender to sleep.

Twenty-Nine

· · · · · · ·

2018

The next morning, we wake up to Liana standing over us and shouting, "Did nobody think to set an alarm?"

Summer and I blearily raise our heads, our hair sticking out at all sorts of odd angles, traces of drool on our chins, in our rumpled clothes from yesterday. Oh God, my neck. I'm too old to sleep splayed out on a couch. I'm not going to be able to move my head right for days.

As Summer groans, I look over to the digital clock on the mantel. It's 10:02 a.m. Rehearsal started at nine thirty. And we're in the outskirts of Bakersfield. I bolt upright.

"We have to go right now!" Liana says.

"Dammit," Summer says as she registers the time. "I'm such a screwup." Her self-loathing fits like an old, familiar sweatshirt, one she's spent too much time in over the years.

"Hey, no," I say. "We're late for rehearsal one day. This isn't that big a deal."

"When I do it, it's always a big deal," she snaps at me with such vitriol that Liana's eyebrows shoot up.

"What did I miss last night?" she asks.

"Nothing," we say in unison, and then we become a flurry of

splashing water on our faces and searching Summer's mom's cabinets for coffee grounds. "Does your mom have Pedialyte?" Liana moans.

"Why would my mom have Pedialyte?"

In the car, I glance over at Summer, who is chewing her lip, hunched forward in the seat, gripping the wheel like it's the throat of her enemy. She's speeding, the radio turned up high, some uncreative rap song blasting through the speakers.

Liana stares at her phone in the back seat, making strange noises.

"What are you doing?" I ask.

"Reading what everybody's saying online about me and Javi."

"Stop right now."

"I need to know what the conversation is!"

"Don't you have a publicist? Can't she wade through all of this for you?"

"She represents us both," Liana says. "And she wants us to stay together. And she's a pushy bitch, so I've been ignoring her calls."

"Okay, *I'll* check," I say. "Give me your phone."

There's the pity, unsurprisingly, and the people posting broken hearts, and the anger at Javi. I read Liana some of the nicer ones about how she deserves so much better, and choose not to read aloud the ones about how she's deadweight in their relationship so this is no surprise.

But also . . . I squint at the screen. There's so much about Noah stepping up and confronting Javier. Yasss, THIS is what an ally looks like! We love to see it! Well, it worked, he distracted the press. But maybe too well. Now he's just as much of the story as Liana and Javier are.

The paparazzi photos of Liana are not flattering, though Noah looks great in them, his muscles bulging, every inch the action hero he's about to be unveiled as. I pause at one photo in particular. Some intrepid photographer captured the moment Noah told me he'd distract the press. He's leaning into me, his mouth against my ear, and I'm grabbing his arm. It appears startlingly intimate in the midst of chaos, and a subset of fans have seized upon it.

- Classic Kat, always carrying a torch for Noah.

- OMG do you think she's going to try to steal him from Summer like she always did in the show?

- Lollll obviously he wouldn't actually go for Summer in real life, she's a mess.

- Doesn't Kat have a boyfriend?

- My friend's friend's sister saw them fighting at the airport, so MAYBE NOT ANYMORE. Anyway I'd ship Kat/Noah, it's like Draco/Hermione.

This is just fans being fans, I think, even as I worry that maybe they're picking up on a tiny kernel of truth. As I'm looking at it, Summer pulls into the parking lot and brakes abruptly, her car outside the lines of the space. Then she storms toward the rehearsal room, me and Liana hurrying in her wake.

When we enter the room, the chorus is going over some dance moves, our spots in front of them conspicuously empty. Noah is all fresh-faced and shining as he strides up to me. "Whoa, was there a party last night? Why wasn't I invited?" I stare back at him and his expression changes. "Hey, you okay?" he begins, right as Michael comes charging over to us, clutching his omnipresent Diet Coke.

"Do you know what a colossal waste of time and resources it is," Michael says, "to have to wait around for you all? We've been here, spinning our wheels, for two whole hours!"

Liana and I brace ourselves. We've been the target of Michael explosions before. But he's not yelling directly at us this time. Summer is the one in his sights.

"Sorry," she says. "My phone died in the night, so my alarm didn't go off—"

"Are you using again? Is that what this was?"

"Don't blame her," Liana says, stepping forward. "She was comforting me about Javier—"

But Michael doesn't slow down. "Or was it simply sheer laziness and lack of commitment? And it's not enough for you to do this alone, you have to drag the others into your shenanigans too?" Michael's so upset his face is turning red. I think, idly, that he might give himself a heart attack, right as he stops yelling, sputters, and falls to the ground.

Thirty

· · · · · · ·

2018

In the immediate aftermath of Michael's collapse, there's some confusion about who should go to the hospital. My instinct is that all four of us should ride in that ambulance with him, like we are his children and he is the father who makes us compete for his favor. But he rides off without us, just one shaky assistant going along. By the time they load him in, he has managed to sit up, dazed but alive, thank God.

We all stand around uselessly, wringing our hands and talking in hushed tones. What is it about tragedy that makes people lower their voices? It's not like speaking more quietly is going to change anything, but still, we whisper.

After about half an hour, the assistant director, Kyle, takes a phone call, then gets everyone's attention. "It was a very minor heart attack. He's going to be fine." People let out sighs of relief, even a few half-hearted cheers. "We're going to ask some people to stay behind, but everyone else should go home and get some rest. Obviously, this is traumatic, so please make sure to do some self-care."

He sends out the chorus members, production assistants, and

everyone else below a certain level. They flock out, concerned, as Mr. Atlas walks in with some representatives from Atlas corporate, ready to meet with the higher-up crew, the four of us, and a few of the more important supporting actors.

"Okay," Kyle says, checking to see that everyone is really gone. He's a gentle, nervous man, almost a boy, younger than we are, and he's clearly bowled over by his new responsibility. Michael didn't want to hire an experienced second-in-command, because he likes to have all the command for himself. This is classic Michael—posture that you're hiring someone inexperienced so that you can mentor them, when really, it's so they'll never challenge you. "Mr. Atlas?"

Mr. Atlas interweaves his fingers, perched in a chair. "Michael is going to be fine. But he needs to stay in the hospital for a day or two for monitoring, and then he should rest and recuperate for a few days after that."

No one wants to be the one to ask the question, to seem so callous and self-interested, but we're all thinking it. Finally, Summer sticks her hand up. "What does this mean for the reunion?"

"We should push it, right?" Liana asks. "If it's supposed to be in two weeks, and Michael's out of commission for half of that time? We don't want to make fools of ourselves—"

One of the corporate people speaks up. "Pushing it will be tough with the advertisers who have already bought space."

"But they'd surely want the show to be *good*, right?" I ask, though I realize as soon as I say it that they'd probably be fine with a train wreck as long as people watch.

"We can't push it," Noah says. "I won't be available." His eyes flit to Mr. Atlas.

"Yes," Mr. Atlas says, almost to himself. "Perhaps we could all use a bit of good news right now." He stands up. "I trust everyone in this room will understand the confidential nature of the following." He walks over to Noah's chair, putting his hand on his shoulder like a proud uncle. Meanwhile, he barely looks at Summer, in the chair next to Noah. In fact, he's barely acknowledged her this whole time we've been back. Still angry with her for screwing up his most profitable show, too offended by her sins.

"We need to keep the live show date. Noah is going on a publicity tour immediately after it. Because we're announcing during the broadcast that he'll be playing Snow Leopard."

Noah smiles politely at the crowd. I look over to Summer, who is hearing this news for the first time. Her body has gone immobile as the rest of the assembled crew and cast breaks into cheers and applause, some of them getting up to clap Noah on the back. I imagine some of what might be going through her head: he's going to become inescapable. He disappears into the mass of excited people while Summer, Liana, and I stay in our seats, Liana clapping weakly but held down by the force of her hangover.

In my pocket, my phone buzzes. Miheer. People are busy mobbing Noah for all the details anyway, so I excuse myself and run out into the hallway, dread piling up in my stomach. It's still working hours for him, not our usual phone call time at all.

"Hey, I can't talk long, shit is falling apart over here. But what's going on?"

"I saw the photos from everything with Liana. Is she all right?"

"I don't know. It's pretty terrible."

He makes a noise of sympathy. Then there's a little catch of his breath as he tries to gear himself up to continue. Normally, the mere sound of his voice loosens whatever anxiety I've got swirling inside of me, but not today.

"What else is up?" I ask, even though I'm pretty sure I already know.

"I also saw the picture of you and Noah, and the conversation about it."

"Ah."

"I haven't been searching it out, but my mother, of all people, called me and was worried. I guess my cousin told my mom's sister, who told her, and . . . I'm trying not to let it get to me. I haven't had experience dealing with random people online having all these opinions about my relationship, you know? I hate being a suspicious, jealous jerk, but I got in my head, thinking about this on top of how we left things at the airport . . . He's not the closure you needed, is he?"

"No, I promise you he's not the reason I came back."

"Okay." Relief shoots through his voice, and for a moment I think we're going to be okay. But then he continues. "And I hate to even ask this, but just so I can fully stop being paranoid . . . Nothing ever happened with you guys, right?" I lean my head against the cold tiled wall. It would be so easy to say the thing that would reassure him, but I can't do that. I may have omitted things, but I will not lie to him.

I swallow. "Once."

Thirty-One

· · · · · · ·

2005

The night of the live finale, all the attention went to Summer, to damage control and frantic negotiations. Liana, Noah, and I were told to stick around—no going out to a restaurant with our concerned families—both to avoid any negative publicity, and in case the higher-ups needed us. But everyone was too consumed with Summer to pay us much attention, so, shell-shocked, we escaped to Noah's trailer with a big bottle of tequila that we'd meant to use for celebrations.

"The movie is off," Liana said. "Right? There's no way we can do it after this."

"Right," I said, trying not to cry. We were *all* trying not to cry as we swigged from the bottle, passing it back and forth. Noah had barely spoken this entire time. "No way at all."

"*The Daydreams* is done," Liana said, pacing around the trailer, kicking one of Noah's drawers in frustration. "She fucked us."

"What we just did, that's the last time we're ever going to play those characters together," I said. "Probably the last time we'll ever perform together at all. Oh God."

I was furious with myself. But as the tequila burned down my throat and loosened my limbs, I became more furious with Summer too. How could she not have held on? I'd told her we would fix things. She had turned my mistake—a shitty, cowardly mistake, to be sure, but one that could have been undone or managed—into something so much larger, a terrible secret I'd have to keep. I could already feel how the guilt would wind its way around me now, inescapable.

Liana's phone began to ring. She stared down at it. "My agent," she said. "I'll be back."

Noah had been reading the news on his laptop. Now, he was lying down on the daybed, staring up at the ceiling, almost catatonic. I came over and perched on the edge of the bed. I had caused this pain in him, and maybe I could do something to heal it.

"Are you okay?" I asked him. He half laughed. "Sorry, I mean, obviously none of us are okay."

"She was a better actress than I ever knew." His voice was hollow.

"Okay, listen. You can't trust what was written in the journal. I was with her at that party, and she definitely didn't have sex in the alley—"

"Maybe she didn't, but that doesn't really matter now, does it? The Summer I thought I knew would never have screwed us all over like she just did. And besides, all those other guys are already saying . . ." He sat up then, rubbing his eyes. "Look, I don't know everything, but I do know that Summer is a liar. And now she's single-handedly ended the show."

I couldn't argue with that.

"I've been so stupid. So fascinated by her that I haven't even looked at anyone else in months, even though there are better girls out there, girls who aren't surrounded by drama all the time." His hand crept over toward mine on the daybed, brushing against my fingers. "Girls like you."

I turned to look at him, and then his mouth was on mine. He must have known all along, consciously or subconsciously, that I would not reject him. I was the safe one who offered him comfort and advice and stroked his ego, and that was what he needed after such a terrible night. This was happening, finally. I was getting what I'd wanted, and all it had taken was Summer's destruction.

I tried to lose myself in the kiss, in the way he pushed me down on the daybed and pressed himself on top of me. I was drunk, just like when I'd had sex with that man whose name I didn't know, and I wondered when I'd get to have sex sober, without having to lower my inhibitions first. When it would feel like something beyond animal instinct. When it would feel like love.

Because I loved Noah, yes, or at least I had, but this was just a pale imitation of what I'd fantasized about, dirty and wrong and sad. And maybe I'd never really loved *him* but what his attention represented: the proof that I could be as worthy as Summer was. Yet I let it keep going, let him unbutton my pants and slip his fingers inside, thinking that maybe if I only kissed him harder, it would feel the way I'd always wanted it to.

The door of the trailer jiggled and we pulled apart, our faces red, our clothes disheveled, sitting up, me frantically buttoning my pants as Liana walked in.

"That *bastard*," she was saying. "He's going to drop me—" She paused and registered the scene in front of her. "Am I interrupting something?"

"No," I said.

"Just hanging out," Noah said.

"Mm-hm." She pursed her lips. "Well, you guys keep 'hanging out.' I'm gonna go to bed. This has been the worst night of my life." She grabbed her things and staggered out of the trailer before we could protest too much. Out into the lot, I now knew, where she ran into Summer and chose to protect her from the full truth of whom Noah was with, figuring that all of our hearts had already broken enough that night.

The door slammed shut behind her, leaving only our awkward silence. Noah leaned in again but I pulled back. "I should go too."

"Come on, no," Noah said. "We still have all this tequila." He attempted his Look, the hangdog smolder, and I wanted to cry. Because I could have sex with him. But I would know the whole time that he was wishing I were Summer. And the thing was, I would be wishing he were someone else too. Someone I hadn't met yet, who wanted me not as a distraction, but as myself.

(Years later, the first time Miheer and I had sex, blushing and shy and slow, it was the middle of the afternoon. Light streamed into my bedroom through my soft white curtains, and we hadn't had a drop to drink. *Yes*, I thought, over and over again.)

"I'm sorry." If I kept going with Noah, I would feel even worse in the morning than I did now. We'd punctured the illusion. "I'm exhausted."

"Fine." He turned away from me, taking another large swig of tequila. I stood clumsily, wanting us to say more; to reaffirm that we meant something to each other even after all this; to promise that no matter what happened, we would try to be there for each other as the world descended on us, hungry for drama and details.

But he had turned back to his laptop, scrolling through Popslop, with the headline **Summer's Sordid Sex Secrets** blasted across the screen.

"We could get breakfast in the morning? You, me, and Liana?" I asked, but he didn't say anything. I walked out the door, and that was the last time we saw each other for thirteen years.

Thirty-Two

. . . .

2018

Miheer is quiet for a moment after I tell him. "So you do have unfinished business with him," he says.

"I guess he's part of it all. But that's not why . . ."

"Why you hit pause on everything we're building together to go do this stupid show?"

Rage flares up in me. "It's not stupid."

"I'm quoting you! You call it stupid all the time!"

Maybe so, but I'm the only one who gets to talk about it like that. "You weren't there. You weren't a part of it, and you never even watched it, so you can't understand."

"You're right, I don't understand. We've been together three years, and for the first time, I feel like I don't know who you are! I just—" He cuts himself off, and I can practically feel my stomach plummet into my toes.

"You just what?" I ask carefully.

He exhales. "You have a lot going on there, and I need to let you focus."

"What are you saying?"

His voice has turned stiff, formal. "I think this is a bigger conversation, and we should wait to talk in person."

"Miheer, no."

"You asked me not to press you about getting engaged while you were away. Now I'm asking you for this."

"But . . . but I love you."

"I love you too." His voice goes gruff. "That's why all of this feels like it's breaking my fucking heart."

Miheer only swears in moments of extreme duress. After he hangs up, I stare uselessly at the phone for a moment. Forget him re-proposing the moment this is all over. He's more likely to break up with me the minute I walk through the door.

My phone buzzes again. Is it him? I nearly hurt my neck again whipping my head down to check. But it's a text from Irene: This is making it very difficult for me to hold down the fort for you. Then a second text: And perhaps I'm the last person who should be giving you "boy advice," but if you throw over wonderful Miheer for some Hollywood beefcake man, you'll be making the biggest mistake of your life.

I knock my head against the wall, relishing the jolt of pain it sends through me. All I've accomplished here is making Summer hate me and literally giving our showrunner a heart attack. I'm livid at everything, most importantly at myself for pouring lighter fluid all over my normal life and sending it up in flames.

When I walk back into the rehearsal room, buzzing with rage, everyone is still slapping Noah on the back, congratulating him on a job he was able to get because he laughed along with the world at the rest of us, because he stole Summer's ideas and made them into a movie everybody loved, because he was buddy-buddy with the guys in power and always, above all, looked out for Number One.

God, how stupid I was, thinking he had changed. Why, because he took me along to a workout session? Because he flung himself in front of the cameras instead of Liana? I need to remember that Noah operates in service of Noah. And it's cool now to be an ally to women, to be a "good" guy. Men are starting to be called out for their bad behavior. I bet he saw his chance to get ahead of the curve. He was probably thrilled that he could yell at Javier and get his name in the headlines. How much regret has Noah felt about everything in the years since it happened? To look at him now, all self-satisfied and tan, the definition in his pecs pushing against his thin T-shirt, it's clear that the answer is absolutely none.

"So we're not moving the reunion," Mr. Atlas says as the clamor around Noah finally dies down. "Kyle here will take over and be in regular communication with Michael to implement his directions. Kyle, would you like to say anything?"

Kyle stands, looking abjectly terrified. "Okay, everyone. Take the rest of the day, and we'll regroup, and come back tomorrow ready to go hard!" It comes out awkwardly, like a boy in his first acting class attempting to deliver the rousing fight speech from *Braveheart*. "Um, and I know we're going to put on an amazing show, and I'm honored to be your new, if temporary, leader. Um, and—"

Mr. Atlas pats his shoulder. "Thank you, Kyle."

The room fills with the screech of chairs being pushed back, the rustle of people packing up. Noah heads straight to Mr. Atlas. Meanwhile, various members of the team hover, waiting for their chance to suck up to The World's Next Huge Movie Star.

Liana, Summer, and I are still in our seats. Liana bends and gathers her bag from the ground with a grunt. "I should go back to the hotel and start dealing with all of this mess." She stands, then gives us a weak smile. "But thank you for last night. I don't know what I would have done without you both." As she walks out the door, Summer gathers her own things, heading away from me without a second look.

I jog after her. "Wait!" She turns, no kindness in her eyes. I've blown up my life to fix things for her. So it has to be worth it. It *has* to be. I clear my throat, glance around, and then ask, "When you said you wanted to bring Noah down . . . could you use some help?"

Thirty-Three

. . . .

2018

Once again, Summer's at the wheel, taking me to some unknown destination. We push through the traffic until we reach a stretch of highway that is, blessedly, empty. Then we roll down the windows and wind along the canyons, speeding out to the ocean, until Summer pulls off and parks at a less traveled stretch of beach, wilder and rougher. She takes a baseball cap out of the glove compartment and puts it on, tugging the brim low, one of those quick camouflage tactics that might dissuade people at a distance from looking closer.

A few people run or sit on the sand. An older couple tosses a ball for their hyperactive dog. But mostly, we have privacy, a rare and beautiful thing. I hug my jacket tighter around me as the wind off the ocean whips around us. Summer slips out of her shoes, leaving them on the sand, then walks down to where the waves meet the beach. She's already standing ankle-deep in the water by the time I take off my own shoes and catch up.

"Gah, that's freezing!" I say as a wave laps over my toes.

She just stares straight out at the horizon, unmoving. She's used to staying stoic as the world hurls all sorts of unpleasantness at her.

Frigid ocean water is nothing. It only hurts the body, and she gave up ownership of that a long time ago.

"You won't screw me over again," she says. I can't tell if it's a question—her voice stays flat—but I shake my head anyway.

"It was bad enough the one time."

"This still isn't going to make everything okay between us."

"I know." I don't expect her to ever be able to forgive me. But maybe, someday, she'll be able to look at me without such hatred and sadness. If this is how she wants to be helped, so be it. Besides, I have plenty of rage for Noah too. My offer isn't exactly selfless.

"Okay, you know law stuff. *Woodlands* being partially my idea . . . that's not the kind of thing that would hold up in court, right?"

"Maybe the court of public opinion," I say. "But not actual court, no."

"That's what I thought." She chews on her thumbnail. "So, I want to make him feel something for me again." A gull soars above us. "I've been trying on my own, but I can't tell if it's working. You're observant. What do you think?"

"He always seems . . . aware of you. Like he knows where you are in the room."

"That's good. But it's probably not enough. You can find out what he's thinking and feeling. Talk me up."

Once again, I'm doing errands for her, but this time I deserve it. I'm working off a debt. "What's the end goal with this?"

"I want him to open up to me. If I can get him alone, loosen him up with a drink or two, and then get him talking about *Woodlands* . . . I want him, on tape, admitting that it was *our* idea, together, and that he never even reached out to me about it. There's a reporter I know. She's always done right by me. If I can get her that audio, she'll publish a story right before the live show. I want this to come out like the journal came out, so that this time, *he's* the one who has to get up on that stage wondering if the world is going to turn on him. I want him to go out there believing that I care about him. And then, when it comes time for our kiss, I'm going to be the one who steps away."

She's shaking now as she talks, catching my eye and then looking back out over the horizon, hungry for me to think this plan is good, pretending my opinion doesn't much matter at the same time.

And what do I think of this grand plan? I have . . . misgivings. But she needs it badly.

"Okay," I say. "I can talk to Noah."

"Good." Her eyes redden. She finally rubs her arms for warmth. "I just . . . do you think anyone will care?" Her voice grows quiet, and I have to stand closer to hear it over the wind and the waves. "I'm scared that no one will care. That maybe it doesn't matter. Any idiot can have an idea, can come up with a plot and a memorable line, but Noah's the only one who could have written that script."

"You're not an idiot."

"It's the only thing of value that I've ever done or thought, but I didn't do anything with it. I went off to rehab. He's the one who made it something special."

"Hey, that's not true." I turn her toward me. She feels so frail, her face drawn, crow's-feet at her eyes. "It's not the only thing of value—"

"What else, then? Name one single thing from the past thirteen years."

I hesitate, and she snorts.

"You asked me, the other day, why I was acting so different. Why I was trying to be like I was the first time around? Because that was the last time I was *good*. The last time people were impressed by me." Her voice catches, but she soldiers on. "Noah is not going to feel anything for the now me. The washed-up, used-up joke of a person, who's angry and bitter and sad and just a shadow of what she should have been, who can't get through a single day in this world without people laughing at her or, worse, pitying her." She wipes her nose on her sleeve, trying to blink away her tears, even as her face threatens to crumple. "That's not the kind of woman Noah Gideon cares about."

I pull her into a hug. She's probably right. The likeliest outcome of this messy, petty plan is that she will fall for him again while he feels sorry for her. She resists my hug at first, but then she softens into my arms, her body heaving against mine, shaking and sobbing, her tears on my shoulder. Thank God that fate and luck and an unpleasant twist to my mouth kept me from being the girl in the spotlight. I wouldn't have survived it. How did anybody?

"Hey, please. You have to know that you are worthy of love as you are."

"You sound like my therapist."

"Oh, you're in therapy! That's good." She pulls back, furrowing her brow at me, and I backpedal. "Not because you in particular need it so much. I think everyone should go to therapy."

"Do you go?" She waits a beat, her face blotchy and drained. "Right. Well, I've been in therapy for years, and I've tried guided meditations and cocktails of antidepressants. I've tried lots of church and no church at all. I've been told a million times that I am worthy of love just as I am, that I need to take a long look in the mirror, that I need to be the bigger person and move forward. But what good is it to become the bigger person when nobody else has to change?" She grits her teeth and takes a step deeper into the water. "I'll move on when everybody else has to look in the mirror too."

"Have you told anyone besides me about this?"

"No. The fewer people involved, the better. Liana's dealing with enough. And I don't want you telling anybody either. I know people in serious relationships always need to tell their partners everything—"

"Don't worry, that's not a problem."

She squints at me. "Oh. Miheer doesn't know, does he? About the journal, and you throwing me under the bus?"

"I . . . I didn't want to change the way he felt about me. Although I think I may have done that anyway." If I think too much about our phone call, I might cry an ocean big enough to surpass the one in front of me.

"You really screwed yourself over too," she says. "Not just me."

"I hope that can bring you some comfort," I say, digging my toes into the grainy sand.

"Hey," she says, gazing out over the ocean, her voice sincere. "You have to know that you are worthy of love just as you are."

"Okay, okay."

"Maybe you should try therapy—"

"Stop teasing me before I change my mind about helping you."

A small smile tugs at her lips. I don't have forgiveness. But I do have an alliance.

Thirty-Four

· · · · · · ·

2018

The next morning is our first rehearsal with Kyle as director, and it does not start off well. We're trying to do the scene that caused such a problem with Michael, the one where Summer bonks her head. Michael didn't do any rewrites before his heart attack—it's unclear if he was meaning to, or if he was planning to string us along until it was too late.

"Um, yeah," Kyle says. "So I talked to Michael this morning. His doctors told him not to overextend himself. He thinks it would be too stressful for him to make changes at this point, so he said to go ahead with the scene as written."

The four of us exchange looks, but we do as Kyle says, moving through the blocking, Summer again pretending to guzzle the punch like a party girl caricature. As she pushes past me to clamber onto the stage, she accidentally stumbles over my foot.

"Sorry," I say.

"It's okay, let's go back," she says. Then she blinks. "That's it. You should trip me."

Clarity breaks over me. "Oh, duh. A classic bit of Kat sabotage."

"Exactly!"

Kyle cocks his head, confused. Noah rubs his chin, his new *I'm listening* look on his face as he watches Summer, though she's not even looking at him.

She's looking at the creative inspiration appearing before her, the puzzle pieces in the air. The words tumble out, like she has to describe what she sees before it disappears again. "Maybe this whole thing is Kat sabotage! Like, if I know that people have heard rumors about me as I'm coming back into the high school reunion, so I'm nervous and want things to go well."

"But I'm jealous and want to keep you out of the picture," I say.

"So you keep handing me punch and then trip me, so I look more out of control than I am."

We smile at each other, almost winded, like we just ran a sprint. We both know it's on the nose. But it's also perfect.

"That's . . . um, pretty different from the script," Kyle says.

"And the script's not working," Liana says.

"I think it's a cool idea. Let's try it," Noah says. "What's the worst that can happen?"

Kyle wrings his hands, uncertain how to deal with this friendly, enthusiastic rebellion. And, of course, the required deference to Noah, who cannot be written off as an unstable diva or a know-nothing like the rest of us. "Well, okay, what are you thinking?"

The next hour is pure magic as the four of us improvise and play around, tossing out ideas, saying yes to one another and almost entirely rewriting this chunk of the script. We change one thing and it ripples, so then we have to change something else.

"I don't want my thing to be all about how much I love my husband," Liana says.

"I think Michael wanted that to be funny," Kyle begins. "Because of Javier, you know?"

Liana stares daggers at him. "I am aware."

"Right, yes, um, I suppose it's not so funny anymore."

"We can make it something else," I say. So we spitball on that too, Liana trying a bunch of different things and making us laugh, Summer throwing ideas her way. When people get too indecisive, I cut through the bullshit and make the choices. The change we made for Summer has loosened her up. She's becoming winsome and glorious in the role, the years almost melting off her as she transforms back into the girl that everybody loved. It doesn't feel fake anymore.

We hand Kyle a computer and have him take notes of what we're saying, and then Noah looks it over and sharpens it up. If Noah didn't have such a pretty face, I wonder if he'd be an English professor, or one of those solid, steady screenwriters respected in the industry, whose name nobody outside of Hollywood knows. He's not the boy ostentatiously carrying around worn paperbacks of classic novels anymore. His intelligence is quieter, but maybe stronger too.

"Are you sure?" Kyle asks as Noah types out a new line for Liana.

"Hey, we've got an Oscar-nominated screenwriter here." I put an arm around Noah, who reddens a bit, eyes shifting ever so quickly to Summer. "We've gotta use his talents."

. . . .

During a break, I make my way to Noah's side. He sprawls in a chair, drinking from a bottle of water, and pats the chair next to him when he sees me.

"Hey," he says as I take a sip from my own bottle. "No offense to Kyle, but Michael should've let you do some directing."

I nearly spit water all over the room at the mental image.

"What?" Noah asks.

"I don't know if you've noticed, but Michael probably hasn't listened to a woman since his third-grade teacher."

"Okay, okay. I just meant that you're good at this. You must be a force to be reckoned with back at your law firm."

It takes me a moment to understand what he just said, because my first thought is, *I don't work at a law firm, what are you talking about?* And then of course, thinking of my life at home threatens to send me into a spiral. No. Concentrate on helping Summer.

Noah lapses into silence, his eyes flicking to Summer, who is reworking some dance movements with the choreographer to reflect the new direction we've given her character. Noah watches her with a puzzled expression on his face, like he can't figure out what to make of her.

In the center of the room, her hair pushed up into a sweaty ponytail, she stretches out her arm, gives a slow swivel of her hips, and then bursts into a quick twirl and a jump. She was always the best dancer among us, picking up the movements fast, investing them with such energy, at times a blur of motion and at other times almost hypnotic in her control. She rolled her body like she was telling each individual piece of it what to do, and those pieces were listening, rapt, just as taken with her charisma as all the viewers of the show.

"Summer's doing well, isn't she?" I ask.

He startles, almost imperceptibly. "Yeah. Yeah, it's good to see."

"I think I was worried . . . based on everything in the media, that she'd be unstable, or unhappy. But we've gotten to spend a lot of time together, and she's really not." I look at him, both of us putting on a performance of being blandly casual. "Have you guys gotten a chance to hang out much, outside of rehearsal?"

"Nah," he says. "With *Snow Leopard*, everything's been so busy.

They're a little pissed that I canceled some of our featurette things for this."

"Mm. Well, we appreciate it. We were just talking about that the other night."

"You and Summer?"

I nod. "You want to know the real reason we were late for rehearsal the other day? We stayed up too late having a heart-to-heart and slept through our alarms. You can just lose track of time talking to her, you know?"

"Yeah," he says, his knee jumping up and down, his voice soft. "I do."

Summer finishes her series of movements, takes a little bow, and then, giddy, looks over at us. Noah and I smile back at her with the same dumb look on both of our faces.

Thirty-Five

· · · · · · ·

2018

By the next day, Kyle has decided to let us fully take over. He sits in his special director chair and nods thoughtfully at things as if he's allowing them to happen, but we all know he's acting just as hard as the rest of us are. During the breaks, he anxiously scrolls through Twitter and Grindr.

We run through what we changed yesterday, and it becomes clear that all of us *practiced*. Without having said we would, we independently memorized our new lines. Sure, it's rough—we just rewrote it yesterday!—but it's funny and tender. It's also maybe a little inappropriate, maybe it calls things out too much, but I love it.

We *keep* running through, past the dream sequence, which hums with joy, and then toward the end even though we've barely rehearsed this part before, nobody wanting to stop the magic that we've got going.

"Summer! Are you okay? Oh, thank God," Liana says as Summer "wakes up" from being knocked out.

"I'm so sorry," I say, improvising based on the new sequence of events we put in earlier. "I want to be the center of attention, but not if it means you almost putting yourself into a coma."

"I'm okay," she says, sitting up. Even in the script we're making, she refuses to say that she forgives me.

We come to the moment when Summer and Noah are supposed to hug—Michael never wrote in a kiss for them, though he said he was going to—and Summer breaks out of character. "I actually . . ." she begins shyly. "I wrote something that I thought we could try." She pulls a couple of creased pieces of paper out of her bag—the hotel stationery that we each have sitting by our beds, her handwriting scrawled all over. "I don't know if it's any good."

Noah swallows. He takes one paper from her outstretched hand and unfolds it. I notice Liana shrinking back, perhaps in anticipation of secondhand embarrassment if the scene sucks.

"You were there, inside my head," Summer begins.

"You've been in mine for the past thirteen years," he replies, and they're off. It's a short scene, no more than a minute or two. But still, she's captured something. A feeling. Regret, but also a hope that maybe second chances are possible. Noah's voice catches. I hardly breathe. And then, it's time for the hug.

There's a sheen of sweat on Summer's forehead from dancing so hard in the dream sequence. Strands of her hair have fallen from her ponytail. Noah brushes them back, out of her face. She looks up at him, her breath all shallow, and he doesn't hug her. He pulls her in, pressing his mouth to hers.

Reviewers sometimes gush about costars having chemistry in the movies or shows I've seen over the years, and I don't really know what they're talking about. Sure, these two leads banter well, or those two go at their sex scenes with incredible enthusiasm, but for my money, none of these people have ever had anything on Summer and Noah, who appear to entirely forget that anyone else is in the room when they're staring into each other's eyes. Maybe it's because I know them as people, but I can feel how every movement between them is fraught.

And now I know what's going through Summer's head as she brings her hands to his face, pressing up on tiptoe, falling into him. Summer kisses Noah like this kiss will save her life, and in a way, if everything goes to plan, maybe it will. The kiss, what it represents, and the way that she will deny it to him, all of this has helped her dig herself out of despair and given her something to work toward. But for Noah, not knowing any of that, all the emotions in her embrace—the revenge and anger and triumph—must just feel like passion. Like love.

Watching next to me, Liana grabs my leg and squeezes. This is supposed to be the moment when the whole chorus runs onstage and we launch into the powerhouse finale, but we told the ensemble not to come in today. So instead, the pianist starts playing the finale, but nobody sings, and the pianist trails off, and Summer and Noah are still wrapped up in each other.

"That was great, you two," I say, and Noah steps back.

He clears his throat. "Yeah, that whole run felt promising."

"Kyle, did you have any notes?" I ask.

"Uh," he says, blinking rapidly. "I thought it was really . . . wow. As someone who grew up watching the show, I found it to be really satisfying."

I smile at him. Of course he's been so nervous this whole time—he's a fan! When no more notes seem to be coming, I turn to the others. "Personally, I thought that, Noah, you're too tentative on the beginning of the duet," I say. "And, Liana, that laugh line on page six is so good, we want to make sure it doesn't get lost."

"Got it."

"But I think we should keep the scene that Summer wrote just as is."

"Hell yes," Liana said. "I did not know you had that in you."

Summer blushes. Maybe she's acting for Noah. But I think—I hope—she's actually reveling in this praise.

Liana's phone buzzes and we glance over—Javier's name on the screen. In a feat of unspoken communication, Summer and I raise our eyebrows at Liana: Does she want to talk about it? She waves her hand through the air: no, she still doesn't know what to do, so let's focus on rehearsal, shall we?

"I don't know if anybody else felt this way," Summer says, "but it doesn't make sense for me to sing lead on 'Butterfly' anymore, does it?"

"No," I say. "Not with the new direction of the character." Summer sang this song—a good old-fashioned soliloquy!—back in an episode where she was getting ostracized for cheating on a test, something she didn't actually do (she would never!) despite me spreading rumors about it. It's an anthem about not caring what people think of you, with this undercurrent of wanting people to see you for who you truly are. (*Shut me down or shut me up, that's what they will try. I could go away for good, or I could turn into a butterfly.*) Michael repurposed it for this, and it worked when Summer was coming in as this party girl. It's her biggest solo in the revival, one of her most iconic songs from the show. But it feels less relevant now that she's playing shy.

"We could try to rewrite the lyrics," Noah says, tapping a pencil against his lips.

"I think Liana should sing it," Summer says.

Liana shoots her a sharp glance. "No. Really? Don't do this because you're pitying me right now. Don't you dare."

"I'm not! It makes more sense for your character. And you've always deserved a solo."

"But then you won't have a big number by yourself."

Summer shrugs, brushes her hand against Noah's shoulder. "I'll have our duet. And plenty of other stuff too." When she takes her hand away, Noah looks down at where it was.

"Will you at least try it?" Summer asks.

Liana hesitates for a long moment. Then she nods to the pianist to begin.

It's a pulsing, poppy song, a forerunner of "Firework" by Katy Perry, starting slower and lower, then racing to a big, bright chorus. Summer always invested it with the requisite girl-power energy, singing earnestly, staying entirely on the beat.

But Liana invests it with so much more. The simple lyrics don't feel *dumb* anymore. They feel like the only possible way to express such big feelings, like Liana has to distill her emotions down to metaphors about butterflies because if she tries to talk about them any deeper, she might come apart.

We watch in awe. Noah's mouth hangs a bit ajar and he nods his head along without seeming to consciously do so. A tear rolls down Summer's face, even though this isn't supposed to be that sad a song. But Liana pours everything she's got into it. Performing is such a lifeline for her, isn't it? I cannot believe that nobody has given her a chance to do it like this before. For me, singing is a pleasant sensation, but for her, it's a way to deal with the roller coaster of life, to acknowledge grief but then turn it into something that *connects* you with other people rather than diminishing you. God, how much I've let my own pain diminish me over the past thirteen years.

Noah's knee moves over, just a few inches, so that it presses against Summer's as they watch. Perhaps he's so caught up in the song that he doesn't realize their knees are touching. Or perhaps the song provides a convenient excuse for something he's been wanting to do anyway.

Summer's spine straightens. Out of the corner of her eye, she catches my gaze, and one side of her mouth lifts in a smile. Then we go back to watching Liana.

In front of our eyes, Liana sings the simple lyrics about being a butterfly, and it's clear to us all that she is a star.

Thirty-Six

· · · · · · ·

2018

A few more days pass as we solidify things and bring the chorus back in. They're all surprised at the changes, but they watch, engaged, some of them even missing their cues because they're so caught up in the show. Kyle talks with Michael each night and tells us his directions each morning, and then we proceed to ignore them. My hunch is that Kyle is not communicating the scope of our changes. Maybe he's a nervous kid whom we put in an impossible situation. Or maybe he knows that Michael would put the kibosh on our experimentation if he heard about it over the phone, and Kyle wants to give us this chance to succeed. Atlas sends a representative to sit in for an hour or two each afternoon to make sure that things are coming along, and we always pivot to the parts we haven't changed, Kyle stepping up and pretending to be a taskmaster who's making us run the remix over and over again.

Finally, with less than a week until showtime, we get word that Michael is strong enough to come back. He wants to start with a run-through to assess where we are and what we need to work on in the limited time we've got left.

I get to the studio the same time as Summer. "How are you feeling?" I ask her.

"Oh, nervous."

"Yup."

"But"—she gives me a sly look—"I talked to Noah yesterday as we were leaving rehearsal. We're going to hang out tonight. To 'catch up,' alone. I'm going to get the audio."

Michael walks in like a returning king, everyone immediately fawning over him, rushing to pull out a chair. I go into the hallway to stretch, and a man comes walking toward me. Mr. Atlas.

"Katherine," he says, actually tipping his hat to me. I swear he is straight out of a black-and-white picture. He's the only person in this whole reunion who actually calls me by the name I've requested. Everyone else defaulted to Kat. Somewhere along the way, I stopped minding.

"Oh! I didn't know you were coming to this."

"Well," he says. "Such a combination of events we've been having. Our viewership will be bigger than we expected. I'm making this my top priority."

The production assistants have set up a row of chairs for the important viewers. Kyle sits in one of them, watching Michael out of the corner of his eye, clearly terrified. He's clutching a thermos of hot tea, but his hands are shaking, the thermos's top the only thing saving the people near him from scalding second-degree burns.

Liana's phone lights up on the chair next to me. A text from Javier, then another: Baby please, can we talk? She turns the phone over. I've typed out about a million similar messages to Miheer and then deleted them, trying to respect his wishes for a break.

The four of us huddle up. "Okay," I say in a low voice. "They're going to be . . . surprised at what we've done. But if we perform it well enough, they'll have no choice but to recognize how *good* it is. So let's be brave."

"Hell yeah," Noah says. Summer nods, her mouth pinched, while Liana makes a humming noise, a last-minute vocal warm-up. We all squeeze hands. And then we begin.

The show starts off normally enough. Then it comes time for Summer to enter.

Hello, party people! That's what Michael had her yelling in his script. Instead, the crowd parts, and she stands there, blushing. "Hi, everyone," she says, all innocent and nervous. "Oh, it's good to be back."

I will not look at Michael. I will not look at Mr. Atlas. I throw myself into the show, just like the others are doing, and we continue, riding on adrenaline, alight and alert and so very connected to one another.

There is something transgressive in what we've created. Making Summer more of an innocent, like she used to be back in the day, causes a cognitive dissonance in the audience. If she comes in like a hot mess, they can laugh and feel superior to her. If she's sweet and blushing, like the last thirteen years have never happened, gears grind up against one another in their minds. Is she really like this, and we've treated her unfairly? Or if she's actually the mess from the tabloids, who is responsible, who is complicit in her falling so far? Are we all?

Liana comes to the fore in a way she never has. Though I manage to avoid looking at Michael or Mr. Atlas, I accidentally catch a glimpse of some of our other audience members while Liana sings "Butterfly," and they lean forward like they're about to fall off their chairs.

Noah fades to the background. He's got greater things in the pipeline, so he doesn't need the spotlight, and I can begrudgingly admit that he's been generous about that. He is having fun, recapturing some of the boyish energy he used to have, but mostly he throws focus to us, charming but not spectacular. Well, except in the kiss, and the scene Summer wrote to precede it. That's spectacular for sure.

And I play my role fine. I didn't come back here to make the world demand my return to acting. I'm capable, like I've always been. Until we get to the end, when Summer's woken back up and I apologize to her. I'm holding back tears as Summer hugs me. Again, I'm not fooling myself that she has really forgiven me, and she will not say the words. But it feels very nice to lean into her embrace.

The final chord of the finale rings out, our triumphant voices blending together, this rehearsal studio filled with our sound. It's so incredibly good, they *have* to see. With this version, Liana will make herself impossible to ignore, so big and bright that Javier can never diminish her again. Summer can get her redemption along with the revenge she craves, and maybe the redemption itself will be so sweet, she'll decide that it's enough, she doesn't need the revenge after all. (Why am I thinking this way? I want Noah to go down!) And I'll be able to go home having done what I came here to do, so I can see what's left there for me.

We take a bow, and then there is silence. I finally look at Michael, who sits very still in his chair. Everyone looks at Michael. Next to him, Kyle's face is green.

"What," Michael says slowly, "the fuck was that?"

"Don't yell, don't stress," his assistant murmurs to him.

"I'm not yelling!" He presses a finger to his temple. "I am very calmly asking what the hell they think they are doing to my show."

Okay, this is not entirely unexpected. Nobody is saying anything, so I clear my throat. "We knew you wanted to write alternatives for what hadn't been working, but we didn't want to interrupt your recuperating, so we worked together to—"

"To make this not *The Daydreams* at all? *The Daydreams* is fun! It makes people feel good, okay?" Michael's voice begins to rise.

"Calm," his assistant whispers, so with great effort, Michael takes a breath, lowers his voice, and keeps going.

"It makes them laugh and tap their toes. It doesn't make them want to hurl themselves into the Pacific Ocean!"

Michael feels protective of what he wrote. But Mr. Atlas is the true boss here, the person whose approval will make the difference, so there's still a chance. Thank God he came today. He is watching Michael rant, waiting for him to tire himself out.

"And don't even get me started on switching up who sings what—the audience isn't coming to see someone else do Summer's signature song."

Next to him, Kyle nods, attempting to look thoughtful. "Mm, mm-hm," he says.

Michael turns to him. "Kyle, you're fired."

"It's not Kyle's fault," Summer says.

"Oh, I'm sure it's everyone's fault combined, but unfortunately, I can't fire any of you four."

"Michael, we really pressured him into this," Noah says.

"And a good director shouldn't let himself be pressured!"

Kyle slowly gathers up his things and begins to slink out of the room. Noah claps him on the shoulder. "Listen, man," he says quietly, "I'll be in touch and make this right for you."

Liana looks down at the ground. There's a stone in my stomach. Mr. Atlas still isn't saying anything. Noah tries one more time, plastering on an easy smile. "Well, hey, maybe there's a middle ground we can find. Keeping it light, but—"

"Creativity is all well and good, but you are not the writers of this project. Michael is." As always, Mr. Atlas's soft voice carries a weight, all of us falling silent in the face of it. Though he's speaking calmly, I notice how tense his body has grown. The changes we've made upset him too. "I'll remind you all that you signed contracts as *performers*. Performers do the script." We stand there like chastised schoolchildren as he continues. "There is a lot of attention on this reunion, and this is not the time to take a chance. This is the time to give the audience what they're tuning in to see. Understood?"

We nod mutely. What choice do we have? We should have known, the whole time, that the Atlas machine always wins.

"Good," Mr. Atlas says.

Michael claps his hands. "Now, we have a lot of work to do, so let's go back to Summer's entrance."

We reset, the ensemble members trying to avoid our eyes.

Summer walks on and flings her arms out, but her movements are hollow. "Hello, party people."

Thirty-Seven

. . . .

2018

After a dispiriting rest of rehearsal where we throw out everything we've worked so hard on and go back to rote recitation of Michael's lines, we walk out of the studio four abreast, our shoulders slumped.

We're silent, until: "My friend owns a bar with a private room not far from here," Noah says. "Should we go?"

I expect an upscale nightclub, but the bar in question is actually a Mexican restaurant—trendy Los Angeles Mexican with complicated mezcal cocktails, but warm and welcoming, and I wish we could stay in the front with the big windows and the brightly painted walls and the groups of friends enjoying themselves. Instead, we scurry to the dimly lit back room, arranging ourselves around one end of the single large table there. A man enters wearing an artfully faded T-shirt and a huge smile, bearing four shot glasses and a bottle of tequila.

"My man!" He claps Noah on the back, and Noah introduces him around to us all—Hector, who owns the place. The two of them exchange pleasantries while the rest of us down our shots and wait for it to be over. Hector refills our glasses and jokes with

Noah for an uncomfortably long time. Summer throws her second shot back.

"I'm gonna get one of my best guys to take care of you and these lovely ladies," Hector says. Soon enough a waiter comes in bearing a basket of chips and salsa, plus four glasses of a tequila cocktail that he declares is "our mixologist's favorite," and takes orders for our next round.

We all dive into our drinks while staring at the chips (stained with grease and sprinkled with salt, heavenly looking), Harriet echoing in our heads, our old hang-ups returning after that disastrous rehearsal, preventing us from being the kind of people who can thoughtlessly eat free chips in a bar. Even Noah just stares, which marks a change for him. Back in the day, he ate whatever he wanted. Now, though, *Snow Leopard* must have drummed some unhealthy ideas into his head too. This, combined with the way that all of his clothing is tailored now (some stylist seems to have incinerated his collection of baggy athletic shorts) . . . the more Noah becomes a major movie heartthrob, the more he's subjected to the same pressures that the rest of us were from the very beginning.

Noah and Liana are making half-hearted small talk about how he knows Hector, when I break in. "It's so frustrating to know how much better we could be."

"If we didn't have to cater to Michael's ego? Yeah," Liana says.

This rejection of our ideas shouldn't feel as bad as it does. Mr. Atlas was right. We're not the writers or the directors. We're the faces and the voices and the drama, and I understand that. Sure, you hear stories of idyllic sets where everyone really *collaborates*, and if someone ever handed me a film to direct, that's how I'd run it. But most projects don't operate that way.

Still, *The Daydreams* is so tied up in who we are. Our characters use our own names, for God's sake, so how come we don't get any say over what they do?

Somehow, I can't quite believe that we're going to give up without a fight. I didn't realize I was such a foolish idealist.

"I keep thinking there's got to be a way to make them see," I begin.

"We won't win, because they're powerful men, and powerful men do whatever the hell they want," Liana says. "Because men are scum. No offense, Noah."

He lets out a sound halfway between a cough and a laugh. "I get why you think that. Let me know if I can do any penance on behalf of my sex." Oh, he has no idea how much we'll make him do. Sure, I've been swept up in the magic of working with him over the past few days, but Mr. Atlas and Michael have very helpfully reminded me that that's not the real world.

Summer is silent, unnervingly so, drinking harder and faster than I've seen her do this whole time we've been back. Didn't she say she was trying to go light on the alcohol to stay professional? She pours her whole fancy tequila cocktail down her throat like a frat boy chugging a beer, then drinks the remaining half of mine.

"I was actually planning on having that," I say, right as the waiter appears again, carrying a tray of glasses.

"You can just take these chips away," Liana says to him, and he puts the full basket onto the tray without even blinking. This is LA, after all.

We sit in silence a little while longer. Liana pulls out her phone, scrolling through the string of messages from Javier, the ones she's been ignoring. She starts to type back—a heart emoji, really?—then catches me looking. "What?"

"Please tell me you're not going to stay with him. You can't."

"I'm sorry, is this your life or mine?" She glares at me, then continues typing.

"But—" I begin.

"Why don't you get your own house in order before you start judging everyone else's?" she snaps. "I haven't heard you talking about Miheer all week."

As my heart drops, Noah cuts in. "Okay, I'd like to make a toast." He holds up his drink. "I know we all feel crappy right now. This is a bummer. But here's to us for giving it our best shot."

Liana and I clink with him, but Summer just brings her drink to her mouth and takes another long sip, before squinting her eyes and holding her glass in the air.

"Oh yeah, bummer," she says. She lowers her voice in an approximation of Noah's, but makes it blithe, idiotic sounding. "Too bad. Oh well."

The rest of us exchange confused glances.

"Uh," Noah says.

She puts her glass down on the table, hard. "Of course it's just a *bummer* for you. This is a rest stop on the lovely vacation that is your life. You can go out there and say whatever mediocre lines Michael wrote for you, and you'll be fine, because you're Snow Leopard. And, by the way, there are a lot of dumb superheroes, but that one is up there."

"Okay, slow down," I say, putting a hand on her arm, but she shakes me off.

"I'm just saying, oh wow, he can stay warm in the cold so he's always running around the frozen tundra bare chested? Spider-Man he is not."

Liana sucks down her drink, her eyes darting between Summer and Noah like she's watching her favorite reality show.

"I know it's not high art," Noah says in a low voice. "But it's an amazing opportunity."

"Well, some of us don't have amazing opportunities. For some of us, this is our last chance. You have no idea what it's like to have your whole life defined by this, because this show only gave you your start." She's getting louder now, her cheeks reddening.

"And let me tell you, that's not because you've got some incredible talent that the rest of us don't. Liana's a better singer and Kat's a better actor and I'm a better dancer, so really, what are you better at? Your superhero power isn't that you stay warm in the cold. It's that you can walk away from anything unscathed."

"Summer—" he begins.

"Save your 'that's too bad' bullshit. I don't want to hear it." She looks around for the waiter, then pushes back from the table and strides out of the room, back into the noise of the front.

Noah's face is ashen. "That was . . . um." He swallows. "I should go after her."

Liana raises an eyebrow. "Right in the middle of a crowded bar?"

"I'll do it," I say. "You guys stay here."

By the time I emerge into the main restaurant, Summer is taking tequila shots with strangers at the bar, a crowd starting to form, people holding up their cameras and cheering as she licks the salt off her hand, then raises her arms in the air and whoops. Modern Mexican pop thumps on the sound system. This place was busy when we came in, but now, it's packed. The girl taking shots next to Summer, a rail-thin twentysomething, throws her arms around Summer, and whispers something in her ear. Summer hesitates, but the girl just grabs her by the hand and leads her out of sight. I push through the crowd, shaking off the people who want to take a shot with me too. "No. Sorry, no," I repeat until I've reached the bathroom. The door is locked, and I pound on it.

"Occupied!" the girl shouts, her voice all giggly.

"It's Kat. Let me in."

"Oh my God, *Daydreams* Kat?" The door swings open. She holds a credit card in her hand, its edges dusted with white powder. "Best night ever! You want in on this?"

In the bathroom, Summer stares at the shelf above the sink, which holds the cocaine that the girl was in the midst of dividing. She looks at the powder like she doesn't know whether to run toward it or far away, so I move to it on instinct, brushing it off the ledge so that it dissipates in the air. The girl lets out a strangled gasp, putting a useless hand out as if she can reconstitute the lines. "That was like fifty bucks' worth of coke!"

I put on my bitchiest face and stare her down. "Get the hell out of here."

She swallows, then turns to the door. "You owe me fifty dollars," she spits over her shoulder before she disappears. The door slams shut after her, turning the noise outside into a faint hum.

"Thank you," Summer says in a low voice, not looking me in the eye. "I was going to . . . I don't know what I was going to do." She slides down the wall and onto the bathroom floor. I crouch next to her. (I'm not going to sit. This floor could probably give a person about five different diseases, and I'm not drunk enough for that.) She stares straight ahead. "I screwed up. I was stupid and impulsive and angry, and there's no way he's opening up to me now." She digs her fingernails into her palm. "Of course I couldn't hold off for one more night."

"I'll get the audio," I say.

She looks up at me, her eyes bloodshot. "You will?"

"Yeah. That's why you let me help you, right? So I can take over when you need to rest. You go back to the hotel, drink a gallon of water, and go to bed."

She nods, brushing her hair against her cheek, then says in a quiet, ashamed voice, "I think I need someone to stay with me."

"I'm texting Liana." I pull out my phone and type, Meet us at the bathroom. Can you take Summer back to the hotel and make sure she doesn't relapse? Please.

Summer climbs slowly to her feet and stares at herself in the mirror, her face haggard, her eyes devoid of any spark. "I hate this," she says to her reflection. "I hate how it's never truly over. There's never one day where you know that, from now on, you'll be better."

I put a tentative hand on her back, feel the rapid rise and fall of it. The door swings open. Liana, slightly out of breath. "Come here, baby," she says to Summer, putting her arms around her, and Summer rests her head on Liana's shoulder. "You and I are going to have a movie night and talk about how the world is trash, okay?"

"You're good?" I ask her in a low voice.

"Yeah, I've already called us an Uber." She turns and leads Summer out into the night.

I appraise myself in the mirror, heart pounding, trying to formulate a plan. Screw it, I'll improvise.

I push back through the bar and into the private room, where Noah sits at the table, nursing his beer. "Are you okay?" I ask him.

"Is she?"

"She will be. Just a tough day for all of us." The sounds from the front buzz in here too, despite the door, the floor vibrating under my feet with the heavy bass. Not ideal for trying to record some secret audio. And a waiter bustling in and out, interrupting any potential soul baring, isn't ideal either.

"Let's get out of here."

"Good idea." He stands up and throws some money down on the table, a large tip for the waiter.

"You want to go back to your place?" He hesitates, so I press on. "The night has already been dramatic enough. I think we should go somewhere where we don't have to be around other people."

He runs his hands through his hair, squeezing his eyes shut. "Maybe we should both just go to bed—"

"Please? I can't go home yet." We lock eyes. Does he think I'm trying to make a move on him, finish what we started all those years ago? Well, if it'll get him to open up, let him believe that.

He looks away first. "Sure. Let's go."

Thirty-Eight

. . . .

2018

Noah lives in a cold gray house on a hill in Silver Lake, slabs of concrete broken up by big windows, one of those homes that looks more like modern art than a place where people can eat breakfast and take a shit. It's not large, but it's formidable. He unlocks the door and ushers me into his big open living room, a high-end bachelor pad feel to it. A leather couch sits in the middle of the room, bookended by metal end tables.

"Do you have anything to drink?" I ask.

"What do you want?"

"We can stick with tequila."

He goes to a bar cart in the corner and pours us a couple of glasses of tequila on ice while I look around the place. There's a record player in the corner; a big window; and an accent wall, hunter green, with a pattern of leaves and nuts painted in black on it. It all feels very well put together and just the tiniest bit like a film set.

"This place is so hip," I say.

"Yeah, my home is hipper than I am." He nudges the record player, a faint smile on his face. "I don't listen to records. I'm not sure I even know how to turn this on."

"Aspirational purchase?"

"Cassie picked this place out, then hired me a designer as a present when I moved in last year. She said she was tired of how my old place looked like it belonged to a college boy. I told the designer I liked music and nature, and this is what happened."

"I was sorry to hear about the breakup," I say.

"Yeah, thanks. She's a good woman. But we got to this point where she wanted to know if I was going to propose or not and I wasn't sure, so . . ." He shakes his head, taking a swig of his drink, then walks over to give me mine. Now that I'm here, alone with him in his home, I am aware in a new way of his presence, how *big* he is, how vital. As he extends the glass and I take it, our fingers touch for a moment. We're trying to figure out each other's intentions. Maybe we're trying to figure out our own. I know what happened the last time Noah's ego was bruised and he was looking for a distraction. And maybe I empathize a little because whenever I think about the heartbreak that awaits me at home, I crave distraction too.

Then Noah lets go of the glass and I take the smallest of sips from it, trying to keep my wits about me for what I've promised Summer I'll do. I wander through the living room, toward the kitchen. "I'm giving myself the tour," I say. "Gonna guess that you've barely used any of the stuff in here either?"

"Yup," he calls back, as I tip the majority of my tequila down the sink. "I'm out of town filming so often, you know?"

When I come back, he's sitting on the couch. I sit down too, close but not *too* close, then hold my glass up. "Refill?"

"Wow, okay. I've got to catch up." He swallows the rest of his drink.

I pull my phone out and pretend to text. "I'm just going to check on how Liana and Summer are doing."

"Of course. Let me know what they say?" I quickly scan the message I do have from Liana, that she tucked Summer into bed but is staying in the room with her just in case. Then I pull up the voice recorder app and turn it on, laying the phone facedown next to me on the leather cushion.

"I think they're okay," I say, then contemplate his accent wall. "You were always a nature guy, weren't you? I remember you said you'd be a park ranger in another life, when you took us all hiking."

"That was a good day." He squints down at his empty glass.

"I finally watched *Woodlands*." He looks up at me, wary. "It was excellent. I cried, obviously."

"Thanks."

"I hadn't realized, those birds were you and Summer. The characters you made up together, right?"

He stands up and goes to refill his glass. "Yeah," he says in a low voice, almost inaudible, as the tequila glugs, and I have no idea if my sound recorder was able to catch it from all the way over on the couch. I grab the phone and walk toward him. "You knew about that? I thought it was a kind of private thing."

"No, I remember you and Summer coming up with those birds."

He nods, an unreadable expression on his face.

"Didn't Summer actually make up that mourning dove character herself? When was it?"

"On that hike," he says.

And maybe this is enough, but it's still flimsy, so I'm scrambling to think of some other way to push him, when he says, "I didn't write that screenplay to get it made. I haven't told anyone this, but maybe you'll understand. Summer had gone to rehab. This was the time when she was supposed to get married, you remember? And I was just . . . worried. You must have felt a similar way."

Conscious that Summer will listen to this, wanting not to hurt her but also wanting him to continue, I settle for a nod.

"I was worried, and writing this thing helped me. It was like I had to get it all out, or I wouldn't be able to sleep. It was supposed to be for myself. We'd come up with it together, and Summer was the bird, and I was going to give her a happy ending in the screenplay at least." He chews on his lip. "But then it was good."

"So you decided . . ." I prompt him.

"Well, Cassie knew I'd been writing something—I mean, I was obsessive about it—and I left it up on my computer one day. She read it and told me I'd be an idiot if I didn't let her give it to her dad to direct. And I didn't want to keep it on a hard drive forever. I guess . . ." He pauses, smiles ruefully. "There's the kid who can get an A in high school calculus, and there's *Good Will Hunting*, you know? I've always been the A student, and *Woodlands* was the first time I felt like I could be more. So, I wanted people to see. Maybe that was selfish. I don't know."

"What did Summer say when you reached out to her about it?" He furrows his brow and I feign surprise. I'm acting a scene with him, like I've done so many times. That's all there is to it. "You didn't reach out?"

"Well, no. She was in rehab. I didn't want to . . . interrupt it. I thought me contacting her out of the blue to say that I'd written a screenplay about us . . . I didn't know what demons she was struggling with, but I didn't think that would help."

"But you at least warned her, when the movie was coming out."

He fumbles a bit. "By that time, she was in rehab again. I asked someone I trusted. My agent. He had loved ones who'd been in and out of rehab, and he said you don't bother people when they're in there."

"Wow, your agent didn't want you to reach out to someone

you should've given credit to? I'm shocked." It slips out harsher than I intended.

"I . . ." he starts, the tequila really hitting him now. "I thought her name being on it might violate her privacy."

"And I think it's pretty selfish to not even give her the choice." He has a million excuses, doesn't he? Each one brings my anger closer and closer to a boiling point.

"But she said . . . she told me she watched it and thought it was beautiful. She's okay with it."

"Oh, pull your head out of your ass! How could anyone be okay with that? And how self-involved do you have to be—" I cut myself off. I've gotten exactly what I need, so I hit stop and save on the recording, then pull up a rideshare app. "Sorry. I should go."

"Kat, wait," he says, grabbing my arm. This is the moment that he's going to try to kiss me, to lose himself in the press of our bodies or to confirm that, despite my anger, I still want him.

And as soon as he touches me, I know with total clarity that I don't. He is my past, and sure, he's caused some . . . disruptions over the past few weeks. But those have been nothing more than aftershocks. My future is a man on the other side of the country, if he'll still have me. God, how I hope he'll still have me.

Noah doesn't try to kiss me, though. Instead, he asks, "Can I tell you some things?" And then he unburdens himself to me.

Thirty-Nine

. . . .

NOAH'S SOLILOQUY

I wasn't looking to fall in love with Summer Wright. I was nineteen years old and starting to become a star, and for the first time I felt like a free agent.

In high school, I told my older brothers that I did theater because the girls there were so desperate for straight guys, it was the best place to get action. But I just said that so they'd stop calling me shitty homophobic nicknames. In reality, once you've hooked up with one of the theater girls, you can't hook up with any of her friends or it'll lead to Hermia and Helena trying to gouge each other's eyes out for real during the fight scene in *A Midsummer Night's Dream*.

So when all of a sudden I was living in Hollywood, full of gorgeous girls whom I never had to see again, I went a little overboard. The group of guys I'd been auditioning with nicknamed me the Pussy Pounder. Don't worry, I hate myself for that too.

The last thing I wanted was to pine away for some girl who had a boyfriend and, maybe even worse, was saving herself for marriage.

But then I met Summer in the waiting room for our chemistry audition. We were introducing ourselves right as one of the guys I hung around with walked out of the callback room. "PP!" he said, slapping me on the back. "Good luck in there."

As he headed out, Summer turned to me, blinking innocently. "What does PP stand for?"

"Uh," I said. "Planned Parenthood."

"Oh," she said. I leaned back, secure in the knowledge that she was just another sweet, slightly dim actress on whom I had the intellectual upper hand. (We should go ahead and establish up front that I was a cocky piece of shit at nineteen.) Then she pointed to my hideous T-shirt. "Because that shirt you're wearing is great birth control?"

I stared at her. She clapped her hands to her mouth and blushed, as if she couldn't believe her audacity. "I'm sorry! That was so rude."

"No, you're right. What was I thinking, wearing this?" I'd barely looked at the shirt as I pulled it out of my clothes pile that morning. Because yes, work was work, so I wanted to book this show. But also, an Atlas show wasn't *cool*. I'd rather have played some haunted loner in an adaptation of a literary novel or, I don't know, a surfer dude on the WB. But sitting there next to Summer, both of us cracking up, I realized I'd do all kinds of things to book this show—cartwheels, blood oaths—if she'd be doing it alongside me.

I understood Summer, or at least I thought I did. She was a people pleaser, always trying to present herself how everybody wanted her to be. But with me, she could let her guard down and be herself—goofy and a little nerdy (her love of musical theater was something else, she could recite the lyrics to any song I threw at her) and creative and smart. Yeah, sure, it made me feel special, knowing that I was the one who brought out her true self. But also, I really liked the true Summer. No, not liked. Loved. I loved her so much, I woke up at six in the morning every day we had to be on set even though I didn't need to leave my apartment until eight. It was like my body set an internal alarm that blared, *Today you get to see her again.*

And then that fucking journal.

The Summer I knew wouldn't lie to me. I was going to go out on that stage and kiss her in front of the whole world. Let them say what they wanted, but *I* trusted her.

I was watching her solo from the wings when that idiot boyfriend of hers came up to me, wearing a laminated VIP pass around his beefy neck. Lucas. God, I hated that guy. I didn't look at him, just stared straight ahead hoping he'd go away, 'cause if he tried to start something with me, I was going to wale on him in the middle of the wings, and Michael would be pissed.

"She really had us both fooled, huh?" he said, like we were brothers-in-arms.

"She didn't write the journal, man. I know."

"How?"

"Because I know her." There was no point in trying to avoid controversy anymore. "Because we're in love and we're going to be together, so you'd better get used to it."

I expected him to punch me, but instead he looked at me with pity. At least I thought it was pity. It was hard to tell what emotion he was trying to convey on his lunkhead face. (Wow, okay. Apparently, I still hate this dude.) "She told you she wants to be with you? That's funny, for months she's been telling me I have nothing to worry about." I already knew that. She had to, because of the movie deal. "She lied to us, she lied to everyone about being a virgin—"

Summer's purity promise was important to her, and I wasn't going to let Lucas drag her name through the mud. My fists clenched. "I told you, the journal's not true."

"I don't know about the alley thing, but I know she's not a virgin. I was there."

I froze. Then I shook it off. So what if she wasn't a virgin? I was trying to be supportive of her choices, but hey, if she didn't want to wait for marriage, I could be *very* supportive of that. She probably had sex with Lucas months ago, years even, before she knew how I felt about her and before she felt it back.

Lucas had the nerve to put his hand on my shoulder. "I think we both got played by a great actress."

I pushed his hand away. "Speak for yourself. It's real with me."

He nodded like he was solving a puzzle (probably one made for children under the age of ten). "Oh. She did tell me you were weirdly obsessed with her. Last week, right before she fucked me in my car."

The expletive wasn't natural for him. It twisted his face, came out wrong, like he knew it was something people said, but he himself had never stooped so low. He rubbed his forehead. "Look, I'm telling you for your own good. She was going to wait to let you down until after the movie contract." Lucas turned to go. "But if you want to keep living in fantasyland, she's all yours." He hulked off into the night.

The thing that killed me was that I knew Lucas wasn't lying. Because he wasn't smart enough to be that manipulative. He wasn't smart like Summer.

The movie contract. She'd used the same exact excuse with both of us. So she saw me as a burden, just another Lucas? Why would she string me along? Our chemistry, that was the only thing I could think of. We were solid enough performers, but our chemistry was what made us special. Maybe she hadn't wanted to ruin it before the movie deal came through.

Someone nearby nudged me. "It's your cue!" I ran onstage for our final scene, doubts piling on top of one another in my mind. From the moment I heard that her dad died, I hadn't so much as kissed another girl. I'd been faithful to her, and what had she been doing?

I'd believed that, out of everyone in the world, she'd shown her true self to me. But everybody believed they were seeing her true self. What made me so different? She turned her beautiful, sweet eyes to me. She moved closer. If I kissed her, I was going to cry, right there on the stage in front of everyone. I wouldn't be able to sing the finale. I'd just break down. And at the time I thought . . . *Forget the Pussy Pounder.* I'd just be a pussy.

So when she stepped forward, I turned away.

· · · · · · · ·

Michael gave good advice. He told me the places to go to be seen, the places to disappear, the people to flatter, and the people to avoid. He believed in my potential. And he knew us all so well. When I woke up the morning after the live show, hungover and confused and trying to see everything clearly, I went to him.

Michael sat me down in his kitchen and made me a coffee. A copy of the *Los Angeles Times* sat on his countertop next to a pile of dirty dishes, open to a headline about us. He rummaged around in a cabinet and pulled out a whiskey bottle, pouring some into his own coffee and then holding it up for me. "Hair of the dog?" I nodded. "So what's up?"

"Do you think there's a chance . . ." I started, not sure how to put my unease into words. I didn't understand what Summer had done the night before at all. But maybe there was something I was missing. "I mean, I don't know when Summer would've even been seeing all these guys that are saying they . . ." I trailed off. In his face, I could see how pathetic I sounded.

He sighed. "Listen. If you want my advice: Have your fun with actresses. But don't fall in love with them. Trust me, I've been there." His ex-wife, he meant. He alluded to her sometimes, how she'd turned out to be a terrible person. "I bet you could pull supermodels, and they're much worse at lying."

"But maybe I should make sure she's okay—"

"And let her suck you back into all her drama?" He shook his head. "You gotta do what you gotta do. But from my perspective . . . ten years from now, you could look back and think, 'Damn, I was so whipped by this crazy chick that I let her destroy all my potential.' Or you take this as a learning experience—we all have them—and push through to bigger and better." He gripped my shoulder. "I want you to be the guy looking back and thinking, 'You know, Summer showing her true colors was the best thing that ever happened to me.' Can you do that?"

I guess I've been trying ever since.

I don't want to paint myself as some tortured James Bond figure. Some closed-off dude who opens up to a woman once, gets his heart broken, and can never love again.

I loved Cassie. Not in the same way, but I also wasn't a teenager anymore when I met her. There were no games with us. We had sex after two dates and went exclusive after two months. I respected her a lot. But somehow whenever we started talking about marriage, I reared back. Because I was getting more famous, and wanted my freedom? The return of the Pussy Pounder? Hell no. If I never hear that nickname again, it'll be too soon. Maybe I wasn't the kind of person who was ever going to be certain about things like that. I'd thought I was certain once, but my radar had been all off.

At the gym one day, trying to get as jacked as possible before my second callback for *Snow Leopard*, I bumped into a guy at the weight rack.

"Oh hey, Noah Gideon!" the guy said. "Big fan."

There was something familiar about him, beyond looking like all the other roided-out bros on the machines. That's right, he was one of the guys who had come forward to tell his story about sleeping with Summer during the second season of *The Daydreams*. I didn't blame this guy for sleeping with her. I'd have done the same thing in a heartbeat. But the tell-all interviews were shitty. Maybe they especially rubbed me the wrong way because I'd implied some stuff, or at least laughed along when other people implied it, back in the year or two after the live show, and when I think about it, I . . . well, I'd handle it differently now if I could.

When this guy saw that I recognized him, he had the decency to look ashamed. "Oh yeah. The Summer thing. You should know I didn't actually steal her from you," he said. "I mean, if you guys did have a thing going on behind the scenes."

"What?" Even as I asked, I knew what he was going to say, and part of me wanted to clamp my hand over his mouth, make him swallow the words and leave me in peace. Because it had been so *convenient* to believe the worst of Summer. It meant I could believe the best of myself.

"I just wanted my name in the paper." The guy shrugged. "So hey, can we get a picture?"

· · · · · · ·

I couldn't stop thinking about that guy at the gym, even as I went through more rounds with *Snow Leopard*, even as I finally told

Cassie that I thought we weren't right for each other, and she cursed me out. I believe her exact words were "emotionally stunted toddler who doesn't understand the meaning of love." I still think the world of her, by the way, even if she doesn't think the same of me. She'll be engaged to some good guy in a year, and he's going to worship the ground she walks on, and I'm sorry there was something holding me back from that good guy being me.

Not long after that, the morning before I had to go do a press junket for *Genius*—this cash grab I did, don't bother seeing it—Mr. Atlas called me. "Truly high-quality work you did at the *Snow Leopard* auditions," he began. "It's my honor to officially offer you the part."

Here it was, the bigger and better I'd been working toward. And when I opened my mouth to respond, I had to stop myself from saying, *Thank you, but no.*

"Noah? Is the connection working?" he asked. "Did you hear—"

"Yes," I said. "This is . . . wow. I can't believe it. I'm looking forward to working together again."

"It will be nice to do so without having to rely on the mood swings of a teenage girl." Mr. Atlas said it in such a jovial, *look at us good old boys* tone, chuckling as if we had been on the same team, the *sane* team, all along. And I guess I had chosen his team. I'd gone toward the power—nights at the club with Michael, listening to him brag about the chorus girls he'd slept with. Dinners with Mr. Atlas at some LA restaurant with a business casual dress code (why did I need to wear a collared shirt to eat a hamburger?), where he introduced me to higher-ups who expected me to perform a certain way for them. I laughed at their well-worn jokes even though whatever you and Summer and Liana tossed out off the tops of your heads was always way funnier. Those dinners felt important at the time, but the best moments of *The Daydreams* were the moments with the four of us together, riding some golf cart too fast around the lot with a bottle of vodka Liana had gotten for us, laughing our asses off.

I'm trying to explain why I was in such a weird mood when I went into the TV studio that morning.

"Knock, knock," the interviewer said, very peppy, as she stuck her head into the greenroom before the show. "Just wanted to go over what I'm going to ask you!" Interviewer-speak for *I know you're an actor, so would you like to rehearse your lines, sweetie?*

"We'll talk about the story behind *Genius*, what you did to get in character. Maybe we'll touch on *The Daydreams* because anyone who knew me back in middle school would be shocked if I didn't ask you about it"—she flashed a grin at me—"but don't worry, your team told me no talk of the finale or Summer Wright or if you'd ever come back."

Interviewers didn't usually want to burn bridges by asking awkward questions. But I'd also started putting firmer rules in place over the past few years as I'd gained more power of my own, thinking about some of the stuff I'd said when I was caught off guard in the past.

And yet on this morning, as this reporter kept chatting away, I opened my mouth and said, without planning it, "Ask me about it."

"Excuse me?"

"Ask me if I would do a reunion. Because I think I would." No matter how or why Summer had been stringing me along, I should've just kissed her like the script said. I should've been a professional. I saw that now. Maybe a reunion was a way to make things up to her. To all of you. If she wanted another shot at being on TV, she could take it. If she wanted nothing to do with any of this, she could say no.

And, okay, sure. It also popped into my head that it could be . . . clarifying to see her again. Help me lay some things to rest.

The interviewer's eyes gleamed. She was peppy, yes, but shrewd. "You'd give me that scoop?"

"Do you want it?"

She smiled. "Obviously."

Forty

. . . .

2018

The video comes back into my mind, clear as the first time I saw it: Noah, on camera, his foot tapping anxiously. I'd thought he was nervous because the interviewer had trapped him, but really it was because he was setting something huge in motion.

He has sunk back down onto his couch, hair sticking up from the way he has been pulling at it, and I want to slap him for doing this to us all, even though part of me is so grateful too. I have felt more in the past month than I've felt in years, both the good and the bad, something dormant and dying inside me sparking back to life.

"Dammit, Noah."

"I know. I'm sorry. I thought this could be a good chance for her. A gift. But now, with the way the show is going . . . maybe I'm putting Summer through humiliation all over again. And maybe it was really for my own selfish purposes anyways." His gaze is far-away, unfocused, until all of a sudden, it's locked right on me. He swallows hard. "Please, tell me the truth. Am I a bad guy?"

I want to tell him the truth. But I'm not sure what it is any-more. "I don't know," I finally say. "But I think . . . I think you're not a good one."

He blinks a few times and hangs his head.

"I'm going to go." I gather my things, leaving him slumped on the couch. And then, with my hand on the doorknob, I turn back to him. "You know, you hurt me too. After the live show, when you kissed me."

"What?"

"You knew I'd had feelings for you, right? It made me feel like shit, knowing you only wanted me because someone else had broken your heart."

"I don't know what to say. I thought we were both trying to feel good on a really bad night."

I shake my head. "And what hurt the most was how, when I didn't sleep with you, you dismissed our friendship like it meant nothing."

"It did mean something to me," he says, red rimming his eyes. "It does. I'm really sorry."

I've spent so much time hoping for forgiveness that I've forgotten I can also give it. But I don't say anything. I just step out into the night, more confused than I've been in a long time, with everything I need on the phone in my pocket.

Forty-One

· · · · · · ·

2018

The next day at rehearsal, it's like we all downed a bunch of Ambien and decided to put on a show. We hit our marks and say our lines, but there's nothing behind our eyes. Each time Liana has to say one of her "jokes" about her amazing husband, she can't quite stop herself from grimacing. She looks down at the ground when Summer sings an uninspired version of "Butterfly." Noah's a little green. Hungover, mostly, but also, it's like he can sense that something bad is coming. His charming grin is nowhere in sight. His kiss with Summer (Michael did at least keep the kiss, as promised) is quick and pained. Summer has given up entirely on wooing Noah back now, and their chemistry is a strange, spiky thing.

After the first run-through, as Michael gives the chorus some direction, Summer comes to my side. "How did it go last night?"

"I got the audio."

She turns, her eyebrows lifting, her breath escaping her like she's been punched in the stomach. "It's everything we need?"

I nod. "You should listen. And . . . how are you?"

She crosses her arms around herself, stiff and tight. "I'm fine." Then she uncrosses them and, ever so briefly, squeezes my hand. "But thank you. For being there."

So during our lunch break, while Liana goes off to do a workout, Summer and I steal away to the dressing room. I put my bag
on the floor, pulling out my phone and some headphones, but then
Harriet comes in carrying our pleather dresses, the ones we almost
had a meltdown about a few weeks ago. "Don't mind me," she says
as she starts to hang them on our costume racks with careful attention. The dresses are still campy and tight but, miracle of miracles,
she's gotten rid of the cutouts. Summer and I raise our eyebrows
at each other, then go through the door to the bathroom.

We lean against the sink and I plug the headphones in, offering
her my phone. She starts to put the buds in her ears, then pauses.
"Is it strange that I'm nervous to listen?" she asks. "After all this
time thinking about it . . ."

"I can let you listen in private. It might be tough to hear some
of the things he has to say."

She nods. "Yeah, I want to do that."

So I go back into the dressing room, closing the door behind
me, and see Harriet fiddling with my bag, which has tilted over
and spilled its contents onto the floor. With no respect for my personal space or privacy, she's scooping up my phone charger and
tampons, putting them securely back in. Harriet was always anal
this way, annoyed that we cluttered up her dominion with our
makeup and our loose change.

I clear my throat and she turns. "All right, all right," she says,
holding her hands in the air, "if you want your things to be a mess,
I'll let them be a mess."

Suspicion hits me. How nice it would be, to have someone concrete besides myself to blame. The way Harriet acted when the
journal news broke . . . we were all in various states of shock, Michael unable to function, and she calmly stepped right up. Almost
as if she were prepared, as if she knew the leak was coming. "When

you were straightening up our things," I say before I can think the better of it, "was that how you found Summer's journal?"

She gawks at me. "What?"

"It disappeared from the dressing room."

Harriet lets out a dazed laugh. "And you think that I . . . ? Why on earth would I do that?"

"Because it was good money," I say. "Besides, you didn't particularly like us. All the nasty comments, whenever we weren't thin enough for you—"

"Do you know how many girls I'd seen get fired because they gained weight?" Harriet purses her lips. "You probably don't remember this, but I have a daughter, and you girls were her heroes. Summer specifically. I brought her to set to meet you all."

I do remember, actually: the girl squealing and gasping as she clutched Summer's hand, barely able to form words, goggling at her in awe.

"Why would I want to destroy my daughter's hero?" Harriet asks, and the righteousness pumping through me turns to a sick feeling. Shame, maybe.

"Harriet," I say.

"Good to know what you think of me, though." She pauses. "Believe it or not, I've always been trying to protect you girls."

"I'm sorry," I begin, but she is already gone.

I stare after her, chastised, as the bathroom door opens up. Summer, her face pale, taking the headphones from her ears. "I sent it to my reporter contact," she says, but she doesn't sound triumphant, just tired, as if sharing the audio involved not pressing a button, but running a marathon. Does revenge heal, or just eat away at you from the inside? "You got exactly what I needed."

Forty-Two

. . . .

2018

It's been too long since they've thrown us to the press like fresh meat, so, the day before the show, they schedule an interview for us with an affable late-night host named Jimmy. (Aren't they all?) The important people have conferred ahead of time about acceptable topics of discussion. Jimmy is not the kind of host who puts his guests in the hot seat, so he'll serve us some softball questions, and we can get out ahead of things like Liana's issues with Javier, reports of tensions on set, how we're bravely soldiering on despite Michael's illness, and more. Our job is to pretend we're all the best of friends who are thrilled that we once again get to suckle at the Atlas teat. One last acting challenge before the big show.

The Jimmy team also films on the Atlas lot, so he pops over first thing in the morning, and we film a sketch where he plays "the fifth Daydream," the Forgotten One, the joke being that he was there all along in the background, trying desperately to get anyone to pay attention to him. We play our parts with the required amount of enthusiasm.

Then, after our final dispiriting run-through, we shower and head over to his studio. We've all gotten gussied up in our own ways. Liana wears this killer gold jumpsuit that strikes me as back-on-the-market chic, though it could also be conveying "he's going to realize how lucky he is and never screw me over again." I'm in a creamy blouse and a tight leather skirt. Noah's got on a button-down, nice trousers, and a maroon blazer. And Summer has chosen one of her virginal sundresses, a soft yellow that flows when she walks, but doesn't entirely convince.

As the band in the corner plays us on, saxophones wailing over a steady drumbeat, we squish onto Jimmy's long couch, Summer and Noah in the middle, me and Liana on either end, waving and grinning at the enthusiastic studio audience, probably about one hundred people in total, with far more women in their twenties than I'd guess is typical for this show. They cheer and scream so long for us that eventually a production assistant comes out and signals to them to calm down so we can start talking. Our interview isn't exactly live—the show won't air until later tonight—but it will remain mostly unedited, with maybe a couple of cuts if we stumble over a word, or a bleep if we swear (though we have promised not to).

I don't want to discount how thrilling, how strange, it is to be here. I've never done a national talk show before. Summer did one by herself during season one, and she and Noah did one together during season two, but Liana and I were never included. Now, the spotlight warms my face, even as the rest of me is freezing. (Why is this studio so cold?) I can feel myself glowing, but I'm not sure whether the perspiration's from nerves or excitement or a combination of both.

My parents know who Jimmy is. They think he's "a good

guy." I've gotten texts from both of them wishing me luck to-day. Now that my mother knows I "made it out," she loves to tell her friends about the brief window of time when I was a child star, my couple of years of rebellion and fame. She and my dad will both be tuning in tonight, my dad with his second wife and their two tweens, my mom with a group of her friends from book club.

I wonder if Miheer will turn it on too. I sent him a text earlier: I know we're waiting to talk so please don't respond, but I'll be on Jimmy tonight, which is sort of a bucket list thing, and it would mean a lot to me if you watched.

"So tell us what we can expect!" Jimmy says, and we're off to the races. We all play up our dynamic, Summer and Noah flirting with each other, me raising the devastating eyebrow when Jimmy makes a lame joke, Liana being so perfectly friendly.

"Was it weird coming back?" he asks us. "For so many of you, it's been a long time since you've acted on TV! And for you, Noah, now that you have an Oscar nomination, well, it must be nice to just have some fun."

"Yeah, we have a good time," Noah says, smiling at Summer. She smiles back at him. "Definitely."

"In some ways, it's like no time has passed," Liana says. "I came back and was like, 'Oh yeah, my best friends and I get to play together again!'"

"And then in other ways, it's really weird," I say. "My body has a much harder time doing all the dance moves."

Jimmy chuckles. "That's right, you're a lawyer in Washington, DC, now! I imagine that you're not breaking into song and dance in the middle of your office. Or are you? Because if so, I want you to be *my* lawyer."

"I'd be happy to handle your business, Jimmy."

"I hope your clients aren't too starstruck when you come back from this." He grins at me and I know I should make a joke here, but nothing comes.

Because in this moment, I can't imagine myself walking back into that office and returning to my life as before. It feels about as likely as me sprouting wings, the idea of once again going back to a skimming-the-surface life. In trying to get away from *The Daydreams*, that's what I built for myself. Thirteen years ago, the three people sitting on this couch with me taught me a new way to feel, showed me that life could hum with passion and creativity, and then the feelings got too big and spilled over. So I ran away from feeling big at all, built a life where I didn't get the lows, but I didn't get the highs either. I didn't realize it until now, and that's because there was one element in that life that was right. One person who made up for everything else.

"It's funny," I say. "I do think I went as far in the other direction as I could, after the show ended. And being back here has made me question if that's what I really want." The others are smiling at me, but I can tell that they're wondering what I'm doing. Jimmy should be moving on to asking somebody else a question, but somehow I'm still speaking, right into the camera, to Miheer himself, even though who knows if he'll be watching. "But the one thing that wasn't just a reaction, the one thing that I have zero doubt about, is my relationship. I know people on Twitter like to talk about rumors, or to ship funny pairings, but I'm in love with a wonderful man back in DC. And I understand if he didn't sign up to love someone in the spotlight. But I hope that, no matter where life takes me after this reunion, he's there too." Oh God, am I tearing up? Also, I think I just effectively quit my job on national TV. Sorry, Irene. Liana gives me a *get it together* look, and I clear my throat.

"That's very sweet," Jimmy says. The producers signal somewhat frantically to him that we've gotten off track. "And now it's time for a game!" He takes us into a rapid-fire "Most Likely To" game, a spin on high school superlatives but reunion themed, where he reads out a prompt like "At a high-school reunion, who is most likely to . . ." and we each hold up a card with one of our names on it as the band plays drumrolls underneath. We didn't get to see the questions beforehand—going for "genuine surprise" in our reactions—but someone from Atlas read them over to make sure they avoided any sensitive topics.

"Most likely to spend all night on the dance floor?" Jimmy asks, and we all hold up cards with Summer's name on them, including Summer herself.

"She's the best dancer of us all, by far," I say.

"Most likely to take over the microphone and sing with the band?" Jimmy asks. This one's a unanimous Liana.

"Most likely to take charge of the planning committee?" All me.

"Most likely to spend the whole time talking about work?"

I pull Liana's name, thinking of all the self-promotion she did on Instagram, although I realize that's a bit of an odd choice as soon as I see what everyone else picked. Noah chose me, and Liana and Summer both picked Noah.

"All right, that's one each for Kat and Liana, none for Summer, and two for Noah. Looks like Noah takes this one!" Summer keeps a smile on her face, but this innocuous question clearly stings—no one chose her name, because she has no work to talk about. "Hey, don't feel bad, Noah," Jimmy says, and I realize that

Noah's noticed Summer's tight smile. "If I'd come up with something like *Woodlands*, I'd spend the whole night talking about my work too."

"Ah, thanks," Noah says. He gives a smile that the women in the audience will read as bashful, although, knowing him the way that I do, I can see that it's strained. Summer's face stays placid, but I can tell it's taking some effort.

"Not to go too off topic," Jimmy says, "but I loved that movie. My wife will tell you I cried on her shoulder the whole time, and I will deny it!" Indulgent laughter from the audience.

"Hey," Noah says, scratching the back of his neck, looking anywhere but at the woman perched next to him. "Don't be ashamed to cry." What a particular type of torture for Summer, sitting next to the man who took their idea while he gets showered in praise for it. At least she'll get her revenge soon enough.

"The mourning dove who thinks her name is about *morning*?" Jimmy holds his hand to his heart. "So good." The audience *awws* and nods. "I think a lot of us underestimated you, but all this time, you were thinking!"

Summer swallows, sits on her hands, as if to restrain herself from coming out with it right here, right now. I knock my knee against hers in an attempt to distract her, remind her that waiting for her reporter friend to publish the story is safer. Accusing Noah of stealing her idea in the middle of this interview will be a terrible look for her. *Don't be impulsive*, I think in her general direction.

"Anyways, enough of that!" Jimmy says, and goes back to the game. I breathe an inward sigh of relief. "Last one: Most likely to leave the reunion for a wilder party?" He raises an eyebrow toward Summer, an *all in good fun* smile on his face, then rearranges his features into the picture of sympathy. "No, in all seriousness, I know things went a little . . . off the rails, should we say? But I'm happy to see you looking so well."

"Actually, there's something I'd like to say about *Woodlands*." The words penetrate. Dammit, I inwardly sighed too soon. But my brain stutters, takes a moment to catch up. Because the person who's leaning forward to talk, voice all strained, isn't Summer.

It's Noah.

"Great, I could talk about it all day!" Jimmy says. A producer signals to him that actually, he can't, because we need to start wrapping up in a minute.

Noah's foot taps away on the shiny black floor. He opens his mouth, then closes it again, rubbing the back of his neck while we all look at him, as the pause stretches on too long. Surely he's going to share some canned *I'm so glad you liked it!* remark, but then why the hesitation? Next to me, Summer has stopped breathing. Her whole body is prickled with goose bumps, either from the chill of the studio or from a premonition of what's coming. Jimmy starts to make a joke ("More talkative on the page, huh?"), and Noah forces himself to plunge into the deep end.

"The mourning dove you just mentioned. Summer came up with that."

Jimmy's face freezes in a parody of itself. Liana's eyes go drama-wide again. Summer's hand grips the edge of the couch, holding on as if the whole world is slowly tilting sideways, her skin stretched so tightly against her knuckles, I worry it might somehow break open. Over in the corner, the drummer drops one of his sticks, and it clatters to the floor. "Sorry," he whispers as he bends to pick it back up.

"Oh, wow," Jimmy stutters. "Really? I had no idea that you two had stayed in touch."

Noah looks terrified, shocked by his own honesty, but he keeps going. "The girl and the boy doves, they were characters we did with each other back on the *Daydreams* set." His hands fidget at his sides, erratic. "I couldn't have written this movie if not for Summer. And the quote that everyone says, 'stupidly hopeful despite the odds'? Summer came up with that line."

"That's my favorite one," Jimmy says, a bit dazed.

"You said that people underestimated me, but more people underestimate her, and that's partly my fault." Noah turns, talking directly to her now. She doesn't blink. This couch is small for four people, so their bodies are pressed up against each other. The two of them sit in the eye of a hurricane, strangely still even as the air crackles around them, as whispers erupt and cameras zoom in close, as the rest of the room loses its shit. "I'm sorry I didn't give you more credit for that before. I should have."

As that beleaguered production assistant comes back out and signals to everyone to quiet down, Summer maintains a dignified posture, a small, bland smile on her face. But I know her. That smile is bullshit. She's gotten the credit she wanted, but still, something is very wrong. Noah knows her too, even after all this time, and his eyes fill with concern, questioning the wisdom of this very public apology without talking to her about it first.

She's not speaking, so Jimmy leans forward. "Summer, what do you have to say to Noah?"

Silence for a moment as she and Noah stare at each other. She's thinking of the perfect devastating dismissal of him, maybe, or the best way to say, *How do you like me now, motherfuckers?* Her voice comes out high and strange, almost as strange as the words she chooses: "Thank you."

Jimmy's producer is signaling that time is up, even as the look on his face clearly implies that he knows it would be far better for ratings if we kept going. "Well," Jimmy says, "I guess I've got you to thank for my favorite movie too! And thanks to all of you for coming by the show. When and where should fans tune in?"

Summer, Noah, and I are silent. Liana steps in as the band begins to wail away. "Tomorrow night on the Atlas Channel, live at eight p.m. We hope you'll all come join us."

Forty-Three

· · · · · · ·

2018

In the aftermath of the interview, things go haywire. Noah turns to Summer, but Jimmy grasps his arm, and Summer starts to slip away backstage, me and Liana on her heels. A producer follows her. "Wait! We'd like you to stick around so we can film an extra segment of the two of you talking about the *Woodlands* origin. Don't worry, we can cut something from the rest of the show, or release it as an online exclusive—"

"No," she says in a terse voice, tearing off her mic pack and handing it to the sound guy.

"But the viewers would love—"

"The viewers would love if you got the hell out of my face," she says, then disappears into the dressing room to grab her things.

"Yeesh," the producer says to nobody in particular. "She really is a disaster, isn't she?"

"You don't know what you're talking about," I say, then rip off my own mic pack, Liana doing the same. We follow Summer as she charges out into the sunlight of the studio lot, as behind us, I can hear Noah calling her name.

"Summer, slow down," I say, but she marches on, past a group of confused tourists here to take a walking tour, all the way to her trailer, clattering up the steps and letting us follow her in. The door slams behind us.

"I just said, 'Thank you.'" Her voice is wobbly, bewildered. "I couldn't think. That wasn't how it was supposed to happen."

"I *knew* the mourning doves thing sounded familiar!" Liana says, oblivious to what exactly is going on. "That was batshit. I bet it'll be great ratings, though."

Summer rubs her face, smearing her makeup in streaks. "How dare he? After everything, he just does it himself, and takes this away from me too?"

"I think he was trying to be kind," I say, reaching a hand toward her trembling shoulder.

"First he won't let me have credit, now he won't let me get him back for it. He just ambushed me in front of everyone and I wasn't ready, and so it looks like he has my forgiveness." She whirls on me, shaking my hand off. "Did he know that it was coming? And now he's decided to get out in front of it so he can control the narrative?"

"I don't think so, I don't know how he would've—"

"Wait, what was coming?" Liana asks, trying to keep up, but Summer ignores her.

"You told him," she spits at me, and I see how destroyed by this she is, just how much she was relying on the relief of bringing him down. "When you went to get the audio."

"What are you talking about?"

"Everything was fine until you talked to him."

"What, you think I warned him to protect himself after I turned off the recording? I'm sorry, but that's ridiculous—"

"I think you had to get up on your high horse and give him a lecture about how much he'd wronged me."

"I . . ." I think back desperately to what I said in Noah's living room. "Sure, I defended you, but—"

"And that was as good as warning him! Because it wasn't enough to get him to admit it, you had to make yourself feel special, just like the first time around—"

"Guys. Stop it," Liana says. "Let's just—"

But Summer barrels on. "Because you're still jealous—"

The weeks I've spent trying to do whatever she wants me to, sacrificing my own needs to make things right for her, all catch up to me, and I snap. "For God's sake, I haven't been jealous of you in years! I *pity* you—" I cut myself off at the look on her face, the way her features crumble like a building being demolished. "I just wanted to help."

"I don't need your help. I knew I shouldn't have trusted you again after what you pulled with the journal." Liana looks back and forth between us helplessly. And if I weren't so utterly heartbroken by this, I'd think it was funny: how we're dressed in our finest, cat-eyes and high heels, all gussied up to rip our relationship apart.

"Please, you have to believe I didn't mean—" I say, reaching for her again, but she jumps back.

"Stay the hell away from me. You ruined my life once and I was dumb enough to let you back in, to think that maybe we could be okay." Her voice clouds with emotion. "That we could be important to each other again."

"We *can* be."

"No. That was a mistake." Tears spring to my eyes even as I try to bite them back. There it is. Some wounds are too deep to heal. Some things, some people, can never be forgiven. My doing everything I could think of to help did not tilt Summer's life back onto the right track. I only shakily propped her up so that, when she fell back down, it hurt even more.

Her eyes are reddening too, but she doesn't soften. She marches to the door, throwing it open, pointing out into the lot. "Get out. I'll do the show with you because I have to. But other than that, I don't want to see you again."

"Summer, stop," Liana says.

"You don't know what she's done. The journal was her fault." She turns back to me. "Get out."

"Stop!" Liana repeats, so urgently that Summer and I can't help but look at her. "Kat didn't take your journal." A deep, weary sadness comes over her face. The look of a woman who has been trying to outrun something, and it's finally caught up with her. She holds her hands up, beseeching, as if trying to make us understand. "Michael was going to cut me out of the movie."

Forty-Four

. . . .

LIANA'S SOLILOQUY

Sure, I live for drama, but I'm not a snoop or a snitch. There's only been one time I stooped so low.

In my defense, I was having a really bad day. Michael called me into his office—this was after Trevor got pulled over for drunk driving with me in the passenger seat. He sat me down across from him, folded his arms, and told me that he'd had enough of my bullshit. "I still have to get approval from the higher-ups to cut you from the movie, but knowing Mr. Atlas, I don't think that's going to be a problem."

My parents didn't push me to be famous, and they didn't discourage me either. When I told them that I would simply perish of a broken heart if I couldn't follow my dreams, they sighed, then did what they could to help me. The investments in singing lessons and dance classes, the month my mom and I spent out in Los Angeles each year when pilot season came around—it pushed them to the brink of bankruptcy and divorce. *The Daydreams* was meant to be the start of something incredible, so that someday, when I was an icon, we could sit around in the mansion I'd bought them and thank God that we didn't give up when the going got tough.

Let's be real—I wasn't going to have anything interesting to do in the movie anyway. There's only so many times you can say some version of *Summer, you're the best!* But getting cut would look terrible. Everyone would wonder why, and everyone would believe Michael's version of it, and people would gossip and gossip until the whisper network in Hollywood was buzzing with the rumor that I was "difficult." There was no market for difficult Black girls, unless I wanted to go on reality TV, which I did *not*. I loved watching everyone else getting messy, but I was too damn talented to make my whole career revolve around who I'd hooked up with in a hot tub.

"What can I do to change your mind?" I asked Michael. "I'll stop drinking. I'll act like a freaking angel. See? I'll even say 'freaking.'"

"The conversation is closed. I gave you warnings, and you kept getting into trouble. And for what, so you could get your rocks off with some Ashton Kutcher wannabe?"

I wanted to yell at Michael that, first of all, Trevor was actually quite talented, and second of all, Trevor was gay. He'd confessed this to me after a fumbled attempt to have sex ("It's not you! You're superfine!"), begging me not to tell anyone because it would destroy his career. (I'm only telling you both now because he gave up on the business and is engaged to a man.) When it came to getting my rocks off . . . look, back then I liked sex as much as the next girl. More, I guess, since I mostly hung out with you two prudes. And FYI, enjoying your one wild and precious body does not make you *kind of a slut*. But I was willing to help Trevor by "hooking up with him" for a few months. Those of us who didn't quite fit the Atlas mold had to look out for one another.

So I bit my tongue as Michael sat back in his chair, putting his hands behind his head. The pose of a man relaxing, taking pleasure in this situation. Was that a *smirk* on his face as he inclined his head toward the door? What a despicable bully. "It's like baseball, you know? Three strikes and you're out."

I stood up, my tone as acidic as I knew how to make it. "Yes, I am aware of baseball."

At the door, I turned around. He'd already moved to something else, clicking away on his computer. This assclown had never given me a real chance. "Why did you even hire me?"

He didn't even give me the courtesy of looking at me as he responded. "The studio thought it would be good to have a Black girl."

"Don't let them see you cry," my mom had told me when I got my first ever job in Hollywood, so I never cried on set, unlike the other girls. And even though I was miserable, even though I couldn't figure out why what I had done was so very bad—I hadn't signed my entire life away! I was twenty-two years old! Sure, I played hard, but I worked harder!—I kept it together all the way back to the dressing room, where I saw that pretty green journal lying on the ground and thought, *Well hallelujah, a distraction.*

But as I read it, the injustice made me want to scream. All this time, perfect little Summer was being just as "bad" as me, if not worse since she was such a hypocrite about it. And yet here I was, getting my career deep-sixed while she got off scot-free? I was going to have to go home and do commercials for my dad's used-car dealership in Atlanta while she became an international movie star? Not if I could help it.

. . . .

Mr. Atlas had a picture of his family on his desk. Two, actually: one of him and his dad, who had started this studio in the first place. And one of him and his wife (fifteen years younger, duh) and their two small boys, the whole family Blond with a capital *B*. I wondered if one of the boys would take over the studio one day. Maybe the two of them would end up fighting each other for control, duking it out and ripping their relationship apart because, in an Atlas world, only one person got to be the best. I studied the pictures as, across the mahogany surface, Mr. Atlas silently flipped through the journal.

Yes! I'd repeated to myself as I marched on over to this part of the lot and asked for a meeting with him. *You are BRAVE. You are standing up for your needs!* But now I wasn't so sure. Mr. Atlas was not cruel like you heard about some studio bosses being. He did not throw things at the walls or at his assistants' heads. I'd never even heard of him raising his voice. But if you displeased him, he simply excised you, and then poof, it was like you didn't exist. Maybe I wouldn't exist anymore after this. But if Michael cut me out of the movie, I wouldn't exist anyway.

He finished the final entry, folded the pages closed, and laid the journal down on his desk, steepling his fingers together on top of it. "What are you hoping that I will do with this? Fire Miss Wright?"

"No, of course not!" I sat up straight and folded my hands in my lap like I was taking a regular business meeting with him. A real professional woman. I should've been wearing a pantsuit or something. Mr. Atlas had always seemed like a man who lived by a moral code, so I was going to appeal to his sense of justice. "I'm saying, how are you going to let Michael fire *me*, when I'm not the only one doing these things? Either you should fire both of us or neither of us, but cutting just me is extremely unfair. Don't you see?"

He was silent for a long moment, peering at me. "What I see is that it is not very nice of you to treat your friend this way."

I didn't give a rat's ass about being nice. "Nice" was code for "boring," and anyone could play that, as I knew from how little was asked of me in my role. But I had hoped that I was kind. In real life, I wasn't the friend who sat around complimenting her BFF all day, but when shit hit the fan, I stepped up. Or at least I had. God, Summer, when I first met you, I wanted to wrap my arms around you forever. You were the cutest, sweetest little sister, and I was going to protect you. But this show, the outsize response to it and the whole Atlas machine, had taken something pure and warped it. The men running our lives had refused to let us grow and pumped us full of resentment for one another, and now it was like my skin was too tight for everything inside me.

So maybe I'd explode, the remaining bits of me scattered among the fibers of Mr. Atlas's rug. (*Oh, these?* he could say to curious visitors. *These bits were once a young woman named Liana who had dreams and ambitions, and she considered herself a good enough person, but then one day she found out she was wrong.*) Instead, I put my head down on his desk, the surface of it cool and smooth against my forehead as I started to cry. Where did I get off, doing this? Breaking down in front of one of the most important men in Hollywood? I just had nothing left to lose.

"I'm sorry. I don't want to be this kind of person," I said, into the wood. When I looked back up, I saw that he was offering me a handkerchief! Nope, this Southern-gentleman act was not it for me. How dare he act so chivalrous, when he'd created the environment that had made this all happen. Oh, I was pissed off too, along with being sad. "I *wasn't* this kind of person when the show started. But you've done this to us, with your competition, and your morality code, and this constant sense that you could . . . end us." A crease in his forehead deepened as I dug myself into a deeper hole. But whatever, everyone already thought I was difficult. I'd dig myself into the core of the motherfucking Earth. "We're just growing up! We want to do what we're good at and make people happy, but somehow that's not enough for you."

"A lot of children look up to you all," he said, so reasonable, so calm. "Being a role model, that's an important part of the job too."

"Atlas is starting to get a track record. Cold and unforgiving. 'The company that ruins teenage girls.' Did you read that article?" Very slightly, he inclined his head. This man had probably never had somebody call him out in his entire life. Time for him to face the damn music. "Fans are reaching out to me, and they talk about what you did to Amber Nielson, the way you cut her loose, and now she's worse than ever."

"Amber has her own demons." He was steepling his fingers again, this time pressing them against one another so tightly, they were turning purplish.

"I watched that video of her about a hundred times, where she says that you made her the way she is. Have you seen it? You should. 'Cause then you'd know that someday, the world is going to look back and forgive us for giving the paparazzi the finger. But you keep this up, and they're not going to forgive you."

While I was talking, I was a righteous goddess, speaking truth to power, the kind of woman they were going to build statues for one day. The moment I stopped, I did not know if I'd ever be able to say another sentence again.

I sat back as Mr. Atlas folded the handkerchief back up into a careful little square and tucked it into his pocket. Then he cleared his throat. "Well. You have given me much to consider."

"Please don't let Michael fire me."

"We will discuss the matter, but I reserve the right to make the best decision for the franchise. Now, you should get some rest for the show tomorrow. I don't want this affecting your performance."

I got up, then began to reach for the journal. "I'll give this back to Summer."

He put his hand down over it. "I do not particularly trust you with this right now. One of my assistants will return it to Miss Wright, with a warning to be more careful about where she leaves it lying about."

"Are they going to tell her that I . . . ?"

He stared at me, then gave me the smallest of mercies. "They will not mention to her how they came by it."

Forty-Five

· · · · · · ·

2018

"So then . . . you weren't the one who leaked it," I say, when Liana finishes her story and deflates.

"No. I'm not a sociopath." Liana turns to Summer. "But you don't know how much I wish I'd given it back to you when I found it. Then, Mr. Atlas's assistant would never have . . ." This whole time, I haven't been fully seeing Liana. I assumed that the Javier situation explained everything about why she was acting strange, closed off. But she's also been carrying around just as much guilt as I have. Now, she waves a hand through the air, her eyes red. "Well. I get it. They could keep fetching coffee and delivering journals for that man, who always gave me the heebie-jeebies, or they could make a huge payday."

Ballsy move, on the assistant's part. It would have been obvious to Mr. Atlas who the source of the leak was. I guess they must have been fine with taking the money and leaving Hollywood forever. Still, something isn't quite clicking.

Summer has been so quiet. Well, of course she has. This reunion has shown her that she has nobody she can actually trust, and that's the kind of thing that could make a person decide to swear off talking to other humans forever. But now she speaks, her voice raspy. "Why would Mr. Atlas want to give something so sensitive to another person when he was supposed to see me that night anyway?"

"What?"

"This was the night before the live show? We had a meeting set up, me, him, and Noah, about the 'future.' He canceled it at the last minute, said something had come up."

The three of us are still, the foundation beneath us shifting.

"No," I say. "No. Why would he want to ruin his own power-house show?"

"He didn't want to ruin it. He wanted to forgive me. It's exactly what Liana said." Summer turns to Liana. "You gave him a lot to think about. We were growing up. People were starting to turn." She looks at me. "And what you wrote in the journal was bad, sure, but it wasn't *so* bad."

"What Kat . . . ?" Liana asks.

"Those later entries were mine. I screwed up too."

"So Summer didn't even do all that shit?" Liana gapes at me. "Dammit, now I hate myself even more than I already did."

Summer drifts around the trailer, putting the pieces together. "He could let the journal come out and make me take my punishment, all the hate and scrutiny that he thought I deserved for not being the perfect girl I was supposed to be. Let me grovel and apologize, cry in a press conference about how I'd let all the little girls down but I'd learned my lesson and would never do it again. And then, when he was satisfied that I'd suffered enough, he could blow away everyone's expectations and choose to be merciful. He could take me back in, and people would think, 'Wow, maybe Atlas isn't stuck in the past. Maybe Atlas is the future.'"

"It's like with the dresses that Harriet made," I say. "Just the right amount of controversy."

"He would have *saved* me. I'd be indebted to him forever."

"But then you took your clothes off on TV, and that was a bridge too far for him," Liana says.

"Exactly."

"Why would he have it come out right before the live show?" I ask.

Summer shakes her head. "Maybe Popslop jumped the gun and published it earlier than they said they were going to. Or he thought it would make more people watch the finale."

In so many ways, I thought Mr. Atlas protected us. Running a company where skeezy men never came into our dressing rooms. His mild demeanor. His quiet force. All this time, though, he was a businessman above all.

"What do we do? Should we just . . . leave? Not do the show?" I ask.

"We signed contracts," Liana says. "And we don't have any actual proof."

"But how do we get up on that stage tomorrow, knowing what we know?"

Summer buries her face in her hands for a moment, pressing her fingers against her eyelids as if she's trying to force back any tears that might escape. Then she lifts her head and gives it a tight shake. "We just do it. And then we never give one bit of ourselves to Atlas again. Agreed? Even if the show goes so well that they offer us a reboot or a movie, we never touch *The Daydreams* with a ten-foot pole, ever again."

"Agreed," Liana and I say together.

"And where does all of this leave us?" I ask.

Summer opens the trailer door. We both stare at her, hungry for even a crumb of forgiveness. Right before she walks back out into the lot, she says, "After tomorrow night, there's no more us either."

@GOSSIPGILLIAN: Ummm, is anyone else watching this Jimmy interview with The Daydreams cast? I think Noah just said that he stole Woodlands from Summer???

@DAYDREAMER23: OF COURSE HE DID. This is what I've been saying for years now! Noah is Trash with a capital T!

@HEYITSMESEB: Calm down, he didn't steal it from her. He still wrote the script himself. Just because you talk about something with someone, does it mean they can never write about it? This happens all the time.

@HEYITSMESEB: And she obviously wasn't going to write it.

@GOSSIPGILLIAN: But to not even ask her?? Did you see this new article with more details???

@DAYDREAMER23: She wrote the line. I've had her words tattooed on me this whole time and I DIDN'T EVEN KNOW.

@CAROLINETWEETS88: He is yet another man profiting off of a woman's unpaid labor and TBH I think we as a culture have moved beyond the need for him.

@GOSSIPGILLIAN: I hope during the live show tomorrow she stomps on his face.

@DAYDREAMER23: YES, MURDER HIM!

Forty-Six

· · · · · · ·

2018

The day of the show dawns hot and windy. And I know this because I wake up at five thirty a.m. and can't get back to sleep.

We have the morning to ourselves to do whatever rituals we need. I drive to a hike and head uphill, a hat pulled low over my face, chugging water, managing to outpace my thoughts until my phone buzzes with a message from Irene: I take it you will not be putting yourself in for partner consideration, then.

I sit down at the top of the hill to type out my response. I'm sorry to let you down. And I know it's selfish to give up my chance to help people.

IRENE: Well. Some might say that art helps too.

KAT: I worry that the only people saying that are artists who want to feel noble about playing make-believe.

Three dots and then: Come on. You're smarter than that.

A tingle starts in my throat as I look out into the skyline stretching before me. We all have stages in our lives that we must move on from and mourn. Maybe some people mourn college. (Not me—

I was two years older than the rest of my class and stayed far away from the campus theater where I might have found my people. College sucked.) Others mourn their twenties, drinking cheap wine and taking the subway home at two a.m., or the stage where they could run for miles each morning before they blew out their knee, or when their children were small and dependent and brimming with love.

Without fully knowing it, I've been mourning a stage labeled Creativity for thirteen years. God, grief is a sneaky bastard. It hides itself for long stretches, only to pop out stronger than ever, and now, at the top of this hill, I sit in the dusty dirt and weep, overwhelmed by how much I missed making things with people I cared about, realizing how many years I lost. I don't want to be done with this stage. I don't want it to be just a stage at all.

A sense of foreboding hits me. I know that I should remind myself that a skittering heart is a normal response to throwing yourself in front of millions of people, and the worst-case scenario hardly ever comes to pass. But it's hard to remind myself of that when, the last time, it did.

We meet at the studio in the afternoon, me, Summer, and Liana straggling into our dressing room for hair and makeup prep. The makeup artist chastises us all for having dark circles under our eyes. Apparently I wasn't the only one who couldn't sleep.

Summer barely looks at Liana and me as we sneak desperate glances at her; she gives one-word answers whenever Liana tries to engage her in conversation. Encouraging sign for our chemistry tonight. The minutes tick away, and my heart rate speeds up. "Do you want to go over the harmonies in the finale?" I ask, even though we've practiced it a million times, as if practicing it a million and one might be the difference between success and failure. Liana nods vigorously. Summer gives a small incline of her head. "Should

I get Noah?" I ask Summer, not knowing if she'll be able to stand being in a room with him, certain that she's barely tolerating being in the same room as us. What will she do tonight, after the show is over? Where the hell does she go from here?

"Might as well," she says, still not meeting my eyes.

So I duck into his dressing room, only to find the makeup artist talking with a production assistant in hushed voices, no Noah to be seen. "Oh," I say. "Do you know where Noah is?"

They look at me with frightened expressions. "Um," the PA says. "We're working on . . . he should be here soon, we think."

What the hell? I back out, then power walk into the dressing room. "Noah isn't here yet," I say. "And we're thirty minutes away from showtime." He's probably just doing a last-minute *Snow Leopard* thing. Still, visions of car accidents or crazed fans taking him hostage run through my mind. Crazed with love for him? Or crazed with wanting revenge for Summer? The reactions on Twitter to his Jimmy revelation were not kind, especially not after Summer's reporter friend published her article early, jumping on the news cycle, confirming that Noah had never reached out to Summer about credit and casually dropping in *sources tell me he's about to be announced as Snow Leopard* while she was at it.

"What? This is not funny, he needs to get his ass here!" Liana says. She's already all ready to go, hair and makeup fully applied. As she scrambles for her phone to call and ask him why the hell he's running so late, Summer sits calmly in her bathrobe. Finally she looks right at me, a strange smile playing about her lips.

I double-take at the look on her face. "Wait," I ask. "What have you done?"

Forty-Seven

· · · · · · ·

SUMMER'S SOLILOQUY (REPRISE)

Last night, after learning that everyone I'd trusted in my life had betrayed me, I went back to my hotel room to find Noah sitting in the hallway.

I couldn't see his face at first. He had a baseball cap pulled down low. Normally, when a strange man is sprawled at my door, it's very bad. Another stalker, deciding that fan mail is no longer enough. I don't get them as much now as I did when I was sweet and young. But there's still an occasional man who feels mistreated by the world, and who thinks that we understand each other. Which is funny, because I barely even understand myself. It's best to have sympathy for them. That helps you feel less afraid. If you thought of them all as men who were out to hurt you, you'd never leave your home again. But you've also got to stay as far away as possible.

I started to back up toward the elevator. But then I saw his Red

Sox cap, which didn't go with his nice, TV-approved suit. I saw how he was hugging his knees and tapping his foot on the floor, and I knew I was in a different kind of danger. "Why are you here?"

He jumped to his feet. As a teenage boy he could dance and run and hurl himself up mountains, but now he had a new discipline to the way he moved. Snow Leopard training, I guess. "Can we talk?" he asked. I was so angry with him and with everyone. But I was also curious.

Where else could we go but my room? As we walked in, I flipped a light switch that illuminated a bedside lamp, and looked around to see what I had left out for him to judge. Not much, thanks to housekeeping, which had made my bed and straightened up the mess of my life.

I wouldn't offer him anything. No drink, no kindness. I sat down in my armchair in the lamp's dim glow, leaving him to stand a few feet away from me, like I was a queen on a throne and he was coming to beg me for mercy. He took his hat off and held it in his hands, completing the metaphor. Good.

"Did you come to get another screenplay idea?" I asked. "Have you not written since *Woodlands* because you haven't had anyone to steal from?"

"I haven't written since *Woodlands* because that was the only story I cared about telling," he said. He knew just the right thing to say up until he decided he was done with you, didn't he? "I came to apologize if I put you on the spot during Jimmy's interview. The way he was treating you was so demeaning—"

"Hypocrite." I wanted to be cold and merciless, but he made me too angry. "You don't get to be a knight in shining armor, riding in to save my honor now after you threw me under the bus back when I loved you."

He stood up straighter. "You did love me, then?"

"Of course I did. I told you!"

"But Lucas said . . ." he began, and a puzzle piece finally clicked into its place.

"You were upset that I'd slept with him."

"I was upset that you lied to me about it." His blue eyes were sincere, searching mine. "And yeah, maybe I was upset that you'd had sex with him the week before—"

"You think I wanted to?" I couldn't sit still in the chair anymore. "But you'd made him so suspicious, he was going to tell everyone I wasn't a virgin if I didn't calm him down—" His expression grew unbearably sad, and I was suddenly so cold. "Besides, I don't need to defend my sexual decisions to you!" I rummaged through the dresser for a sweater, something comforting to wrap myself up in and hold on to. Now, so many years later, it seemed ridiculous that I hadn't told Noah about sleeping with Lucas. I've come to believe in a forgiving God, who doesn't particularly care what I do with my body. But back then, virginity was everything. I'd thought my mistake was giving it to someone besides Noah. But really, my mistake was thinking I was worthless without it.

"I wish you could have trusted my feelings for you." I didn't look at him as I pulled the sweater on, clutching the cuffs in my hands. If I focused on something solid, I didn't have to focus on regret. "But there's nothing to do about it now. You made your apology. You can go."

"Wait." He caught my hand, his palm so warm, mine like ice. I pulled away. "I'm also sorry that the show tomorrow night won't be our version of it. I didn't mean to dismiss that, at the bar. I wanted to come back and make things right."

I had to get farther away from him, so I moved toward the opposite wall, steadying myself against it. I knew I should ask him to leave. Instead, I asked, "What does that even mean? What does my life look like after this show, in your mind?"

He rubbed his cheek. "You get to have the career you should have had. Maybe you get to do a sitcom, be funny like you always said—"

We both knew how hopeless that was now. "Even if tomorrow night goes well," I said, "I think fame has ruined performing for me. I liked losing myself in a character, but I don't know how to do that anymore. The constant scrutiny, the pressure . . ." I paused, struggling to articulate it. He waited, giving me the time. "The camera used to feel gentle, like it was capturing the best of me. Now it just feels unforgiving."

"I understand that."

"Okay, Snow Leopard."

"No, I don't . . ." He sat down on my floor. "You don't say no to an offer like that. I know I'm lucky to be in this position. But it feels like I'm on a treadmill that's speeding up faster and faster, and someone's removed the button to control it, so I have to keep going. You know what I mean?"

"That's how I felt during the second season." I slid down to the floor too. "Sometimes I wish *The Daydreams* had never come along, and I'd made a life where I had a nice family and, I don't know, did regional theater. People would come see me in *The Music Man*, and afterward, they'd say, 'You know who did a lovely job? Marian the librarian.' But they wouldn't remember my name, or even my face, just that I made them feel good for two and a half hours. I think that life would have been really nice." Here we were talking again just like when we were teenagers on the telephone, everything so easy, but also impossibly hard at the same time. I twisted my hair tightly around my finger so I didn't have to look at him. "Too bad I was so smoking hot."

I made him laugh with that. "Too bad."

We lapsed into silence. Again, I knew I should ask him to leave. It was time to end the danger, the dance, of letting someone who has hurt you stay.

But this time, he spoke up. "If it's any consolation, my agent called—it sounds like some article is coming out about how I screwed you over with *Woodlands*." He'd already gotten out in front of it. It would slide right off him. "I think Kat talked to a reporter."

"No," I said. It came out sharper than I'd meant it to, and he furrowed his brow at me. I tossed my head, shooting him a defiant look. "*I* talked to the reporter. I'm the one who had Kat ask you about it."

He stared at me. Then he put his head in his hands. "You . . ." He made a noise, and his shoulders shook. When he looked back up, I thought I might see hurt on his face, but instead, it was admiration. Like I'd surprised him, but also, somehow, he wasn't surprised at all. "Of course it was you."

"I'm done with not getting credit for the things I do."

He nodded, opened his mouth to say something, then closed it again.

"What?" I asked.

"It's funny that we thought we were the loves of each other's lives, and we never even went on a date."

"Hilarious."

Looking down at his shoe, he said, "We could, you know."

Now it was my turn to laugh. "What? Go on a date?"

"Why not?"

"Because you broke my heart and took our idea. Because you're going to be Snow Leopard, and I'm a joke."

"You're not a joke."

"You should watch some late-night comedy monologues from the past thirteen years."

"You're not a joke to me." He spoke softly, with a hesitation that seemed unnatural on a man so used to being beloved. "Haven't you felt something, since we've been back here?"

"I've barely been myself. I've been playing a role."

"Not when we were making the show our own. Not when you were yelling at me in the bar the other night."

"Oh, and that's the moment I recaptured your heart?"

"Kind of. Yes."

"Stop being ridiculous." I squeezed my eyes shut. The audacity of him. After all of this, he still thought he could have everything. Men always thought that. A simple apology couldn't undo all the damage. I pushed myself up to my feet. "I already have enough to think about, with not completely humiliating myself tomorrow night, and facing Mr. Atlas now that I know he leaked the journal—"

"What?"

I told him then, the whole situation. By the end, he was on his feet too, pacing, his fists clenched. "I'm supposed to be the face of a franchise for that man? And you have to get up onstage and *dance* for him?"

I sat on the edge of the bed, picking at the duvet cover. "I wish I could just fly away and leave him to pick up the pieces."

"Yeah," he said, sitting down next to me, half a foot away. He reached out and put his hand over mine, a gesture of comfort. "Wouldn't that be nice."

A throwaway bit of agreement, that was all it was. But suddenly I knew how I could hurt him. He'd turned away from me and taken our idea and then had the nerve to apologize before I could hold him accountable for it, but there was still one more thing I could try. Slowly, as if inspiration were breaking over me, I said, "So why don't we?"

"What?"

I turned my hand over so our palms were touching, tingling. "Let's not show up tomorrow night. Let's just . . . go to the airport and fly away from Atlas." He was staring at me, either in awe, or as if I were speaking a language he didn't know.

I've spent many years battling my own impulsivity. But as many times as it has hurt me, it has helped too. Stopping me from an ill-conceived marriage—I'd been in the car on the way to my getting-ready location, my wedding dress in a dry-cleaning bag beside me, and all I could think was that I'd hardly spent any hours with this man sober, and in fact I'd hardly spent any hours doing anything sober in recent months, and I'd checked myself into rehab instead, the best decision I could have made. Now I had enough of an impulsive reputation that Noah might believe I was serious.

"You want to leave Kat and Liana high and dry?"

"After what they did with the journal, I'm not going to lose any sleep."

"You know what this would do to our careers?"

"I don't have a career. But yes, you wouldn't get to be the face of Mr. Atlas's franchise. I understand if even still, you don't want to give that up." He pulled his hand away, running it through his hair.

I studied him, a man glowing in the lamplight. "You can't half-ass making things right. So if you mean what you say, you could get us two tickets to wherever you want and we could fly away from this toxic company." He hesitated. He wanted to lift me up, but didn't he know that was impossible? I'd grown too heavy. I'd have to get my satisfaction from dragging others down.

"Doing this show for Mr. Atlas tomorrow night . . . it will break me. If I fly away on my own, I'm an unreliable disaster. If we fly away together, we're making a statement the world can't ignore." It was the best performance I'd done in years, so stirring that I almost believed it myself. "And then, sure, when we get off the plane, we can go on a date."

He looked into his lap, his chest rising and falling with his breath. The silence stretched out, so long and complete I could hear the hum of the air conditioner, the low blur of TV from the room next door. I could even, I thought, hear the faint thump of Noah's heartbeat. Of course he wasn't going to do this. Of course I didn't have that power over him.

"Okay," he said.

"What?" Electricity lit up my body all the way to my fingertips.

"We don't do the show. LAX, tomorrow night." I suddenly had trouble breathing because everything I breathed in was *him*. He was joking; he had to be. I took his face in my hands and turned his head. I needed to look him in the eyes.

"You're serious?" I asked. Once, I'd had him memorized like the lyrics to our old songs. Now, he was coming back to me with new verses: faint lines in his forehead, a controlled stillness in place of his boyish animation.

He held my gaze, his pupils dilating. Back when we first got famous, I learned that magazines sometimes photoshopped your pupils larger. That way, whoever looked at your picture imagined that you wanted them. Noah's pupils nearly crowded out the blue of his irises as he looked at me. Messy, frustrating me, holding his golden, beautiful face. His jaw moved beneath my fingers.

"I'm serious," he said, his voice husky, hardly louder than a whisper.

He was a good actor. He was going to change his mind. So what I did next, I wanted to do quickly, in this brief, intoxicating moment when I could still believe he would give up everything for me. I pulled his face in closer and I kissed him.

It was stupid, maybe. But I'd denied myself when I was young. For years after, I'd told myself I would never have him, that I didn't even want him, but then I'd see pictures of him with a girl-friend and think before I could stop myself, *But he's mine.*

For Noah, maybe it felt like the beginning of something as he pulled me tightly to his chest, as I tugged off his shirt and we fell back on the bed, but I knew this would be our only time. So I was going to focus on every moment of it.

I wasn't coming to him as a blushing eighteen-year-old girl, all potential, pretending he was my first. So much had happened since he loved me. His body had grown more powerful, and I didn't want him to be disappointed by mine. I didn't think I could take that, so I reached to turn off the light, but he pressed my arm down on the bed. "No," he said in a hoarse, low voice, a hidden voice that no one else got to hear. Holding me in place, he studied every inch of me. My breath caught in my throat. Time seemed to break free from all its usual rules. Then, urgently, he bent his head and kissed me again.

I gripped his strong, smooth shoulders and thought, *This is Noah, moving on top of me.* And then, although I meant to focus, to memorize, I stopped thinking. I lost myself in the feelings, fragmented at first, then all-consuming. When we were done, I tasted something salty that I thought was sweat, but Noah traced his thumb against my cheek, his eyes tightening in concern. "Did I hurt you?" It was only then that I realized I'd started crying.

Forty-Eight

. . . .

2018

"Holy shit," Liana says. "So he's on his way to the airport right now?"

Summer nods and starts changing into her costume for the opening number.

"But you're not going?" I ask.

"He won't even make it there. He'll think the better of it, turn around, and run in here with ten minutes 'til showtime. But at least he'll have gotten a good scare, and people will get to talk about what a difficult person *he* is for once."

"Sweet Jesus." Liana stares at the sky for a moment, pressing her fingers to her temples. "And what the hell are we supposed to do if he gets stuck in traffic?"

"I don't know, throw out the script and sing the songs," Summer says. "But he's going to be here. He's Noah Gideon, and we all know that when it comes down to it, he cares about himself. Besides, he already got to have sex with me, so it's not like—"

Liana's phone buzzes, and she looks down at it, then pulls up a link. "My friend just sent me this." She holds the screen up to Summer and me, the three of us bowing our heads over it as a video on Twitter plays.

It's shaky, taken by a young woman on her phone as she walks around, starting out front facing. "Am I seeing things, or is this Noah Gideon at LAX right now?" The video flips to reveal a guy sitting in a row of uncomfortable airport seats, clutching a Dunkin' Donuts iced coffee, his leg jiggling. "Isn't he supposed to be doing *The Daydreams*? Should I go say something, or am I going to feel so dumb when it's not him?" The video ends.

"He went." I'm light-headed. "I mean, that *was* him, right?"

"Oh. Well, good," Summer says. Her body has gone rigid beside me, her breathing shallow as she realizes the pickle she's gotten us into. How are we going to rework the whole show in half an hour? I can't quite wrap my head around it all. Summer Wright is officially no longer the messiest of the Daydreams. Noah just took that heavy mantle onto his broad shoulders, muscled for a superhero he will never play. After all these years building a career as a reliable heartthrob, leaping over people and obstacles, he threw it all away. And he left the three of us in deep shit.

"Okay, he could still make it back, right?" Liana says. "If he left right now?"

"In time for the start of the show? In Los Angeles traffic?" I ask. "No."

"Oh goody, there's more," Liana says, shooting an accusatory look at Summer as she pulls up the next video in the thread, just posted a minute ago.

"I'm so nervous," the young woman says as she approaches the man. She flips the camera around. "Noah Gideon?"

Noah looks up. It's definitely him, all right. Liana clutches my hand, squeezing so hard I worry she might break my fingers.

"What are you doing here?" the fan asks. Noah starts to shield his face, to turn away as the fan persists. "What's going on?"

Then Noah seems to make a decision. He stops hunching his shoulders. He takes his baseball cap off. "Call it a mental breakdown. Call it going to rehab." He smiles, but it's not his charming movie star smile, nor the unrestrained one he sometimes couldn't stop from spreading over his face with Summer. It's the shaky smile of a man who knows he is being a fool, but chooses to believe anyway.

"What?" the girl asks. "You're going to rehab?"

"Actually, wait," he says. "Are you posting this? 'Cause if so, I want to say . . ." He looks right to the camera, his voice catching. "I know that I'm going to wait and wait, and you probably won't come. I understand. But I'll be here. Like you said, you can't half-ass making things right." The girl starts to move the camera, but he holds up a hand. "Oh, and if you end up doing the show, break a leg."

"This is so wild," the girl says, and then, as if she's just remembered something, "and is it true that you're going to be Snow Leopard?"

"Screw Atlas," Noah says. "I'm never working with them again."

The video ends. We stare at the screen, shell-shocked.

"Okay. Shit," I say, scrambling for a foothold in this new reality. "So we'll make the show a concert, and sing his parts?"

"Dammit, Summer!" Liana says. "Great revenge, but you messed this up for the three of us real bad."

Summer stares down at the makeup counter. "I'm such an idiot," she says.

"No," I begin as Liana says, "Yeah."

Summer stands, finally, ready to take charge of the situation she created. She looks around our dressing room, but her gaze is unfocused, as if what she's really seeing is inside her own head—visions of what we need to do, how we will explain this to Michael and the audience. She reaches down to grab something from her bag.

No, she's grabbing her whole bag and putting it over her shoulder. "I forgot that I always come back to hope," she says, turning to us with a bewildered expression. She is luminous, her cheeks flushed, lit from within. "I'm sorry, but I have a plane to catch."

I'm temporarily at a loss for words. Liana, however, lunges forward to block Summer's path. "How are we supposed to do the show without you?"

"You were always the more talented one anyway, so go out there and show everyone."

"But—" Liana sputters, putting her arm up so that Summer can't leave.

"After what you told me yesterday, you don't get to be mad." Summer steps forward and kisses Liana's cheek, then ducks past her to me.

She hugs me tight, strokes my hair. She's so fragile in my arms. "By the way, I forgive you both," she says, and runs out the door.

Forty-Nine

. . . .

2018

"What do we do? Oh God, what do we do?" Liana asks as she sinks into a chair. She puts her head between her legs, alternating deep breaths with shuddering moans. I pinch myself hard. This is a dream. Surely it can't be that our stars just ran off together in some misguided attempt to say *fuck you* to the network.

They've both always been good with stories. Noah wrote a whole movie to give himself and Summer a happy ending. Maybe he's telling himself one now too, living his life so it is the most thrilling narrative, completing the redemption arc—he stands up for what's right and ends up with the dream girl! And Summer's self-destructing yet again. They're going to crash and burn within the week.

Or maybe this kind of gigantic gesture was what it took to make amends, and these two reckless kids were made for each other. Her obsession with bringing him down . . . perhaps you don't get that obsessed with someone unless you love them a little bit too.

I could deliver a full semester of college lectures on all the reasons that they're going to regret this. But I don't have time to do that right now because it's twenty minutes to showtime, and we are in crisis.

I'm not a fainter. But my head is suddenly so light that I have to brace myself on the counter where we have our touch-up makeup, our hairbrushes, my phone.

And then I pick that phone up and call Miheer.

"It's all a mess," I say as soon as he answers. "And I can't go out there, and I love you and I do want to marry you more than anything but first I need to tell you about the bad things I did back when—" I cut myself off, because it's so *noisy* wherever he is. "Wait, what's going on? What are you doing?"

"Um, I am here."

"Where?"

"In the audience. Surrounded by a lot of enthusiastic women in their twenties. I feel a little creepy."

"You came?"

"Yeah. I watched your Jimmy interview last night and, wait. Hold on . . ."

Tears well in my eyes. My phone buzzes with a text from him. He's sent me a photo he just took of himself, in the throng of bodies, giving a thumbs-up and smiling shyly at the camera. Oh, my heart: he's wearing a T-shirt that says **TEAM KAT** on it.

"You look amazing," I say.

"Thanks. Wait, what do you mean, you can't come out here?"

"Summer and Noah ran off."

"I thought— There's a rumor flying around out here, my new friends next to me were saying that someone who looked like Noah was at the airport, but they didn't believe it was true."

"It's true. And Summer's going to meet him."

"Are they really in love? That's exciting." He's acting like a little fanboy. I would be tickled, if I weren't absolutely panicking.

"So we have to cancel the show."

"No," he says. "You're not going to do that. You're Kat Whitley, and you make things happen. The audience came all this way."

"They didn't come to see me."

"Well if they didn't, they *should* have! You're so funny in this role—the episode where you shut down the Ferris wheel? But tender too, like your duet with Summer—"

"Hold on, have you been watching old episodes?"

"After our last call, I started thinking: this show is a bigger part of who you are than I'd realized. And sure, I could get upset with you for not telling me more about it, but also, I'd never really asked."

"You watched the show." It comes out as barely more than a whisper.

"Every episode." I have trouble articulating words, but somehow I have found a port in the storm, or it has found me. "If nothing else, *I* came to see Kat, so do the show for me."

"If we fail, the media will rip us apart."

"You survived that once before. You can survive it again."

"I love you," I say. "I'm going to go."

"I'll see you very soon."

As I put the phone down, Liana watches me, a temporary pause in her hyperventilation. "Calling Javi for comfort didn't even cross my mind," she says in a small voice.

I step forward to hug her as my phone dings again. A message from Summer: I hope you can forgive yourself too. And can I ask you for one more thing?

Liana and I both stare at it. As Summer's next text comes through, there's a commotion, Michael's voice booming all the way from the greenroom. "So go after her! And get Mr. Atlas. Yes, I'm talking to you." People spill out into the hallway and toward the greenroom, whispering anxiously. I push through the panicking masses toward Michael, who is pacing back and forth as frightened assistants scurry out of his path. "Those *idiots*," Michael says when he sees me, steadying himself against the wall. "What are they thinking? Did you know about this?"

"Not until just now," I say.

"We're canceling the show," he says, not to me but to himself. "We'll have them put up an old rerun of something." He presses his head against the wall. "Shit, but the advertisers."

"And the fans."

"Right, them too."

Mr. Atlas comes rushing backstage, his jacket slightly askew, his face white, an assistant filling him in on everything that has happened. He presses a handkerchief to his lips. "Michael, what is your plan?"

Michael looks behind me, and I turn to see that a crowd—the whole cast, all the assistants and backstage crew—has formed, talking and whimpering.

"Michael?" Mr. Atlas prods.

"I don't know, I can't think, I can't—they're trying to kill me. I'm not supposed to stress like this!" Michael sinks down onto the couch, useless.

So I step the fuck up.

"We can do it concert-style," I say to Mr. Atlas.

His eyes narrow in skepticism. He doesn't want to hand the reins over to me. But what choice does he have? "Explain," he says.

I turn to the crowd. "Does someone have a piece of paper?" An assistant rushes over with a yellow notepad, and I start writing out the list of songs in the order that we were supposed to do them. First and foremost, I reassign "Butterfly" to Liana. For the big group numbers where Summer and Noah have small solos, I ask chorus members if any of them want to fill in, and pick from the raised hands. Everyone watches me, on tenterhooks. "Tape?" The assistant rushes back over, and I tape the set list to the wall. "Okay, team, no script. Instead, we sing and dance our asses off. We'll get some of the fans up onstage to do the Summer and Noah songs from the old days. They know all the words, and everyone loves audience participation, right?" I look to Liana, who is still breathing rapidly, her eyes locked on mine. "You good to banter with me in between numbers, fill in the exposition and such?" She gives a quick jerk of a nod.

"This won't fill the entire allotted time slot," Mr. Atlas says.

"So get your people to edit together a montage or something to play at the end."

Liana speaks up. "Kat and I can tell some behind-the-scenes stories if you need us to buy you more time—"

"Family-friendly ones only," he says.

She juts out her chin at him, this man who took her momentary lapse in judgment and destroyed our entire show with it. "Don't worry, we understand how much Atlas cares about protecting its brand."

After a beat, he looks away from her and back at me. "I don't know about this. It will be messy."

"But at least it will be something."

He considers it, then nods. We've got the go-ahead. I turn back to the crowd. It's actually, weirdly, exhilarating. "Go finish getting ready, and then let's do this, okay? And wait." I grab one of the production assistants. "I need to talk to a cameraperson."

Everyone scatters except for me and Mr. Atlas. "Thank you for taking charge." He stares at the set list with my notes on it, his nose twitching. "And I am sorry that they have left you to perform in an uncomfortable situation. I'm sending my legal team after them, don't worry."

"That's not a good idea." I stare straight ahead at the set list too, my voice lowered.

"What do you mean?"

I take a deep breath and go full lawyer. "From my extensive experience working with contracts, I'd imagine there's a clause about how signatories have the right to renege if damaging information comes to light. And the head of the network leaking an employee's private journal to the press is pretty damn damaging, wouldn't you say?"

He blinks at me. But he doesn't deny it. Doesn't say anything at all. Summer told me that, backstage during the finale, he could barely look at her, loathing all over his face. She thought that loathing was for her, and I'm sure it was. But maybe a little part of it was for himself too. I hope it's haunted him the way the rest of us have been haunted. I hope that he'd also like to make amends.

"You caused enough damage," I say. "Let them go."

He fiddles with his glasses. Then he swallows and taps the set list. "I look forward to watching the show."

Fifty

· · · · · · ·

2018

The crowd chants the word "Daydreams" over and over as Liana and I stand backstage, slick with sweat, waiting for our cue. Liana trembles, muttering something under her breath. At first I think maybe it's a calming mantra. But then I hear the words. "She screwed us. She screwed us."

The cue comes and she throws her head back, always the professional, running onstage for the opening number as I follow. We sing and dance with the chorus, filling in Noah's place in the choreography, and the crowd screams when we finish the number and fling our arms out, chests heaving, in our final pose.

I can see people in the first few rows craning their heads, wondering where the hell Summer and Noah are. I step forward with Liana and address them all. "We're doing things a little differently than planned tonight. But hey, it wouldn't be a *Daydreams* live show if it didn't go off the rails, now would it?"

A rumble of confusion goes up. Liana holds out her hand. "Summer and Noah have had a last-minute . . . emergency, so we're going to be your leads tonight." People's faces fall, cries of anger and concern piercing the air.

I hit them with the devastating eyebrow. "*Excuse* me! I've been thirsting for stardom ever since I was born. This is my moment, so don't you dare boo."

There's a low wave of laughter, people now uncertain whether this is reality or plot.

"And they'll hopefully be joining us at the end," Liana says.

"In the meantime, as much as I think I should sing every number in the world by myself, I need to be gentle with my beautiful instrument," I say, stroking my throat, hamming it up. "So do any fans want to get up here and help us out?" I pick a few people from the crowd, two who are raising their hands so enthusiastically their arms are in danger of dislocating from their sockets, one guy whose friends are all pointing at him even as he hides his face in (faux?) embarrassment.

As a commercial break rolls, I tell them each what part they'll sing, where they'll stand, reassure them through their nerves. And then we are back, and holy shit, we've been strapped into a roller coaster and there is no getting off.

The adrenaline is unlike anything I've ever felt. It's strange and messy, what we're doing, but slowly, people get into it. They are having *fun*, cheering for the fans who have bravely taken the lead. Liana and I tell a few G-rated backstage stories from the first time around and banter capably. And, sure, it feels good to perform. But what's really making me float ten feet off the ground is the big picture here, the sense that I gave other people what they needed to shine.

Then it's time for "Butterfly." Liana steps forward into the spotlight, and the crowd goes silent as she sings. It's even more raw, her voice even fuller, than it was when she did it in rehearsal. She's a game-day player, and besides, she is feeling a *lot* right now, and when she's done, a full-on roar emanates from the audience.

This night is going to be the beginning of something for her, I would bet my life on it. She turns to me, tears streaming down her cheeks as the crowd chants her name, and I take her in my arms.

"You are amazing," I whisper in her ear.

"I am, aren't I?" she says, stepping back, glowing. She looks deep into my eyes for a moment, and the courage clicks into place. Bringing the microphone up to her lips, she turns back to the audience. "And, Javier, if you're watching, I want a divorce."

That sets everyone off into a fresh round of hollering. But there's always a naysayer, always a troll. And as the applause dies down, a woman toward the front of the crowd begins to shout, "Where the hell is Summer?"

"She should be coming any minute now," I say, looking off into the wings. The production assistant standing there shakes her head, mouthing, *Not yet.* Mr. Atlas stands next to her, arms folded. He looks entirely too pleased about how this show is turning out. In some ways, this is better for his ratings, isn't it? If we'd done our mediocre show, we'd have gotten coverage for a day or two, some reviews here and there. But this? People will be talking for weeks.

The woman who asked about Summer boos. This is the thing you can forget about fans, when you suddenly have so many of them. They're not a mass of people who feel the same way about everything. Each one has their own beating heart of a story, their own reasons for being drawn to what you've made. This particular woman feels differently from the others here, and, as she makes a stink, more people join in, the ones who paid good money for something specific that they've been denied.

"She's still the same mess," the woman shouts. Others chime in, words like "typical" and "disaster" piercing through the roar. We are losing control now, people arguing among themselves in the crowd.

"Okay, I've got a backstage story for everyone," I yell, "about what really happened with Summer's journal."

That gets their attention. My throat goes dry as the hush descends, as everyone stares at me. There's a moment in so many movies when the villain takes the spotlight and monologues about their dastardly deeds, and this is mine.

Liana shoots me a look of warning: *You sure about this? Don't be stupid.* But I force myself to start talking. I'm doing this to calm the people who were booing, but maybe I owe it to the people who have devoted themselves so fully to us too. "All those things in there, the judgments about everybody else, the man in the alley, everything the world ripped her apart over. She didn't write them." Miheer is out there, in the dark, watching me, and even though I'm scared, I know it's time for him to hear this. I have to believe that he can still love me on the other side of it. "I did."

A rumble of confusion, of shock, from the crowd. "I'd been using her journal. And when it got out, I let her take the blame. Because I was terrified of what Atlas would do to me. What *everyone* would do to me."

Mr. Atlas is shouting from offstage. "Katherine, stop this now!" He makes a motion that I should cut it out. But I don't listen. Because my name is Kat.

"Oh, what the hell," Liana says from behind me, and steps forward. "It was my fault too. I found the journal and trusted someone with it that I shouldn't have because I wanted to save my job. The environment had gotten so cutthroat, with the men in power playing us against each other."

Mr. Atlas charges over to the production assistant, grabbing her walkie-talkie, seizing the connection to the control room. "Cut the feed," he says into it. "Go to commercial, play the montage, do whatever you have to."

I don't know if they do or not. Regardless, I keep going, Liana clutching my hand. Maybe the rest of America won't see it, but this place is packed with fans, and they will hear. Forget the villain monologue. I am more than just The Bitch. I am human, and I messed up deeply. Someday I'll mess up again. We always do. The thing that makes us good isn't whether or not we mess up, but whether or not we try to make it right.

"I let Summer take my punishment. And for that, I will always be sorry. But why the hell did we have to punish her so much anyway? We destroyed her for our own entertainment, but we can find better ways to be entertained. We *have* to."

Total silence from the crowd now. I see little beams of light in the audience. Phones, recording. Even if Atlas stopped airing, the footage will get out.

From the wings, the production assistant calls my name. I look over, and she gives me a thumbs-up.

"And now, for the grand finale," I say to the crowd. "Summer and Noah."

A screen on the stage that has been projecting close-ups of our faces begins to show a new setting: the airport.

Now, the cameraman I sent after Summer follows her through the terminal at LAX as Noah comes into view, slumped in a seat at the gate, legs splayed in front of him while fellow travelers point and stare.

Summer whirls around, throws her shoulders back, and, straight to camera, says, "I wrote this scene." Then she calls out to Noah. "You were there, inside my head." It's one of the lines she scribbled on a piece of hotel stationery for the two of them to read. Lines they committed to memory and did so well in a rehearsal room until they were told to stop because it was too raw, too much.

Noah whips his head up at her voice. A million thoughts seem to hit him as his gaze settles on Summer. His relief and joy that she's there. His awareness of the cameraman following her. His sudden understanding of what she's doing. He stands, takes his hat off, and says the next line in the scene.

"You've been inside of mine for the last thirteen years."

They move toward each other as they recite the rest. It's not long, only a minute or two, but it's momentous. Their eyes shine. Everyone in the terminal stops what they're doing to watch.

Summer says her final line. And then she runs into his arms and he lifts her up. If this were a movie, the way they press together now would be the only nominee for the Best Kiss category at the MTV Movie & TV Awards, this single kiss taking up all five slots, nobody else daring to compete.

They break apart slowly, him putting her back down again as the people in the terminal around them whoop, as our crowd cheers too, not that Summer and Noah can hear it. I don't even know if they can hear the people around them.

Then, Summer breaks their gaze. She turns and speaks directly into the camera. "There's your kiss." She takes Noah's hand, and says one final thing before the video goes black. "Now, please. Leave us the hell alone."

Epilogue

. . . .

2019
Eight Months Later

Miheer and I pull into a dirt driveway, a small white cottage rising up among the trees before us.

"Are you sure you want me to come in?" he asks as he turns the car off. "I can go drive into town and look at antiques or something, let you all be alone."

"No. It'll be good for you to help, since we can trust you not to leak it. Besides, I want them to get to know my husband." The word still feels weird in the best possible way. I smile at him giddily.

He shoots me back a matching giddy smile as we get out of the car. "Okay then, wife."

When Summer opens the door for us, I almost don't recognize her. Who is this healthy-looking brunette in front of me? "Hi," she says, giving us each a brief, distracted hug. "Come in, Liana's already here." She turns over her shoulder as she leads us through the entryway to the cozy, old-fashioned kitchen. "Do you want a cup of tea or something? We have a shitload of tea."

"Ooh," Miheer says. "Chamomile?"

Summer nods toward some double doors as she starts clattering around. "Go ahead into the living room."

On the other side of the doors, Liana sits on the couch. She squeals when she sees us, and begins to struggle to her feet, although she has to push aside about five different throw blankets.

"Sorry, I'm being suffocated," she says, then calls to the kitchen, "Summer, do you buy a new blanket every time you're bored?"

"No!" Summer calls back. "It's cold out here."

"They're *nesting*," Liana says confidentially to us, opening her arms for a hug. "Congratulations! I want you to know that I'm happy for you, even though I'm a bitter divorcée and you didn't invite me to the wedding."

Miheer laughs. "We didn't invite anyone, we promise. DC lets you do a self-officiating ceremony, so we just put on nice clothes and went to the park."

"Okay, fine, I forgive you."

When Summer emerges from the kitchen with Miheer's tea, Noah comes with her, carrying stacks of printouts. His body is softer, like a human's again. There's something easy between him and Summer, something content. Their one date turned into another and then another. For the past couple of months, as they've dealt with the ruins of their careers, they've been shacking up in this cottage in upstate New York. The press hasn't exactly left them alone, but nobody's camping outside their house either.

After Noah hugs us, he hands each of us one of the stacks of paper, and we settle in our seats as Summer assigns us roles to read, her hands trembling. Noah squeezes her shoulder and she calms.

The thing about going scorched earth on your employer is that it makes it hard for other employers to trust you. People are interested in us, yes, but hesitant. Liana's doing the best of us all, as she should be, having just wrapped a feature, in the process of recording an album. Still, for every producer who was obsessed with her rendition of "Butterfly," there's someone reminding them that she also shit-talked Atlas's "toxic environment" onstage. I've been shadowing some directors and starting production on an extremely low-budget short film, but I get the sense that Mr. Atlas may have done some subtle blacklisting, spreading the word that I'm not to be trusted with a set of my own. Summer and Noah? They've been flooded with offers for terrible reality TV and tell-all interviews, but nothing else.

At least Michael's career is also in the shitter. Word spread about his backstage meltdown under pressure, and about how difficult he has been to work with over the years. Someone else will be helming *Disaster Ship*'s fourth season.

Our one big opportunity came from the most unexpected place: Atlas, asking if we wanted to do a limited series, as a peace offering. Because they've been suffering too. Noah and Summer's grand gesture inspired a host of journalists to start digging, a bonanza of opinion pieces and retrospectives about the network's past failures. And besides, we did get them excellent ratings. The new show they proposed would be pretaped, *not* live, but with more creative control for the four of us. We could come back, make a bunch of money, show the public it was time to forgive and forget.

Maybe it was stupid, but we turned them down.

And then Summer called to tell us that she'd written a draft of a screenplay. Liana would be perfect for the leading role. I might be a good fit to direct. Noah had been helpful in bouncing ideas around, and could play a smaller part along with producing. Would we want to get together to read it out loud, and see if it was any good?

So, we are here, showing up and trusting one another and taking a gigantic leap of faith.

Because maybe the script *won't* be any good. Or maybe it will be, but the funding will fall through. Maybe Liana will get offered the role of a lifetime and need to bail on us. Maybe Summer and Noah will break up in the middle of filming and refuse to be in the same room as each other, or she'll relapse, or he'll start to resent all that he gave up when the publicity for *Snow Leopard* (now starring one of the Chrises) begins. Maybe some disaster—natural or man-made—will befall the world right before the premiere and be all that anyone can think about. There are a million maybes.

Still, we turn to the first page. Electricity crackles in the air. I look around at the people who taught me a new way to feel. Then, stupidly hopeful, we begin.

ACKNOWLEDGMENTS

· · · · · · ·

In some ways, this book is a love letter to good creative collaborators—people who get you, support you, and make you better. I've been lucky to work with some of the best collaborators around. My editor, Jen Monroe, pushes me hard in the kindest way. Without her brilliant insight, these characters would probably be cardboard cutouts of themselves, and I'd be banging my head against the wall, wondering why this book hadn't lived up to its potential. Stefanie Lieberman, Molly Steinblatt, and Adam Hobbins are one hell of an agent team: fierce and funny and smart. Their enthusiasm for this idea from the very beginning made it all possible. Can you believe we've all been able to work together on THREE books now? Here's to many more!

I'm so thankful to the whole Berkley team, starting with my publicity and marketing all-stars: Jessica Mangicaro, Danielle Keir, and Tara O'Connor. I'm the luckiest to have you in my corner. Candice Coote wonderfully provided a fresh set of editorial eyes, Anthony Ramondo and Sarah Oberrender made my dream cover, Angelina Krahn caught my mistakes in copyediting (and correctly pointed out that maybe I shouldn't use the phrase "buddy-buddy" so many times), Liz Gluck was an amazing production editor, and

ACKNOWLEDGMENTS

Craig Burke, Jeanne-Marie Hudson, Claire Zion, Ivan Held, and Christine Ball are all excellent champions of the books they publish. Thank you as well to Jin Yu, Emily Osborne, and the others at Berkley and Janklow & Nesbit who have helped support this book in countless ways.

I'm also grateful for the author friends I've made along the way. I know if I try to list all of you, I'll wake up in a cold sweat in the middle of the night after this book has gone to print, remembering all the names I forgot, so I'll just say, if we've had a chance to connect and support each other in this wild, wild industry, thank you. We don't really get "coworkers" in the same way that other people do, but I sometimes think of you as mine (but, like, good coworkers, with whom I'd like to spend more time hanging out around the watercooler). A special thanks to those who have taken the time to provide such generous blurbs for my books.

I'm consistently bowled over by the passion and talent of the Bookstagram and BookTok communities, the booksellers and librarians, and everyone else who devotes themselves to spreading the word about the books they love. Book people are the best people.

Sash Bischoff, Lovell Holder, Blair Hurley, and Daria Lavelle gave me perceptive and encouraging feedback on this book from the very first rough pages. To Kate Emswiler, Becca Roth, and Celey Schumer: it's an honor to be part of the Popslop cinematic universe with you. Thank you to Paavana Lepard for teaching me about lawyers, Will Wagner for telling me which car the rich girls at his high school would drive, and Becca Mohr for all her helpful notes.

As the characters in this book know, the world of Hollywood can be confusing and overwhelming, but Olivia Blaustein has helped me navigate it with her enthusiasm, hard work, and fantastic judgment.

I also want to acknowledge the women who came of age in the spotlight back in the early 2000s. As research for this book, I read articles and interviews from that time and watched a lot of old videos that could be pretty soul-crushing. I hope that all these women are able to get the reevaluation and appreciation they deserve. If this novel whetted your appetite for more 2000s pop culture content, I particularly loved reading *Open Book* by Jessica Simpson, in which she was able to tell her story in her own words.

To all the friends who have so kindly encouraged me through the writing of this book and told me they were excited to read it: here it is, I hope you like it! Thank you to my family, which I'm thrilled has expanded to include the Christie/Handelsman clan. My father, Mark, and brother, Matt, have seen me through many books now with love and support. My mother taught me so much of what I know, even if she can't be here to read this book. And finally, to my husband, Dave: thank God it didn't take us thirteen years to realize we should reunite.